STAR-TOUCHED STORIES

ALSO BY ROSHANI CHOKSHI

The Star-Touched Queen
A Crown of Wishes

STAR-TOUCHED
STORIES

ROSHANI CHOKSHI

Wednesday Books
New York

STAR-TOUCHED STORIES. Copyright © 2018 by Roshani Chokshi. All rights reserved. Printed in the United States of America. For information, address St. Martin's Press, 175 Fifth Avenue, New York, N.Y. 10010.

www.wednesdaybooks.com
www.stmartins.com

The Library of Congress Cataloging-in-Publication Data is available upon request.

ISBN 978-1-250-18079-7 (trade paperback)
ISBN 978-1-250-18080-3 (ebook)

Our books may be purchased in bulk for promotional, educational, or business use. Please contact your local bookseller or the Macmillan Corporate and Premium Sales Department at 1-800-221-7945, extension 5442, or by email at MacmillanSpecialMarkets@macmillan.com.

First Edition: August 2018

10 9 8 7 6 5 4 3 2 1

FOR THAO AND EILEEN,

WHO GAVE THIS WORLD A HOME

ACKNOWLEDGMENTS

This collection of stories wouldn't have been possible without my incredible readers. Thank you so much. You're the most generous-hearted, joyous, creative bunch, and I'm humbled every day by you.

As always, my friends and family have watched the cycle of madness that is my writing and have never once batted an eye. Mom, Dad, Cookie, Pog, and Panda—I love you. To my grandparents and the rest of my family who always took the time to read me stories, thank you. Victoria, Niv, Bismah, Marta, Zan, JJ, Renee, Lemon, Ryan, Stephanie—you're phenomenal human beings.

A thousand and one thanks to my family at Wednesday Books and Sandra Dijkstra Literary Agency, who transform and transport these tales.

Last, but never least, to Aman, who holds my spirit together.

DEATH AND NIGHT

·»· 1 ·«·

DEATH

I stood outside the home, watching as the light beaded and dripped down the length of the Tapestry thread. I waited. There was never any rush. Not for me at least.

The light dangled from the end of the string, clinging and reluctant. A passing wind stirred the ends of the thread, teasing out strands of memory. The memories plumed into the air, releasing the scent of a life lived in love. One by one, the memories unraveled— a pillow shared by two heads bent close in secrecy, a frayed blanket kept inside an eternally empty cradle, a table that sagged from the weight of uncertain feasts. Happiness stolen from the edges of sorrow.

I stepped over the threshold.

The lights in the hut extinguished. Shadows slipped off the walls to gather around my feet. Inside the hut, someone had propped up a stingy fire. Cinnamon scented the air. Past the dusty vestibule, rows upon rows of bay leaves hung from the ceiling. Strange runes scratched into small animal bones and ivory hairpins lay in carefully constructed patterns. I laughed. Someone had tried to ward me away. But there was no door that didn't open to me.

At the far corner of the house huddled two people. A man in the arms of a woman. Old age had blessed him, yet for all his gnarled veins and silver-streaked hair, the woman cradled him as if he were a child. He murmured softly into the crook of her neck. I watched them. She wasn't crying.

The woman looked up . . . and saw me.

How refreshing.

"Greetings, Dharma Raja," said the woman in a clear voice.

I took in the bay leaves and bone pins. "You were expecting me, I take it."

"Yes," she said, hanging her head. "I regret that I cannot serve you any food or drink or treat you as a guest in our home."

"Don't let it trouble you," I said, waving my hand. "I am rarely a guest. Merely an inevitable occurrence."

Her husband did not stir in her arms. His breath had grown soft. While the woman had kept her eyes trained on me, I had taken away his pain, siphoned it bit by bit. I was in a generous mood.

"You have come for him."

"As I will for you, one day. I could tell you the hour, if you wish it."

"No."

I shrugged. "Very well."

She clutched him tighter. Her hands trembled. I knew she could feel his life unspooling. She may have seen me, but she did not see his life pooling beneath him.

"May I ask something of you, Dharma Raja?"

"You may."

But I need not honor it.

"We always wished to leave this life together."

"I cannot change your appointed time, even if I wished."

She closed her eyes. "Then may I request, instead, that you not let him pass to the next life until I may join him there?"

Now this was interesting. I sank backward into the air, and an onyx throne swirled up to meet me. I tilted my head, watching her.

"Why? I haven't weighed your life yet. What if you were far more honorable than your husband in this life? I could pour your soul into the mold of a princess blessed with beauty and intellect, riches and wonders. I could add silver to your heart and fortify you from any heartbreak. I could give you a life worthy of legends."

She shook her head. "I would rather have him."

"You'd rather have him, and whatever life that entails?" I leaned forward, eyeing the dingy room.

Her eyes flashed. "Yes."

"He may not even come back as a human. Believe me. I've remade emperors into cockroaches and cockroaches into kings. You seem like a reasonably intelligent woman. Would you truly like to keep house for a bug?"

She lifted her chin. "I would be his mate in any form."

A curious emotion prickled my skin, nudging the back of my thoughts. My hands tightened on the shadow throne. Before I could stop myself, the question flew from me:

"Why?"

"Because I love him," said the woman. "I would prefer any life with him than any life without him. Even the deities know love to the point that they will chase their counterpart through thousands of lifetimes. Surely you, oh Dharma Raja, understand how extraordinary love can be?"

I knew very well what could come of love. I had seen it. Been cursed by it. Even now, I thought of her. The way she ran away and left a shadow in her place. Love was extraordinary.

Extraordinarily spiteful.

Extraordinarily blind.

Extraordinarily misleading.

"Bold words," I said.

"They do not move you?"

I shrugged. "You may appeal and supplicate and wheedle as you wish, but I have heard every excuse and plea and sputter, and my heart has never been moved."

The woman bowed her head. She gathered her husband to her chest. Her wedding bangles clanked together, breaking the silence. When I left, custom dictated that she must remove those wedding ornaments. Widows did not wear such bracelets. I had not considered until now that the sound itself was a thing near death. And that chime—gold against gold—struck me far louder than any keening. In the echoes, I heard something hollow. And lonely.

I dropped the noose. It slid through the man's skin, noiseless as silk. Life had left him. All that was left was his soul.

You never forget what it's like to withdraw a soul. It is an unclasping. Sometimes a soul is tough and hard, surrounded by sinews of memories gone brittle with age. Sometimes a soul is soft and bursting like wind-fallen fruit, all bruised tenderness and stale hope. And sometimes a soul is an ethereal shard of light. As if the force of its life is a scorching thing.

This soul belonged to light.

When the woman looked down, she knew that her husband was gone. The thing she cradled was nothing more than meat soon to spoil. Tears slid down her wrinkled cheeks.

"Come now," I said, standing from the throne. "I have taken husbands when their wives still wore the henna from their wedding. I consider you lucky."

"I beg of you," she said. "Don't let him move on without me. He would have asked the same."

I swung the soul into a satchel and the light faded. I headed for the door, more out of formality than anything else. If I wanted, I could've disappeared right then and there.

"Please. What would you do for someone you loved?"

I stopped short. "I can't say I've had the pleasure of that provocation."

"You love no one?" she asked, her eyebrows rising in disbelief.

"I love myself. Does that count?"

And then I left.

I had lied when I told the woman I loved nothing.

Standing in front of Naraka—taking in the flat gray lands and stone trees, the crests of mountains like jagged teeth, and the night sky stretching its stars above my palace—I felt the closest thing to love. Night understood me. Night held the promise of secrets slinking in the shadows, of things that conjured fear and bewitched the sight. Nothing was more beautiful than a night sky dusted with stars. Nothing was more terrible than a night sky scrawled with a thousand destinies.

Night was inevitable. Like me.

Yelping and the scratching of paws greeted me the moment I walked inside the palace. My hounds snuffled the folds of my cloak, whining loudly.

"Souls are not chew toys." I sighed.

They huffed, slinking away to the shadows. If they were upset now, they would soon forget. My hounds were my usual representatives to the worlds above and surrounding Naraka. They fetched the souls too stained to lure me aboveground. They'd taken queens from their deathbeds and maidens from the throes of childbirth, soldiers in war and priests at their altars. I was certain they'd find a murderer among the dead to rend and chew with perfect contentment.

I envied them. They could forget what had upset them. But I saw the reminder of what had unsettled me in the empty hallways and silent vestibules, in the solemn and in the eternal. Everywhere.

Envying a mortal and now a beast? Pitiful.

Gupta walked into the hall, his arms full of parchments.

"How was it?" he asked.

"Normal. Less tears than I expected. The wife could see me, though, and she asked for a boon."

"Did you grant it?"

"I'm undecided on whether I should."

Gupta stepped back, brows crumpling. "You look—"

"—preternaturally handsome?"

"No."

"Record keeping is ruining your eyes."

"Impossible."

"Well, one can hope."

"If anything, record keeping has made me more observant," said Gupta.

We started walking down one of Naraka's halls. A thousand mirrors glittered around us, reflecting cities and ports and seas. I never bothered to look at them anymore. There was nothing new to see in this world or any other.

"And what do you observe?"

"Emptiness."

The woman's parting words flitted to mind. *What would you do for someone you loved?*

"Don't let that trouble you. Probably just the reflection of your own mind."

Gupta primly rearranged his papers. "When you decide to stop being a churlish infant, and talk to me about what's bothering you, you know where to find me."

"I am not bothered."

"You are irritated for some reason," he said loftily. "But I'm sure you'll find the answer in the Tapestry." He glanced down at his parchments, checking off names and underlining cities. "Anything else to tell me?"

"You have ink stains on your nose."

Gupta shrugged. "Admittedly, I can be too close to my work."

"Exactly how close? Do you roll around with the parchment afterward, murmur love songs to the paper, and profess your undying love for the written word?"

"I would never roll around in my parchment. It would get wrinkled." Gupta turned to walk away before pausing. "Oh, I forgot . . ."

He snapped his fingers. Ink splashed on my face. "You've got something on your nose."

And then he stuck his tongue out at me, and disappeared.

The Tapestry was a lesson in light and dark. When I stood in the throne room, I felt the threads from a hundred lives pass over my palms, snagging and spinning against one another in an unfathomable web of cause and effect and balance. It was my duty to uphold the balance, to throw dark where there was too much light and sew light where the dark grew too thick. Sometimes the Tapestry showed me a life thread out of place. Sometimes it showed me forest fires approaching a village or a cure for a disease that the world should not yet see. Today it showed me . . . myself.

The threads shimmered like light upon water. My reflection changed, stretching into the halls of Naraka itself . . . the stone halls and the marble courtyards. Empty, empty, empty. The reflection quivered: an ivory counterpart to the onyx throne, a shadow curled around mine in the night, a voice that balanced and weighed. A garland of flowers placed around my neck. My heart tightened. I felt that image opening inside me, as if my whole life had been something lopsided in need of righting itself. The Tapestry's demand knifed through me:

I needed a queen.

Once more, the threads twisted, and the sight wrapped tendrils of ice around my heart—the palace of Naraka split in half, the moon hanging in a torn sky. Without warning, the Tapestry fell back on itself, threads looping and dancing until it was still as a pool.

I sank into my throne, staring at the Tapestry. The message was vivid and vague at the same time. It wanted me to fill the halls, not with the dead, but with . . . a bride. I sat there. Numb. For years, I had considered the possibility of finding someone to share this gift and burden. But whenever I closed my eyes, I saw her. The way her eyes had squinted against the brightness of the Sun Palace. The shadow she left standing in the doorway as she fled. Wearing her smile. Wearing her eyes. Did she think I would not notice the substitute she had left behind? If I had stayed silent, I would have committed a grave injustice.

If I had stayed silent, I would never have been cursed.

The longer I sat there, the more the palace fidgeted. Annoyed. Perhaps it felt neglected in the past few days. Voices grew out of the floor, suddenly taunting and cruel.

> Let us show you a jewel that is not yours.
> Let us show you a door that will never open to you.
> Let us show you a soul that you can never claim.

In the Tapestry, I saw a smile fashioned for me alone. *A jewel that is not yours.* I saw a man standing in a field, someone's arms thrown around his neck as if she had created a hidden world just for them. *A door you will never open.* I saw two people walking with their fingers threaded together, and I felt transfixed by the impossible wonder of a bond so powerful that it was a living thing. *A soul you can never claim.*

I slammed down my fist. The sound trembled throughout the room, and small fissures netted their way down my onyx throne.

"Enough," I said harshly.

I abandoned the Tapestry and the door slammed shut. My head throbbed. I knew what I had to do. Stepping into the hall, a familiar door winked in the half-light. Gupta called it my Inspiration

Room, which sounded vapid, but I suspected he did this on purpose. The room was so much more. It was my thoughts poured into shape. The moment I stepped inside, a burden lifted from me. Here, I was not the Dharma Raja. Here, I was no destroyer.

Here, I was a creator.

The onyx floor expanded, and the shelves—littered with my old thoughts—bent forward as if in polite acknowledgement. Around me, I saw decisions that had weighed heavily in the past: all conquered, all organized.

In the corner of the room, a pair of heavy wings caught the light. Each feather was a braided bolt of lightning. On another shelf, a ship with an ever-changing prow crafted from an eclipse's halo glowed. There were jars of materials floating in the air: the velvet-silent tread of panther paws on the forest floor, buttons of lies and garlands of nightmare teeth.

Even looking at them gave me peace. My creations served as reminders that my thoughts could be conquered and tamed. It was a reminder that even with all that I destroyed, I could create too. Even if no one was there to witness it.

I took a deep breath and tasted the crackling of magic on my tongue. I flexed my fingers, closed my eyes, and concentrated on the darkness.

Darkness has a sound if you know how to listen. Around me, darkness sounded like the roaring space between thoughts and the chaos of possibility. Nothing was born of light. Everything was born of shadows. I caught a ribbon of lustrous shadow notes and snatched it from the air. I twisted the dark in my hands, and thought of the Tapestry and the Shadow Wife's curse. When I opened my eyes, I faced what my thoughts and energy had created:

A lustrous horse with milk-pearl eyes. It drew its lips back over its teeth and in the unshaped dark of its mouth, a city glinted—steel spires and iron trees, paved walkways of jasper and agate, squares of amber windows glittering in the makeshift night. A hidden world. The horse snorted, nipping at the charcoal shoulder of my *sherwani* jacket. The longer I stared, the more I saw it for what it could be. What made a thing a horse? The content or the shape? Was it some-how . . . both? And maybe that wasn't so impossible. Maybe I could have a marriage and not a marriage. I could have a bond that looked like marriage, but have none of the inner workings that made its essential marriage-ness. My queen could have everything she wanted. Except my heart. I didn't need the Tapestry before me to imagine what that future would look like: perfect equality, and perfect balance, with none of the intimacy. None of the risk. I would escape the Shadow Wife's curse, and still keep Naraka whole.

I smiled to myself before realizing that a critical part was missing from my plan:

I needed a queen.

Gupta was hanging upside down in his favorite hallway, a bone-white corridor lined ceiling to floor with crackling tomes, glowing branches, and sweet-smelling parchments. He swung back and forth a little when he saw me.

"Don't look at me like that," he said, glaring. "Sometimes I need a new perspective when I'm writing."

"I was not going to comment. I recognize a hopeless case when I see one."

Gupta frowned at me upside down. "What do you want?"

"A bride."

"And I want dinner."

"I'm serious." He fell to the floor. I kicked at his foot. "Shocked?"

"Floored," said Gupta, and then he cackled at his own joke.

"This is no time for humor. I need a queen. Now."

"What brought this on?" asked Gupta, still not bothering to collect himself from the floor. "I believe I send you a list of prospective brides at least once a year. If memory serves, you burned each of those lists . . ."

"Not true. With the last couple of lists, I tossed them into the air . . ."

"You mean that tornado of paper that chased me down the hall?"

"See? I don't set fire to everything," I said. "Now to answer your question, it's become a necessity because I've seen it in the Tapestry."

Gupta paled. In a blink, he was upright, floating with his legs crossed and scribbling on parchment.

"But what about the . . ." He trailed off, and I knew what word had made him stumble.

"I found a way around the Shadow Wife's curse."

"How?"

"Simple," I said. "I won't fall in love."

Gupta raised an eyebrow, but said nothing.

"Now I need to find out what—"

"Not what," said Gupta. His gaze was unfocused, fixed somewhere on the cut of night sky through one of Naraka's windows. "Where. And *when*."

I couldn't remember the last time I'd been dragged to the Night Bazaar. It was the riotous, pulsing center of the Otherworld.

Here, merchants peddled all manner of strange wares—bones that told the truth, rare blooms that toyed with memories, harps that sang their players' emotions, and even edible colors shorn off from a single rainbow. It was a place I avoided as often as I could. Far too noisy. Full of simpering beings eager to pay false homage.

"What are we doing here?" I asked, ducking my chin to avoid making eye contact.

He cut a path through the merchant kiosks. From the corner of my eye, I spied a *kinnara* woman with bright gold feathers laying out a series of small weapons—bows and arrows that shifted diaphanous and half-invisible in the light; an *apsara* adjusted her anklets and threw her henna-stained hair over one shoulder; a *bhut* with its feet pointed backward peddled a cursed cup of alms. After years of walking leisurely—what was the point of running to something or someone when they could never escape you anyway—I found myself walking briskly. Impatiently.

And then, rising out from the crests of the merchant kiosks loomed a strange dais. Small birds carved of amber soared against a silk screen. Lotuses a violent shade of pink and purple released a drowsy perfume. I caught a whiff of it even where we stood and I drew my hood back. *Desire.* Heat coursed through me. Need gathered low and furious at the base of my skull. But I pushed back. When I chose a consort, those emotions would not drive me. If I had my way, we wouldn't feel them at all.

"*This* is where you will find your bride in two months' time."

"What's in two months?"

"Do you never keep track of holidays?"

"No."

"It's going to be *Teej* in two months."

My eyes must have widened because Gupta's grin stretched widely.

"Not so brooding and hidden in the dark that you could forget what that means."

"Apparently not."

Teej was the time when the members of the Otherworld selected a consort. Lovers would often arrange to meet and declare their choice of a consort by placing a single red bloom in their beloved's palm. But there was a strange rule to *Teej*. A heavy samite curtain separated them from each other's sight. Lovers would have to identify one another by the sight of their palm. Some didn't bother with choosing a lover beforehand. They would peruse the line of assorted hands and choose the one that called to their soul.

Foolish.

"You expect me to make this momentous decision by chance and simply show up at *Teej* and let someone choose me? Based on my *hand*?"

"You could do that."

I waited, then caught the smug tilt of his grin.

"Or?" I prompted through clenched teeth.

"*Or* you could take the two months you have available and find someone. And arrange to meet them at *Teej*."

"What if the right one doesn't come to *Teej*?"

Gupta scoffed. "Every Otherworld maiden will be at *Teej*. Trust me."

·» 2 «·

NIGHT

"You could promise me a palace of spun sugar and I wouldn't go," I said.

"What if I—"

"You could hang me upside down and tickle me with lightning and I would not be persuaded."

"Rather vicious, don't you think?" asked Nritti. She shook her head, and the small golden ornaments strung through her hair chimed sorrowfully. Three chimes. That never boded well.

I had lost count of how many times I had heard the chiming of Nritti's golden bells. To everyone else, the bells distinguished her as the chief *apsara* of the heavenly courts. Everyone else heard the bells and saw the cosmetic appeal—the glint of gold against the black fall of her hair, a trill of precious metal to silver her immaculate dance, a glittering crown that belonged to none else in the court of Svargaloka.

To me, the chimes were something to be translated. One chime meant: *Here we go again.* Two chimes meant: *I am questioning our friendship.* Three chimes meant: *Once more, I must rescue her from the depths of bad choices.*

Three chimes.

I shook my head. She sighed, and resumed kicking her feet in the pale blue river before us. At this hour, the river looked like a shard of sky. The reflection of rose-colored clouds floated down the still water. Soon, indigo would stain their edges. Like bruises. For a handful of moments, the sky would turn monstrous, purpled and marbled as if someone had beaten it senseless. One might call it cruel. And yet without it you'd never notice the stars.

Maybe the horror of dusk made the stars beautiful. You had to prize apart and flay the sky just to notice them. And for that cruelty, they bared their cold and unflinching beauty, their fixed and fervid glory. That beauty held truth—destiny and doom listed in the space between those burning silver infernos.

Nritti hugged her knees to her chest and followed my gaze. "You were the first person to tell me there was nothing violent about the night."

I smiled. "And you believed me because there was nothing violent about me."

She raised an eyebrow.

"Not entirely violent," I allowed.

"Not entirely scary."

We turned our gaze to the heavens and waited. There was beauty in the night, if you chose to see it. Some did. Some didn't. For some, night was the time of dreams and rest, of balance reasserting itself. For others, the hours crowded between dusk and dawn belonged to the ghosts. I knew what they feared: the uncertainty of nighttime, the lightlessness of those hours that were not the black comfort of sleep but the shadows at the bottom of a monster's throat. I glanced at my reflection and saw their fear staring right at me. Why could I not be dreams and nightmares both?

Nritti reached for my hand. I looked down to see our knitted fingers. Even though we had known each other all our lives, sometimes I never recognized myself beside her. Her skin—a lustrous gold—paled next to my own violent shades. *Almost time,* I thought. Vespertine ink bloomed across my skin, spelling the calligraphy of dusk and near-night. Stars winked in the crook of my elbow and a constellation curved around the bend of my thumb.

"Already?" asked Nritti.

"Shorter days."

"And longer nights."

"I don't mind."

"Of course you don't," laughed Nritti. "Self-loathing would not become you."

Behind me, the strange silver trees of the ashram stretched longingly toward the sky. I understood how they felt. It was only natural to want to feel part of something bigger than yourself. I glanced at my arm. Violet clouds shivered to life on my skin. A storm cloud kissed my wrist. And yet for all that I wore dusk and night . . . I was not part of the story. It is the price of immortality and eternal youth to never recognize your own fate in the stars. If we must live forever, then we must live blind.

I guarded the stars with my body. I let the constellations dance across my skin as if they could draw sustenance from the air I breathed. I coaxed nighttime into the world and guarded that sacred cusp of time before the world slipped once more into a tomorrow. I kept the past and present divided by a dance.

But it didn't matter how many days and nights or dusks and dawns passed. The truth was that no one could do what I did. And yet the entire world was as blind to me as the stars were blind to us all. As much as I loved the night, I wanted to break free of it as well. I wanted to be more than a canvas for stars and stories. I wanted to make my own.

Nritti looked behind me to the ashram. "Everyone wants to know where this place is. I bet there's already a crowd waiting for those dream fruits."

I followed her gaze to the orchard behind us. When I came here, the ashram became renowned for the strange fruit that sprang from the earth—slender, silver trees where fat purple fruit dragged the boughs to the earth like soul mates inexorably pulled to one another. The fruit always tasted cold, no matter how hot the day. All day I labored on those dreams, on what snippet of reality would be stretched thin and packed inside that fruit. When midnight fell, I came to the Night Bazaar and sold them for the price of someone recounting their day. I learned and listened, and they ate and dreamed.

"Your point?" I asked.

"You know, in my despair of you not joining me for *Teej*, I may accidentally let the location of this ashram and your famous orchard slip . . ."

I narrowed my eyes. "You wouldn't."

"I would never!" she said, feigning hurt. "But maybe I would."

"And you call *me* manipulative."

"I'm just trying to—"

"—look out for me, do what's best for me, instruct me in all the ways of living and point out the sun in case I mistook it for an orange."

She considered this. "Yes."

"I'm not hopeless."

"But you are sheltered. And stubborn as a mule."

"It could be worse. I could have the face of a mule too. I'm counting my blessings."

"Or you could have my face," she said. "Count your blessings that you don't."

In the fading dusk, Nritti looked silvered. *Apsaras* were always beautiful, but she was a gem even among them. It didn't matter that her hair had fallen out of its braid or that her clothes were crumpled. She looked more polished than a gemstone that had gulped down the moon.

For as long as I had known her, Nritti had the kind of beauty that earned her a place among the stars. When she entered a room, light clung to her. When she left a room, light seemed a mere legend. No radiance compared. But it came with a price. One that wore on her. I nudged her arm.

"How many marriage proposals this time?" I asked.

"The usual."

"About a hundred?"

"Give or take."

"Any entertaining acts of idiocy amongst all your besotted suitors?"

She smacked my arm, laughing in spite of herself. "Don't mock their love."

"Why not? They mock you with the assumption that you'd say

yes." I rolled my eyes. "More than that, they mock you by assuming there's nothing more than your beauty and dancing."

"Isn't there?"

"You sing too."

Another smack. Another laugh. But this one a little more hollow.

"One of them said he'd write my name in the stars," said Nritti. "He was a mortal king, invited to the court of the heavens for a great *yagna* he held honoring the gods."

"And so . . ."

"And so he fell off a balcony with a sword in his hand. I think he intended to cut a path through the stars."

Now it was my turn to laugh.

"Did you catch him?"

"Oh yes. Eventually. But I did let him fall a great deal before I stood up."

We laughed for a long while, stealing seconds before my evening duties called me from her side.

"Is that why you want to attend *Teej*? To find a consort and hopefully put an end to all these unwelcome marriage proposals?"

She shrugged, and her hair ornaments chimed delicately.

"I don't want simply to *find* someone. I could've done that years ago."

I raised an eyebrow. "You want love."

"Is that bad?"

"Of course not. I want that too."

It'd been something we'd talked of since we first met. She'd been asked to perform a solo dance for the grand Festival of Lights. I'd barely started making dream fruit, and the night was so new that it was hardly flecked with stars. She was nervous about practicing in the light, so I conjured shadows for her and we became friends.

"Then I want love," she said simply. "And I'm willing to believe that I can find it. I'm willing to be brave enough to search for it, even if that means failing."

"Are you hoping the God of Love will be at *Teej*? Crouching behind the curtains and stringing his sugarcane bow and arrow of honeybees?"

She laughed. "Will you let me know if you see him?"

"Certainly. I'll be the one bribing him to make you fall in love with a cow."

"Not a bull?"

"I prefer the scandal."

Just then, the clouds in the river began to break apart. The silver trees behind us shivered in wait. The crossover from day to night was complete. I glanced up and saw the faint impression of hoofmarks against the clouds. Ushas—the goddess of dawn—had already driven away her chariot, and magic had eagerly poured back into the world.

We were in the human world, but just barely. Night thinned the boundaries of the mortal and Otherworld. Small amber lanterns no bigger than a thumbnail danced across the river. A handful of scarlet *kinnara* feathers drifted down the stream, releasing smoke and sparks of gold into the air. The *gunghroo* bells of *apsaras* ignited the silence. Nritti heard it too and stiffened as her own bells began to chime and keen.

But not all the magic that poured out at night was full of light and feathers and music. In the distance, I heard rough hands pounding on a stone drum, and the hollow knocking of skulls garlanded around a *raksha*'s belly.

"I have to go," said Nritti, standing.

"I know. So do I."

Soon, I'd have to shuck off this sari. Someone would notice if a disembodied dress started dancing and floating around. Nritti thought it was scandalous to run around naked. Technically, I was not *running around* naked. I was *dancing around* naked. Which sounded worse. But was it scandalous if no one could even tell?

"I'll see you afterward?" asked Nritti, breaking my thoughts and nodding to the orchard.

"Always."

"Prepare yourself for a crowd, sister. Tonight, we are entertaining a princeling."

From time to time, mortal rulers were invited as personal guests to the Otherworld to reward them for certain prayers, offerings, or even aid in battle against demon spirits. And from time to time, some of them returned with an *apsara* for a wife. Their first wives were rarely pleased.

"What did this one do for the honor?"

Nritti shrugged. "I think he helped in some battle or another."

"Poor thing. I don't envy the attention he'll get."

The Otherworld had a bizarre fascination with humans. But they often expressed it with zero decorum. I'd once seen a curious *naga* girl tugging at a human boy's neck, bemused because he hid no cobra hood behind his ears.

"It seems like fitting punishment for dragging me from your side," said Nritti. "I hope he leaves with nothing short of four hundred proposals of marriage and a cursed sandal that causes him to stub his toe every day. But I'm glad, at least, that you get something out of that crowd."

She stared past me to the silver trees heavy with fruit.

A human prince meant a huge Otherworld crowd. And a huge crowd meant more people to buy dream fruit. Maybe I'd buy some new trinkets after they bartered. An amphora of honey from moon-bees. Or a bolt of silk culled from sea roses.

A s soon as Nritti left, I began.

Night heralded sleep and shadows, demons and dreams. But I heralded night.

Sometimes I wondered whether that made me worse than a demon. But I supposed no one berated a door for allowing a robber to cross the threshold. Then again, people could be unforgivably stupid.

The sky broke. Black, starless waves poured into the ether, hovering over the world like a blanket that refused to fall. This was the very essence of night. The eerie scent of shadows perfumed the world. It smelled like fear at an unexpected bloom of cold between your shoulder blades; like the prickling of ice at feeling inexplicably watched; like a breath yanked from your lungs when you had run out of stairs on a staircase and couldn't figure out how. But the dark didn't scare me.

Quite the opposite.

I rose into the air, letting the wind whip my hair around my face. Where did the sky end and I start? I never wanted to find out. I let myself sink into that feeling of being infinite. For a moment, I had neither edges nor emptiness. I was everywhere. Everything. A cut of stars. The shadow of a crescent moon. The satin sand beneath the wave. The bistre loam beneath the land.

I reached out and snatched the darkness, dragging it down to earth with me. It needed to be sewn into the world, tucked beneath every leaf and stone, hewn to every mountain crest and sculpted into the bowl of every lush valley. But the only way to make the night stick to the world was to dance it into place.

And so I did.

Unlike Nritti, I had no *gunghroo* bells to transfix my audience. But the sound of my feet hitting the forest floor caused the birds in the trees to tuck their heads beneath their wings. When I pressed my fingers into *mudras*, no crowd roared with applause. But the earth sighed, as if it had finally accepted the weight of darkness and chose to sleep rather than spar. I bent, ready to unfurl the last shadow when I heard twigs snapping underfoot.

Cold pierced my spine.

Whenever I danced, every mortal thing that may have been able to see me would instantly fall asleep. In the mortal realms, everything could die. Not even the trees watched.

Yet, something . . . *someone* . . . was doing the impossible.

I spun around. "Who's there?"

From beneath the heart-shaped leaves of a *peepal* tree, something rustled. And a voice, so lush it made ambrosia acrid, answered me.

"Only the lowly painter who tries each night, in vain, to capture evening herself."

"What do you want? Show yourself."

The stranger stepped out of the *peepal* tree. He was broad-shouldered, his features as severely beautiful as a strike of lightning.

He wore a crown of blackbuck horns that arced in graceful whorls of onyx, catching the light. But it was his gaze that robbed the clamoring rhythm in my chest.

His stare slipped beneath my skin. And when he saw my eyes widen, he smiled. And in that moment, his smile banished my loneliness. He moved toward me, grasping my hand, and his touch hummed in my bones like an aria. A song to my dance. The beginning of a promise.

Which is just about when I realized that I was wearing nothing.

And also when I realized that he didn't seem to mind that I wasn't wearing anything.

I yanked my hand away in the same instant that shadows rushed out of the ground to hug my body. Granted, it was hard to tell what was what when the sky and I looked the same. You had to look close. But this stranger had looked at me the way no one had before, and I wasn't taking any chances.

Shock forced me to stare at him, and my heart plummeted. The blackbuck horns. The leather bracelet around his wrist that I knew could swing into a noose at any time.

"Gods," I breathed.

"Just one," said the Dharma Raja, grinning.

I raised an eyebrow and gestured at myself.

"You specified gods," he said. "Not goddesses."

I raised one brow. "I am glad you acknowledged me, oh Dharma Raja. For a moment, I thought you had confused me for a mortal and meant to take my soul."

"I'm not here for your soul."

But he was here for something. My eyebrows soared up my forehead. The Dharma Raja never left Naraka unless a pristine human soul had called him to the human world. He never wandered through the Night Bazaar. And Nritti told me that he rarely attended the festivities in the heavenly courts. When he did, he was notoriously somber. The only time he enjoyed himself was when he was tormenting any visiting mortal kings by dropping his noose beside their knees by "accident."

"What are you here for?"

Without any hesitation, he said: "I am here to make you my bride."

Shock rooted me to the spot. All I could do was stare. And as I stared, I had the strange observation that he had the kind of beauty made for nighttime. Not because the darkness blurred his features or hid any imperfections. But because the shadows understood him. The shadows silhouetted his impressive frame, so that he looked cut from the sky. And when he grinned, I saw some of the beauty that belonged to night alone. Moon roses unfurling in quartz caves. Midnight rivers swollen with stars. Secret sights that were never meant for sunlight.

I met his eyes levelly and folded my arms across my chest. "Why now?"

He frowned, as if that was not the question he had prepared to answer. "Not 'why me?'"

"I don't need a recitation of my virtues and beauty. Although I wouldn't say no to an epic ballad dedicated to them either . . ."

"I shall start composing immediately . . ."

"You wouldn't be my first suitor, and you probably won't be my last. So no. I know why you would ask. What I want to know is why you have chosen *now* of all times to come out of hiding in unmarried bliss . . ."

"People think I've been hiding this whole time?"

"What did you want them to think you were doing?"

"Something more sinister."

"Brooding?" I suggested.

He considered this. "It would be less insulting than cowering from potential brides."

"Have you met the women of the Otherworld?" I asked, laughing. "I assure you that no one would find you cowardly for hiding from them. We are fearsome to behold."

The corner of his mouth tilted up. "I've gathered."

"So? Why now?"

He drew himself up, squaring his shoulders. Had he practiced this? I wanted to laugh, then thought better than to humiliate him.

"I would like a companion. The duty of my existence is to tend to the balance of things and I have failed in that regard toward my own personal life. Besides, I think you and I would suit well. I wish for a queen who would rule beside me and not be afraid of the dark. You wish for recognition. There will be no love between us, but there will be tranquil balance without the complication of passions and I will be true to you and honor you above all others."

My fingers tightened in my sari. Had a more bland and lifeless proposal ever been delivered? Nritti's proposals always involved men jumping out of balconies and trying to cut a path through the stars, or women making declarations of unending love and swearing it on every hair of her head.

"I've heard about you," he said quietly. His solemnity broke, and curiosity took its place. "Every night you peddle dream fruit. Every night you ask for someone to tell you a part of their day. Every night you ask if they remember the dreams you gave them. Someone else might think it's a routine check of your merchandise, but I suspect it is more. I suspect that you feel a flicker of hope every time someone remembers the dreams you gave them. I suspect that you want them to remember and perhaps even *act* upon it. Why do you do it?"

No one had ever spoken to me like that.

"I thought kings prided themselves on subtlety."

He shrugged. "Death is not subtle. Death is a slam in the chest, a sudden extinguishing of lights. Why should I be any different?"

Fair.

"Then to answer your question, I do it because I want to be more than the stories reflected on my skin," I said. I'd never spoken those words aloud, not even to Nritti. And once I had freed them from my thoughts, I couldn't seem to stop: "I want to make things that are true. I want to write my own legacy in the stars instead of simply having the stars be my legacy."

As I spoke, rage flickered in my voice. I thought of all the times I had tried to push for more and all the times the world had pushed back. When you had everything, what was more? When I looked into the Dharma Raja's eyes, I saw a shadow of that craving. That desire for the bone-deep contentment of wanting nothing. I craved that fullness. I craved it every time I woke to a fresh dusk and fell into my solitary work, knowing that this copse of trees and slice of time was all I possessed. I craved it when I walked through the Night Bazaar, arms full of dream fruit and wondering if any of their flavors would last beyond sleep's fickle memory.

He tilted his head, considering this. "You want power."

"Recognition."

"Same thing," he said, waving a hand. "My kingdom could use

someone like you. A queen with fury in her heart and shadows in her smile. Someone restless and clever."

Queen. Being queen—especially of a realm like Naraka—was a position bristling with power. But simply because time grew in abundance didn't mean that it should be squandered. Besides, the Dharma Raja himself said that I should expect no love in our marriage. Who would ever want that? I'd forgotten how many times Nritti and I had spoken of finding love. And the truth was that I wanted to spend my life with someone who made eternity too short. I wanted a love that time could never erode, a foundation that would grow spires and turrets large enough to swallow constellations. And yet I wanted love like a home, a corner of the universe built for two and snug as skin. I wouldn't settle for less. Queen or no.

"I will not have you," I said.

"Rather hasty."

"So was your proposal. Choose another."

"I choose you."

His cold arrogance splintered. And beneath it, I saw someone who looked as hesitant as I felt. My hands dropped from my body. For a split second, I let myself revel in the knowledge that he *wanted* me. He, whom so many others had blindly tried to discover behind the samite curtains of *Teej.* He, who ruled Naraka with an iron fist and a flinty gaze but was as notorious for his honor as he was his isolation. He . . . who had introduced himself as a *lowly painter who tries each night, in vain, to capture evening herself.*

I narrowed my eyes.

"Regretfully, oh Dharma Raja, I must reject your proposal," I said, dropping into a half-curtsy that could best be described as an unfortunate flop. "And out of the goodness in my heart, I must warn you that should you inflict that horrific introductory line on any other woman, she will probably reject you too."

His gaze dropped. Nritti would be horrified with me. I had insulted the Dharma Raja. As I watched him, I noticed that his shoulders had begun to shake. He was . . . *laughing.* He threw his head back, laughing all the while. When he finally stopped, he looked me in the eye and said:

"May I visit you again? If you do not wish it, I will not return. I would not disrespect your wishes."

"But . . . but I just rejected you."

"I prefer the challenge of courtship."

He made it sound as if this was a game. I found myself intrigued, but not enchanted. And certainly not in love. I pushed out the memory of the first time I saw him and that inexplicable surge between us that felt like a secret I'd forgotten. If he wanted to play a game with me, then so be it. I have never lost.

"I have nothing better to do, so I suppose I can indulge my curiosity," I said, lifting my chin. "For your own sake, please don't imagine that means I'm interested in becoming your queen. I won't marry without love. And you refuse to marry with love. So it seems we are at an impasse."

"So it seems. But you may surprise yourself in finding what matters more to you," he said smoothly. "I've spent eons wandering. Do you know how many times I've been offered everything if only I would let them live? Men have offered their wives in their stead. Mothers have sometimes tried to exchange one child's life for another. Lovers will suddenly have a change of heart when one meets the dagger and the other is left wondering whether life without them is quite so dismal after all."

Even as he spoke, ambition lit up my thoughts. If I never found love, would it be so bad to possess every other dream of mine but that one? But then I steeled myself. I had seen the loss of love too often and soothed too many lonely hearts to sleep that I refused to live that way.

"We will see whose thoughts win out in the end."

"I never lose."

I smiled. "Neither do I."

"I suspect that over the course of our courtship, you may feel differently."

"You'll court me with tales of bitter disillusionment and jaded tales of love? Please excuse me while I swoon at your feet."

He fell quiet for a second and pain flickered over his face. Then, just as quickly, he resumed his collected demeanor.

"It is customary to bring gifts when courting," he said. "Do you . . . want anything?"

"Of course I want things." I laughed. "I want the moon for my throne. Stars to wear in my hair. A garden unlike any in all the realms."

He considered this. "It shall be done. I will take my leave of you now."

"You'll come back tomorrow?" I asked.

He looked at me, bewildered. As if the thought of not coming back was nothing short of impossible.

"And the next day. And the day after that."

"For how long?"

"As long as it takes."

"And if I never say yes?"

"If that is the case, then I hope you'd take pity on me and tell me never to return. Even death shows mercy, for at least it is an ending."

When he left, sticky warmth seeped into my grove of trees. I never liked the heat. Nritti loved basking in the sun, but I preferred the cold. When the Dharma Raja stood before me, the very atmosphere had turned cool and winter-scented. Maybe that's why I had relaxed in his presence. Even now, my body hungered for the cold of him. I stared at the spot where he had disappeared. *As long as it takes.*

What exactly had I agreed to?

And why would he ask for a marriage without love?

When the Dharma Raja left, I collected the dream fruit. I placed my hand against the bark and found it perfectly cold and polished as a pearl. One by one, I plucked the ripest fruits. They were dusky as plums, and yet there was something of the Otherworld to them. An uncanny chill to their flesh. A strange gemstone sheen to their deep violet. The moment someone ate them, the flesh would break apart—inky and star-flecked as the night sky. It tasted like the outskirts of consciousness. Of wanting. That's what made the Otherworld so ravenous. This was why I asked every night for them to tell me about their day. I wanted to hear the lilt at the end of their sentences. How they had yearned for one last piece of moon candy. How they had been pulled from their beds too early. Sometimes the act of wanting was more intoxicating than the pleasure of realizing the act.

I arrived in the Night Bazaar just in time to watch Nritti's last dance. Every time I crossed into the Otherworld, a wave of shock fell over me. There were so many people. So many *things*. Life pulsed all around me and I reveled in the surge of sounds, so different from my usual quiet haunt where sleep and shadows frosted the world.

My collection of dream fruit floated behind me, kept cool in its shadow bundle. Soon, I'd have to make my way to the side of Night, which was the only place where the fruit wouldn't spoil. But for a moment, I tilted my head back and stared at the sun. I had to settle for this half-view of daytime and this ripped sky. As always, my imagination wandered over what the sky truly looked like during the day. When I awoke each dusk, the world looked bloodied, as if the sun had waged a war to stay in the sky and lost. Nritti said morning and day were soft and golden, an infinite crown fitted over the world. She said it looked like peace. I wished I could've known peace.

The passersby began to jostle back and forth. Some inclined their heads to me in respect. Others turned away, disgust flitting across their features. I steeled myself. Whenever a mortal prince visited the Otherworld, the large crowd diluted the true denizens of the Night Bazaar. For the most part, the Otherworld understood my role in the balance of light and dark. They never perceived me as some harbinger of evil. But when beings poured in from every crevice of the world, they dragged along whatever local superstitions had gathered in the places where they haunted and guarded, ruled and treasured. The human world was still young. To them, night brought no dreams. Only nightmares made real.

"It's her," a *naga* whispered to his mate. Their cobra hoods flared around their faces.

Beliefs in fear had a way of tethering minds. I couldn't help that once I had tucked night around the world that things with empty backs and hollow grins began to look for sustenance. Night was not meant to be protective. Night was meant to be restorative. Most days,

I let that knowledge spread through me like a balm. But today I felt exhausted. I moved away from the *naga* and his mate without glancing into their eyes.

Around me, vendors hawked all manner of objects. There were sweets for sale—handfuls of stardust shaped into glittering whorls and shimmering blossoms. A beautiful *nagini* grabbed a fistful and waved it through the air.

"To enhance the beautiful visions dancing before your eyes! Guaranteed to taste sweeter than an *apsara*'s kiss or one year of your life will be returned to you free of charge!" she promised.

More vendors. More tables. Enchanted flutes for sale. A tonic in an emerald bottle guaranteed to honey the voice and ensnare listeners. Tins of cosmetics, kohl made from pressed shadows, and pots of deep red and scarlet stolen from the last flames of sunset.

In front of me, a couple playfully argued as they made their way to the podium of celestial nymphs.

"What if you prefer their beauty to mine and leave me?" teased the woman in front of me. She was a lovely being. Her slim torso disappeared into elegant golden feathers and shining talons. Golden pearls wreathed her wings and her smile was lustrous. Content.

Her mate leaned toward her. Light winked out in the space between his head curving to hers, like day flashing to night. He traced her feathers.

"Your beauty rivals the sun. Your sweetness rivals the moon. You are every beginning and end," he said, brushing a kiss to her temple. "You are entirely inescapable."

The tenderness between them sharpened into an edge, and I felt cut. I remembered, suddenly, what loneliness looked like. Loneliness looked like a gaping hole where there should have been your reflection in a mirror. My throat tightened. I couldn't look away from the couple, and yet the longer I stared at them, the more I felt a heaviness weighing on my chest.

I walked faster, and my thoughts slipped into familiar daydreams. Daydreams of shadows fitted together, eager hands waiting to trace a beloved face, warmth blossoming between two hearts. In those dim spaces behind want, a face emerged in my dreams. A hard and unforgiving face, whose beauty belonged to the night and whose eyes looked cut from stone. The Dharma Raja. As soon as the image came to mind, I jolted. I couldn't picture the Dharma Raja walking beside me in the Night Bazaar. But for some reason, I could picture him walking beside me in other places. By a grove of silver trees. By a sea of pleated starlight. By a palace of marble and glass.

A horrid bellowing broke my reverie.

I spun around to see a *raksha* with the head of a water buffalo twirling a pair of eyeballs around his head.

"Enchanted pair of eyes! Useful for seeing through all kinds of things," he shouted. "Like deception and jars of wine. Or even"—he stopped and grinned—"a lovely *apsara*'s clothes."

A group of men crowded the *raksha*. I moved past them and flicked my wrist. A night wind rattled through the bazaar, kicking up the silk skirts of tents and display tables and stealing the eyeballs straight out of the *raksha*'s hands and into my palm.

The *raksha* blinked. "What happened to it?"

"You lied to us!" yelled one male.

"THIEF!" roared the *raksha*.

I grinned, ducking beneath a silver rope strung with colored glass lanterns before disappearing into the crowd. Nritti hated the way some of the men and women of the Otherworld looked at her. Some women would lust after her. Some women would blame her for love unrequited. Some men would lust after her. Some men would blame her for love unrequited. And when everyone in this world had power, beauty could become a dangerous thing.

By the time I got to the *apsaras'* dancing podium, a huge crowd had gathered. I watched as the *apsaras* soared through the air, silk trailing behind them. Each time they stamped their feet, the *gunghroo* bells around their ankles released tiny blooms of petals and gold dust. The crowd sighed. Tablas dropped low beats and the sky broke, sending golden flakes to rain down on the audience. They were near the final movement of the dance. Flutes and bells, horns and silvery voices grew louder in urgency, spinning a story to which the *apsaras* danced. A tale of kings vanquishing demons who wandered beyond their realm and invaded the mortal world in the dead of night. Nritti had mentioned that tonight's performance would be held in honor of the human prince. Maybe the song was about him and his deeds. I spotted an opening near the back of the crowd and edged closer. I couldn't stay for the finale, but I always tried to see Nritti's dance before I set up the vendor stall of dream fruit.

From the sudden intakes of breath, I knew that Nritti had taken over the stage. She leapt into the air, soaring above the others. The light clung to her, and her steps echoed in the very vaults of the heavens.

Here was why they called her the Jewel of the Heavens.

When Nritti danced, the world felt too small. Spectators leaned out, crowding themselves elbow to elbow to watch her. Except one. Seated at the front of the stage and flanked in an ivory throne carved of clouds, sat a young man. His crown was mortal-made, for it did not gleam with Otherworld jewels and even his finest silks were not as resplendent as the most common of our garb for it did not contain a single thread of moonlight. In profile, he was handsome. When he turned his head, he was shockingly beautiful. Even Nritti—who had walked past the god of love himself without a second glance—could not keep her eyes off of him and he, even though he was not looking at her, seemed to tilt toward the sound of her. His whole body seemed shaped to the light she cast. It was only when he turned his head to face the crowd that I saw why he didn't bother to look at her:

He was blind.

". . . I asked him *twice* about the talon marks down his back," said a harried *yakshini*. She had a long multicolored beak and bright gold hair that ruffled furiously about her face. "And do you know what he said?"

I faked a grin. Sometimes I'd get customers who considered purchasing a dream fruit little more than telling someone all about their horrific day. This was one of those occasions. The line had been long at first, but once this *yakshini* had gotten in line, half the beings behind her had dwindled. The other half were either smiling smugly—probably thinking of how to leverage the long wait time into their haggling methods—and the other half were one word away from leaving. I wanted to scream. This woman was jeopardizing my ability to empty out the Night Bazaar of its sari collection.

"No, I don't. But I do think that you've paid generously for a dream fruit. Perhaps even two!"

She cocked her head to one side. "Two?"

"Yes."

I shoved the fruit into her arms.

"One for you and one for your mate," I said loudly and quickly. "Nothing makes a couple stay together more than mutual dreams."

"I suppose so," she said, gathering the fruit. "Thank you."

"Thank you."

I did not say: *Please come again soon.*

The next person in line was a handsome *asura*. He was tall, broad-shouldered, with sparkling eyes that glinted green as the jungle in one moment and blue as the sea in the next.

"That line was horrifically long, but had I known that a thing as lovely as you waited on the other side, I wouldn't have complained."

A thing. I suppressed a recoil.

"I am sorry about the wait."

"I could wait forever."

Please stop talking.

"But compensation is necessary. My time is precious. I'm a king, you know."

So are half the people here.

"What do you want?"

"Three dream fruit."

"For the price of what?" I asked, bristling.

"Oh no, beauty. I'm not paying. This is compensation. I can guarantee you that just by standing here in your line and letting my presence be felt, I've increased the size of your customers."

Or chased away a third.

"That's out of the question."

"Forget the dream fruit then," said the *asura*. He leaned forward, bracing his elbows against the table. "Let us talk about what I may offer you."

"Remove yourself."

"You know what I find interesting?" he said, reaching for my hand.

I yanked it back.

"Half the people here always think that you summon demons to your side. How would you like to prove those rumors true, beauty?" He smiled. "What do you do all day? Tend to your dream orchard and wait on nightfall? Surely, you would prefer my company to all those lonesome trees?"

"I would prefer the company of feral tigers with foul breath and a lightning bolt for a tail instead of you. Get out. You're not interested in these wares. And I am certainly not interested in yours."

"Oh, dear Night. So delicate. So lonely. So unfamiliar with the ways of demons and men. Let me teach you. You are wrong, you know. I am interested in your wares," he said, grinning. "Just not the fruit."

"You're interested in my wares?" I asked, tilting my head. I smiled, looking at him through the veil of my lashes. Light skittered over my skin, as if my fury had piqued the stars' interest.

He was hardly a hand span away from my face. Up close, his eyes were pond swill. His breath reeked of blood. "You see, no one else would ever want you. You spend so much time in that human world, you might as well be one. Who would ever pair themselves with something so sullied? No husband would share your bed for fear that you may bring demons upon him when he sleeps. But me? I'm different. I would touch you. Only I could ever bear to touch you."

Wrong, I thought. An image of the Dharma Raja bloomed in my mind. He was at my side, a cold smile and poor flattery on his lips. I raised my hand to the *asura.* White light winked in my palm.

"Could you truly suffer my touch? Me and all my delicate, lonesome, cursed weakness?"

"Yes," he said hungrily.

"How selfless of you." I brought my palm to his skin. His eyes widened, ringed around with white. My arm tensed in the struggle, the star-spangled and black velvet of my skin twitching in restraint. *I could burn you*, I thought. *But that wouldn't bode well for my reputation.* Still, I kept him there and for a terrible moment, the knowledge that I *could* burn him to a stunted pair of horns rushed through me in a delicious wave.

"The stars are rather delicate, aren't they?" I whispered low in his ear. He was sweating now. The air had the metallic tang of flesh collapsing under heat. "Do you forget that I wear the stories of the world on my skin? I don't care that demons take advantage of my hours to kill and plunder. That is not my concern. You are too small for me, little monster. I keep time aloft. I keep the promise of tomorrow. And you are nothing."

He broke away, gasping. A ghostly imprint of my hand spanned across his cheek. Glittering bits of stars clung to his singed eyelashes and burnt ear.

"Monster," he hissed.

I grinned. "Only at night."

He ran.

"I'll be back tomorrow if you want some more!" I hollered after him.

The line went quickly after that. A few of the customers rushed through their orders. Eager to get away from me perhaps. The last person in line slithered forward, sinuous and languid. Small gems sparkled off her serpent tail. Dramatically, she flung back her cobra hood. Then again, she did everything dramatically. Uloopi, the princess of the *nagas*, braced her elbows on the table and winked at me.

"I see you've been making friends," she said, nodding in the direction where the *asura* had disappeared. She grinned.

The first time I opened the stand for dream fruit, no one came. No one wanted to pay the price with their own stories and secrets. And yet they all wanted to dream. Uloopi was the first to slither toward the stall. She had promptly scattered all the passersby who refused to purchase anything and loudly proclaimed: "Finally. I've been waiting to tell someone all the sordid details of my life." Most of her sordid details were other people's gossip, but I reveled in it anyway. Every day since, Uloopi left her subterranean palace to wander through the Night Bazaar, criticize every person's outfit, reluctantly tell me her secrets and eagerly tell me other people's, and buy a dream fruit.

"Are you going to *Teej*?" I asked.

She shuddered. "What would I want with an immortal consort? They live far too long for my taste."

"You prefer human princes."

"Always."

"It doesn't hurt to love them?"

She looked at me sharply and then her gaze darted to something behind me. "Of course it does. But I'd rather feel that pain than nothing at all. That is always the problem with immortality, is it not? That one day we will outlive our love of life."

"You may find someone who makes you feel otherwise."

Uloopi waved a disinterested hand. "That day has yet to come."

"I'm sure you'll tell me all about it when it does."

"If I do, I want your whole supply of dream fruit."

"Deal."

"Excellent," said Uloopi. She raised one slim eyebrow. "Want some gossip?"

"Absolutely not!" I fluttered my hand to my neck before leaning over the counter. "Why? Who's it about?"

Uloopi laughed. "Did you see that man who grew three other heads last week?"

"I think I'd remember if I saw that."

"Well, *I* heard that it's because he wanted to keep a couple extra eyes on his wife. Honestly, if you want to keep your wife, is your head the thing you should be investing in?"

I swatted her. "Blasphemy."

She held out her hand: "Dream fruit, please. Or I'll tattle on you to Nritti."

"You know you don't get any dream fruit until you tell me something about yourself. And besides, Nritti wouldn't believe you."

"A serpent tail was not the only thing I inherited from snakes, you know. I have hypnotic eyes."

"That's just myth."

"Am I a myth so soon? You're making me feel ancient. Only thing noteworthy today was that I've nearly perfected a resurrection jewel."

"That sounds useful considering you can't die."

"I wanted to see if I could make the impossible and as usual I outdid myself." She flipped her hair over her shoulder. "Is that exciting enough for you? We can't all have absurd and tragic tales like the Shadow Wife."

"Who's that?"

Uloopi rolled her eyes. "Don't you know anything?"

"I spend most of my time outside of the heavens and in the human world. I don't get much gossip."

Uloopi huffed, which I took as tacit acceptance that she thought I had a point.

"The last scandal I remember was when the Lady Saranyu, the wife of the Sun god, decided she could no longer stand the brilliance of her husband. So she ran away and left her shadow, the Lady Chayya, in her place."

"He didn't notice?"

"Of course not! They were twin images of one another."

"But they were different people?"

Uloopi's gaze turned sly. "Of course! But men can be fools. And so it was not the Sun god who discovered the deception, but the child that the Lady Saranyu had left behind. The Shadow Wife bore her own children from the Sun god. And she favored them above Lady Saranyu's child."

"What happened?"

Uloopi's voice dropped to a conspiratorial whisper. "The child knew and told the Sun god. He was furious and went out into the world to bring back the Lady Saranyu."

"And the child?"

"Cursed by the Shadow Wife."

"With what?"

"My friend, *that* is the question. No one knows."

"What happened to the Sun god?"

"He ended up with two wives."

I shook my head. "And the child?"

"I have no mind to ask *him* how he's faring since that incident."

"It's a boy? Who—"

Uloopi jumped back, smiling. "Ah! Look who it is. The Jewel of the Heavens."

Nritti floated down from the air and sank into a graceful curtsy. "I've come to pay my respects to the Terror of the Deep."

"Is that what they call me?" asked Uloopi, her brows creasing. She smiled. "I love it."

"Of course you do, monster."

Uloopi stuck her tongue out. I tossed her a dream fruit, and she caught it with one hand. Nritti summoned a cloud and fell back into it like it was a bed, while Uloopi settled into her emerald coils. I leaned against the table where I'd sold dream fruit and surveyed the Night Bazaar. The three of us went through the same ritual at the end of every day. We'd huddle together, watch the beings, and recite all the things about our day that had gone right and wrong.

Nritti took a deep breath. "Something happened today."

"The blind princeling," Uloopi said, not taking her eyes off the sky. She had an obsession with the sky, perhaps because she saw so little of it in her sea palace.

"What's his name?" I asked.

"Vanaj," she said. Sighed, rather. She exhaled his name like it was something precious and teased out of her.

I narrowed my eyes. "Did you have anything to drink?"

In answer, she swatted my arm. "No. We talked for a long time."

"*Talked.* That's a modest euphemism," said Uloopi. "And for a long time you say? My, my."

"Don't be crude."

"Too late for that." I smiled. She seemed happy, and my heart welled in happiness for her. Nritti was kind and giving. She deserved joy. "You seem smitten."

"Perhaps a little."

"I'm sure he feels the same."

She smiled. "I hope so."

Uloopi spent the next hour mercilessly teasing Nritti, while I tried not to laugh. I kept fighting the urge to tell them about the Dharma Raja. But I was still in disbelief. And part of me didn't want to reveal this secret. I didn't want it prized apart and examined under Uloopi's harsh humor, or poked and prodded by Nritti's questioning. So I kept silent.

When a new day lightened the sky, we stood up and made our way to the edge of the Night Bazaar. The market had already begun to shift and gather itself for the next day. Tents turned transparent as glass before spiraling into pillars. Golden motes of pollen fell through the air and landed on the discarded and the spent. Broken jewelry clasps, silk cones full of half-eaten iced fruit, trampled *shatranj* pieces and bits of paper with predictions of true love. No sooner had the golden dust touched them, and then they disappeared into the ether.

"I met someone too," I said, so softly that neither Uloopi nor Nritti heard.

The words still felt unfamiliar and impossible on my tongue. I wanted to savor the sound of them, each word a bright candy for me alone. I knew they'd be supportive and teasing, loving in their own way.

But I wanted to keep the secret of him close.

· » 3 « ·

DEATH

YESTERDAY

I n Naraka, the mirrors gloated. Behind their silver faces, cities spied on me just as I spied on them. I wondered what they thought of this pacing mess of a king. From the corner of my eye, I could have sworn that I saw a tree quivering with laughter. Even the palace, which was usually restrained in its mischief, taunted me, and voices from a hundred directions whistled smugly:

Is the Dharma Raja nervous?

I ignored them and tipped backward just as an onyx throne spiraled from the ground to catch me. Leaning back, I squinted up at the glittering mirrors. In the smudgy darkness of the palace, they looked like shards of stars.

The sight of the *Teej* podium had unsettled me. I could not forget the scent clinging to those lotus blooms, the way a specific desire had been fitted to every gap within me. Every time I closed my eyes, I thought I caught the perfume of the companion in my dreams. A girl who smelled like night-blooming flowers and silver on roses. I needed to meet her. And yet, a part of me couldn't stomach the thought. A word echoed in my thoughts: *cursed, cursed, cursed.*

I had to be careful not to love her.

"Hungry?" called Gupta.

He was whistling as he walked toward me, carrying a silver platter full of the strangest fruit I'd ever seen. It was night-black; each inky slice looked flecked with stars. A curious smell filled the air, like a dream that had ended at the best part.

"Where did you find this?" I asked. I didn't want to take a bite. I already felt unfulfilled as it is.

"You should really read my reports."

"Not in this life."

He rolled his eyes. "They're dream fruit. Created by Night herself."

"What's her name again?"

I'd never seen her in the courts of the heavens, but that was because she spent so much of her existence in the human world. I had heard her name before on the lips of the dead and dying. They thought she heralded *me*. Ridiculous. No one could summon me.

"Oh, many . . . Kalindi, Yamini, Syamala . . . surely you've heard of her?"

"In passing."

"Met her?"

"No."

This, for whatever reason, seemed to be the correct answer to Gupta. He drummed his ink-stained fingers against his arm.

"Rather intriguing guardian. When the day is gone and the night descends to take her place, many people in all the realms consider it a time that belongs to the demons and the dead. And you, naturally. Some perceive her as something of an ill omen."

I smiled to myself. I knew that feeling of never walking somewhere without a thread of fear unspooling in every living being. Where the shadow of you fell like a veil over every conversation and every interaction. I enjoyed it entirely. No reason to waste a single word on etiquette. It was considered merciful not to speak and thoughtful to avoid, essentially, everyone.

"I imagine she must revel in it," I said.

"Quite the contrary," Gupta said. He tossed a slice of fruit in the air to catch it with his teeth. It bounced off his mouth and fell to the ground. "Nooo . . . that was the last piece."

"So get more."

He flailed an arm at the fallen slice. If it were me, I would've immediately swiped it off the ground. Actually, if it were me, it would have never fallen in the first place. But Gupta had a deep fear of dirt.

"Can't," he grumbled. "She grows them and extracts quite the strange price for one. I had to steal this one."

"What does she demand in return?"

"She asks them to tell her stories about their day. She asks them to tell her things that no one else knows about them. And if they're recurring customers, she asks about the dream they purchased."

A strange feeling prickled in my chest. "Do they remember the dreams she gives them?"

Gupta looked surprised. "No. I don't think so. But why does that matter?"

"Perhaps she wants to give them dreams they remember."

"But then it's not really a dream," said Gupta.

"Exactly. Then it becomes something else. Something that guides you."

"I think she just wants to follow up on the quality of her merchandise," said Gupta dismissively.

"No," I said softly. "She wants recognition."

I stared at the fallen piece of fruit on the floor. Even from where I stood, I could sense the cold of it. How it glistened and lulled. Simple, but beautiful magic. No one ever did anything new in the Otherworld. Too often, it was a place of staid contentment. But this gem of a fruit looked like restlessness. Curiosity flared through me.

"She's quite beautiful too," said Gupta. "Albeit, not in the traditional sense."

I shrugged. Beauty meant little to me. Silken hair, clear skin, arresting eyes? I could manufacture all those things and more in the reincarnation pool. Traits like cleverness and creativity? Those could not be made. The longer I sat there, thinking of this guardian I had never met, I realized something strange. I *wanted* to meet her.

"Is she . . ." I stopped and tried again. "That is to say, would she even—"

"No consort, but not for lack of interest from others. She went to *Teej* once, from what I gather. Although the acacia trees near where she dances say that she has no desire to attend *Teej* ever again. It was quite the point of contention between her and her friend."

I eyed Gupta a little more sharply. "You had that answer on hand."

He snorted. "I have *most* answers on hand. I am the scribe, after all."

I grinned. Problem solved.

"I have decided. She should be my queen."

Gupta stared at me and then laughed. "*Her?*"

"What's wrong with her?"

"There's nothing wrong with *her*. In what world do you imagine she would have *you?*"

I frowned. "What's wrong with me?"

Gupta considered this. "Nothing so repulsive."

"Thank you for that winning endorsement."

"You are a little arrogant. And sometimes moody and broody, which are such uninspired traits for the Lord of the Dead. And you are *obsessed* with tinkering with things. Plus, you're quite blunt. You probably have no idea how to speak to a woman."

"Of course I know how to speak to a woman."

Gupta raised his eyebrows. "Do you wish to meet her?"

"Not *wish*," I said, heaving to my feet. The onyx chair swiveled and disappeared. "*Will* meet her."

"And say what?"

"That I think she would make an excellent consort. I want a companion. She wants recognition. It's a victory for us both and sound reasoning too."

I started walking toward the door when Gupta jogged up to me. "*That* will be your opening statement? You need to make a good impression. Bees are drawn to flowers, not rocks, for a reason. And that is a ridiculous number of assumptions about someone you don't even know."

I stopped short. He was, as much as I hated it, correct.

"I pray that these next words never cross my lips again."

Gupta cupped his hand to his ear and grinned like a fool. "Do go on."

". . . teach me."

One more example of how to describe someone's eyes and I would destroy someone.

"You want to give off an air of refined elegance," said Gupta. He was gliding to and fro across the mirror-paneled hall. I leaned against the wall and tried not to glower. "You want to be coy but not so reclusive. And you want to be inviting without being too available."

"I hate this."

"Last time we'll practice," said Gupta. For his own sake, he better be right. "Now. Pretend I'm her."

He disappeared behind a corner. A thick brume of ink rose up from the floor in Gupta's impersonation of night. Tiny lights poked holes in the mist. Were those supposed to be stars? And then. Singing. Gupta ran into the hall flailing his arms over his head. Then, he twirled in a circle:

"I am a beautiful maiden!" he trilled in a high-pitched voice.

Please stop.

Gupta stopped spiraling in manic circles when he saw me, and clasped a hand to his chest. "Who are you?"

"It is I . . . the Dharma Raja . . ."

"And what do you want, handsome man?"

I glared, but Gupta remained in character and blinked furiously. There were times I wondered what dying was like. This was one of those times. Except I wanted to die out of necessity. Not curiosity.

"I was captivated by your beauty," I deadpanned.

Gupta—curses upon him—ran his hand through a false pile of hair that was more or less a strategically placed ink blot. "What beauty?"

"You look like a"—*nightmare*, my mind supplied—"dream."

The shadows and ink vanished and Gupta clapped. "That wasn't so miserable, was it?"

"You made me resent immortality."

"Now you have a place to start in your conversation. And you owe it all to me," he said, grinning. "Now go."

"You do not need to tell me twice."

When I saw her, the world ceased to exist beyond where she danced. I forgot Gupta's lessons. I forgot why I stood there. I forgot what I wanted. I even forgot the curse the Shadow Wife had placed on me all those years ago.

Night's dance thrummed with purpose. Her grace sharpened into a lathe, and with it she sculpted the promise of tomorrow from nothing but shadows. She was *potential* incarnate. When she shaped shadows to every sleep-creased fold in the earth, she was balancing time, wiping slates clean, allowing any beginning to take shape. When she frosted night over the world, dawn whispered the lyrics of every tomorrow: *here is a thing not yet started, here is a thing of magic.*

My own halfhearted attempts of invention paled before her. She was the beginning of all ideas.

And before her, I was humbled.

Her laughter was still ringing in my ears when I arrived back to the palace. Gupta was meditating upside down and cracked open an eye when he heard me.

"Oh no," he said, paling. "Not a single insult? My *sherwani* jacket is practically around my head."

"I can see that."

My hounds ran up to me, snuffling my palms with bemused expressions. I scratched their ears absentmindedly.

"What did she do to you?"

She had laughed at me. And made me laugh at myself. And she had been freely honest. People always threw their honesty and last secrets at me, as if by expelling them in a dying breath, they could shorten their time in the less savory parts of my kingdom. But she had given her honesty without expectation. And her honesty was a gift.

"How did the introductions go? Was she adequately wooed and smitten courtesy of yours truly?" asked Gupta.

"She hated every word your 'expert tutelage' forced me to say."

Gupta gasped, and his eyes narrowed. "Impossible!"

"She is."

"Don't take it personally. Women are hard to please," he grumbled. "Especially beautiful ones."

Beauty. I hadn't thought much of it before. Beauty seemed too random, too flimsy to pin any true value to. Her features were lovely, but that wasn't what made her memorable. Stars and constellations had knitted their way from her forehead to her toes. She wore the stories of the world as if every story had only ever been about her. And wasn't that what beauty should be about? A rhythm of features and colors trying to be remarkable enough to earn a tale? If so, she had that in infinite quantities.

"What did you tell her?" asked Gupta, hopping from his upside-down perch.

"That I wanted to make her my queen."

Gupta squeaked and tugged at his hair. "Where is the *mystery* in that, you fool? What did she say?"

I laughed, thinking of her response. Sharp tongue. Clever.

"She said no."

"Just like that?"

"Just like that."

"But I thought . . ." started Gupta, before he frowned and tented his fingers. "Don't despair, there's always—"

"No," I said. "If not her, then no one."

"But she rejected you."

"And she said I may see her tomorrow. And even court her."

Gupta raised a skeptical brow. "Seems like you've met your match in cruelty."

"I'm not cruel," I said, waving a hand. I was pacing back and forth. How many hours until nightfall?

"There's only two months until *Teej*. Even by your normal standards, you seem a little overconfident."

"I think she's far too ambitious to refuse my offer."

Gupta muttered something that sounded a lot like "arrogant cow." Then, with a flick of his wrist, a flurry of heavily inked parchment papers soared into his arms. "If that is what you wish, then how can I help?"

"First of all, never instruct me on the art of courtly coquettishness again."

Gupta winced. "Noted."

"Second. There's something I want to give her."

Gupta clasped his hands to his chin and made a strangled cooing sound. "Is it your *heart?*"

Cold prickled down my spine. And I heard the Shadow Wife's taunts echoing in my thoughts: *You should have learned from the beginning that when someone leaves, it is because nothing was valuable enough to make them stay. You were not enough. And with this curse, I bind your heart.*

"Better than a heart," I said tightly.

Before I left, she had asked for a garden unlike any in all the realms. She would have it.

I wandered through the room where I kept my small creations. On a shelf beside some discarded thoughts, a miniature glass garden caught the light. I had made it on the day I retrieved the soul of a celibate gardener. I had to decide whether he should be reborn as a vivid, but short-lived rose, always pressed to the bosom of the queen he had chastely loved. Or if I should make him into a king, someone who would marry the queen he had loved when she too was reincarnated into a new form. There was something about the garden that reminded me of Night. The way hope grew in every crystal blade, unsure of what it would be next. This would be my starting point. But I could make the garden larger. Grander. Something filled with translucence and light, crystal roses and quartz lilies, emerald ivy and moonstone jasmine vines. Things that were themselves even as they took on the reflection of the world around them.

Like her.

When I was nearly finished, Gupta called out to me. And I knew from his face what it meant:

Dusk was about to fall.

"Do you have your gift?"

"Yes."

"What about your *sherwani* jacket?"

"What about it?"

He looked appalled. "That's the same one you were wearing this morning."

"It will be fine."

"*I* would notice if someone courting *me* was wearing the same jacket."

"Hence, why no one is courting you."

The grove where she danced stood next to the Chakara Forest, where the human and magical world had somehow woven together. Here, small gray birds fed off the moonlight and chirped remnants of children's dreams. It was a popular haunt of gentle *rakshas*, those demons who preferred to disguise themselves as boulders for years upon years rather than participate in the blood sport of their brethren. And it was here where Night's orchard of dream fruit sprouted cold fruit and silver limbs. The more I thought about seeing her, the more something within me gathered into a tight knot.

In the clearing where I had first seen her, I let go of that clamoring sensation in my chest and opened my palms. Tiny glass seedlings drifted and swirled into the ground. Translucent roots expanded into tessellations. Before my eyes, the glass garden grew:

Thick *ashwagandha* shrubs, orchids with pale quartz petals, arrowheads fat as palms and bright as topaz. There were jasmine vines with pearl buds, water lilies with diamond petals. Nilofars and lotuses. Beneath the sunset sky, the glass garden transformed into a grove of lush flames.

Behind me, I heard a fierce intake of breath.

I turned around, and there she was. Livid as the sunset. Red and gold streaked across her skin. Her hair was tied back in a loose braid. Mirth filled her eyes even before she smiled and I found myself hungering for the sound of her laugh.

"You asked for a garden unlike any in all the realms."

"You listen well," she said. She touched each flower reverently and I knew, with a sudden surge of pride, that she liked what I had made. Crouching to her feet, she held her arm to a glass lotus that resembled her flaming skin. "A garden to match me."

"Yes," I said. "For a guardian unlike any in all the realms."

She raised an eyebrow. "That's a far better compliment than your last attempt."

Lowly painter. I shuddered and inwardly cursed Gupta. "I relieved my instructor of his duties."

"Ah, see. There is your problem. You consulted a man." She laughed. And I wanted to catch the sound and play it forever. "You should have asked a woman."

"Then I shall make amends now. What should I have said to you?"

She shrugged. I couldn't tell whether the faint scarlet bloom across her cheeks belonged to a blush or the sunset. "The truth. What was the first thing you thought when you saw me?"

When I first saw her, I remembered how the sky crouched low over the world, its black belly swollen on thunderstorms and stars. And when I saw her dancing, I remembered the edge of a cloud sliding across her neck. I remembered the ghost-pale cut of its silhouette before it disappeared beneath the fall of her hair.

"I thought you looked like edges and thunderstorms."

"Should I be flattered?"

"Be anything you want. But I would not have you any other way."

The sky leaned a little further to the call of night. The red of her skin faded to a dull plum. That brilliant incandescence of the flame-filled sky softened. She looked away and when she looked back, something like mischief sparked in her eyes.

"I was thinking of you."

"How flattering."

"I was thinking of your stubborn desire to court me despite inevitable rejection."

"Less flattering."

"But mostly I was thinking of how I don't know you."

"What do you want to know?"

"I'm glad you asked."

With a small wave of her hand, a richly patterned rug sprawled across the grove. Silk pillows landed with soft thumps onto the covering. The black and white tiles of a *shatranj* board caught the light and small onyx and alabaster figurines hopped into their respective places.

She seated herself at one end of the game and gestured for me to sit. "For every move I make, you must answer a question."

Before she could reach for a piece, I flicked my wrist and a wave of shadows rose out of the ground, swallowing up the board. "If you want to know me, then I want to know you too. We are equals. If you may ask a question, so may I."

She rolled her eyes. "Must you be so dramatic?"

"Is that your first question?"

"You *could* answer out of the kindness of your heart."

"I'm not known for kindness."

She laughed. "Then here is my question. How did you make my garden?"

I liked the way she called the garden hers. "How did you know I made it?"

"My question. Not yours."

"I took whatever rain slicked each of those flowers and froze the impressions to look like glass. I took every color from dusk and dawn and midnight. I poured hope in every flower, though I must confess that the hope originally belonged to a gardener of an ancient kingdom. He was in love with the queen who spoke to him only three times in his whole life. And yet he hoped that she would know that each bloom and their beauty was for her alone. His hope never wavered," I said. "That is why this garden of yours will never break."

Her lips formed a soft O, and she glanced back at the garden as if seeing it with new eyes. "A rather huge undertaking for someone who told you they won't have you."

"Do you like it?"

"I love it," she said fiercely.

"Then I don't consider it an undertaking at all. Now. My turn. What do you think of when you dance night into the world?"

She kept her eyes on the board, evaluating her next move. "I could refuse to answer since you already asked a question."

"You *could* answer out of the kindness of your heart."

"Like you, I am not known for kindness," she said. "But I am known for vanity about my own importance, and your question appeals to that." I bit back a smile as she braced her elbows on her knees and tapped her lips. "When I dance, I think of . . . stories. I can't read any of the tales written in stars and inked across my skin. But I think about how we retell them a thousand times over. And when I dance, it's like pouring ink over a thousand tomes and letting people start anew."

"Retelling them," I repeated slowly. "I understand that. Every day I decide a story."

I told her about the Tapestry. I told her how a single death could change the outcome of a hundred lives. That duty—to move between the fixed and fated moments—weighed on me, but there was more than just sacred purpose in the responsibility. I didn't have to walk along mortals to know the weight of their dreams, and even though they did not know what they entrusted to me, I was still honored with the task. When I finished talking, she eyed me like she knew a secret.

"I hadn't realized we were both creators."

I laughed. "I am no creator."

"Are you so certain?" she asked, tilting her head. Violet bloomed around her neck, and for the first time I had no wish to see night. I wanted to stay in these stolen hours between sunset and true dusk. "You created this beautiful garden. You create a new tale with every ending. That sounds like the role of a creator to me."

I had never thought of it that way. There was something freeing in the way she spoke, the possibility of it all. I envied her. If I stood by her side, how different would the world look? Between us, the *shatranj* board lay forgotten. Faint stars bloomed across the dusky purple of her arm. She followed my gaze and frowned.

"I have to go now," she said. Perhaps I was deluding myself, but she sounded reluctant.

"This has been . . . enlightening."

"That's quite the opposite of what I do," she said, gesturing at the darkening length of her body. I tried to look away from her, but my sight kept snagging on the way her full lips danced on the edge of a grin. Or how I'd never seen hair as dark as hers, lush and starless as an eclipse.

I dragged my eyes up to meet hers and found her stare questioning. Curious.

"Pity our game went unfinished, but I'll take my leave of you," I muttered quickly.

Her hand brushed against my arm. Her touch was cold and burning. Just as quickly, she withdrew her hand. But she stayed close.

"Tomorrow, I think Nritti will be keeping me company from sunset to dusk."

"Who?"

"You don't know her?"

"Should I?"

She seemed stunned by this. Nritti, as it turned out, was an *apsara* who had earned the nickname the Jewel of the Heavens. They were friends.

"I see. Then I suppose—"

"Come at night," she said, the words spilling from her.

"I knew you'd want to see me again."

She leaned closer, placing a cold hand against my chest. My heart raced. She brought her lips to my ear:

"Or perhaps I just want my other presents," she said. "If you remember, I did ask for the moon for my throne and stars to wear in my hair."

She drew away, but did nothing to increase the distance between us. Mischief flickered in her eyes. Cruel queen, indeed.

"I have not forgotten a single word that has passed your lips."

"Is that so?" She raised an eyebrow. "I'm glad my words were memorable."

I reached out, my thumb just barely grazing her lip. She stilled as I bent my head to her ear:

"It wasn't the words."

When I left, I left with the taste of her laughter and the sound of her thoughts. I left with the scent of her hair clinging to my skin. I left imagining the world seen through her eyes. A world of stories folded quietly between stars, where the ink of night poured star-touched dreams into the world and whispered to the earth of all the things it could be the next day.

When I left, I understood a shard of human grief. Not the pining or the despair. But that bone-deep craving to spend a moment longer with someone.

·» 4 «·

NIGHT

I would not have you any other way.

Above me, the sky was on fire. The sun's last rays illuminated the land, but the light stretched thin and haggard. I hugged my bright red knees to my chest. I glanced hopefully at my skin, searching for a telltale stain of blue. Nothing. I sighed. There were still hours left until nightfall. I walked to the glass garden right outside my grove and sat in the middle of its wonder. Around me, flat flames burned inside the translucent petals. Light crested off crystal buds, dancing from flower to flower before breaking on the inside of a garnet lotus. When the light broke, all I could think of was how every piece of this garden had been crafted from a shard of hope. A gardener long dead had hoped that someone he loved would see how every blossom and beauty was for her alone. And the Dharma Raja had remade that. For me. Hope—that colorless light—snuck into the fissures of my thoughts and bloomed. But what that hope wanted to grow into, I couldn't quite name.

"I have so much to tell you!" hollered a voice from outside the grove.

I leapt to my feet in time to see Nritti gliding toward me. She stopped short at the sight of the glass garden.

"What is that?" she asked, frowning.

"A gift."

"From *who?*"

"Not important."

"Tell me."

"You're the one who ran—"

"Flew," she corrected.

"*Flew* into my grove about having so much to tell me. You first."

I still wasn't sure whether I would tell her about the Dharma Raja or not. I still wasn't sure what it meant. The garden was a beautiful and thoughtful present, but it wasn't a vow. And I wouldn't marry without love. And it's not like I *loved* him. I hardly knew him.

Having sufficiently talked myself out of revealing anything, I fixed Nritti with an expectant stare.

"I saw Vanaj yesterday," she said.

The blind princeling. I nodded.

"He is like . . . a cold winter breeze when you need it the most on a summer night."

"Did you tell him that?" I cringed. "If I were Vanaj, I'd wish I was deaf instead."

Nritti smacked my arm. "I am sharing my emotions!"

"Could you do it without bad metaphor?"

She exhaled. "I like him. He is sweet. Kind. Funny. He *listens* to me the way no one else has." Nritti darted a glance to me. "Well. Not *no one*."

"I understand that," I said softly. "I'm happy for you, sister."

"I thought . . . I thought maybe you wouldn't be."

"Why?"

"Because then we'll spend less time together and I know that it can be too quiet for you here, by yourself. And what if you're in the Night Bazaar and I'm not there? Who is going to decipher your foul sense of humor?"

I smiled even though her words stung. "Don't worry about me. Less time together isn't no time at all. And besides, we have an infinite amount of time."

I didn't tell her the other thought weighing in my head. Vanaj was a mortal, with a mortal's life span. Many kings lived until they were as old as eight hundred, but they always died in the end. No matter how much she loved him, they were already running out of time together.

Happiness turned her beauty from striking to transcendent. Whatever dying light was left in the sky rushed to illuminate her.

"Thank you," she said, squeezing my hand. "Now, tell me about this person."

I revealed as much as I could without giving away who he was— the game of *shatranj*, the ease of our conversations, even his beauty. And at the end, Nritti said nothing.

"I hope you know what you're doing, sister," she said quietly. "Sometimes we women are our own worst traps. Our hopes snatch us like quicksand. Our loneliness forges a cage. Sometimes all it takes is one sweet glance and kind word to make us forget ourselves. I just don't want to see you trapped."

I bit back any hurt. Perhaps she was right. What if what I felt was nothing more than all my collective loneliness rising up at the first sign of affection?

"You don't trust him."

"I don't *know* him," she said. "But it sounds as though you are starting to know him. You have to trust yourself above all. Even me. For your sake, I dearly hope I am wrong. I want nothing more than for you to be happy."

We spent the rest of the sunset hours talking and watching the sky transform. It looked like any other day between us, but something else had crept into our thoughts. Longing. I could see it plainly in Nritti's face and the way she kept worrying the ends of her sari and tugging at her braid.

"If you want to spend time with your Vanaj, then go."

"First, he's not *my* Vanaj." She bit her lip. "And second, if I went to him, don't you think I would seem too eager?"

I splashed water on her face and she sputtered angrily. I wished Uloopi was here to talk some sense into Nritti, but word had leaked about the resurrection stone she'd made and a handful of mortal demons were after the jewel. She had to come up with demon-proof security measures to safeguard her invention. *Queen problems*, Uloopi had said yesterday, before tossing her hair over her shoulder and slithering away. *I'll tell you all about them next time, my friend. In the meantime, keep that dream fruit ready for me.*

"You're like a bull fighting with its reflection," I said to Nritti. "Stop getting in the way of your happiness. So what if it seems eager? Don't you think he would feel just as eager to see you again? Besides, I'm sure he's already infatuated with you."

"You think so?"

"He must be. He's blind, so your beauty is insignificant. And I can't think of a single other trait left to recommend you, yet he managed to stay by your side for an entire evening. Thus, he must be in love with you."

"You're horrible," she said, but she grinned widely as she smoothed down her hair and adjusted her skirts. "Will you be at the Night Bazaar later?"

I looked over my shoulder to the silver orchard. There wasn't enough fruit to sell. Relief flickered inside me. For the first time, I wasn't eager to run away from my grove.

"Probably tomorrow. I will give the world a rest from dealing with me."

Nritti eyed me knowingly, but if she guessed my reluctance, she didn't share it. When she stood, she walked to the glass garden and traced a petal delicately.

"Fine workmanship. Whoever he is, he has the eye of an artist."

I smiled. "I think he'd be pleased to hear that."

"Not an artist by trade?"

"No."

"What does he do?" she asked. "I am assuming he is one of us."

"He is. But his duty is . . . unique."

"Unique enough to tempt you to attend *Teej*?"

Without answering her, we hugged and said our good-byes. Nritti ran. She turned from a silvery silhouette to a thread of shadow and then . . . nothing. Even though I knew in my heart that she was not running from me, I still felt like something left behind.

For as long as I had lived, I had always belonged to two worlds. My duties nourished the human world, and there I learned my dances. My life belonged to the Otherworld, and there I learned my duties. But I was Night. And it meant that I was forever a threshold, a space between past and present, yesterday and tomorrow.

If not content, I had at least grown accustomed to not quite belonging. I had Nritti. I had my grove and my garden. And I had tried, endlessly, to change the world around me. I had tried to make dream fruit that would last, tried to craft a story that would last beyond sleep, tried to *influence* the world. But nothing changed.

Many people thought that ghosts filled the night. They were wrong. True ghosts lay in people's minds, in that space between curiosity and blindness. I didn't want to be a ghost anymore. I didn't want to haunt my own shadow. I wanted more.

But how?

The Dharma Raja's proposal pushed to the front of my thoughts. At the thought of him, something in me softened. But Nritti's words unfurled like a bed of thorns in my heart.

I just don't want to see you trapped.

If there was anything I had learned from the Otherworld, it was that nothing was freely given. Everything demanded a price. And the truth was that I did not know what the Dharma Raja wanted from me. And when I discovered the price for all he offered, would I pay it just to have what I wanted?

I was still lost in those thoughts when I heard the trees creak and groan, as if they had sunk into bows. But of course they would. Every tree was mortal. And every mortal thing knew whose voice they would hear at the end:

"As you asked, I have brought you the moon for your throne."

Warmth spread through my bones. The Dharma Raja stood tall and imposing, but not nearly bulky enough to conceal a whole throne. And he stood before me with his hands at his sides, relaxed and handsome.

"Have you?" I said, raising an eyebrow. "I hope I'll fit in the seat."

"Not quite a throne," he allowed. "And it's not here."

"Where is it?"

"In the Chakara Forest. It was far too heavy to drag over here."

"Too heavy? I didn't realize the Dharma Raja had any weaknesses."

I was only teasing, but when he looked at me, the taunt died in my throat. His gaze moved slowly from my lips to my eyes, and when he spoke it was from a place shadowed and unused. A place still feeling out its own existence.

"Only one."

We walked side by side, leaving the grove behind until we had entered the Chakara Forest. I had wandered here many times. Few came here after dark. Even humans could taste the magic coating the air, the way it lifted your hair from the back of your neck and promised beautiful and terrible things. The trees sank into bows, brushing moon-silvered branches against the forest floor. Half-hidden in the loam, a woman's sapphire necklace glinted a bruised blue. A dead bell chirped in a child's rattle. A love letter printed on the underside of a leaf waved its secrets to the wind.

And in the middle of it all stood an imposing polished black mirror. My breath caught at the sight of its beauty. Carved alabaster and ivory framed the surface. Moon pale and just as magical. On the edges, small illustrations moved back and forth—a water buffalo ambling through still woods, a *nagini* diving into the depths of a watery castle.

"You made this?"

He nodded. An image flickered in my head, of the Dharma Raja alone in his cold kingdom, head bent and mind brimming with images he couldn't wait to unlock from a block of stone. I thought of the other day when I had called him a creator, and the quiet wonder that had lit up his face.

"It's beautiful. But—"

"—it's not a throne," he finished. "But it is, I think, what a throne for the moon should be like. The moon travels the world. And a throne should survey all the lands you touch and influence. You deserve no less."

He brushed his fingers against the mirror, and the black reflection rippled.

"For someone draped in all the stories of the world, how much of it have you seen?"

Stars flickered against my skin, and I wondered whether they were listening to him, tilting a little farther out of the sky to hear the lustrous dark of his voice.

"Very little."

His words grasped at a yearning I barely acknowledged. I didn't want to tell him how dearly I wished to see the world in all its states. To see how the night transformed other cities and landscapes beyond my grove. Or the ocean. Or how much I wanted to see the true sun, and not some torn half of it.

"I thought so," he said. "Where would you like to go? This will take us anywhere."

"How did you come across something like this?"

"Hundreds of mirrors fill Naraka's halls. You could see and visit any world and any city you wished." A note of pride struck his voice. "In my kingdom, nothing is impossible."

"I don't think I'd like to live in a world with no impossibilities."

He frowned. "Why not?"

"It strikes me as . . . uninspired. What property is left to dreamers when every idea has been tamed and conquered? What about the poet who dreams of embracing the night sky? It's utterly impossible. And yet the thought of it sparks song and dance, poetry and philosophy."

The Dharma Raja fell silent. "Then I hope I am wrong."

"There's always impossibilities in dreams. Dream more."

He looked at me. "I'm beginning to."

I reached out to trace the place where his fingers had graced the mirror. "Will you take me to see the ocean?"

"I know just the place," he said. He held out his hand to me. "May I?"

Sparks of light danced down my spine. His thumb ran over my knuckles. Together, we stepped into the mirror. Black and cold. And then *falling*. My heart raced as a swoop and weightlessness feathered inside me. On instinct, I clung to him and his arms folded around me. Still, my heart raced.

A moment later, we stood along the shore. I caught my breath, dizzied from the sudden jolt of solidness beneath me.

"You were wrong," he said.

"About what?"

"I have done the impossible," he announced. "I have embraced the night sky."

"You did no such thing."

"Is that so?" he asked. His voice felt too close, and I realized that I hadn't stepped out of the circle of his arms. It had felt too natural to lean against him. I looked up to see his brow arched, his lips tilting into a knowing grin. "Then what do you call this?"

I thought about the fall and how he had offered *zero* warning. I lifted my chin: "Opportunistic."

A wolfish grin lit up his face. "You caught me."

"Now who's performing impossibilities?" I smirked. "Someone should write a story about me, for I have ensnared Death himself."

"Not ensnared," he said, and his voice burned low in my ear. "Enchanted."

"You're getting far better at flattery."

I stepped out of the circle of his arms and into the silky sand that hugged the ocean. When I turned to look at the water, I forgot everything. The ocean churned the constellations, rearranging a thousand tales in its ink-dark water. Water always had a calming effect on me. But standing before the ocean, I felt awed. The ocean stretched infinite, so that nothing but a delicate thread of land kept the sky and sea apart.

"What do you see?" asked the Dharma Raja.

I told him what I saw—ink and starlight, torn stories and new endings. And as I spoke, his obsidian eyes seemed to gleam in longing.

"I would give anything to see the world the way you do," he said softly.

"And I would give anything to *see* the world as you do. You travel everywhere. Never tethered to one place or one allotted time."

"True. But my eyes have squandered every sight I have been given," he said, resentment deepening his voice. "I am trying to change how I see the world."

"Are you following advice from the same instructor who taught you how to pay a compliment?" I asked, teasing. "If so, I might counsel you otherwise."

"In truth, I think you have been my instructor in seeing the world differently," he said. His fingers brushed against mine, just soft enough to be coincidence. "Lately, I have tried to summon wonder like a lens. But it does not come to me until I stand beside you."

We walked along the shore. Water pooled around our ankles, and the shock of it was cold and welcoming. The Dharma Raja murmured something under his breath, and colorful glass *diyas* and white petals sprang up along the waves. Like wading through a festival.

"I envy you too," I said suddenly. I couldn't stop thinking of the legendary Tapestry in Naraka, an object where every mortal life possessed a thread and every life was held in fragile balance. "When a thread is frayed in a thousand directions, no one but you gets to decide which path to choose. Only your voice counts in that tale, and there is no story more potent than life."

"So this is why you ask for your patrons to tell you about their dreams and their days. You wish to know whether the dream fruit you created made a difference?" I nodded, and the Dharma Raja murmured: "You want your voice to be heard. I understand."

His words—simple and unfettered—rang in my ears. He *understood*. In the Otherworld, striving for things beyond what you were given was unreasonable. Even Nritti and Uloopi couldn't fathom why I *wanted* so much.

I hadn't realized, until now, how understanding could coax a small, shared world into existence. When I answered him, even my words felt new. Like they were spoken in a language birthed into being for this very moment.

"I believe you," I said. And then, I gave away a secret. "Night resets the world. It is a blank page for a story to be writ upon. But I have no hand or voice in the matter. That is why I envy you."

He stopped walking, and reached for my hand. "Is that what you want?"

His face bent to mine. This close, it was impossible to ignore the nocturnal beauty of him. This close, it was impossible to break his fathomless gaze.

"I do," I said. "And now that I've told you what I want, it's only fair for you to tell me what you want."

"Fair?" He laughed. "No one is guaranteed fairness. Not in any life. And not by any god or goddess."

"Fine," I said, waving a dismissive hand. "Keep your secrets."

I turned away just as his hand snaked out for my wrist.

"It's no secret that I want you," he said. He bowed his head to mine, and his eyes burned black. "Come with me. I will make you a queen among storytellers. I will give you a kingdom. A place full of mirrors where you can step into any world you please. With your perspective and my position, we could rewrite the world."

I want you . . .

We could rewrite the world . . .

It was more than tempting. His offer sang to me. When he stood this close, my heart didn't race. It slowed. As if my heart and mind had conspired to live in this moment forever.

"As your bride?"

"As my queen," he said. "What can I offer? What can I give to persuade you?"

For one glittering moment, I wanted to press my lips to his. To taste all that he offered. But then I stepped away, and the moment between us broke.

"I will freely give away my opinions and perspective," I said. "But I will not marry without love. Not for all the power in the world. Life, for us, is too long to live without it."

"Love," he repeated. He thought it over. A strange expression drifted over his face, as if he was remembering something.

"What do you have against it?"

"Nothing."

"Have you been in love before?" I asked. The question had burned inside me ever since I met him. Had his heart already been bruised and that's why he wouldn't consider giving it away once more? Which forced another question in my head: did I want his heart?

"Never," he said.

"Then what's the problem?"

"The problem is that I can't. I . . . just can't."

He dropped my wrist.

"If it's my perspective and opinions that you want, I would give that to you freely," I said. "As a friend."

"I have no need for friends. I have enough of those."

"You do? How many do you have?"

"One."

I laughed, choosing to drop the subject. "Come, I want to walk farther along the shore."

And just like that, his offer seemed swept away by the waves. Once more, we lapsed into conversation. He told me of the places he had seen in the mortal realm. Places where lush jungles pulsed and swallowed ancient temples and kingdoms with forgotten names. And I told him of the people I had met in the Otherworld. People who sold fantastical ornaments in the Night Bazaar and sung prophecies in reverse or got drunk on bottled lightning.

"There are people with curses too," I said. "One *apsara* was cursed to lose her beauty for half her life for the next five hundred years. Her husband had to choose whether he wanted her beautiful by day or beautiful by night. It was said the right answer from him could break the curse."

"What did he choose?"

"I'll tell you, but I want to hear what you would pick if you were the husband."

We walked in silence for a bit. In the distance I saw Airavata rise out of the ocean. The great white elephant trampled over the waves, his trunk working quickly with a needle and a gauzy mist. He was spinning fresh clouds for dawn. A tightness in my chest gathered and fell. It was nearly time for me to return.

"Whichever she wanted," said the Dharma Raja.

"Why do you think that would break the curse?"

"You said that the right answer from the husband would break the curse. But we all know that true curses are broken from within, thus the answer from the husband must have been one that gave his wife the power. Not him."

I smiled. "Most husbands would not have thought that."

"I would not be like most husbands."

"Pity you had not married the *apsara*."

We continued along the shore. My thoughts turned to the *apsara* with her ruined face for day, and the resentment she carried for night. The curse would break, eventually, but five hundred years was enough time to lose whatever love she once had. Even if her husband had chosen right . . . would she still love him?

Around us, the ocean changed. At once, my limbs yearned to sleep, to fold myself up in the remnants of night until tomorrow. The Dharma Raja must have sensed my exhaustion because he placed his hand gently at my back and steered us once more toward the ivory mirror.

"I wish you would come away with me," he said softly.

My smile turned drowsy. "Not without love. Although I will not say no to a whole host of presents until then."

He laughed. "You're exquisitely greedy."

And then I was back in my grove. What was left of night looked like a flimsy sheath of ice upon a pool. And dawn chipped away at it with pink hunger. Slowly, slowly, sleep claimed me. I felt the cold of the Dharma Raja slipping from me. He was leaving. I reached for him then, taking his hand and holding it close as an oath. Exhaustion unraveled my thoughts. And I was glad, then, that I was too tired to speak. Because all I could think was how the last thing I wanted before sleep was his hand in mine.

5

DEATH

She faded with the dawn. One moment, her hand in mine. The next moment, I held nothing. When I finally left the grove, the sun had devoured the last vestiges of night and drenched the whole sky a sticky rose gold. I walked away half full of glee and half full of hurt. The best was feeling the ghost of her touch. The worst was knowing she'd simply touched me from exhaustion.

And then, a mind-numbing idea entered my thoughts. I hadn't had the chance to ask whether I could visit her tonight. Or what gift she might want. Unease filled me.

This was . . .

This was *awful.*

In Naraka, Gupta greeted me with a steaming cup of *soma.* I downed the goblet in one swallow. My hounds circled my feet, ears raised and muzzles hopeful for some evil soul to chew on for a year.

"Once more, I am empty-handed," I said to them, holding up my palms. The hounds slinked away, annoyed.

"You sound pitiful," said Gupta. He crossed his arms. "You look pitiful too."

"She didn't say if I could come back."

I told him what had happened. Gupta stroked his chin. For reasons I can only assume were meant to heighten his cognitive madness, he hovered upside down with his feet crossed and jacket flapping about his ears.

"She never said anything like . . . until next time? Or later I will see you?"

"No."

I was pacing. *Why was I pacing?* It hit me, then, that I was anxious. Like I was hungry but wouldn't taste the food. Thirsty, but nothing would slake me.

Gupta righted himself and lightly tapped my forehead. I batted away his hand.

"What are you *doing?*"

"Experimenting."

"Can you experiment on someone else's forehead?"

"I could. But I won't."

Tap tap tap.

"Gupta. I realize you cannot die. But there are many ways to make—"

"You're smitten," he said. Matter of fact. As if he was remarking on the phase of the moon.

"You're a fool."

"So are you. Love has made a fool of you," he said. And then he frowned. "There's a poem somewhere in there, but I am miserable at structure and rhythm, so I will spare you my attempt."

"How merciful," I said, crossing my arms. "And I am not smitten. I simply like order in my universe. And there's no order because I don't know *where* I'm supposed to be this evening."

"Just go back to whatever it is that you used to do during the evening."

I opened my mouth to speak, but the words caught in my throat. For a moment, I struggled to remember what it was that I used to do during the evening. But when I closed my eyes, I only saw her face. Day and night. That was the difference she left within me. Every day after that had become a lesson in seeing.

Night fell. I waited. I didn't know what I expected. A message? Some sign? A flock of eagles attacking me and dragging me to her? But maybe I waited too long. Because when I finally arrived at her grove, it was empty. Night had already been seamlessly sculpted into the land.

She was gone.

When I got back to Naraka, Gupta was dressed in a simple cotton-spun *sherwani*. He wore a *pagri* over his head, strangely molded so that it looked like he wore a pair of horns. And he was holding out a length of black silk to me.

"Where are you going?"

"Correction," said Gupta. "Where are *we* going? Stop pining. Your beloved is probably in the Night Bazaar surrounded by every other anxious and amorous person. It's a big day today."

"What's today?" I asked miserably.

"Stop feeling sorry for yourself."

"Or what?"

"Or I'll take it upon myself to read you a bedtime story as one would to an infant who has fallen ill. We can start with *The Way the Mountain Grows over a Handful of Centuries* and move onto dissertations of the benefits of semiaquatic creatures guarding temple treasures. Once upon a—"

"Noooo."

"Then put this on."

I snatched the cloak from Gupta, tied it around my shoulders, and flung it over my head. The hood was enchanted, so I could see perfectly through the material. I found a blank mirror and grimaced. The top half of my face was obscured.

"You want me to enter the Night Bazaar like *this*? I look ridiculous."

"You always complain about drawing attention to yourself."

"Gupta. I have a hood covering my face. What part of this does *not* draw attention to myself?"

"The part where if your full face was showing not a single person would come near you. At least this way, they're curious."

"She won't be there."

"On the contrary, I expect she will. She'll be curious. You see, there's an interesting rumor floating around the Otherworld. It is said that this *Teej*, the Dharma Raja himself is seeking a consort from among the lineup of eligible demon maidens, nature spirits, goddesses, and guardians. And this marks the last full moon before *Teej*, so it's bound to be full of people and celebrations, would-be lovers and betrothed couples."

"Who. Spread. That. Rumor?"

Gupta tapped his chin and a thousand little ink blooms erupted behind him, shaping into tiny arrows that all pointed . . . to him.

"But I don't *want* to look through a lineup of maidens, I only want her."

"She doesn't have to know that."

"Doesn't that defeat the purpose?"

"She'll be intrigued. She's used to expecting you every day. Every day you've gone there and professed your undying love—"

"I never said those words . . ."

"Fine, you bored holes into her eyes with an intense be-with-me-forever gaze."

I said nothing, but I felt my jaw tighten.

"Naturally, she will grow accustomed to that! Where's the excitement? The tension?"

A few moments later, we were walking through the Night Bazaar. Every avenue was crowded with people of all shapes and sizes. The *Teej* podium floated over the crowd, a gliding bird with impossible wings.

Gupta kept patting his makeshift horns. "Do these make my head look big?"

"Yes."

"Excellent," he said, smoothing his jacket. "I had to do my best to look unattractive. Difficult to do, you know. Can't have men and women falling over themselves because of me."

Above us, small golden lanterns careened to the center of the Night Bazaar. Music poured out from unseen instruments, and the rhythm was heady with wonder and yearning. Even Gupta had begun to bob his head to the beat. We walked closer to the sounds of dancing, the raucous cheering and countdowns. When a clearing appeared beneath the split sky, the *Teej* podium transformed into an unopened lotus bud. With one thunderous clap, the petals peeled back, revealing a golden stage filled with *apsaras*. The opening act before the dance of would-be lovers. I stifled a yawn, and kept looking.

Vendors crowded around the stage, hawking their wares before an entranced audience. Every time I looked around the room, something within me leapt eagerly. *Was she here?* A wisp of stars and smoke caught my eye. But it was nothing but iridescent serpent scales on a beautiful *nagini* woman. Across the room, I thought I saw the fall of impossibly black hair. But it was nothing but a ribbon of slow-moving shadows, eagerly wrapping themselves around whichever dancing couple most desired the privacy.

Beside me, Gupta inhaled sharply. I followed his gaze to the split sky above us. It was *breaking*. Rain. Rain from the side of day danced toward the ground like chips of amber only to transform into golden-throated birds. Rain from the side of night danced toward the ground like chips of opal only to transform into silver-tailed fish.

"The sky belongs to birds. The ocean belongs to fish. But love belongs to all," said Gupta.

"Another horrific poem of yours?"

He pointed behind the stage, where the words stained a wall of ivy.

"This is nauseating. I'm leaving. She isn't here anyway."

"Are you sure about that?" he asked, jerking his head to the floating podium.

The *apsara* dance had ended. A *yakshini* with sea-foam hair lifted her arms to wash the stage of its discarded rose petals and broken bells. Shunted to one corner of the stage stood a small onyx podium. Halved fruit spilled across the counter. Dream fruit. And there she was, pointed chin resting in a star-touched hand. Her hair thrown over one shoulder, twisted around with opals and jasmine. She was *laughing*. With a man. A human man, no less. A moment ago, the sight of her had crowded out my very thoughts. Now, the sight of her—with *him*—left me feeling strangely punctured. Like the air had gone solid and I could not possibly breathe it in. I watched them.

He was, I allowed, handsome.

But in his next life he could be a wild pig with a persistent gum disease. For one black second I tapped at my noose.

Gupta swatted my hand.

"Could you have a little faith in my self-restraint?"

He considered this. "No."

And then, a shimmering *apsara* appeared beside her. Gupta's mouth fell open. I jabbed him. He closed it. This must be Nritti, the Jewel of the Heavens. Her title was indisputable. Her skin was peerless, but it wasn't drenched in night and scrawled in stars. Her eyes rivaled sapphires, but they didn't shine with wonder or restlessness. Her lips would shame roses, but they didn't tug into sly grins or tighten at the thought of something funny.

Her beauty made me ache.

But not for her.

Nritti reached for the princeling. The princeling reached for her. Music fell through the air. Golden-throated sparrows collapsed into dew. Silver-tailed fish shivered into feathers. I could breathe the air and it tasted like relief.

"A dance for lovers," said Gupta, jabbing me with his elbow.

The princeling and Nritti whirled off and into the stage, leaving her alone. Alone with her chin perched in her palm, an arch smile stretching her lips. But I knew her smile. The details of it had somehow emblazoned itself into my bones so that I couldn't smile myself without feeling the weight of her grin propping me up. The smile she wore now was only a memory of how a smile should look.

Gupta grumbled, and I was shoved forward.

"Move, fool."

I moved. And when I walked to her, I certainly felt like a fool. A crowd watched as I cut a path to her. She hadn't noticed yet. Her gaze was distant and unfocused. A comet's tail left a trail of smoke across her shoulder. Today, she was dressed in all her finery. Thin rings of beaten gold and amber circled her wrist. A delicate chain of silver bells fell across her waist.

"Who is he?" whispered a *naga*.

His would-be mate shrugged, her cobra hood flaring out so she could gossip in privacy.

"Not a demon," whispered an *asura* to the *yakshini* with sea-foam hair.

"Not a human," she replied.

I felt the silk of the hood tickling my neck and drew a sigh of relief. In this way, at least, I was safe from their gaze. No line flanked her vendor stall, and yet she had returned to rearranging night fruit and sprucing up the plate of sample slices. When she felt my shadow across hers, she spoke without looking up:

"I've poisoned all the fruit, so think twice before you . . ."

She looked up and stared.

"Poisoned fruit?" I asked. "What a romantic thing to sell on this momentous occasion."

A corner of her lips quirked into a grin. I felt it in my bones.

"I am certain there is at least one lover out there who will thank me."

"The unfortunate thing is that I believe you. But if you did such a thing, then I would have to work on a holiday."

"We can't have that."

Why did I thrill when she said *we*? *I* and *you* were thin, solitary words remade by her lips the moment she spoke *we*.

"No," I said, savoring the next words, the unshaped wonder of them: "We can't."

She looked behind me, and the smile slid off her face. I followed her gaze to see a small crowd milling from the outskirts of the stage where couples leapt and danced.

"Dance with me," she said. Commanded.

And I nodded dumbly. As if I could do anything else.

Her hand rested on my shoulder and my thoughts splintered at her touch.

"I almost didn't recognize you with that hood on," she said.

I spun her in a circle and a constellation slipped from her wrist to her elbow.

"I would have worn it the first time we met if I knew it would make you laugh."

"It makes me laugh only because you look ridiculous," she said. "And I can't tell what you're thinking or feeling when it covers your eyes."

"Maybe I don't want you to know. Maybe I am intentionally obscuring my feelings from view."

She looked at me, her gaze suddenly hooded. At first, I thought she would speak. But instead, she sipped on her lower lip and turned from me. The music fell thick and honeyed around us. I spun her again. But she did not come back to me. She frowned, like she was remembering something.

"I thought I'd see you here, but perhaps not under so strange a disguise. They said the Dharma Raja was looking for a wife," she said lightly. Too lightly. "I suppose my rejection has finally sunken in. Did you think I wouldn't recognize you with a hood?"

"Those rumors were started by my advisor, Gupta."

"The same one who taught you how to speak to a woman?"

"The very same."

"That almost explains it."

But there was still a frostiness to her voice.

"He started it because I came to see you in the grove and you weren't there. Gupta thought you would be here. I only came here for *you*." She fell quiet, but she looked up at me. Her expression, for one sliver of a moment, was unguarded hope. "Do you truly think I meant to disguise myself from you? That this hood would be enough to hide my identity?"

She crossed her arms.

"It only exposes your jaw and lips," she said. "That's hardly enough to recognize."

"That's implying there's nothing memorable about the lower half of my face. My lips are certainly memorable."

She moved closer. Or I moved closer. Or the music had grown so greedy that it ate away the distance between us.

"I wouldn't know," she said. Lightly. Mockingly. But there was something uneven in her tone.

The music made me bold. I slid my fingers into her hair. Her hair was cold silk against my palm. Her eyes fluttered shut. Then opened. And I knew what the unevenness in her voice had been: want.

"Would you like to?"

I waited for the moment of waiting, but it never came. Without answering, she tipped forward. Her fingers tapped a secret rhythm across the nape of my neck before she pulled me to her. Her lips met mine. *No, not met.* She was not capable of something so gentle. Her lips conquered mine. But I didn't mourn my loss for long. I braided my fingers in her hair, fire edging my thoughts when she sighed against me.

In that strange lightlessness that belonged to closed eyes, I thought I could see inside myself. Whatever was inside me was no stage like the one upon which we danced. *Kissed.* What was inside me could not fit beneath the sky even though it was lit up by an inferno of stars. Her lips opened beneath mine. She tasted the way she looked—like wonder and cold, velvet shadows and hidden paths beneath too-dark woods. She tasted like the edge of imagination, like the shadows of a new idea, which chases away your thoughts and leaves you lost in dreams.

I was lost.

But as long as it was with her, I never wanted to be found.

6

NIGHT

The kiss changed everything and nothing.

When we emerged from that strange stage, no one commented. No one saw. The whole world turned joyously selfish and curled inward. We left the Night Bazaar behind, hands entwined. We didn't speak of *Teej*—mere weeks away—or what the kiss meant. We had torn a chunk of that enchanted silence from the stage and carried it within us like a talisman, something to ward off every worry.

"Will you come back tomorrow?"

"And the next day. And the day after that."

I bit back a smile. "For how long?"

"As long as it takes."

Every night, he visited me. And every night we walked to the moon-mirror throne, which was not quite a throne, but all that a throne should be, and got lost together. On the third night we walked through an enchanted desert where the mirages took on the forms of fantastical bodies of water—ice braided along a ravine, quartz-clear puddles shot through with small violet flowers. The mirage promised cold, clear water. But at a single touch, it was nothing but singed weeds and dry sand.

"It's maya," I said. "Illusion."

"They say that is all the world is."

"How pessimistic you are," I teased.

"What do you think?"

I had not realized until I met the Dharma Raja that I had a favorite question. But now I did. And this was it.

"I think it's utterly wrong to say that the world is nothing but illusion. They say that Night is just an illusion of a new tomorrow and a story not yet written. And, as you know, I am very real."

I laced my fingers through his, smiling at the shy grin that slipped onto his face.

"Perhaps," he said thoughtfully. "But if there is anything I have learned at your side, it is how every sight is open to a thousand and one interpretations. So perhaps the world is a bit of illusion after all. We simply choose which mirage to see, and draw meaning and stories from that."

This was another thing I had not expected about the Dharma Raja. He liked to think through problems. He was stubborn. But more than anything, he wanted to question things.

"Perhaps," I allowed.

"That reminds me," he said, withdrawing his fingers from mine. "I made you something."

He reached into his robes and drew out a small glass orb. Light sparked and whirred within it. He tossed it into the air and the small crystal orb unfurled, spreading tendrils of light over us until we stood in a room full of stars. He reached out, grasping the stars between thumb and forefinger, like they were nothing more than glass beads waiting to be plucked and refashioned. One by one, he stole the false stars out of their false sky until he fashioned a small headpiece in the shape of a glittering sparrow. He slid it into my hair, and the false sky peeled back to reveal the desert.

"I have given you the moon for your throne, an impossible garden, and now stars to wear in your hair. As I promised," he said softly. His eyes cut to mine. "And I always keep my promises."

I had not kissed him since that evening in the Night Bazaar, even though I wanted to. I couldn't stand the thought that maybe each kiss would tease away something precious, something I wasn't ready to give. Nritti's words floated back to me: *What does he want from you?* I didn't know. Worse, I was beginning to suspect that whatever it was, I would give it. That small truth left me exposed. Almost resentful.

He stood before me, his hand outstretched, stars nestled in his palm. And we both knew this was not just a gift. What he offered me was soft and glittering, inflexible, and it wasn't just stars.

It was his heart.

He fixed his fathomless black gaze on me, the same gaze that brought kings to their knees and snipped a season in half. But what I saw was this: I saw that when he walked beside me, some alchemy transformed my voice and thoughts to gold. When we spoke, the world bent beneath our views and adjusted itself accordingly. When we imagined, infinity became something I could grasp. When he touched me, I felt charged with possibility, as if every dream tucked inside me had been chiseled out by his hand. When he looked at me, it was like drawing breath for the first time.

Unease flickered across his features. Guilt squeezed my chest. If I stayed silent any longer, I would hurt him. And the thought of that chilled me. Perhaps he suspected that my silence meant that I was rejecting him. But that wasn't the truth at all. When someone offers his heart, you could not give anything less in return. My silence came not from my reluctance to give away my heart, but from the shock of knowing that I already had.

Here is mine, I thought, closing the distance between us.

His unease melted into hope. Then awe. He gathered me to him, and kissed me. And between our bent heads, the starry sparrow fluttered silver wings and took off into the air.

Here is my fear and my wonder, my hopes and my doubts.

Here I am.

7

NIGHT

There were only two weeks left until *Teej*. And still, we hadn't quite found the words to lay meaning to what had happened. To what we wanted. Sometimes, when no one was there, I tried out the words in my head, feeling out their unfamiliar weight and texture: *queen of Naraka. Consort. Beloved. Friend.* Sometimes, I whispered them aloud and thrilled in the sparks of light that danced up my spine.

That night, he appeared as usual. He touched my hair lightly, as usual. But then, unusually, he looked behind my shoulder to the untamed silver orchard and the dream fruit weighing each bough. The whole grove was lit up with the scent of wind-fallen fruit, the bruised and over-sweet fragrance of wanting gone to waste.

"You no longer sell them."

"I have decided to stop," I said. "Permanently."

I'd made the decision a while ago. The Night Bazaar would have to find a new way to dream. I'd sent Uloopi all of the last batch. She would have been furious with me for not telling her, but hopefully the remaining fruits would appease her. I sent along a small note: *To dream and dream, and dream some more. One day, I hope they pale before your reality.*

Her reply: *There better be more where this came from.*

The Dharma Raja leaned against a tall poplar, his thumb worrying at his lower lip. Once, I might have thought it was a contemplative gesture. Now, I recognized it as mischief.

"Before, you seemed quite determined to change every mind of the Otherworld. I recall you making a very impassioned speech about only having the ability to tell a story with a voice. Now how will you change the world without a piece of fruit?"

Teasing fool. I twisted my hand and a tiny river pebble soared to his head. He dodged it with a lazy swipe of his hand. And then he tossed it back to me, only this time it became a stone bird that hopped across my shoulder before collapsing into smoke.

"I learned a new way of storytelling," I said primly.

"I noticed," he said, nodding at the grove.

Over the past weeks, I had changed things. The orchard had fallen to neglect, but I had tied its silver boughs and strung a net of pearls between the trees. Ruined, dark things squirmed in the net. Caught nightmares. The other week, I had coaxed a well to hollow out the earth. The Dharma Raja sensed it for he leaned his ear toward the direction, as if he could hear all the things whispered in the water—good portents and well wishes. In the well's reflection, the stars churned and pinwheeled above, never keeping the same shape. I hoped that it would remind people who drank from its water not to believe in the first thing they saw.

"I was wondering when you'd come to realize this," he said. "Most storytellers are already familiar with this tenet."

"And that is?"

He moved toward me gracefully.

"That the best story is shown. Not told." He grinned. "I could've told you that. I've been practicing that for years."

He was right. It both delighted and annoyed me to no end. I wanted to make a difference, to be seen as more than I was. All this time, I had been so caught up in what the Otherworld thought. I had lost so much time trying to push my thoughts and self onto them, but it made no difference because they were just words without meaning. If I made the Dharma Raja see the world differently, then he let me see myself differently. I was enough unto myself. I would not let myself be held back by what anyone thought. And that was what I wanted to coax into life with these dream wells. I wanted someone to look inside of them and see something else. It was different from dream fruit because it knew it had no desire to last beyond the veil of sleep. It was simply an idea. A *nudge*.

"You could have advised me from the beginning to show more and tell less."

He arched an eyebrow. "Would you have listened?"

"I would've very convincingly pretended."

He laughed. And I caught his laugh in a kiss.

A week before *Teej*, Nritti and I sat side by side—as we always had—our feet scraping at the bottom of the river, toes digging into the bank in search of gold. Ever since I stopped going to the Night Bazaar, she would find me here in the red hours between sunset and true night. Sometimes, Vanaj would come with her and then the three of us would play *shatranj*—Nritti and Vanaj on one side, me on the other. Most of the time I lost, but I felt like I was winning every time Nritti laughed or grinned. Today, she was doing both, even though Vanaj could not visit with her this dusk.

"You're glowing with love," I teased. "It's beginning to hurt my eyes."

She laughed, and the bells strung through her braid shook with mirth. "There's that viper tongue. I was wondering where it went. You're so . . . *kind* around Vanaj."

"It's only for your sake. I had to provide one wonderful thing about you. Me. There's not much reason to like you, what with your horrific looks and grating voice."

Nritti gracefully fluttered her hand. "You are most merciful."

"And beautiful," I added.

"And beautiful."

"And charming."

"Let's not get carried away."

I laughed. "So. Where is your smitten lover?"

Nritti blushed.

"There's something I want to show you," she said, hesitantly. She drew out a delicate golden necklace strung together with black beads. I breathed in sharply. A *mangalsutra*. It was the piece of jewelry that defined a married woman. "We pledged ourselves to one another in the *gandharva* tradition. He went to ask Lord Indra if he could take me away from the court."

I think she knew all that I couldn't say because she reached for my hand. As always, I was struck by our differences. Already, the red of sunset had begun to peel back . . . revealing rose-tinted smoke sky and rain-cloud skin. Hers was the sun as seen through water, an Otherworld dream of gold and light. But our differences were only in looks. I felt her heartbeat pulse against my skin. And I knew that no matter what changes would come, we would always be sisters.

"I'm not leaving you," she whispered.

"I would never stop you." And I meant it. Nritti may not have believed in me the way the Dharma Raja did, but she loved me and she supported me the best way that she knew how.

"I will always send word. I will visit often. I will sing your praises to the stars and back."

I laughed, but my throat felt tight with tears. "Oh, please don't sing. Has Vanaj heard your voice? He's already blind, Nritti."

She held my hand a little tighter. "Besides, you will have some-one to pass your days with." She looked at me slyly. "And your nights."

My cheeks heated beneath her gaze. I had told her a little about the Dharma Raja and his visits. But she had never met him, and I had never divulged his identity. With *Teej* approaching, I couldn't help but think of Nritti's original advice. What did he want from me?

I had been courted before, but no one had gone to such lengths to know me. No one had dared me to dream of more for myself. No one filled me with dreams of my own. I'd come close to telling him on many nights, but couldn't. I hadn't forgotten that he had asked for a bond without love. Every time I imagined his rejection, my heart stuttered.

"He has never said he loves me," I said quietly.

"But you think he does?"

I nodded.

"Do you love him?"

"I don't know."

"When you are with him, what do you see?"

I closed my eyes, thinking of his presence. He was the burning thing in my heart, a caught flame that challenged and inspired me. He was the winged thing in my soul, something carrying my dreams aloft and freeing me from the ground. He was the nightmare of night, the tragic ending to a love story, the shadow over the cremation ground. My memories summoned him—night and smoke, embers and wings. I would not have him any other way.

Nritti's voice fell to a hush. "You see, sister? That is your answer."

Some insipid voice at the back of my head whispered to me anyway. And in its echoes, all I heard were my doubts. My fears. Vanaj had already given Nritti a *mangalsutra*. He had declared his love and married her in the manner of the *gandharvas*. Whereas the Dharma Raja had never once offered me that commitment. He had never once said that he loved me. *But he gave you the moon for your throne and a garden unlike any in all the realms. He gave you stars for your hair and offered his heart in his palm.*

I felt Nritti's hand smooth the hair away from my face.

"Sister. You are courageous and clever, creative and compassionate. But your doubts will ruin you if you let them. Choose happiness. Choose love."

Soon after, she left. And it was just me and the yawning sky and the pale stars shuffling sleepily into place. There was only one week left until *Teej*. All this time, he had yet to name what this was. The Dharma Raja had stated his intentions ages ago, but intentions change. Change was the only thing that could be counted upon. I knew that better than most.

For hours, I stood in the glass garden. Touching the tips of the crystal flowers and palming the diamond-paned jasmine vines. Every cool brush of the glass reminded me that what I felt was real. When I touched the glass, something crystallized within me. I loved him. I knew that now. And I wasn't going to wait around for him to tell me that's how he felt too.

Tonight I would tell him. I prepared the grove, arranged my hair. I waited, my heart full to bursting, my mouth brimming with all things I wanted to say. *Needed* to say.

But he never came.

· » 8 « ·

DEATH

I had lost myself. Sometimes I didn't think I'd drawn breath until her lips touched mine. Sometimes I saw the world as she did, and it was no longer an old and creaking thing, but a song I had not been able to hear until now. I told myself it was nothing more than the perfect companionship. Devoid of love but full of understanding. And every time I told this to myself, I thought the whole palace of Naraka shook with laughter. I ignored it.

For the past few days, I had imagined the world as it might be and not as it was. I had collected souls and spun them into new forms. There had been no need to visit the Tapestry. Until now.

The moment I stepped into the room, it sensed that I had changed. And like any beast that sensed weakness, the threads pushed and pushed until they broke into my thoughts. They rummaged with cloth fingers, ignoring my protest and fury. They spoke over me with taunts, dragging a noose of my past around my neck until I was yanked into a memory I never wished to revisit:

The Shadow Wife wore my mother's face. She crouched by my side, grabbing me by the shoulders.

"Do you know what you've done?" she asked.

"I've done nothing but tell the truth. Something you should have done years ago."

I had been younger and more foolish then, eager for justice. My mother had been missing for centuries. Some said that the Sun Palace was so bright that the light could cut you if you weren't careful. Some said that the light had cut my mother, splitting her heart right down the middle and blinding her heart to the love she should have carried for the child she left behind. I never asked why she left or where she went. When I was younger, I thought I had not loved her enough and that was why she left. When I grew older, I saw how love was sometimes not the tether but the whip. The thing that made you run far and fast and never return.

"You exposed me. But every truth comes with a price," said the Shadow Wife.

I would never call her Mother. I would never call her Lady Chayya. I would never speak her name.

"You don't frighten me."

She tilted her head to one side, worrying her lip the way my mother did when she was considering something.

"But love frightens you. Love and the loss of it frightens you, doesn't it?"

I said nothing.

"You should have learned from the beginning that when someone leaves, it is because nothing was valuable enough to make them stay. You were not enough. For this, boy, I curse you. And with this curse, I bind your heart. The

woman you give your heart to will leave you just as the Lady of the Wind left your father. And the heartache you feel now will be nothing to the loss of her."

The Tapestry taunted the words over and over. I reeled back, and the cloth fingers that had carded through my memory like so much silk suddenly crumpled and fell limp. My breath rattled in my lungs like the dead. I left the Tapestry behind me, determined to sort out my thoughts when Gupta appeared carrying a bundle of parchment roses.

"What are you doing?" I asked.

"Getting the palace ready, of course!"

"For what?"

"For *her*," he said, rolling his eyes. "It needs to be fitting for a queen. You already made her that garden, but I thought she might like something a little more intellectual. Look!" He tossed one of the parchment roses into the air and it opened into a mouth, shouting out snippets of Gupta's reports:

It really comes down to opposable thumbs.

And:

There is something rather grotesque about pearls. Why does anyone like them? It is spit. Congealed spit.

"You can't be serious," I said. "You expect her to walk through a garden of reports?"

"It's better than what you did! You gave her a garden of *glass*. That is actually hazardous to life."

It struck me then. Gupta was preparing for her to come here. Because he assumed she would become the queen of this kingdom. I turned slowly on the spot, staring at the halls where she might walk down, the mirrors where she might pause to consider a strange reflection. The dining table where she would sit across from me. The bedroom where I would sleep by her side. And as I imagined these things, the truth of the Shadow Wife's curse took hold.

If I fell in love with her, I would lose her. Maybe she'd come here and hate this place and leave. Maybe she'd realize that she couldn't stand the thought of eternity with me after all. The Shadow Wife's curse was true. I had felt it press itself into my bones the moment she spoke, and there it stayed, biding its time. Waiting until I fell in love.

The only difference was that I could stop this before it ever started. I could spare us all a world of pain. Even if it broke me.

"I'm sorry," said Gupta. "It's not a hazard. If she likes your garden, then who cares?"

"She . . . she can't come here."

Gupta stepped back, stunned. "What? Why?"

Because I am dangerously close to falling in love.

"It won't work."

"I thought you said that if it couldn't be her, you'd have no one?"

"I did say that. I choose no one."

"But you love her . . ."

"Don't say that," I said under my breath. "Don't say those words. I don't love her. I can't love her and I won't love her."

Gupta raised an eyebrow. "You do realize you have little choice in the matter."

"I have control over life and death, but not love?"

"Yes."

"I made a mistake. I see that now."

"Why are you doing this?" he demanded.

Because I'd already lived this. Under a shadow, I'd known a cursed existence and emerged into a cursed life.

"I'm cursed," I said.

Gupta knew that, but I'd never told him the details until now. Over the years, he liked to guess what the curse was. Lack of personality was his favorite guess. When I finished telling him, he stared at the ground.

"I still believe there is a way around this," he said. He spun a pen in his hand, which meant that he was about to rummage through the archives and find a solution. "But even then, what does it matter? You already love her."

"That's not true," I said, even as something sparked and tugged within me.

"If you can't see it now, then perhaps that is the true curse."

He turned, leaving me standing in the middle of the palace. I couldn't move from this spot. Moving meant that I had to put an end to something I liked far too much. Night came and went, and still I could not find the will to end what I had known. For the briefest space of time, I knew what the Tapestry had first taunted. A jewel no one else possessed: our time together. A door within reach: her arms around my neck.

A soul claimed: my own.

When the next dusk fell, I moved. I commanded my feet to move and they did not question me. But I could not command my thoughts to fall still.

Death was not always inevitable. But pain was. And right now, I couldn't see beyond the shape of that pain opening inside me. It wasn't that I could not control myself around her. It was that I had no desire to. Beside her, the world seemed impossible with wonder.

When I stepped through the final gate of trees, there she was. Burning like a star. She softened and then frowned. One look and I knew how impossible it was to live without her. I could exist without question. But *live?* Think, dream, create?

All those things I had learned in her presence. For a crazed moment, I wondered whether someone could survive on the threshold of love, like leaning over the lip of a cliff. Or would the lure of the fall always prove too great? Maybe I would risk it. For her. But then she stormed toward me and her next words pronounced me cursed:

"I love you."

Time stammered. Or I stammered. It didn't seem to matter because she just continued talking:

"I want to be with you because I love you. Not because I need you. I don't," she said, gesturing with her arms at the number of dream wells she had set up and the dream fruit that had gone to waste on the trees. "You inspired this, but I did it on my own. And I know I could do more at your side, but that's not the reason I choose you—"

"Wait," I said. I felt like I was choking on the word.

"And yet what I can't understand," she continued, "is why you insist on a bond with no love. I think you love me too."

"I don't."

She raised an eyebrow. No lip biting. No harsh intake of breath. Nothing but a raised eyebrow.

"Yes, you do," she said calmly.

"Why is everyone saying that?"

"And I've also figured out why you refuse to say it aloud," she said. "I know who you are."

"So you've guessed what that curse is, have you?" I asked, the words coming out crueler than I expected.

"Not fully. Tell me."

"If I love you, you will leave me. And it will cause me great pain. That is the curse."

She stared at me and then she disappeared on the spot. I stood there, stunned for a couple of moments. And then I heard her voice behind me:

"There. Curse fulfilled. You loved me. I left. I will imagine in my infinite vanity that it caused you pain."

"You're not taking this seriously."

"Why should I?" she retorted. "How many people suffer a cursed life simply because they didn't know how to listen to what the curse meant? Her curse was nothing more than the risk we take to live each day. All I hear is your cowardice."

"I am *not*—"

"You're scared," she said. "I am too. But I would rather live in fear than live without love."

"I'm sorry I'm doing this to you . . ."

"You are not doing anything to me. You are doing this only to yourself. If this is what you choose, then so be it."

For the first time, her resolve shook. She would not meet my gaze. She reached into her hair, tugging on the little sparrow fashioned of stars.

"Fear is like a curse, Dharma Raja. Like a curse, it lays down lines where none should exist. It squeezes your thoughts into a pattern until you become convinced that there is no other way to see. But I choose differently. I wish I could say the same for you."

Once more, she left. But this time, she did not return.

· » 9 « ·

NIGHT

When he didn't show up the first night, I wasn't sure where I should go. Nritti would always welcome me, but I didn't want to intrude on her and Vanaj with my pathetic tale of rejection. I needed someone with experience, which was how I found myself in the city of Nagaloka.

Down here, the kingdom of the *nagas* was cold and miraculous. Glossy seaweed wrapped around the turrets, sea roses bloomed down paths of pearl and salt stones. Everything glowed from the small drifting silver thuribles that lit up the city with moonlight. Beautiful *naginis* showed off their new gems or sharpened fangs and twice I heard their seductive singing through a flurry of waves. It was the thick of night, and her kingdom was nearly empty. Everyone let me pass without question. I walked through the palace until I found Uloopi at the end of an emerald hall. Her face looked a little pinched from the recent flurry of stress, but she grinned the second she saw me.

"Dream fruit?" she asked.

"Hello to you too."

"What brings you here?"

"Either delusions of love or the confusions of securing it."

"You know I hate seeing you sad, but I do love a good drama."

Uloopi and I walked—well, I walked, she glided—to a court-yard strung with seashells. Night was different under water. The waves took on an eerie texture. Almost feathered.

At Uloopi's prodding, I told her about the Dharma Raja. About the visits where he had promised me a throne, but not his heart. I told her about how each visit was a lesson in wonder, why I had abandoned the dream fruit in search of something more.

"I forgot how little you know," she said, reaching for my hand. "And I do not mean that in terms of your intellect, my friend. I think I know why your Dharma Raja refuses to utter those words . . ."

"He is not *mine*."

Uloopi raised one bronze shoulder. "He wants to be. And you want him to be. Therefore I am calling it as I see fit."

"But—"

"Do you want to know or not?"

I nodded.

And she told me the rest of the tale of the Shadow Wife and the cursed boy.

When he visited me, I was ready. I was armed with knowledge far greater than his past. Knowledge was powerful, but it was made powerful by the person who held it and spoke it. Knowledge was little more than footsteps pressed into the earth and called a "line" so repeatedly that the act of telling made it true. But I knew better. Perspective propped up the world on stilts of belief. I knew that better than most. And now I had to convince the Dharma Raja.

When I finally saw him, something in me unfastened. Here was someone who would have given me a kingdom and a throne without the expectation of my heart or my bed in return. Here was someone who saw me as no one ever had. When he looked at me, he didn't see night but the potential it brought: dreams and songs not yet sung, potential and creation.

Uloopi's and Nritti's words surrounded my heart and I spoke nothing but truths. I wasn't afraid of being scared. Life was too long for that. But the more I spoke, the more he curled in on himself. Over and over, I laid my heart bare.

Over and over, it crumpled.

A day and a dusk. A day and a dusk. A day and a dusk. I was losing track of it all. I was sitting in the middle of my garden of glass when the trees rustled. Hope plucked at my bones, playing me like an instrument until I thought my whole body was singing. But when I looked up, it was not the Dharma Raja standing at the edge of the horizon, but Nritti.

"Have you no smile for me, sister?" she asked, beaming.

But one look at my face told her everything. She ran to me then, her arms soft around my shaking shoulders.

"What do I do?"

At this, she lifted my chin. "Go to *Teej*. If he doesn't come, then you know that you have lost nothing but time. And we have plenty of that to spend without consequence."

I nodded, but the truth was that I did not want to spend time without consequence. I had glimpsed something more, a purpose that I was beginning to unlock day by day. The visitors to my dream wells had doubled and tripled in the past couple of days. Little by little, they were remembering the images I had spun. Little by little, my voice was being carried out into the world. The Dharma Raja's words floated back to me: *We could rewrite the world, you and I.*

I didn't need him, or anyone, to rewrite the world. But beside him, I had felt as if there was a world for me alone. A place that lived at the seams of my heart and grew there, wrapping glass vines around my bones and burying stars in my heart. It was a place of quiet and creativity. And if I had the choice, I never wanted to be without it.

But it seemed that wasn't my choice to make.

"I'll go to *Teej*."

· » 10 « ·

DEATH

The days blurred. I walked the halls, fed the hounds, stood before the Tapestry. Everywhere I moved, thoughts of her robbed me to the point where I sometimes didn't recognize where I stood or where I was going. *Fear is like a curse. But I choose differently. I wish I could say the same for you.* I couldn't shake those devious thoughts out of my head. She bent the way I saw the world. But she couldn't bend it to the point that it broke a curse.

Today was *Teej.* I tried to forget it, to lose myself in some other thought. But I couldn't.

The sky tilted to dusk. I fled to a part of the kingdom where souls waited to be categorized and organized, remade and reshaped. There, a familiar soul caught the light. And I remembered the request of the wife from so long ago, the woman whose words had spurred the listless existence that would very well be my future.

"Do you wish to wait for your wife?"

"Yes."

"Why?"

"Because I love her."

"Why?"

"Because life does not look how it should without her. It is a piece gone missing, a perspective that reminds me what it means to live. Without her, my life would be colorless. Life does not owe me fairness. But I will see beauty, even if I must fight for it. So will you let me stay beside her? And wait until she comes?"

Maybe the words hadn't truly come to me until now. But finally, finally, I saw it. And the truth was a latch in my heart. The soul reached out and touched me, and in it, I saw the barren wasteland of my thoughts. How the world had lost shape and color and texture since I had not seen her. What she coaxed out of me was a visceral need to live, and wasn't that what fueled immortality and made it worthwhile anyway? That there were wonders still left to be uncovered? Perhaps she could not bend the world such that it would break a curse. But she had bent my thoughts until I saw hope around its meaning, silver in its bleakness. I wanted to believe the curse had broken. Because I did love her. I couldn't remember where it started and I couldn't fathom it stopping. And she had left. And the pain of it had sucked the color from my world.

"I grant you this request," I said.

And then, I ran.

Gupta was waiting for me, a dark green *sherwani* jacket in his hands.

"I have been waiting out here for so long, I thought I had started aging."

"I don't have time for this. I have to get to her—"

"She won't be at the grove. She's at *Teej*."

My heart dropped.

"Even if I go, how will she recognize me? Don't most of those lovers use ridiculous signals or secret words on their palms or something?"

"Maybe that's the test," said Gupta, shrugging. "You saw through a curse. Now she has to see through you."

*C*hoose me.

I stood behind the podium, curtained off from everyone else. There were all kinds of tricks to *Teej*. People tattooed their hands with hints so that they would not end up with the wrong mate. But there was the leap of faith in this exercise, the same leap of faith required of a relationship. Maybe it was a fool's errand, but I had made my hand indistinguishable. We had never studied each other's palms but perhaps that was where the beauty lay. Whatever form she took, I would recognize her. Because it was not me that knew her, it was my soul. And it could never forget her.

·》 11 《·

NIGHT

Hope is light. It shines its way into crevices and shadows you wouldn't recognize. I held that hope within me, and I let it flare into a fire until it laid to waste my every doubt. I hardly remembered walking to the *Teej* celebration and waiting my turn in that line. Nritti held my hand tightly and waited beside me.

"Uloopi told me to give you this," said Nritti, opening my palms.

A necklace with a round-cut sapphire and strung with delicate seed pearls fell into my hands.

"What is this?"

"She said this was what she created the first time she tried making the resurrection stone."

"Does it bring back the dead?"

"No. But it calls forth our happiest memories."

I clasped the necklace around my neck, savoring the strange warmth of the pendant between my collarbones. It was magical, but not enchanted. No memories surged before my eyes. And yet, I felt a thread of warmth from my head to my toes. Like the afterglow of a long laugh.

When I ascended the stage, some of the lesser beings taunted me. But I pushed past them, clutching that hope within me. This was a beginning. Maybe it would not be the beginning I wanted, but it was a beginning I deserved. I surveyed the row of hands, one by one, stopping when I saw the hand covered in soot. At first glance, it looked like it belonged to a *raksha*. But when I looked closer, I saw cracks in that paint. I saw that the monstrous was little more than a flimsy coat of color. More than that, it was an invitation—to start a life with a different way of seeing. Starting now. I reached out. The curtain fell back with a crumple of silk. Dimly, I heard the audience suck in their breath. There . . . there he stood. Tall and shadowed, with a crown of blackbuck horns threatening to pierce the split sky above us. Guilt flashed in his eyes, before it became something else entirely: relief.

"I hoped you would choose me," he said.

I fought back an impossible laugh as that hope and light broke inside me.

"I have no dowry."

"I don't care."

"Then what do you want from me?"

"I want to lie beside you and know the weight of your dreams. I want to share whole worlds with you and write your name in the stars. I want to measure eternity with your laughter. Be my queen and I promise you a life where you will never be bored. I promise you more power than a hundred kings. And I promise you that we will always be equals."

"Not my soul then?"

"Would you entrust me with something so precious?"

I reached for one of my slippers and held it out, grinning.

"Here, my love, the dowry of a sole."

He held me closer than a secret and when our lips met, the world between us became a charged and living thing.

·»12 «·

DEATH

I knew little of curses, but much of stories. These were the tales collected in teeth, passed down from the mouth of one generation to the next. I heard the dead murmur them like talismans when they walked through my halls. They shared stories of curses shattered by moonlight or splintered by kisses. In all the years since the Shadow Wife had pronounced my heartbreak, I had never believed them until now. Because here, with Night's lips to mine, and the world yielding its treasures one by one . . . I knew that I was free.

POISON AND GOLD

・》 1 《・

Aasha glanced around the sumptuous throne room. For once, it was empty. Though not for long. Any moment now Gauri would enter through the heavy, golden doors. Aasha could picture her friend. Radiant and powerful, every bit the queen she would soon become. She could already see Gauri smiling broadly, relaxed, in a way she hardly ever did in public. She only did that because she trusted Aasha. A trust she hardly deserved. Gauri might smile at her, but that was only because she did not know the terrible secret that lurked in Aasha's heart.

And she must never find out, thought Aasha.

She glanced around the room. The two thrones that would soon officially belong to Gauri and Vikram looked foreboding. Around the thrones' raised dais were gilt chairs and cushions for the councilors and diplomats. Four large windows stretched across the tapestried walls. Today, the scarlet curtains had been pulled back to let in the morning sunlight. Normally, a gossamer net hung from the eaves of the palace, a barrier that kept out any curious birds. But it must have been damaged. The proof lay in Aasha's cupped hands. She opened them a crack, as if peering slowly might change the outcome. In her hands lay a small bird that fit in the hollow of her palm. It was dead.

In her hand, it looked asleep. The bird's small body was still warm. The glossy feathers of its chest stuck up as if it had very recently been wind-ruffled. Tearfully, Aasha smoothed down its blue feathers. The bird was blue, as blue as the five-pointed *vishakanya* star printed on Aasha's throat. The very star that had ended its life.

For a *vishakanya*, all it took was one touch to end a mortal life.

"I am so sorry," murmured Aasha to the bird.

"Who are you talking to?"

Aasha looked up. She hadn't heard Gauri opening the door. Gauri walked toward her, smiling, until she saw what lay in Aasha's hands. Gauri looked at one of the windows, frowning.

"It must have flown in and gotten trapped," she said. "But you really shouldn't touch that, Aasha."

Gauri was right. She really should not have touched the bird. The truth was, she had not even noticed. It had flown in silently. Aasha had been sitting down with her back turned to the window when the bird alighted on her shoulder. The animals of Bharata always crept a bit closer to her, as if they knew she was not human and therefore less likely to harm them. But all Aasha had felt was the rasp of claws along her shoulder. She had jolted upright. In her panic, the *vishakanya* star had flared to life on her throat and the small bird's life had gone out like a light. Aasha should have been able to control it. That was the wish that the Lord of Wealth and Treasures had granted her after all. A choice. To live as a human and know the touch of a new life, and still be able to turn into a *vishakanya* and know that a life could fall at her touch. But lately, she could not rein in her power. It made her a deadly risk. Gauri had no idea.

Slicing a section off one of the silk banners, Gauri used it to pick up the bird and set it aside. Someone else would take care of it.

"There is something I must ask you," began Gauri. "Do you remember the meeting with Ujijain's intelligence committee?"

Aasha . . . remembered. In a fashion. She remembered that someone had brought in a strange arrangement of flowers with the spikiest, glossiest leaves she had ever seen, and that she had been entranced with them for nearly an hour. Normally, she could control when her touch was deadly. And though she had been in Bharata for nearly a year, she was still enamored with the feeling of living things beneath her hands. Every texture was a lesson in wonder. Every animal muzzle that pushed into her hand was a gift.

Which was all to say: no.

She had no memory of that meeting.

Gauri must have sensed as much because she laughed.

"To be fair, I do drag you to far too many meetings."

"I know," teased Aasha.

But she did not mind. She liked having a duty. She had never really had one in the *vishakanya* harem. Besides, acting as a sort of guard for Gauri allowed Aasha to indulge in her favorite pastime: watching humans. Humans had so much etiquette. Their desires hardly ever matched their actions. To Aasha, they were fascinating contradictions that spoke a language she only knew in snatches and phrases.

With their wedding fast approaching, Gauri and Vikram spent most of their waking hours in the company of their councilors. Once they were wed, their kingdoms—once ancient rivals—would join. It was a dream that the people of both kingdoms held tight to their hearts. Their two monarchs, young and beautiful and already legends in their own right, would steer the world into a new age.

But as beautiful as that sounded, the reality of merging the two kingdoms was less like a dream and more like a nightmare. Political plots were subdued with all the regularity of sunrise. Conspiracies thrived in the shadows, and loyalties to Gauri and Vikram changed by the day. Which was where Aasha's abilities came into play. As a *vishakanya*, she might have a deadly touch, but she had another power too. She could read the desires of others. All she had to do was reach forward with part of her mind, and card through a human's intentions as if they were cloth. From intentions alone, she could discern who meant Gauri and Vikram harm, and in this way keep them safe.

Looking at Gauri, she did not need her powers to know how her friend felt. Dark presses hollowed Gauri's eyes. But she wore an exhausted smile like a badge of honor.

"Why did you wake up so early to speak with me when what you really want, and quite probably need, is sleep?" asked Aasha.

"As a queen, I don't always get to do what I want," said Gauri tiredly.

"But that's the whole point of being queen," said Aasha. "You get to make rules."

"True," allowed Gauri. "But 'let the monarch nap' is a far less important rule than the one I wish to speak with you about."

Aasha plopped into one of the thrones.

"Speak!" she said, clasping her hands in her lap.

But then she remembered that she was not supposed to sit in the throne, even though it was a chair and chairs were for sitting in, and promptly stood.

"You know I don't care for those rules," said Gauri, waving a hand.

Aasha sank back into the seat, her cheeks flaming. The first time she had done that had been in front of a handful of councilors who nearly accused her of insurrection. How was she supposed to know that humans had all kinds of rules about which people could sit in which chair? It wasn't as though the chairs minded.

"You've been in Bharata for almost a year now," said Gauri. "During that time, I don't believe I have ever once asked you what you wanted. Not for the day or for a meal, but what you want out of, I suppose, this . . . life."

Want.

The word prodded at her. In the *vishakanya* harem, her want had been so simple. She wanted a choice that had not been given, to experience the human life that had been denied. But in Bharata, that want had warped. Now she could be a human too. But she did not know how to do that. She did not know the right things to say or how to act. Though she was nearly three centuries old as a *vishakanya*, the human life-form that she could take was hardly more than a young woman stumbling through the darkness. Which made her wants . . . complicated. She wanted, now, what any human wanted. A place among people. A home in someone's heart.

She wanted to be a person.

A true person.

But she did not know how to explain that to Gauri. And lately, she did not feel as though she were flesh and bone at all, but poison cleverly disguised as a girl. All she had to do was look at the small silk-covered lump off in the corner of the room as proof.

"I don't know," she said finally. She did not meet her friend's eyes. "Right now, I would most want a pistachio cake."

Which was not a lie.

Gauri's eyes narrowed. "I can see Vikram's influence on you quite clearly."

Aside from Gauri, Vikram was Aasha's other friend. The sly-eyed emperor of Ujijain had made it a point to guide Aasha through the intricacies of court life. Under his tutelage, she had learned how to insult a person with the highest degree of elegance, how to keep a straight face through a lie, and how to curse. Gauri had not been amused when she had displayed that last talent in front of a group of visiting dignitaries. Vikram, however, had been delighted and let her pick the desserts for an entire week. It had been a very good week.

"What do you want me to do?" asked Aasha.

Gauri shifted, uncomfortable. "Walk with me through the gardens. Vikram should be there. He should be awake by now."

The two of them rose and left the throne room behind. By now, dawn had fully stretched into morning. The servants in their scarlet and green livery had just begun their daily chores. Water was being drawn from wells and purified for morning prayers. Beyond the ornamental gardens, Aasha could hear the clang of swords as the soldiers moved through the day's first drills. In the gardens, birds with bright feathers roosted in the trees as if they were living jewels, and the slender pools carried the clouds' reflection in their waters. Out of habit, Aasha touched her neck. Her *vishakanya* mark flared, and a new sense overtook Aasha. Sensing desires was like perceiving another dimension. She stretched out her senses, feeling for any human intention that desired violence. In her first weeks at Bharata, it had been hard to differentiate nuances of desire. She had nearly attacked a courtier who had desired to kick another man down the stairs. That, she now realized, was impulse. Humans had many violent impulses, but they were rarely brought to fruition. The desire for true violence felt like a river of cold. It ran deep, made more intense by how long the desire had lived there. It was her sense for this intention that kept Gauri and Vikram safe.

"There's been a problem of late," said Gauri.

"A problem?"

An undercurrent of fear ran through Aasha. Was it possible that she was wrong and that Gauri in fact knew of her ailment? Scared, Aasha caved in her shoulders as if she might exist in this world just a little less.

"Yes," said Gauri. "And that's part of the reason why I was asking what it was that you wanted. I wasn't sure if, perhaps, with all the changes going on in the kingdom, you really wanted to stay here . . . with us."

A cold knot of horror grew in Aasha's belly.

Was Gauri trying to say that she was no longer wanted here? That she had to leave? Aasha felt stricken. Of course that would make sense. They would have the security force of two great empires. They would have no need of her. Perhaps her blunderings in front of other people had become too burdensome.

"Aasha. Where do you see yourself in the future?" prompted Gauri.

By now, they had reached the end of the pathway. Vikram slouched against a pillar, hands shoved in his pockets. He looked bleary with sleep. He managed a smile, but the moment he saw Aasha's face, his smile fell.

Vikram strode over immediately.

"You're scaring her!" he said to Gauri. "Just look at her! She thinks we're kicking her out."

Gauri stared at Aasha, horrified.

"That's not what I meant at all!" said Gauri.

"*I told you* we should have started this whole thing a different way! You always make everything sound ominous," said Vikram.

"Your version sounds like too much pressure and like you're not giving her a choice!"

"Oh really? Let's try," said Vikram. He turned to Aasha. "You are like family to us. You know that. In the process of merging our kingdoms together, a very important position has opened up in our innermost circle of advisors. We were hoping that you might consider staying with us for at least a couple more years—"

Aasha didn't even let Vikram finish. She threw her arms around him and Gauri. Her shoulders shook as she muffled one critical word:

Yes.

Yes, *of course* she wished to stay. Nothing horrified Aasha more than the prospect of a human life without friends. Growing up, Aasha's only family had been the sisters of the *vishakanya* harem. But then the Otherworld kingdom had held the Tournament of Wishes, and Aasha had met Gauri and Vikram. Back then, they were merely contestants, a young prince and princess fighting to retain a wish. But though they were champions, they were not the only victors. For her role in their story, Aasha had received the wish that let her out of the harem's confines. At Vikram's words, gratitude overwhelmed her. She was not yet ready to tire of the human world. With this promise of a new position, she would not be forced to leave.

When she finally lifted her head, she saw Vikram mouthing: *I told you so* to Gauri, who rolled her eyes.

"Well then it's settled," said Vikram.

"You haven't even told her what the position is," said Gauri.

"Oh right," said Vikram.

Aasha didn't much care for the name of the job. Kingdoms handed out titles that hardly made any sense. There was a secretary of Interior, but the person did not stay inside all the time. There was a Royal Taster, whose main task was to set out the food and never commented on the taste of a dish at all. Whatever they asked of her, she was certain it would be simple.

"What is it?" asked Aasha.

Vikram reached for Gauri's hand.

"We would like you to be our Spy Mistress."

S py Mistress.

    That title was nothing at all like the royal titles that dealt with interiors or tasting. In fact, just the way Vikram spoke the title sounded strangely heavy. Gauri looked at her expectantly. Hopefully. All traces of lightness vanished from Vikram's face. This was no light or meaningless task. To them, it was both an honor and a burden. She could see that now.

    Aasha had to grit her teeth and focus all of her energy to keep the *vishakanya* star from showing on her skin. If it showed, then Gauri and Vikram would know that she could no longer control when it appeared. She would be forced to reveal that sometimes—like when she was frightened or surprised—the star would show and her touch would instantly become deadly. She would be forced to reveal that she was a threat to their lives. Lately, she had taken to barring her doors just in case Gauri ever thought to wake her up from sleep. The thought that she might hurt the very people she loved filled her with nausea. And now they had given this great gift to her. A sign of their trust. Their love. She was not worthy.

"Aasha?" asked Vikram.

Aasha knew she could not force a smile. Vikram was too shrewd. He would know. So she mimicked the humans she had watched all this time. She sank to the ground, her chin tipped toward her chest. The posture of a subject to one's sovereign.

"Oh, Aasha," said Gauri, embarrassed.

Gauri placed her hands at Aasha's shoulders, drawing her upright.

"It will not be an easy task," she said. "Although we want you to be our Spy Mistress, the final approval falls to Bharata's current Spy Mistress. You will have to leave court and train with her. If, in three months' time, she finds you worthy, then you will become her equal and work alongside her."

"Bharata's Spy Mistress is . . ." Vikram's brows drew together. "How do I say this? Well. It's said that her temper makes Gauri look soft-spoken in comparison."

Gauri glared.

"I mean that in the most affectionate way possible," he said.

She did not seem appeased.

"And if I do not succeed?"

"Then you return home," said Vikram.

But there was a silence there. In the past, Aasha had not always been able to recognize such pauses for what they meant. In the past, she would've simply said "very well," and then turned on her heel in search of diversion or entertainment. Now, she knew better. Humans always paused before sharing bad news. She did not know why they waited. Perhaps they thought to give the air a break before assaulting it with sorrow.

"And then?" prompted Aasha.

Gauri, always the braver of the two, spoke first. "If you do not secure this position, we have been informed by our joint councils that they would prefer you not to be in the room during meetings of state."

Aasha's eyes widened. "But why? Have I not done my job well? Or—"

"You've been a boon to us," said Vikram. "The problem is that we cannot reveal what it is that you actually do."

It was of utmost importance that Aasha not reveal her true nature.

"I understand," she said. And she did.

Aasha tried to put herself in the mind-set of the human councilors. If she had no official position, then she would be forced to the margins of court. All those hours spent in activity, in *purpose*, would be replaced with loneliness. Without a purpose, what would she serve to Gauri and Vikram except as some bizarre ornament or relic from a long-ago adventure? She would be a burden to them.

"I do not want to go," she said. "I'll just stay and continue on as I have before."

Again, that pause.

"Our joint councils have been strict," said Vikram miserably. "Either you earn an official position or . . ."

"Or you cannot be in our company. Period."

Aasha's heart began to race.

"I have to . . . to leave to stay?"

They nodded.

The world now felt terribly larger than it had just a moment ago. Bharata was safe. She might be ridiculed for her oddness, but at least it was in an enclosed space. As it was, Aasha could hardly mimic the correct human mannerisms. Her blunderings were only tolerated because of her friendship with Gauri and Vikram. Even *tolerated* was a generous word. Some dared to whisper that the queen of Bharata kept company with a witch. Not all citizens were eager for the kingdoms of Bharata and Ujijain to join together. They would take whatever observation they could and twist it cruelly. Aasha was reminded all too often that every blunder she made had consequences beyond her.

Once, when Gauri had been in a meeting with various diplomats, Aasha had started yawning. She tugged on Gauri's sleeve, interrupting her, all to ask whether or not they could go outside instead because she was terribly bored. Gauri had turned to her, and in a voice so low that no one else could hear her, said:

"Do you not realize how deeply you are embarrassing me? Stop."

There was no malice. Or heat. And it was the calm, flat of Gauri's voice, spoken while her face was still a mask of pleasant calm, that had set Aasha's insides on fire . . .

She had done wrong. There was no other way around it. Gauri had apologized for speaking so harshly the moment they were alone, but the humiliation felt sticky for weeks to follow. It had not even occurred to her how her actions might look to another person. Interrupting the queen of Bharata was tantamount to insulting her control of court and even her fitness as a sovereign.

And now, she would have to leave even this behind. What strange terrain awaited her? She could feel the weight of Gauri and Vikram's expectations like a hand pushing down on her lungs. In the Otherworld, she had been called too curious for her own good. Now it seemed as though she had traded curiosity for cowardice.

"Do you accept?" asked Gauri.

Aasha wanted to say yes. But the question was not whether she could accept, but whether she *should*. All she had wanted was to know what it meant to be human and all that that entailed. But it had come at such a jagged price. In her panic, she felt her blue star prickling. Aasha tamped it down, and stared at her two friends.

They had fought through so much. Could she not do the same? And then she saw their smiles fall just a bit. As if they'd been stung. And all fear drained from Aasha's heart. Her friends needed her. Love, fierce and sharp, grabbed her heart.

"Yes," she said. "I accept."

Aasha could not remember falling asleep.

In her dreams, her thoughts tangled and stuck together. The dreams lost their edges—she was in the *vishakanya* harem, the heat forcing her hair to stick to the nape of her neck. In the next moment—or perhaps it was an hour later, or perhaps it was at the same time—Gauri was running toward her. Blood on her mouth. Hands full of thorns. Aasha's blue star wouldn't disappear in time. She tried to warn her that she could no longer control her powers. She tried to warn her to stay back. But Gauri didn't hear her. She flew into her arms, then wilted.

Aasha bolted upright.

Failure sat heavily on her chest. For a moment, she could hardly draw breath into her lungs. Her heartbeats roared loud, an unruly cadence that seemed to scream at her in that gray fugue of sudden waking:

You failed. You failed. You failed.

Her head dropped into her hands. Something sharp and dry scraped against her skin. She shrieked, drawing back.

There, in her lap, lay a perfect circle of black roses. She must have forgotten to take them out of her hair before sleep. Now they looked like something she had dragged out of her nightmare.

Last evening, Gauri and Vikram had been so happy.

Already, there were plans being made for her journey to where the Spy Mistress lived. Already, there were political whisperings afoot. More desires to comb through. To make sure that she was not leaving them in a nest of vipers.

It was not anxiousness that drew her from sleep.

If anything, part of Aasha thrilled at a new opportunity. She was still scared to leave Bharata, still nervous that she might embarrass herself there as she did here. But there was urgency in this task. In the harem, everything was slow-moving and planned. In Bharata, it was much the same. Routines, tasks, feasts. No competition to be seen. In the harem, none of the *vishakanyas* competed with each other. They were all beautiful. All intelligent. All gifted in some way, shape, or form. And long life, at least amongst the *vishakanyas*, had all but extinguished any burning desire for recognition. But now she felt that desire. It almost felt like an ache settling against her ribs, this need to *show* just how much she belonged.

Initially she did not know what it was. She told Gauri that perhaps she had eaten the wrong dish at dinner the previous night. But Gauri had laughed:

"That's just the teeth of ambition chewing at the heart of you," she said. "Let it bite. It's good for you."

Ambition had not shaken her from sleep. It was fear . . . fear that her horrible secret might hurt the ones she loved.

Yesterday, Vikram had been confident that she would earn the Spy Mistress's approval and be taken on for the position.

"You can wield and control such force, Aasha," he'd said proudly. "We're not worried."

Control.

She couldn't. Not anymore.

The blue star on her throat pulsed. Sweat cooled against her skin. She hadn't summoned her *vishakanya* powers, and yet they had reared up anyway, forced to the surface by her own panic.

She couldn't name the point where it started. It was sometime after she came to Bharata. A courtier had asked where she hailed from, and she had answered that she was a *vishakanya*. Luckily, the court had taken it to be a joke and pretended to faint if she brushed past them. After that, Gauri and Vikram had forbidden her from revealing her true nature.

At first, she had been stubborn. *Vishakanyas*, though deadly, were not inherently evil. But she quickly learned that nuance meant little to humans. Over the past year, Aasha had grown used to the rumors that snaked after her. It was around the third month of her stay that courtiers—mad with envy over her proximity to Gauri and Vikram—had taken to calling her a witch. In the beginning, Aasha did not mind. She had been called worse. Not all patrons of the Otherworld were kind. She did not mind what someone else thought because she knew who she was.

At least, she used to.

But her greatest desire—to experience a human life—had changed nearly everything.

"If I told people what I was, then they would not be scared," Aasha said. "People are only scared of things they do not know or understand."

She knew that better than most.

In the Night Bazaar, there worked a fear monger. He sold pinches of fear—dark purple blooms with thorns so thin and sharp and crowded together that they looked deceptively like velvet. All one had to do was stroke the bloom, and the fear would seep through the skin and lace through the bloodstream. Aasha had seen ancient *rakshas* fall to their knees, their eyes ringed with white, just to make the torture stop. They were highly sought after by the kings and queens of a thousand different realms. No need to kill a person with this interrogation device. Merely blow out the candles, and let the darkness do the rest. Aasha had asked the fear monger what he had distilled to create the kind of fear that trailed ice down spines and yanked people from dreams.

"The unknown, child," he had said, for Aasha was young in the eyes of immortals. "I gather the shadow moving swiftly out of the corner of one's eye. I gather the creaks in the floorboards when the sleeper balances on the precipice of dreaming. I gather the doubts that turn knuckles pale and hollows the stomach with an invisible kick. And I burn them down to this."

But Vikram had explained that even if their fear was gone, a new emotion would take its place: malice.

"Imagine what someone would do if they found out that you could sense desires?" said Vikram. "They might try to fool you. Or hurt you. And in doing so, they might even put Gauri and me at risk."

"But that is horrible!" Aasha had said.

"It's human," Vikram had answered with a weary grin.

All it took was a few months in Bharata to see that Vikram was right. Aasha had never realized how much humans lied, both to themselves and to those around them. Their desires were so tangled and nuanced. If they knew what she could do, they would just bury their intentions further. Humans were beautiful and deceitful. Even with fury in their hearts, their actions could be virtuous. Even with virtue in their hearts, they could act with cruelty. Why? Did that make them bad or good? To fit in here, she was expected to act like them. She *was* one of them, she supposed. But now all the things that made her who she was had been called into question. No longer could she act on impulse or simply do as she wished. It led to a horrible gap within herself, this sour hollow where all she did was wonder what was *wrong* with her. Why could she not do as others did?

And then came the day her powers faltered.

Even now, shame rattled her bones.

It was such a small thing too. To cause such devastation.

Last winter, she had tamed a mynah bird in the gardens. It had hurt its wing. Aasha had created a small splint and fed it bright berries and slivers of sweet nuts. For a time, the bird had been her companion. It liked to sit on her shoulder, and nibble at her bright earrings. In the spring, the bird disappeared, and Aasha, though she mourned it, was happy that it could come and go as it pleased.

By summer, she had nearly forgotten about the bird.

Then came the afternoon where she had been walking outside, having just left one of Gauri's meetings.

She had been deep in thought, turning over a point in the meeting. One man had smiled at her. But his desire . . . his desire spoke of revulsion. For *her*. Had she done something? Did she wear her differences so obviously? What else could she do to try and be human?

At that moment, something warm knifed against her cheek. Aasha didn't think. She only reacted.

A shudder ran through her.

She didn't even have to raise her hand. She felt the star prickle to life on her skin at the same instant that she heard a low *cheep* of surprise. When she turned around, the mynah bird that she had loved and nursed back to health was dead at her feet.

From then on, she had kept at a distance from the others. When there were invitations for festivals, she had stayed behind. What would startle her next? Unannounced fireworks? The belly of a thunderstorm skimming over the city? She wanted to go. Every part of her yearned. This was why she had come to the human realm in the first place . . . to see and live and dance. To slake her wonder in sips of a life that had long been denied.

But she couldn't.

Every time she heard laughter outside her suites, she thought of the mynah bird at her feet. She heard its hurt cry of surprise replaying over and over in her head. The mynah bird became the citizens of Bharata, fanned out in a circle around her, struck dead all because she had been . . . *surprised.*

Just last week, she'd nearly killed a child. The little girl had accidentally tripped her. Aasha, caught off guard, had reached out her hand to steady herself. The child, thinking to steady her, had tried to grab her hand.

In the last second, she'd gripped a marble column. The blue star flickered and faded in a blink. But a blink was all it took to kill.

Now, Aasha looked around the room.

It would be so easy to pack her belongings and leave in the middle of the night. Aasha slid out of bed, her heart racing and breaking at once. But then she stopped. She couldn't leave her friends. And even if she did, who was to say that she would be able to control her powers if she returned to her sisters? What was to prevent her from being startled and suddenly turning mortal? What if one of her own sisters, thinking to help her, reached out and killed her with one touch?

Tears sprang to her eyes.

No matter how she looked at this world, she was trapped.

She had traded one prison for another. By tomorrow morning she'd be leaving for the home of the Spy Mistress. She closed her eyes, feeling as though every undeserved hope Gauri and Vikram had placed in her had suddenly sprouted thorns. If they knew what was wrong with her, they would have never given her this honor. Or believed in her. They might have even banished her. She deserved as much.

Outside, the moon was a rind of silver growing on top of the mountains. Aasha leaned back against the cushions, staring at the empty space beside her. A strange ache dug into her bones. Even the shadows had found stillness. Peace.

Of all the human desires and emotions that fascinated her, love was the most mysterious of them all. The texture of that desire manifested differently in every individual. She had sensed the desire between two people and found it scorching to the touch, or desperately entangled with emotions of grief or envy, or desire so light and delicate that it seemed as if it were wrought from strands of daydreams.

In her wish to live a human life, she had discovered so many human emotions. She had felt envy quite sharply when Gauri had asked to spend time alone with Nalini and she had not been invited. She had felt a flicker of desire when a young man or young woman held her gaze and flashed a smile full of invitation. Though she knew sorrow best of all these days . . . not once had she felt love. Romantic love. She knew full well that both Gauri and Vikram held part of her heart. But if she could hold so much in her heart, could she not give it to someone as well?

She knew what love was supposed to look like. She saw it every day with Gauri and Vikram. The moment they beheld each other, it was as if a trail of light had been instantly forged between them.

She would never forget the first time that realization had struck her. Aasha had been leaving the kitchens, her favorite haunt when no official duties pulled her to Gauri's side. There was a shaded path that wound through the orchards of Bharata. That was where she had spied Gauri and Vikram through a gap in the trees.

A swing hung from the sweet-scented branches of the gulmohar tree. The blooms were plump and garnet red. A crimson so striking that Aasha had once expected the petals to scald her like a flame. Vikram was pushing Gauri, laughing. She smiled up at him, her chin perched over her shoulder. Vikram had cupped her upturned face and kissed her smile until their expressions twinned the other.

The memory made Aasha want to curl around her shadow. She couldn't possess such a thing. She dreamed, sometimes, of a smile fashioned for her alone. A smile that only she summoned. That only she knew the secret contours of. That only she could find in the dark with neither candle nor moonlight but only the illumination provided by a beloved memory.

Beneath her arm, the blackened rose petals fell apart. It was as much a reminder as it was a warning. She should not want such things.

She'd only char them and be left with nothing but ashes.

D o you have everything you need?"

"Yes."

"Did they pack enough food and water, you think?"

"Gauri . . ." said Vikram softly.

Gauri ignored him.

"Do you have a knife?"

"She has something better," said Vikram wryly. He wriggled his fingers.

Aasha tried not to pale.

"What about desserts? Did you say good-bye to the kitchens? Half of them are so used to seeing you they probably think you're part of the staff."

Aasha had said good-bye to the kitchen workers. One of them had given her a favorite earthen pot, and if she inhaled it deeply, she could smell the ghost of spices that had settled into its cracks. Learning how to cook had become her favorite human pastime.

Only a few people had gathered to see her off. Outside the gates of Bharata, dawn had scarcely touched the skyline. A rosy blush gleamed through the trees. In the early morning chill, Aasha could see her breath plume before her. The cold hardly bothered her, but she pulled her shawl tight anyway, as if it might insulate her from the chill of her own fears.

The horses had been teamed to the chariot. In a few minutes, this carriage would take her far away from the confines of the palace. Aasha felt like an exposed wound, her heart raw and bared. But deep within her, some remnant of the old Aasha remained. Curiosity flickered to life. What was beyond these walls? And how interesting would it be to learn something *new* for a change instead of spending her days listening to others?

"We will see you in three months' time," said Gauri. "At our final ceremony before the wedding."

"Thank every pantheon of deities," said Vikram. "So many ceremonies. I can feel myself aging. Look," he said, pulling his cheek taut. "Do you see any lines?"

"The only lines I see are the fine cracks in your sanity, my love."

Vikram scowled.

Aasha stifled her laugh. Was it allowed? She had taken so much care to unlearn parts of herself that now everything she did felt stilted, made slow by every second-guess.

With a final good-bye, Aasha stepped inside the chariot. It lurched forward. A cloud of red dust gathered. The silhouettes of Gauri, Vikram, and their small entourage gradually faded until Aasha was all alone.

Aasha had seen cities of legend. She had visited the realm of serpents, and wandered through the mother-of-pearl and moonstone palaces. She had walked in the Night Bazaar and felt the moonlight silver her skin and the sunshine warm her face at the same time. But nothing compared to human cities. They reeked. Even from her chariot, Aasha could smell the animal sweat wicking from oxen dragging ploughs. She could smell the paste for brick-making, and the char of cooked food. Human cities were imperfect. To her, it made them all the more beautiful. All the more real. There was no magic here where someone might simply lift a palace from the ground. Everything demanded time. Patience. And yet the very nature of human existence—little more than a gasp of breath and a blink—seemed at odds with human marvels. A man might spend his whole life building a work of art, and never see it finished. But it was that dream—of what it might become, of knowing he had contributed to something immortal—that fed his soul. That was the magic of humans. Aasha felt humbled even to glimpse such endeavor.

For four days they traveled through Bharata.

Eventually, cities gave way to towns, then villages, then . . . forests. Aasha dearly wished to stand at the front where the charioteer drove the horses. She wanted to stretch out her hand, and feel the firm silk of vines dangling from the branches. She wanted to step outside and feel the damp earth squelch between her toes. But when she had asked the charioteer, he had been appalled.

"No lady of the court would do such a thing," he said.

Perhaps a braver person would have pushed back. It was not as though the court of Bharata were there to see her stare wide-eyed at the jungle. But the man's condescension cut her. Ashamed, she did not ask again. Instead, she stayed curled up in her seat, leaning out the window with her chin tipped toward the ceiling of tangled trees and her mind lost in daydreams.

On the fifth day, they reached the Spy Mistress's tower. The chariot in front, full of Bharata's soldiers, stopped first. Aasha wanted to get out with them, but she was told to wait. Not wanting to offend the Spy Mistress before she had even met her, Aasha did as she was told.

Once she was allowed to descend, Aasha surveyed her new home for the next three months.

A thin frost hung in the air. It was nearing dusk, and the gathering darkness made the roads look unattended and lonely. She had imagined that the Spy Mistress would live in a palatial mansion hidden in the trees, disguised by mirrors so that the eye didn't register its grandeur. Or perhaps a home cut into a waterfall. Something fanciful that said "Here Be Secrets."

But this was not it.

It was a slab of sandstone along the side of the road. Obvious, and yet unattended. There had to have been a village nearby, and yet there were few signs of life aside from some stray cattle wandering by the road.

A crow circled overhead. Aasha looked around, but there wasn't anything *dead* for it to consume. Unless it was somehow feeding off the sad, empty energy of this whole place.

There was no one out here.

No sentinels.

No guards.

Not even a large fence with chinks cut into the stone, so that someone might be able to peer through it and find another person.

"Does she know we're coming?" asked Aasha.

The soldier, Suraj, squinted up at the tower.

"She should. But then again, that's never made much of a difference to her."

"Is she truly so awful?"

"Certainly!" said Suraj. "She wears her hair shorn like a widow, but she has never married. She curses like a man. Wears pants. I bet she was the one who decapitated the Spy Lord of Ujijain."

Aasha felt a bristle of indignation. She had heard people talk the same way about her own kind, how they were wild and consumed men out of spite.

"Have you met her?" she asked coldly.

"Not at all," he scoffed. "And I hope I never do."

Frowning, Aasha looked back at the door to the tower. It was half-open. But it didn't look like an invitation. It had that same tense quality of a monster sinking back on its haunches. Waiting.

Not even the evening light—hungry as it usually was to spill over the land before it was reeled back into the sky—dared to step past the tower's threshold. Aasha tilted her head. It looked strange. Flat, somehow.

"Spy Mistress!" called Suraj.

But no one answered.

The other soldiers had begun to discuss the best way to enter. The Spy Mistress was known for laying all kinds of traps around the place.

Aasha walked forward. Strange. The light did not reach over the threshold.

But neither did the dust.

Instead of going in front of the door, she walked off to the side. She reached around for a pebble on the ground, throwing it directly into the door. It ricocheted with a metallic, pinging sound. Aasha almost grinned. It was false darkness. The first trap.

Sure enough, the ground right in front of the entrance to the door crumbled into a pit. If anyone had been standing there, they would have fallen instantly into a hole.

Aasha had seen something similar to this at the entrance of Nagaloka, the realm of serpents. A trapdoor that punished those who were disrespectful enough to enter an open space. It was far more polite to sit at the side, and wait to be noticed. That was the true entrance.

Suraj jogged over to her.

He walked cautiously toward the edge of the hole that had widened where the trapdoor fell. And then he hopped back.

"How did you know?" he asked, staring at her wide-eyed.

Aasha did not know how to answer. Some things were instinct. A human of Bharata would see a tiger and run, thinking it meant to harm them. An individual of the Otherworld would see a tiger and stop, thinking they might know them.

"I just did," managed Aasha. And then she wondered what Suraj had seen that would make him leap away from the edge. "What's down there?"

"I do not wish to alarm you. I do not think a well-bred lady would have ever seen such a thing."

But Aasha was not a well-bred lady.

Ignoring him, she walked to the brink of the trap and looked down. Would she see a pile of bones or a pit of iron spikes? But no.

Open water met her gaze. A scaly tail whipped the water into waves, thrashing hungrily. She jerked backward. There wasn't anything that would save a person, and the Spy Mistress hadn't even bothered to warn them about the kinds of horrors that might be faced in their halls.

Perhaps someone else would have seen such things and called the Spy Mistress ruthless. It did not seem human to punish intruders this way or to be so cunning. But for the first time, Aasha breathed easier . . .

This she understood.

This cunning. This testing. This crouching.

Gauri and Vikram had thought that the Spy Mistress position would suit her. This was the first time that Aasha believed that perhaps they had seen something within her that even she had not.

At the side where Aasha had thrown the pebble, a scraping sound filled the emptiness.

They walked over to see that the dry and twisting vines that had covered the side of the building were nothing more than artfully painted whorls of steel. Now, they were being pulled up, like chain mail, over the side of the tower to reveal a sturdy black door. The true entrance. There was even a note nailed to the center:

Speak true
Speak fast
Or I'll kill you

Aasha appreciated her bluntness.

She did not doubt that the Spy Mistress meant her words

and she found it exhilarating. In Bharata, everyone hid their spite behind silk. They hid murderous ideas behind well-bred manners. Here, she did not have to think too hard.

Just as she had at the brink of the well, Aasha reached for her own instincts.

If anyone thought it was odd that the strange advisor of Queen Gauri was clutching her throat, no one said anything. Which was a good thing too because Aasha was reading *them*. She cast out her will like a net, gathering what desires floated to the tops of people's minds like oil separating from water.

Desires were gauzy blooms of heat—they flared or subsided. But always, they were there. If there were any humans present, that soft dent of heat would have revealed them.

The Spy Mistress couldn't be here, she thought.

"You brought me a gawker?" called a peevish voice on the other side of the door.

Aasha jumped back.

It was impossible. How could she have avoided Aasha's reading?

Suraj appeared behind her. "Yes, Mistress. This is the Lady Aasha, personally selected by Emperor Vikramaditya of Ujijain, and Queen Gauri of—"

"Did you not the read the door?"

"I beg your pardon—"

"Please don't. I never cared for beggars."

"Yes, I read the—"

"When I say speak fast and speak true, it's not me showing off my sparkling wit and humor. It is the baldest plea of: DO NOT WASTE MY TIME!"

The stones shook.

"Yes. This is her!" shouted back Suraj. "Take her. Train her. Make her like you—"

"Truthfully?" laughed the voice. "The new sovereigns must have a sense of humor. Or self-loathing. To the untrained eye, they can look remarkably similar."

The Spy Mistress still had not opened the door.

"It is my duty to dispatch her," said Suraj, growing more red-faced by the moment.

"Is she a letter? Or a prisoner in need of execution?"

"She is not," said Aasha rather forcefully.

"Lo!" called the voice. "It speaks."

Suraj shot her a look of sympathy. The luggage was placed by the door. The soldiers, fierce creatures that they were, had already closed the door to the carriages.

"We will be back at the third new moon to take Lady Aasha back to the palace," said Suraj. "At that time, you will be asked to accompany us and either name her as co–Spy Mistress or rescind any recommendation."

"Third moon?" taunted the Spy Mistress. "We'll see if she lasts that long."

Aasha was left standing outside of the door.

The court of Bharata had taught her how to wait and stay still. The *vishakanya* harem had taught her to fold her hands and look demure. But Aasha . . . Aasha for all that she had learned, could not unlearn her curiosity. Her fingers twitched even as she tried to lay them flat against the tops of her hands. The sense of useless waiting grew from barely tolerable to scalp-burningly impossible.

Unable to stand it anymore, she stepped aside from etiquette. "Hello?" she called.

The door swung open. But the Spy Mistress was not there.

The moment Aasha stepped inside, a fugue of magic hit her. Not the kind fashioned of hopes and unexplained wonders, but the kind wielded by demons and deities. It took Aasha by surprise, as if she had wandered to the end of a dark tunnel only to find a secret entrance to her room. The enchantment fanned the blood through her veins, and the blue star, without any summoning, burned on her skin. She clapped her hand over her throat.

Hide yourself.

That was the first and only condition that Vikram and Gauri had imposed.

Not even two steps inside the door, and you've already failed, she chided herself.

But the Spy Mistress could not have noticed. For there was no one inside.

Although Aasha could feel the weight of enchantment in the air, she could not find its seams. She did not know where things started or stopped, and she found herself wondering how the Spy Mistress had ever come to wield such magic. If she was a magical being, her desires still should not have been obscured.

No furniture touched the bare stone. But veins of warmth ran through the floor. Life was not here, but *below.* It had to be, because the smells of cooking had seeped through the stone. Luxuriant smells that gnawed at her stomach. Roasted vegetables and rice fluffed with strands of saffron and mixed with ghee. Iced fruits. Bread glistening with oil.

A voice called out from the stone:

"If you can't find the food, then you can't eat it," taunted the Spy Mistress. "Think of it like a secret you're supposed to sniff out."

Annoyance flickered through Aasha. Cast out of Bharata, separated from her friends, and now dying of hunger, she had no patience for cruelty too. Perhaps in another time she would have tried to intimidate this Spy Mistress. Perhaps a demonstration of her deadly touch to suggest that she was not someone to offend. But the deadliness of her touch was not a thing to use frivolously. A rush of texture flew through her mind. The iridescent silk feathers of the mynah bird, the warm damp of the child's palm, and the bird as blue as her star, its feathers still ruffled from a wind it would never again feel.

Outside, the sun had begun to sink slowly, light dribbling over the horizon. Her stomach ached. From a distance, the light looked like a plush mango split open. She licked her lips. Why didn't she think to bring any snacks with her? Soon, evening fell. Aasha's hunger sharpened. But so did her sight.

For so long, she had tamped down the instinct of the Otherworld that to reach for it once more felt almost shameful. And yet, even as she tried to read the room once more, it yielded no secret desires. Aasha felt blind.

"You cannot possibly mean to starve me!" she called. And then, in a smaller voice. "Do you?"

That would not be very kind. Bharata hadn't always been kind either, but at least they had never denied her the pleasure of a full stomach.

"I can and I will," replied a haughty voice. "If you can't find your way to the food, you don't deserve to eat."

"But you are to be mentoring me," protested Aasha. "Surely this cannot be your version of such a responsibility."

"It's my version of ridding my home of unwanted guests."

"I am not a guest," said Aasha. Her hair was beginning to free itself from the stays. She brushed it back furiously. "I am supposed to work alongside you as the next Spy Mistress . . ."

"You'll be the next casualty if you spend your time screeching instead of searching," said the Spy Mistress.

Aasha huffed in frustration. She searched every corner and scanned every wall, but still she was no closer to finding the food. Aasha forced herself to collect her thoughts. She sat in the middle of the stone tower and looked around her.

The stones set in the floor and the wall made no difference whatsoever.

Now the sun had completely sunk out of view. Slow moonlight pushed through the window, and beyond Aasha could see a silver crescent perched along a tree. Hunger was unfastening her thoughts. She sat there, letting her eyes slowly unfocus when she saw it . . .

A web.

It was dancing just out of sight, dangling and unspooling from the ceiling. Aasha tilted her head back. It hadn't occurred to her to look *up*. After all, how would a ceiling possibly be the entrance to the kitchens? Then again, in the Otherworld such things had been possible. A headache fuzzed at the edge of her thoughts. In Bharata, her Otherworld instincts kept her from being accepted. Here, her acquired human instincts kept her from being fed. She could not decide which was the worst evil.

What had the Spy Mistress said? She racked her brains. *Think of it like a secret you're supposed to sniff out.* A human might have thought that meant to follow a trail on the floor. But what if she did not think like a human at all, but instead, like . . . like herself? *Sniff.* What a strange word. It meant to smell something out, but what if that was not what the Spy Mistress had meant? The word itself played on one sense, but perhaps she intended another. That, at least, is how things would have been done in the Otherworld.

There was no scent to follow here. But there was a window. There was something she might see rather than sniff. Aasha walked to the window. She positioned herself with her back to the light, and watched how it flowed out before her, snagging on the ends of a couple of threads. In the moonlight, they were as insubstantial as spider silk. An idea came to her. She stepped forward, piling her belongings on top of each other until she had formed a sort of ladder. Then she wrapped her hand around the silk, and *pulled*.

The threads may have looked like silk, but they were strong as rope. They didn't snap off in her palm the way she expected. In fact, she had to drag herself down using most of her body weigh just to move the threads.

Not far from where she stood, the stone tiles shifted. A sound like the gnashing of a monster's teeth rang in her ears. Within moments, a small hole in the floor had opened up. Kitchen smells spilled into the air. Aasha clambered down from her stacked possessions, approaching the opened floor delicately. Staircases wound down to the bottom.

Aasha gathered her things and took the first step.

To break food with another was no small act. In Bharata, even sitting down for tea with a stranger was considered the first step to thawing unfavorable relations. With some courtiers, it was considered a strange act of intimacy. This was something Aasha had not realized until she had sat down for tea with a woman and immediately heaped spoonfuls of sugar into her cup *without* tea, which—she blushed to remember—indicated interest in a scenario that had startled her.

With tea and eating, parts of oneself were exposed. Not just their teeth or tongue or the slow-flutter of eyelids when something particularly tasty demanded the denial of one facet of the senses. It was the method. Whether they stirred sugar into their drinks or balanced a sweet cube between their top and bottom teeth, sipping like a sieve. These things meant something.

Aasha used to love tea. She loved the lemongrass scents and the sharp spicy note of ginger. But after she had choked during a formal tea with Gauri and an ambassador from the mountain country of Patnagar—and very nearly started a war all because she had served the tea for herself instead of letting the ambassador's companion pour as dictated by Patnagar custom—she had stopped. She hadn't thought she'd done anything wrong. She had even read the ambassador's desire and it was clear that he desired for all of them to drink. But desires are served without instruction. Nuance was a thing taught by constant engagement, something that Aasha had never had the chance of doing until she came to Bharata.

"Even I didn't know about that rule," Gauri had confided.

But strain showed at the edges of her eyes. From then on, Aasha had started to take meals alone and in her room if she was not to eat with Gauri or Vikram.

And so it was with great humility and wariness that Aasha entered the dining area of the Spy Mistress. There was a great table, carved of onyx, and beset with ethereal decorations. An enchanted swan of smoke and glass swam from the front to the back end of the table. A chandelier of black roses bloomed from the ceiling. Each center emitted a shower of sparks that disappeared the second they drifted toward the onyx table.

And yet, for all that beauty . . .

There was no food.

She glanced behind the dining table to where the Spy Mistress was mixing a number of concoctions in a vial. It was a rough kitchen. Of sorts. Pots and cups. Measuring accoutrements, and a built-in well that Aasha imagined brought water into the subterranean space.

A door led out from the dining room, but Aasha could feel the presence of magic. As if this place might hide multiple doors that would lead to parts unknown.

All she could see of the Spy Mistress was her sharp profile. Her nose was slightly bent. She wore a small diamond in one nostril. Her hair was swept back in a knot, most unusual for a woman holding one of the government's most distinguished positions. Even more unusual was her dress, which was not a *salwar kameez* or a formal sari, but a brushed black silk tunic over cotton jodhpurs. Her only concession to the fashions of the harem women was a low-slung belt resting over one of her hips. Except where so many of the women Aasha had seen had used the belt as a kind of decoration, the Spy Mistress had sprays of glowing herbs, tools with sharp edges, something with an end like polished glass, and a pouch fat with coins.

"Tempted by the smells?" asked the Spy Mistress without turning.

"I—" Aasha stopped, gathering her wits.

This was not how she was supposed to act when she met an official from Bharata. There was supposed to be a careful dance of manners and gilded words. Maybe the woman was testing her?

"Forgive me, but—"

"You might as well get out," said the Spy Mistress, bored.

For the first time, she turned to face Aasha. Aasha bit back the urge to gasp. While the skin on half of the Spy Mistress's face was smooth, unlined and brown as a ripened nut, the skin on the other side of her face looked puckered. Pearly scars netted their way across her nose, tugging one side of her mouth into a sneer. One eye pinned Aasha beneath its gaze. So black it looked nearly garnet. The other eye was sea-blue pale, its pupil tapered like a snake. It did not look at Aasha. It seemed to look beyond her. And whatever it saw made her snake pupil dilate.

"Spy Mistress," started Aasha, trying to borrow the right order of words from Vikram. "I believe we might have misunderstood one another from the beginning."

"I understand that you're someone who simpered cleverly enough to get a government position. You understand that I'm not remotely interested in training you," said the Spy Mistress, spinning around. "How's that for misunderstanding?"

"I'm sorry, but—"

"Don't be sorry. Just don't be *here*. This is no place for apologies. Or sniveling."

"I—"

"You don't belong here."

It was said without heat. Without malice. Like so many other pronouncements about Aasha. It was spoken like a fact, which made the aim of the Spy Mistress's words all the more cutting for their clarity.

Aasha felt as if someone had taken a flame to her patience.

"That's . . ." she struggled.

She gathered her thoughts. Her self. Gauri had handled those who challenged her rule with calmness. Politeness. Vikram handled his dissenters with humor. Disbelief. But Aasha . . . Aasha had never wielded calm nor charm. Until Bharata, she simply confronted. She simply asked. She was just so . . . *simple*. The poisonous sneer of an adviser snuck into her thoughts: *"The Lady Aasha? A disgrace. At best, she's nothing more than a common wildflower among roses. Why the queen keeps company with her will not reflect well upon Bharata."*

Everyone had seen how well she did not fit except Gauri and Vikram.

The Spy Mistress was just like all those courtiers.

But unlike those courtiers, the Spy Mistress seemed to be angry that she was just like them . . . and yet she wasn't. The Spy Mistress did not know that. She did not know *Aasha*. The Spy Mistress did not know that cowering came as easily as breathing to Aasha these days. She did not know that her innocence of etiquette had received a brutal training.

She did not know her.

She expected nothing.

And so she could be anyone. She could even be . . . herself.

"That's . . . entirely wrong," said Aasha.

The Spy Mistress froze. "What did you say?"

"You're wrong," said Aasha. "Wrong, wrong, wrong."

She sang. She grinned. This was her former self—maybe her only self—breaking free.

The Spy Mistress just stared. And with every second that stretched without comment, Aasha felt as if she'd shaken off a heavy weight.

"Gauri and Vikram sent me here because they know I'm the best equipped for the job," said Aasha. "I want to learn. And you will train me, Spy Mistress."

The Spy Mistress raised her eyebrow for one fleeting second, before facing the assortment of vials in front of her. She seemed to have reached a conclusion.

"Spy Mistress?" she scoffed. "What a hideous title. It's not as though I leap from the rooftops of Bharata like a masked vigilante. I am Zahril."

Aasha bit back a laugh. *Zahril?* A name that meant poison. How strange.

"As for your tenacity," she said, nearly spitting the word. "Don't think you're particularly special just for being as persistent as a roach. Simply because that little show of 'feistiness' charmed their majesties does not mean that you're now my star pupil."

"But I am your pupil?" ventured Aasha.

Zahril snorted.

Aasha took this to be a yes.

"Everything in this place is more precious than your life. I can't have you fainting. You might fall on something precious. Eat."

Aasha hadn't noticed the measly plate of food sitting at the end of the dining table. One would think that a place as secretly sumptuous as Zahril's home meant that the food must be equal in glory.

One would be wrong.

There was one shallow bowl full of wilted, unseasoned vegetables, a stack of thin *paratha*—*without* ghee, Aasha noticed with a pang—and a jug of water.

Those sumptuous food smells had been nothing more than perfume wafting from the vials that Zahril kept measuring and consulting.

As she ate, Aasha watched the Spy Mistress.

The desires of others came so easily to her that she never thought to seek them out. But with Zahril, Aasha found herself wondering. What did one eye see that the other did not? What made her stand so straight and pull her face into lines of fury? What made her . . . her?

But she didn't dare to read Zahril. Not when she stood so close.

"Stop staring," said Zahril.

The word *sorry* fluttered in her throat. She had said it so often of late that she reached for it more than any other word. When she wasn't talking to Gauri or Vikram, *sorry* preceded every complaint or question or suggestion. *Sorry, but I hoped that . . . Sorry, but I think you . . . Sorry, but this was supposed to be . . .*

Emboldened, Aasha spoke.

"How long have you been the Spy Mistress?"

"Long enough for the respect I earned to ripen into fear."

"How long was your training?"

"Nigh on a century."

It was strange how Aasha felt at once surprised and not surprised at all. Despite the centuries she had been alive, Aasha passed for a young woman in the human realm, though she was hardly more than a colt when it came to her experiences. Zahril was like her. Perhaps even older. It was not unheard of for proximity to the Otherworld to extend the life of a human.

Something in Zahril's gaze turned daring. She lifted one eyebrow. Aasha looked down at her miserable food. She did not like the Spy Mistress's glare.

"Why do you go through the trouble of creating the scent of beautiful food when you will not eat it?"

Zahril's hand twitched.

"Because it is beautiful," she said. "Beautiful things spark all manner of problems. Twisted things often carry the guise of something beautiful, and people let them into their hearts. They smile at the knife aimed at their throat. More fool them, but it is useful in espionage."

Aasha didn't know how to respond, but it didn't matter. Zahril exhaled sharply.

"Have you ever seen a *vishakanya*?"

Aasha stilled. *Yes, in fact, I am one* was not the right thing to say. She had heard the name *vishakanya* uttered and draped in longing. She'd heard it hissed in shadows and chasing an averted gaze.

She had never heard it spoken as if it had broken someone.

"I know of them," said Aasha finally.

"Think of those wretched creatures then when you consider the poisons. Think of how they might be beautiful and treacherous. Think of how all their kind is nothing more than a pretty vase full of venom."

Zahril's words clung to her skin. Hate was nothing new to Aasha. She'd heard the fury before, but she had never heard something so . . . personal. It was a hate that had not sprung up single-minded and empty, but was faceted like a cold, hard jewel. And when Aasha looked into Zahril's hate, all she was herself was reflected back a thousand times. Aasha stood a little straighter. What did it matter to her that Zahril despised her and all her kind? She was only here to learn. Not to make friends.

Still, her hate made her curious. What had happened to the Spy Mistress?

"Perhaps not everything is quite as it seems or looks," tried Aasha.

Zahril sneered.

"Leave me. Your room is the first door on the left down *that*," said Zahril pointedly.

A door shivered to life on the wall. Whoever had made this home had constructed illusions in the Night Bazaar, Aasha was sure of it. She made her way across the dining room and kitchen. Zahril said nothing, but her back was turned and so, Aasha let her curiosity take hold. She touched her throat. The raised edges of the blue star puckered against her fingertips. She waited. Something felt *off*.

Zahril's desires should have plumed like smoke.

Aasha should have been able to pluck them from the air.

But she couldn't because the unexpected happened—

Of all the people in the world, Aasha couldn't read Zahril.

Aasha woke up in the darkness. She shook her head, and immediately turned toward the wall. There were no windows here. Though there were paintings full of startling lifelikeness. An image of Bharata, and a painting of a forest bright with fruit. They were even signed, although Aasha hadn't noticed this until now, with a small symbol: a star balancing on the peak of a mountain.

Aasha wondered whether Zahril had made them . . . but there was a softness here that seemed distinctly *not* like her.

Perhaps they were drawn by the hand of another Spy Mistress. Someone who had lived long enough to make paintings and infuse them with love. Aasha placed her hand against the canvas, the glossy ridges where thick daubs of paint stuck out tickled her skin.

What did you do to last so long? How can I do it too?

But the painting yielded no answers.

Aasha left the paintings behind, performed her ablutions, and then opened the door to the maze of hallways. Unlike yesterday, there were no food scents for her to follow through the sprawling labyrinth of Zahril's tower. It was lovely, if sparse. And dark. The dark did not bother Aasha. There had been plenty of times in the *vishakanya* harem when they had not emerged from their den for nearly a month because it was not deemed safe to perform their arts. But this darkness was different. Not the kind of cozy shadows that spoke of something lived-in, but rather damp. Aasha's skin felt tighter. She had only just gotten used to that sharp scent of green, growing things, and the rough texture of dirt beneath her fingers. She hadn't traded a prison of silk for one of stone.

"Hello?" she called, when she entered the kitchen.

There was a basket of food on the dining table. She rummaged through it, finding a spiced potato *paratha*, a couple of oranges, and a milk pouch. Her throat felt scratchy. Wasn't there any tea in this forsaken place?

The food had to be delivered. By what means, Aasha wasn't sure. There might have been a chute in this place that led straight to the neighboring village's kitchen for all she knew.

"I guess if it can't even spare sunlight, there's no chance of tea," she lamented.

There were several shelves lined with jars. Some held pieces of agate and polished moonstone, others held mustard seeds and candied fennel. At the way back, she finally found it: a tin of tea. The leaves looked brittle, but the aroma was still there: earthen and sweet.

She took it out, and measured out the spices. Grated nutmeg, cinnamon sticks, cardamom pods, star anise, and cloves. In a small pan, she toasted them together, and then ground it with a mortar and pestle. The water, tea, and milk were bubbling when she felt a slice of cold in the air. It was the cold of parting space when another body has just entered.

"What do you think you're doing?" snapped Zahril.

Aasha froze. "Sor—" she started before shaking herself.

"I'm making tea," she said. "I made some for you too."

A chair leg scraped. Followed by some reluctant shuffling.

"I didn't realize they sent me a kitchen maid," needled the Spy Mistress.

Aasha just shrugged. She'd been hassled before by others. If they chose to displace their fury and frustrations on her, she had about four hundred years of practice.

"I'm not, however I enjoy preparing food," said Aasha, throwing grated ginger into the spiced milk.

"How quaint."

"It's not the worst habit," said Aasha. "I could enjoy rolling in manure, for instance. And that would make me far less enjoyable company."

She'd borrowed that line from Vikram. She muttered a thanks to him in her head.

Aasha strained the tea into the two mugs, and set one down before Zahril.

She looked at it for a long time, her features still entirely obscured.

"What's this?"

"It's called tea. From common knowledge, I've gathered that one sips it when it's cooled down a little. Sometimes you can dunk a biscuit into it, if that suits you."

If Vikram were here, he would have grinned widely. Over the

past year, he'd gone out of his way to cure what he called her wide-eyed-cat approach to life. The first time Aasha had made a rather vulgar joke, Vikram had been so proud, he let her choose all the palace desserts for a straight week.

"Don't be condescending to me," snapped Zahril.

Aasha's bravado withered and snapped. A braver person might have retorted: *don't drink it*. But she did not feel very brave anymore. She felt as if she had been stripped of her skin and with no armor, every word and insult bruised her heart. Every word had to be placed into the context . . . human or Otherworld? Every reaction required a well to draw from, and hers had gone dry.

Aasha turned around, giving a show of privacy. Faintly, she heard a dainty sip. And then a splutter.

Zahril choked. "How much ginger did you butcher for this?"

Aasha glanced at the cutting board. She knew ginger made food spicy. But she liked spicy things. She liked when her nose burned and her throat felt as though it had caught fire. It seemed that she was quite alone in this.

"A little bit?" she ventured.

Zahril glared. She waved her hand. Out of nowhere, a hand made of smoke appeared. It plucked the steaming tea from off the table, then tipped it. Aasha imagined that it would spill on the ground, but instead it disappeared in some enchanted, concealed pocket of air. At another wave from Zahril, the enchanted smoke hand collapsed into a spiral of tea steam. Aasha stared at the space in the air where the hand had disappeared. Zahril could do *magic*.

"How did you . . . ? What—"

"I traveled extensively and made friends. Those friends gave me gifts and taught me many things," said Zahril. "As one does."

Friends?

With that?

Aasha found that hard to believe.

She'd no sooner be friends with Zahril than she would cuddle a basket of razors. When she glanced at Zahril, she saw the near-creature blankness of her sea-glass eye. Her black eye was just as cruel. Little more than chips of obsidian. Aasha was sitting across from her, her elbows perched on the polished wood. Without realizing it—or even thinking it—she had leaned forward, the better to peer closer at that one black eye . . . and maybe it was the way the chandelier light rippled across her face or the remnants of steam left over from the discarded tea cup, but Aasha thought she caught a certain glint there. A sheen not quite rubbed away, no matter how much the person wished to conceal it.

"What. Are. You. Doing," hissed Zahril.

Aasha was hardly a foot away from her face, risen up on her elbows, leaning awkwardly across the table.

"Oh! I—"

Zahril shoved herself back from the table.

"Come with me," said Zahril flatly. "In three months' time, I will decide whether or not you're worthy of the position. And so far your only talent has been to show me how poorly you make tea. No doubt that will be useful should you choose to kill someone during lunch, but that's not enough for this duty."

Zahril walked toward one corner of the kitchen. While her back was still turned, Aasha drained her tea. The spice felt like a living beam of light twisting down her veins. Gauri said that anything was better with tea. Even battle. Aasha had not understood at first. It was not as though someone could pause warfare for a steaming cup of liquid. But now Aasha realized that Gauri had not been referring to the tea. Not really, at least. She had been referring to the beauty of ritual. The way routines lay tracts in the soul that when they were performed felt like a gentle propping up of a weary spirit.

In the kitchen corner, Zahril reached for a hanging rope of garlic in the corner of the kitchen and pulled. A little ways from where Aasha stood, three of the stone tiles shimmied out of the floor. In the gaping darkness, Aasha heard the *clip-clip* unfurling of wood slatting against wood as the shadows birthed a set of stairs.

Part of Aasha crumpled. *More* darkness? Did this person never bother with the sun anymore?

Zahril took the steps briskly, and Aasha followed.

At the bottom of the spiral staircase, she felt something in the air, a slight hook and tug beneath her navel as if the last step she'd touched wasn't a step at all but a threshold *elsewhere*. She thought there would be another hall at the bottom, but instead the room peeled back into something blinding.

Soft dirt pressed back against the soles of Aasha's feet. The milky-sweet scent of leaves crushed underfoot and wet animal pelts stung her nose. A bolt of blue-silk sky arced overhead, and sunlight spilled from the tops of trees, dripping down between the leaves and leaving pools of gold. They were standing in a forest clearing. For a moment, Aasha was so shocked and then blissfully delighted by being outside that she did not realize where she stood. But when she noticed Zahril out of the corner of her eye keeping to the edges, she had the prickling sense that she was missing something. Aasha glanced at her feet. She was standing in a circle outlined by small, glowing stones. Near her stood a large pile of stones nearly double her height.

"There are five senses to conquer. Sight. Smell. Sound. Taste. And touch," said Zahril. "Your duties will require a little of all of them simultaneously. I don't suppose you have any military training?"

Aasha shook her head.

"Typical," said Zahril. "This is what happens when bureaucracy rules the day. What *can* you do, Aasha?"

It was the first time that Zahril had ever spoken her name.

"I can sing. Dance. Make tea. Albeit poorly. I can . . . read," she said softly.

But she did not specify what, exactly, she could read.

"And I'm told I can fell a man with a touch," she added.

She summoned her best smile from her courtesan training, and when she spoke the words, she remembered how Vikram had taught her how to tell a truth so wryly that its meaning stayed hidden.

"Flirtation only gets you so far in life," said Zahril. "Here's your first lesson then, Aasha. If you see it, you can stop it."

Aasha frowned. "What does that mean?"

"You'll see."

The pile of rocks began to shift. They cobbled together, forming a living spire that grew and grew. The rock giant swiveled its faces, stretching one arm up. It sailed through the tree, knocking a handful of sleeping parrots from the branches. They squawked, took one look at the thing, and flew off in a different direction. Before, Aasha had been standing in a puddle of sunlight. Now this thing had choked off the light and she was plunged into shadows armed with nothing. Not a branch or a rock. Not as though that would have helped her.

"You've got everything you need," said Zahril.

The rock giant advanced. Aasha took a step back. The thorny bark of a tree dug into her back.

"You're just going to let it kill me?" she asked.

"The selection process is rather brutal, I'll admit."

As the giant marched forward, Aasha no longer wondered what had happened to the other contestants for the role. The rock thing roared. No true sound or yell echoed from its stone throat, but the effect was like the noisy cascade of rocks. It swung its fist up. Then down. Aasha tried to run, but the moment her feet touched the rim of the circle she was thrown backward.

She glanced up sharply.

Trapped in the circle.

That murderous Zahril had trapped her here. She glanced at her.

Zahril waved her fingers.

Aasha skirted around the edges. She didn't have training in this at all. She'd never run an obstacle course, let alone *run*, unless it was to the kitchens for desserts. As the rock giant swung another punch, Aasha cursed. How many times had Gauri tried to drag her to the training grounds and teach her how to use a sword? The idea *sounded* nice, but waking up at the crack of dawn to Gauri grinning broadly was terrifying enough.

If only she could *touch* the creature.

But it didn't have any thoughts. It wasn't a sentient thing that had desires twisting above its head. And even if it did, the last thing she wanted was to expose her true nature to Zahril.

She thought of Gauri and Vikram and a raw ache opened up in her chest. She missed them. She missed Bharata. She missed that sense of belonging.

Think think think.

The creature had gotten its hand stuck in the earth from slamming it so tightly. *It even looked* frustrated, she thought.

Off to the side, Zahril inspected her hands.

"Don't bother with pleading either. I simply won't hear it," she called lazily.

The last thing she was going to do was ask for Zahril's help, thought Aasha. Her hands clenched. The spice of the tea that had warmed her veins now twisted through it, sending sparks to the outmost of her limbs. Those teeth of ambition nipped at her once more. Aasha had never felt this in all her life. This burning desire to meet a goal imposed by another person. She wanted to reach it. Smash it. Throw its remains across the smug grin of the Spy Mistress.

Zahril had said that she had everything she needed to defeat the creature. Maybe she couldn't fight like Gauri or outsmart her way like Vikram, but she did one thing better than them all . . . she could read. People. Expressions.

That was her whole training.

This time, when the rock giant raced toward her, she didn't run. She stood her ground. The creature didn't pause. This time, Aasha didn't look beyond the circle, didn't pay attention to the arching boughs that would give her no protection. She focused on the face, forgetting its terrifying limbs and quickening pace. She treated it as she would any visitor to the Night Bazaar. What did they want? What did their faces say that their bodies didn't?

Aasha searched its gaze. She had thought that it would be nothing more than crude, rudimentary features, a product of the rough-hewn magic. But there were subtleties too. The granite mouth sloped in a grimace. The brow, a jutting shelf of diorite, had been cleaved like a frown.

The rock giant roared.

She held her ground.

Secrets hid in gazes. She'd seen it so often in the Night Bazaar—a hungry gaze skimming over her skin even when the mouth was twisted in disgust, grief like a lightless aura around the pupil, pain tugging down eyelids into a heavy-lidded gaze of indifference. A gaze was like a prayer murmured under the breath, something swift and sacred and secret.

The rock creature had great hollows for eyes. But they were softened. And in the crease near its inner corner, Aasha caught a glimmer like a teardrop. It was hardly a foot away from her. Its trembling footprints gusted dirt into her eyes. Still, she didn't take her gaze away from the creature's face. She waited until it had leaned forward, jaws flung open and then she moved . . .

She'd never had the best reflexes. Even when she was learning how to dance, she sometimes lumbered after the rhythm instead of embodying it. But this was more like a punch that just had to glance off the object. Not connect.

One jump into the air. Her feet lifted. Wind fluttered against her jodhpurs. Her hand stretched out, reaching for the rocky ledge of the creature's eyes. Her fingers brushed against that teary glimmer.

It stopped. Aasha was left dangling, her fingers turning white from the tight grip.

Finally, she dropped to her feet.

Adrenaline jolted through her and Aasha felt a burst of awareness. She felt and saw and heard *everything* in that second. Bird wings knifing into the sky. Stones settling in the creature's joints as it turned still. Even the shadows creeping over the trees. It felt . . . divine. For a split second she wondered whether this was what Gauri felt when she whirled through battlefields and led military drills. Maybe she should start getting up at the crack of dawn with her . . .

"Well, that was entertaining," said Zahril.

Aasha grimaced. What was the point of imagining training with Gauri if she couldn't even guarantee that she'd be let back into Bharata after this?

Zahril stood unmoving, arms crossed. The indifference sobered that surge of power.

"Entertaining?" she repeated.

"It's always entertaining to watch sheer panic collide with danger. It forces the body into survival mode, producing feats that are otherwise unexpected."

It took a moment for Aasha to unpack everything she was saying.

"You think it was a onetime incident," she said flatly.

"Tomorrow will put that theory to the test."

"I did it on my own merits!" she said.

And that, Aasha realized, was true. She had been trained to do a great many things, but the things that she picked up, the things that spoke to *her* abilities, were unique. It made them all the more precious for they belonged neither to her acquired human instincts nor her natural *vishakanya* charm.

"Did you now?" asked Zahril. "On your own merits, you forced your perspective to search for a spot of calm? On your own merits, you stared down a thing that scared you? No. That was a construction imposed by myself. Your only merits were your reaction, and even that was a product of circumstance rather than any actual initiative on your part."

Aasha deflated.

"But who cares?" repeated Zahril, twirling her fingers. "What do you want from me, Aasha? A pat on the back? A congratulatory embrace?"

Her cheeks flushed.

"No, I just wanted—"

"That's the first mistake," she snapped. "Don't *want* anything. Do you understand? When you take on this role and you've saved a group of people with nothing more than a word, you don't get to run out to them and tell them all about it and demand their adulation. It will never go to you. You may even be poisoned, spat upon, cursed from a distance. Pandering to anything or anyone other than yourself will earn you a swift death if you're not careful."

If she could, Aasha wished she could unzip the earth and throw herself into it. Was it so hard to say "good"? Maybe the other contenders for the role hadn't been brutally squashed by a rock giant. Maybe their egos had just shattered and cut them all from the insides and they had no choice but to leave. If Zahril wouldn't acknowledge what she'd done, then so be it.

She could do it herself.

"Aasha, you're an upstanding individual. And also almost obscenely attractive," she said out loud. She patted her head. "Your reward is a foot rub. That you will give. To yourself."

And then she gave herself a round of applause.

Zahril stared.

Aasha was smiling so widely that she almost didn't notice until it was too late. Beneath her, the ground turned black. A flower that she had plucked as a celebratory reward withered between her fingers. Without intending to at all, the *vishakanya* star had flared to life on her throat.

She tamped it down, willing it away and holding her breath until it disappeared.

When she looked up, Zahril was clomping out of a stairwell concealed in a mess of banyan tree leaves.

She hadn't seen.

Aasha shuddered. She still remembered Zahril's venomous words from yesterday when it came to *vishakanyas*. She didn't want to imagine what would have happened if she had seen the blue star. Because it wasn't the rock giant that she should be worried about when it came to her livelihood.

She was staring at the greatest threat to her life right now.

·》 6 《·

For three straight weeks, Aasha avoided death. She avoided death in the form of a colorless gas that she only noticed from catching sight of leaves faintly curling. She avoided death in the form of a shadow pool that lay beside the stretched-out darkness of a massive statue. And she avoided death from a wall of hands where every hand offered a poisonous beverage except one, and she was forced to take a sip of one glass. That had been the hardest. Not because she was worried about death in the form of a poisonous drink, but because if she took a poisonous one and didn't die then Zahril would have surely noticed and probably killed her.

The way a Spy Mistress had to think appealed to Aasha. It was less about anticipating, and more about looking. During those weeks where she avoided death, not once did she reach for the mannerisms that she had learned in Bharata. And neither did she reach for her *vishakanya* abilities that she had learned in the harem. Instead, she reached for . . . herself. The space between her two lives where she existed in moments of stolen peace. A place of curiosity. Questioning. The kind of place where a horizon may not be a horizon at all, but a sword of light laid flat upon the land and glimpsed only if one tilted their head *just so*. Aasha felt as though she breathed easier here in a way that she never had in Bharata or the *vishakanya* harem. In both places, she was either too much or not enough. If her soul had been fluttering from the harem to Bharata, here it had fallen still. Not still, like death. But still, like sleep. Rest and repose to an era of restlessness.

It was the start of the fourth week. Aasha had just survived a grueling lesson of mismatched scents. Bananas that smelled like burnt rope. Bitter almonds on an apple rind. Musty sweets. Pine-sharp perfume on pistachios.

"This doesn't smell like what it looks like," Aasha had protested.

Zahril had scoffed. "You think a poison is going to announce itself just for your convenience?"

"That would be nice, yes."

They had fallen into a rhythm. Zahril would insult. Aasha would ignore. A lesson would ensue. Each time she didn't die, Aasha imagined that a small tool chiseled out a little more of Zahril's smile. Her face, though scarred on one side, was still . . . beautiful.

Aasha hadn't noticed until today. It was at the end of the lesson. Aasha's hair was plastered to her face, damp from the steam room where Zahril had laid out the various poisons and scents. Zahril had been leaning out over those poisonous fumes, one sea-glass eye swiveling, the other—garnet-black and glinting like ice under a new moon—pinned to Aasha. The steam and smoke and venom had plumed into the still air. A watery phosphorescent light had burst from a broken vial. Zahril had averted her gaze just in time, bringing her almost face-to-face with Aasha. Aasha, who had no cause to worry about venom, had no cause to flinch. She stayed still, her eyes wide open, which was how she noticed that Zahril had squeezed her eyes shut. It was such a strangely childish gesture that Aasha fought back the urge to shelter Zahril in her arms. But within seconds, that urge faded. Something else replaced it . . . a nearly painful desire to reach out and touch. It was all because of the light from that broken tube. Silvery light burst from it, illuminating the smooth planes of Zahril's face, the crescents of her cheekbones and dark spill of her eyelashes, the wide bow of her mouth, which—when not pulled into a sneer—was full as a fruit. Zahril had opened her eyes to see Aasha staring at her. A moment too long passed. And then it was broken.

A week passed.

Aasha still hadn't been able to shake Zahril's face from her thoughts. And, if she was being honest with herself, she didn't really want to.

There had been something secret, unguarded in her expression. An ease that Aasha had only recognized in her own reflection. It didn't make sense to imagine that the Spy Mistress might share anything with her, but Aasha felt as though she *knew* that fear. That gap of belonging and not quite fitting, wondering if the parts of her that overlapped might somehow be worn smooth with time and simply fall into place.

Nearly two months had passed in the Spy Mistress's company. Aasha, who hated the taste of the bland food delivered from the neighboring village, had taken to preparing the dishes herself. Zahril generally claimed her food was either inedible or fatally spicy, but Aasha noticed that her dish was always clean after a meal.

Tonight she was making *pakoras*. Zahril had only just started sampling the things Aasha attempted to make.

"That doesn't smell right," said Zahril. She was eating whatever bland offering had been prepared by the people in the neighboring village. "If you poison yourself, I will feel like a very poor instructor."

"I will try not to hurt your feelings," said Aasha.

Aasha did not turn as she spoke. But she felt, like a bend in the space, as if Zahril was smiling. Yesterday, Aasha had simmered apple slices in cloves and honey. Zahril, whose hands were full, had said:

"Just give me the thing, if you're so desperate for me to insult your culinary ability."

Perhaps she meant for Aasha to put it on the plate. And leave it there. But she hadn't.

She placed the fruit between thumb and forefinger, twirling it like a spiral, so that it might catch any threads of golden honey. Then she'd held it up to Zahril. Zahril tensed. Not looking at her. But her lips had parted, and Aasha placed the fruit on her tongue. If she saw the barest flush of red on Zahril's cheeks or if Zahril had noticed the slight tremor in her fingers when her skin had brushed the damp velvet of her lips, neither of them said anything.

Aasha had never made *pakoras*. But she understood the basics. Chopped cauliflower, tomato, plantains, and chili peppers dipped in a batter made from gram flour and deep-fried into crispy perfection. The smells soon overwhelmed the kitchen . . .

But so did the popping oil. It bubbled faster than Aasha expected. Leaping out of the cast-iron pot, and landing everywhere. Including her skin.

Aasha gave a sharp cry.

Zahril was at her side in an instant.

"What's wrong with you, girl?"

"Wait—" she started.

Aasha saw it before it happened. The ladle poised too close to the handle. The sharp jut of Zahril's elbow, and the sudden shift in weight.

"Move!" cried Aasha.

She pushed. Zahril stumbled. The pot of oil teetered. Spilled.

It only took a blink.

The oil sprayed up and out, catching Aasha's bare toes and lapping Zahril's arm. A strangled gasp escaped Zahril's throat just as Aasha pulled her into a shadowy corner of the kitchen, safe from the oil.

"I would curse your whole line if I knew your surname," hissed Zahril between winces.

Aasha ignored her. She recognized the outline of a dusty firestone hanging near a large copper pot. She ran to it, breaking the stone on the counter. A white plume of gas escaped, snaking toward the oil and the burning vegetables, drowning the heat until it was covered in thin, spidering frost.

"Are you all right?" asked Aasha, returning to Zahril.

"Never better," she said, through gritted teeth. "I've always wanted to be equally burned. If only it got on—"

"Stop that," said Aasha sternly. "This is no one's fault. You came to the stove because you were concerned. For me."

Zahril said nothing.

"How can I dress this wound?" she asked.

Zahril cradled her arm close to her side. She glared up at Aasha like a wounded animal.

"My bedroom," she said, finally.

In that moment, Aasha felt as though the entirety of the Spy Mistress's tower was an unfamiliar maze. It did not matter that she had crossed its stones and knew its secret doors and memorized the rough stones of the staircases. Now it was an unfamiliar land because she was going to see Zahril's bedroom. It was as if the sky had pulled back a corner of itself, revealing a vast, beating heart.

Aasha held her by the elbow, gingerly. It was only as they walked through a new passage of stone that a realization caught Aasha by the throat . . .

For the first time, her blue star hadn't flickered to life in response to surprise. Or danger. In fact, it hadn't happened at all since that time with the rock monster. The work that spoke to Aasha's soul had calmed something within her. Weeks ago, she would have been too scared to move Zahril out of the way. Too convinced that to touch her during one of those moments would only end her life or injure her another way. But there had been a strange shift within Aasha.

Even now, she didn't feel that pang of worry that she might harm Zahril. It was only concern. It was only them moving through the familiar darkness of the Spy Tower, the light from the lanterns tense and pale, not illuminating anything more than two girls making their way over the stones, their arms linked, worry etched in their faces. Their care for one another enough to chew down the pain. If only for another moment.

And to Aasha, that was all anyone needed to see.

Zahril stopped outside of Aasha's room.

"Did the oil get to your head too?" she asked. "That's my room."

"And mine is beside it," said Zahril.

At an alarmed look from Aasha, Zahril managed a single, power-ful snort.

"This is tradition with every potential Spy Mistress," she said. "You're not special."

Special. The word stung more than it should have. It's not like she wanted to be the only person that had inspired Zahril to spend each night, unknown, near her. But she wanted, she realized, to *be* special to someone even if it meant being ordinary and unnoticed to everyone else.

At Zahril's touch on the wood paneling, a door shivered to life.

"Who made this tower?" asked Aasha. "I only know of one *rakshasa* king who can make illusions like this."

"Do you now?" Zahril smirked. "You're getting better at inter-rogation. Well done. Always ask when you perceive a person is at their weakest. They're far more likely to open up."

"Are you at your weakest?"

"Certainly," said Zahril with the kind of breezy casualty as if Aasha had asked something as inconsequential as the time of day. "But my weakest is leagues above everyone else's strongest."

She stepped through the door, leaving the question unanswered. Aasha followed after her. It took a moment for her eyes to adjust to the sudden dimness of Zahril's chambers.

When her eyes finally did understand what they were looking at, her imagination pulled her vision off center. Aasha hadn't even realized how secret corners of her mind had wondered at Zahril's personal chambers. Sometimes, after grueling exercises, she thought Zahril slept on a stone circle. She thought that there was nothing but one candle guarding her. Her imagination had coaxed forth a place of bareness. Cold.

The reality was anything but.

Sumptuous.

That was the only word Aasha could summon. Though the kitchens were barren, and the other chambers empty of warmth, it was as if this was the one place where Zahril had shoved every facet of her personality. The room was multileveled.

Couches and sofas on one side—far more than one person would need for themselves—piled high with silken throw pillows and velvety blankets. Chandeliers of raw amethyst and unpolished garnet unraveled from the ceiling, as if this bed chamber had been carved into the mouth of a wondrous cave. On the second step down, there was a wide bed and several tables covered with amphorae of perfumes and bone-boxes cut into the shapes of jewels that held powders and cosmetics, lip stains and an assortment of crushed metallics for eyeshadow.

A fire roared in the other corner. Books—hundreds with gem-toned spines—lined an entire wall. There was something else too. Paintings. Paintings on every wall. They seemed familiar even though this was the first time that she had seen them. The scenes depicted a life Aasha thought she had left in her past—the Night Bazaar, its split sky cradling both a moon and a sun, the light feathering over softly rendered vendors and creatures. How could Zahril even know about such a thing? Few humans had ever gained access to the Otherworld. Even less had been admitted into its shops and allowed to leave.

"Are you going to help me with this wound or let me bleed out?" snapped Zahril.

Aasha hastened to her. She was standing beside her bed. When Aasha approached, Zahril nudged her chin to a small chest of drawers.

"The green bottle," she said.

Aasha opened up the lid. The contents of the chest unfurled like a miniature staircase. There were slim bottles emblazoned with roses and interlocking vines, bowls of raw quartz filled with bright pigments, and a thousand slender amphorae. It smelled strong. Chemical. She traced the bottles quickly before finding a small green bottle.

"Unstopper it," said Zahril.

She did.

"Now pat it onto my arm."

"With what? My hand?"

"A cloth," said Zahril.

Aasha cast her glance around, but didn't see anything. She reached for a strange, dirty-looking rag beside Zahril's pillow.

"Not that!" she snapped. "That's . . ."

For the first time, Zahril *blushed.*

"That's not mine," she said finally.

"It's in your possession," pointed out Aasha.

She held up the rag, and that was when she noticed something printed along its edges. A star balancing on the crest of a mountain. It was the same signature that she had seen on the painting in her room. It was also, she noticed as she took in the surroundings with a new eye, the same signature emblazoned on every painting here. The symbol, the scrap of cloth, the sudden glisten in Zahril's eyes. It spoke of grief.

"Who was she?" asked Aasha.

Zahril bit her lip. "How do you know it was a she?"

She didn't know. Not for certain, anyway. It wasn't as though there was something distinctly feminine about the signature. Maybe it was the scent that lingered in the square of fabric. It was silk, she realized. Perhaps, once, it had been pristine and white. Instead of the threadbare and moth-bitten thing that it was now. Maybe it was the memory of love that had preserved something about it— a scent like milk steeped in roses. All delicate cream and new blossoms.

"I don't know," said Aasha. "Instinct, I suppose."

Aasha cast around for a different cloth, but Zahril sighed.

"Just use it."

"Are you sure?"

"Am I stuttering?" she snapped.

"Let's not forget that I'm the one wielding the potion."

"Don't threaten me unless you intend to follow through with it."

"Maybe I will," said Aasha. "I could leave you."

She wasn't even sure where the words had come from . . . maybe it was exhaustion. For pushing herself further than she ever had, for conquering her fears and for winning when she was told she wasn't. Maybe it was childish to want just a *yes*. *Yes, you did it.*

"Then go," said Zahril.

If the air itself solidified and turned them into those strange insects forever pressed between glass, Aasha would have found it more comfortable than standing in front of Zahril. For a girl that didn't look much older than nineteen, Zahril looked as if life had made her heavy. As if it had carved a dimension and a space for a world of grief that she had no choice but to carry with her. A dare lingered in the knifelike balance of her gaze. It said: *well, were you threatening me or not?*

Aasha, even as she gritted her teeth and felt a little part of herself cave inward with hate, did not go.

She poured some of the green bottle onto the edge of the thread-bare handkerchief. She reached for Zahril's hand, forcing her eyes not to drift upward when she heard her wince. Zahril's hand trembled.

The burn was livid. Skin flaked and curled at the edges. The skin beneath was raw and shiny.

"You should go," said Zahril, once Aasha had bandaged her hand. "Tell them you learned from me. I'll even sign the thing agreeing that you are fit for the job. That's what you want."

Want.

It was the underbelly of wishing. A wish was fantastical. A want was . . . fleshy. It was a snake biting its tail—devoured and devouring.

Foolish or no, she felt betrayed at having any wants. A wish was supposed to remove all of that. And look how far a wish had gotten her?

It had brought her outside of the world she knew—took her dreams and made them nightmares, unstitched her nightmares and turned them into dreams. She had wanted choice. In its wake, she had found uncertainty. Human. *Vishakanya.* What was she?

Aasha said nothing for a couple of long moments. Maybe a week ago everything that Zahril said had been what she wanted. A week ago she would have said that all she wanted was the seal of approval that would make Gauri and Vikram happy, and let her stay in Bharata. But the weeks had worn away those edges of her. It wasn't that things had changed, so much as that parts of herself felt peeled off. She wanted to earn this.

"No."

Zahril raised her eyebrow. "No?"

"You're wrong," said Aasha. "I don't just want you to say that I'm fit for the job. I want to earn it."

"So be it," said Zahril.

She turned her face, but Aasha caught the glint of a smile.

As if she had passed some test.

· » *7* « ·

Zahril had taken with fever.

Aasha had caught her in the hallway that morning.

"Good reflexes," said Zahril hoarsely.

Her attempt at sounding like an impartial mentor were thwarted by the sweat beading across her forehead.

"Why are you trying to turn this into an evaluation?" scolded Aasha. "You're not well. Let me take care of you."

Zahril grumbled. But Aasha ignored her. She half-carried, half-dragged her down the hall and back to her room. As she had observed from yesterday, she placed her hand against the wall, watching as a door shivered to life.

"You haven't managed to fit an arena in here, have you?" asked Aasha.

"The thought had never occurred to me."

"Well then I guess we can do a different kind of lesson for today."

"Don't lecture me," said Zahril.

Aasha helped her to bed, pulling the covers up to her chin.

"We've already done sight, sound, and smell—"

"Taste," said Zahril, tiredly. "There will be a glass tray in the kitchen. Bring it."

Aasha nodded. As she took the stairs she called: "I'll bring you tea too!"

Just as the door closed, Aasha heard a grumble of protest and faintly:

"Am I not in enough pain?"

Aasha piled a tray with cut persimmons, mugs of tea, and handfuls of mint leaves. She preferred mint in her tea. Zahril preferred mint as an extension of violence. When she wasn't talking, she chewed down the stalks to a green pulp.

In the other pantry, Aasha found a second glass tray. It was heavy, weighed down by a number of unguents and bottles that had been welded to the metal. A few weeks ago, Aasha would have found it intolerably heavy. But her arms had grown stronger. They even looked different. There were callouses on the pads of her fingers from not noticing one of Zahril's killing contraptions fast enough, and a couple of small welts on her wrists and palms from brushing against a hot pot from forgetting her cooking. A steady ache pulsed between her shoulder blades, along the curves of her waist and down her thighs. Soreness from muscles shedding their weakness.

Inside Zahril's room, the lantern lights drifted across the ceiling. Zahril sat like an imperious queen, the pillows forming a mini-fortress. There was an armchair and a low table at her side where,

Aasha realized, *she* was expected to sit. The moment she set down the glass tray, Zahril held out her hand.

"Tea?" asked Aasha.

Zahril just pushed out her hand a fraction farther.

"Don't look so pleased with yourself," said Zahril once she had wrapped her hand around the mug. "I know people who chew the bitterest roots and eat the strangest things simply because they've grown accustomed to the taste."

Aasha just shrugged. It was a thank you, and she knew it. What did strike her as strange was how Zahril said *people*.

There must have been a time when she hadn't shut herself in this tower. Just looking around at the room, Aasha saw that half of the things here must not have been picked up at random . . . they must have been *given*. As gifts. There were glass dolls, and dresses sewn from the colors of a sunset. Jewelry that shimmered, the gemstones and setting changing by the minute. Once, Zahril must have had friends. Even Gauri, as far as Aasha knew, had never repaid Zahril's services with anything more than land, title, and a fair chunk from the coffers. In the past twenty years, no sovereign of Bharata had died at the hands of espionage and even when the kingdom had been plunged into wars, their intelligence had never failed. Surely that deserved a gift. As Spy Mistress, Zahril could only be around people in secret or in highly controlled situations. She was as shut off from the world as Aasha was.

"Open the glass tray," said Zahril.

Aasha did so.

"There are many ways to poison a sovereign," said Zahril. "Most often in their food or drink. Everything that the king or queen tastes, you must taste."

Aasha frowned. "But I've never seen you in Bharata. How are you able to taste their food? And what about when—"

"You think Bharata is without its magic? What about the plate of food that is always offered to God first and then carted off?"

Aasha had not considered this. But in Bharata there was always one plate of food presented before the deity. She had never asked herself what happened after that.

Now she knew.

"But the deadliest thing to a queen or king is not poison, but the truth," said Zahril. "A truth serum could make them reveal the truth about a child's parentage or a war strategy or even the reasons why they might be entertaining a particular diplomat. I've seen the truth crumble kingdoms. A monarch bears a heavy burden, and nothing is more precious than the secrets they keep."

"How do they even get them?" asked Aasha.

Truths were an easy currency, but difficult to harvest. A shop-keeper in the Night Bazaar would have to collect five hundred truths for a single drop. It was far easier to trade truths between merchants. Only the Night Bazaar would have sold anything like that. And it was already impossible to imagine one human wandering through its strange split sky, let alone several high-ranking officials. Zahril must have read her mind because her smile was slow and grim.

"The Otherworld knows who will keep its secrets."

She sighed. "There is only one way to do this. It is something I learned from the one who came before me, and it is something you must do for the one who will come after you."

Aasha held her breath at these words. Zahril had not been as serious about the Spy Mistress position when she had first asked, but now it sounded like an inevitability. The words freed up some peace within her. As Spy Mistress, Aasha would not have to be torn between human and *vishakanya* instinct. She could only act as herself.

"The people who will report to you, the agendas and scheduling, that's something even a baboon could learn. But this is the difference between espionage that anticipates and espionage that defends. We have survived this long on anticipating. On knowing and feeling as intimately as if we were every victim," said Zahril. Her eyes flicked up to Aasha's. "Secrets are leverage. They are full of invisible sinew and height. Never underestimate the space they take up in a room."

Zahril opened up the cabinet at her side, taking out a small glass box that held one bright cherry. Aasha recognized the fruit from Kubera's Grove of Plenty. The orchard had every fruit tree of the nine worlds. And yet for all those trees, they only bore one fruit each. One cherry that looked lustrous as wet rubies. One plum that looked scooped from the lining of nighttime. One apple that looked rolled through the sunrise, gathering blush and pink and even speckles of white. Once a year, *yakshas* and *yakshinis* harvested the fruits and carted them off to the Night Bazaar. There, they sold for as much as eighteen years of one's life and even the love you had for another person. But the benefit was just as outlandish:

The fruit never faded.

Even eaten, all that was needed was that the seed was set aside. In the blink of an eye, it would plump once more. Ready to be devoured.

Zahril dipped the cherry into the truth potion. The potion was translucent, and dripped off the cherry like a thick stream of water.

"One question," she said. "And one only. It is the kind of taste that has no flavor, but rather carves a place of knowing inside you.

It is the reason why monarchs never suspect it because they can't know it until it has happened."

"How often are they slipped this?"

Zahril's face darkened. "Often enough."

Aasha had a memory of days when Zahril bolted the door behind her. Music blasting through the walls. She had thought that it was her just being prickly. Now she saw it for what it might have been: protection. What would have happened if Aasha had asked a question about Gauri? Zahril would have had no choice but to respond. The moment she did she would have placed the empire at great risk . . .

No wonder she hid in a tower. Away from where people might take advantage of all the ways she laid herself open out of duty to her country.

"The truth is a poison," said Zahril.

Then she slipped the cherry between her lips, and ate.

One question.

Aasha had a thousand burning ones. She ran through them as she went through the ritual, dipping the cherry in the serum and raising it to her lips. But there was one difference.

She had already tasted this.

She knew the flavor . . . it had been one of the first things she had eaten. The *vishakanya* harem had given it to her, snapping off a diamond-bright icicle that had dangled from one of their fountains. She had drizzled the icicle with the poison and rolled it in sugar, giving it to Aasha like a present. *We must make sure that our blood knows every poison. You are lucky to eat this so young, when your thoughts are not so dangerous and your truths are not so cutting, little one.* Aasha had still been embarrassed by the serum. Especially when one of her sisters

asked if she looked pretty in blue, and Aasha—who had no choice
but to tell the truth for a whole week as she consumed the poison—
had told her: "The sky would be so offended to see how you wear its
skin that it would plunge us into night forever." Her sister had not
been pleased.

But knowing the poison also meant that it could no longer af-
fect Aasha. She let the familiar taste settle on her tongue. The truth
tasted different to everyone. For Aasha, who had never had much
reason to lie, truth tasted light and sparkling. It tasted like fresh snow
licked off a pane of sugar.

Zahril, on the other hand, made a face.

Aasha grimaced, wondering how the truth would change for her
when she became the Spy Mistress.

"Now that you know the taste you will never forget it," said Zahril, dragging her uninjured arm across her mouth. She pulled a
shawl tighter around her, as if she could protect her heart better that
way. "You may ask me a question."

Aasha hesitated. This truth was supposed to be a moment
freely exchanged. Zahril was letting down her guard . . . letting her
in. Aasha couldn't give her the same. The serum simply didn't work
on her.

She wondered whether she should tell her the truth, but how
would she explain it without giving away *what* she was?

Zahril raised an eyebrow. "This wears off, you know."

"How long does it take?"

"For this, an hour. But that is because it is half a drop diluted in
water. It is an example. If enough was slipped into food, it could force
a monarch to speak in nothing but truths for an entire year."

Aasha glanced at the tattered scrap of silk on Zahril's bedside.

Zahril caught her eye, her mouth tightening to a thin line.

"I have nothing to hide."

Aasha swallowed. *I do.*

Questions were tricky things. Aasha had grown up amidst the riddles of the Night Bazaar. A question must be as precise as if it had been turned upon a lathe.

Something about that silk held her fascination. Looking at it was like not recognizing one's own reflection in a pool of rippling water. She couldn't quite place it, and yet she knew she should. She thought of how Zahril had clutched at her mug of tea. How her hands were fine-boned and delicate, made more unsettling against the razor-cruelty of her tongue or the cold leanings of her mind. She thought of how Zahril cradled that silk. Kept it beside her. It was not a talisman, kept for protection. It was a penance. Aasha was not one of those Otherworld beings who could suss out pain. But this was obvious.

"Ask and be done with it, Aasha," said Zahril.

One chance to know.

Even as she uttered the question, she didn't know why she cared. Why she even bothered to discover.

"Why did the girl who gave you that silk die?"

Years later, Aasha would remember this as the moment when she knew silence was not invisible. One could see it by looking at the shape it left behind, like an impression of shadows. She saw silence in the way the light pulled back from the space where she and Zahril sat, as if it were carving out a place of darkness.

In Bharata, Aasha had seen a thousand expressions of surprise. Eyes widening, lips parting, brows lifting. She'd seen men and women grow pale or turn red, goose bumps erupting on their arms or nails turning white from digging into skin. But Zahril's expression did not change. If anything, it had gone flat. Affectless. It chilled Aasha.

"She died because she loved me, and I loved her," said Zahril.

Her gaze did not lift to Aasha's. Aasha knew that there was no reason for her to continue, but Zahril shifted, uncomfortable. As if she couldn't just let that truth exist without context.

"This was early in the reign of the raja who united the cities that became Bharata. This was a time when the Otherworld had not yet closed its borders. The flow of goods and services between the two worlds was not a strange thing. The rival empress of Ujijain sent a *vishakanya*. They're the worst kind of creatures. Human children snatched from their mother's breast, thrown into a dingy harem where they are force-fed poison and brainwashed into becoming some of the deadliest assassins the worlds have ever seen."

Aasha forced herself to take even breaths. She could not afford any panic to reveal her true nature.

"They can kill with a touch, you know. And it was during the . . ." Zahril steadied her voice. Her throat bobbed. ". . . the dance. A courtesan that we did not recognize came to the table. All she had to do was kiss Sazma, as one would kiss a sister. Joyously. I was not looking closely, too reliant on the protective amulets. Too dazed from a recent victory. I didn't even see that cursed blue star on her throat until Sazma dropped to the ground."

Zahril closed and opened her hands, as if she were testing her strength. She started rubbing her palm violently.

"But I got that thing," she said fiercely. "I opened her throat right there on the banquet. Her blood splattered."

Aasha looked at her face. For the first time she saw that those scars were not ropy twists of skin. They were like lashes of rain against a window.

Not rain, she thought. She corrected herself.

Blood.

"But it was not without its benefits," said Zahril.

Her voice was acidic. It could have melted glass. She raised her hand. There, on the outer curve of her palm, Aasha saw it:

A blue star.

"It wasn't simply the touch of that monster's blood, but the—" She cringed. "*Taste.*"

Aasha took sips of air. She felt light-headed. But if she gulped down the air, Zahril would see. And notice. Worst of all, she might *wonder*. Wonder about the scarf Aasha wore around her throat despite the warm air. Wonder about the speed with which she completed any lesson that had to do with poison. Wonder what lay beneath that cloth.

Because now she knew why every time she tried to read Zahril's thoughts, she was met with a foggy wall.

Zahril had not simply touched the venom of a *vishakanya*. If that were so, she would have died on the spot. Aasha knew of only two ways to remove a *vishakanya*'s poison from someone's body. Either another *vishakanya* could sense the threads of poison and draw it out like a great net. Or the person touched must drink the blood of a *vishakanya*. Both earned immunity from poison. Like Gauri. But only one rendered someone wholly immune to a *vishakanya*'s abilities.

"*It has never happened,*" her vishakanya *sisters* would croon. "*No one has ever guessed our secret.*"

But they were wrong.

It was clear that even Zahril didn't understand how it had worked. If she did, maybe she would have hung the *vishakanya* like meat from a hook. Turned Aasha's blood into a precious elixir, and sold it to every king and queen in danger of the poisonous courtesans.

Aasha heard the words. *Creature. Vile. Monster.*

They echoed inside her thoughts, sprouting thorns that were far more venomous than any poison in her veins. It was as final as death too. If Zahril knew what she was, she would have never let her into her palace. She would have never let her eyelids flutter shut when Aasha had placed that food upon her tongue last week. It was such a small thing . . . that flare of trust. And yet, nothing had ever been more precious to Aasha.

Before, the emotion she didn't want to name had felt distant. Something beheld underwater. But she felt it now—the rush of it— just as the possibility of it ever coming true shattered in front of her.

Want.

She wanted Zahril. Wanted to trace her lips with her own, to listen to her grumble, to catch her fingers between hers.

To thank her.

All this time in Zahril's company and not once had Aasha lost control. Before she had come to the Spy Mistress's tower, she had been too torn between being either human or *vishakanya*. But now she saw that the key to controlling her abilities was simply to be *herself*. That the very act of freeing herself from trying to be anyone *but* herself had released the grip of her worst fears. Zahril was, in part, to thank. Now, if Zahril found out about her *vishakanya* heritage, she might take her life over her thanks.

"I have told you the truth," said Zahril. She placed the hand with the *vishakanya* star flat upon her leg. "Now it is my turn. What do you not want me to know about you?"

It was a clever question.

Then again, Zahril was no fool. Aasha felt a burst of relief that the poison did not work on her. Otherwise she would have found herself on the floor. Her throat cut.

A truth that Zahril did not know about her . . .

She did not want to lie even though she could. It would have felt jagged inside her, like a bone set poorly. So she spoke a truth. As bluntly as she would have done if they were just two girls that had met somewhere else . . . like a flower market beneath a tent where raindrops dangled like jewels. Or in the fierce glow of a festival's fires, their foreheads slick from sweat, mouths sugary from sweets. Or in a world where they did not have to drag their past selves alongside them.

"I want to kiss you."

8

Aasha was not sure what she expected to happen.

She watched her face, looking for some hint as to what she felt. A small quirk of her mouth would have been enough for Aasha. Even the flash of a frown would have at least thrown her out of the limbo of not *knowing*. But Zahril did nothing. Said nothing.

Aasha almost wished she'd just laugh at her.

Instead, the words had grown so heavy between them that Aasha half-wished she could pluck them out of the air and hide them out of sight.

"It is fine to want things," said Zahril finally. "It is far worse to need them. That is the risk of acting upon want."

Her tone was hesitant. Altogether wrong. Zahril never said anything hesitantly. Everything she did was injected with purpose. But that wasn't what twisted inside Aasha. It was the softened feel of her words. Zahril was so embarrassed for Aasha that she was comforting her.

And that was how the dismissal became a rejection so fierce that Aasha almost wanted the *vishakanya* star to flare onto her throat. At least then Zahril would throw her out of this place, and she'd never have to look upon her mismatched eyes or wide lips.

But of course it didn't.

"I have done everything I can to teach you," said Zahril. "The final examination will be tomorrow. Your appointment depends on your performance. After that, Bharata has requested our appearance at the final engagement ceremony of Queen Gauri and Emperor Vikramaditya. I will alert the village to prepare enough food that you don't kill us with your cooking."

A feeble joke. Aasha just nodded. She knew she should have been glad.

Zahril could have decided that she could no longer instruct her when those were her true feelings. Or she could have demanded more than one truth, and Aasha's cover would have been blown. Zahril was not so embarrassed by her declaration that she would give her false hope though. And the fact that she was already planning on food from the village could only mean one thing:

She believed Aasha would pass.

Aasha, even, believed that she would pass.

The only thing that had changed was that she wanted more than an appointment from Zahril. Zahril knew it. And as Aasha gathered the tray, mumbled her excuses, and left the room, all she could think of was whether that sliver of confidence was Zahril's own offering. That this—her belief and her faith, and perhaps even a little of her trust—was all that she was willing to give.

Aasha set down the tray. In the emptiness of the kitchen, she summoned her *vishakanya* star. A leaf had snapped off the *tulsi* plant that lived at the edge of the counter. Aasha swiped it off the marble, watching as the edges of the leaf blackened and smoldered.

For as long as she remembered, her touch was an extension of her that she hardly gave any thought to. It was like a shadow, forgotten until it loomed stark and vivid upon the ground. And yet her whole life, Aasha could always blame being a *vishakanya* as the source of her pain. It had kept her in the Otherworld. Then it had threatened the lives of those she loved in Bharata. She wanted to blame it. Wanted to curse it. Wanted to hold out this part of her and say *you are the reason.* But she couldn't. Zahril hadn't even bothered to reject her. She simply ignored it. And Aasha was left staring at her reflection on the polished copper of the kitchen pots. Wondering what fault her reflection hid from her.

The morning of the final examination was black and dark.

But Aasha had grown used to this. She fell asleep and woke up in darkness. For the past couple of weeks, she hadn't let the darkness get to her. And yet sometime in the space of last night and this morning, she felt cracked. The velvet fingers of the shadows had found them. Heaviness dogged her steps. Hope, that familiar brightness that she could always reach, felt distant.

If she didn't pass, she'd not only leave in disgrace. She'd leave with her heart swollen and bruised. Maybe it would leave her chest altogether. Then what?

She stepped outside and immediately winced.

Warm liquid hit her toes. Something sharp grazed her ankle.

She looked down to see what had been the culprit, and found the broken shards of a teacup.

That darkness lifted its fingers at the same time as the corners of her mouth:

Zahril had made her tea.

A asha had been to enough tournaments of the Otherworld to know what to expect. Her heart didn't race when she walked to the end of the hall and found that the passageway to the kitchen had disappeared, replaced with a tunnel of darkness.

A sign floated in front of her, written in light:

Get Out

A different version of Aasha would have taken it personally, but Zahril's command was clear. Her task was to find her way out.

The moment she nodded, the darkness rippled.

Walls peeled off from the tunnel, stone grinding together as the slabs of rock closed around her. Her breath tightened. She didn't like tight spaces.

Earlier in their lessons, when Aasha had fought back on what the use of these lessons were, Zahril had only laughed.

"The purpose of this is to teach you how to think," she had said. "Everything else can be learned on the job."

Think, thought Aasha. *You already know how to do it all.*

It was that one thought that comforted her, especially when she found herself looking at a bright, empty room devoid of windows and doors. The light seemed to emanate from the walls, like a cave threaded through with quartz. Maps littered the floor. Aasha knelt, touching them, searching them for a riddle. How could she get out when there was no exit? It's not like she could burn a hole through the ground and escape. Zahril was sneaky. She may have drilled Aasha on the five senses, but she shifted them out of obvious focus. Taught her to think in the manner of absurd things. Taught her that using her senses meant not trusting them at their core level.

She studied the maps.

Maps of cities she'd never traveled to, of oceans where creatures rendered of ink and ash widened their jaws, ready to swallow an empire. She trailed her finger up . . . a square of black.

A series of triangles. Mountains.

Close-knit spirals. Ocean cyclones.

A broken line. Treacherous roads.

The symbols all stood for something, and she realized what it was from wandering through the Bharata archives. A map key. She pressed her palm to it, and felt it—that sensation of magic, an unexpected burst of cold, like mistaking pulverized ice for a dusting of sugar. Zahril was not averse to using magic in her lessons, and when Aasha drew away her hand, she felt something cold and metallic against her skin . . .

A key.

She grinned.

But if she had the key, she needed a door. There was nothing in the maps in the shape of a door. Nothing that might even be the semblance of one.

"What makes something a door?" she asked herself aloud.

It was a barrier. An entrance. An exit. And all doors had thresholds, a line that split one place from another.

She stared at the maps. An idea struck. She gathered them one by one, until her arms were heavy with thick papers and sweet-smelling scrolls. Then she arranged them in a line down the room. With the key in her hand, she stepped over the line.

The room split.

Beneath her, the floor shattered. Dark earth flecked the threshold of maps. The smell of damp, growing things and something else . . . something rancid and sharp dug into her nose. And then she heard it. The snuffling. Scuffing of creature paws.

The room had warped and pinched, darkening as it transformed into the mouth of a cave. Only this time she wasn't alone. Something was making its way to her. A creature like a rat.

But Zahril hadn't left her entirely in the darkness. The smell of growing things revealed itself. Bushes with sprays of berries. Some were the bright purple of a new bruise. Others were the toasted yellow of turmeric. The creature ambled toward Aasha, and she could smell its breath. The rank, bitterness of food gone un-picked. She stifled a cough, and pressed her arm against her mouth. The creature had a row of needle-teeth, and a long, furred nose. Its eyes were pale as pearls. Nothing at all like the milky eye of Zahril that gazed at something else at all times. She watched it from a distance. It brushed past the purple berries, shivering as it moved, and then nibbled at the yellow berries. Then it licked its small, red mouth.

It started advancing, as if it smelled her.

Aasha shivered.

Was she supposed to get past it?

A part of her mind chastised her. *She didn't teach you stealth.* But panic gnawed at her logic. She tried to skirt past the ratlike creature

ROSHANI CHOKSHI

that loomed tall as an elephant and wide as a building. Its tail, bald but for a few coarse hairs, whipped to her.

It saw her.

With something like a roar, it came toward her. Aasha tried to run. It loomed over her. One paw poised to slice her open. She felt something damp and disgusting matting her hair. She tried to rub the gunk onto her arms, wondering if that would make her invisible to it, but the rat hissed. It didn't make a difference. It would eat its waste with as little distaste to eating her.

Aasha ran to the other end of the cave. The only things were the bushels of thorned berries. She dove into the thicket of their leaves.

The rat trotted after her. Snuffling. Easy. It knew that it didn't have to rush because there was no way she could get past it. Around her, the purple and yellow berries scratched at her face. Aasha breathed fast. She watched as the rat moved closer, forcing her to keep her eyes open. Something caught her eye. A shudder in the creature's skin. She frowned. Watching again.

It didn't like the purple berries.

Every time it brushed against them, its own skin crawled.

Aasha grabbed a handful, pulverizing them in her fist and rubbing it onto her hands and arms just as the creature found the bush where she hid. She waited, back pressed against the rocky ledges of the cave. The creature's nose was hardly a foot away from her. She could count the pores on its nose.

It snuffled her, a pale tongue trying to lick over her face. With a disgusted snuffle, it shuffled backward. Aasha could hardly breathe. She just grabbed a handful of more purple berries, then crept behind the creature. Its ears perked. Head swiveled. But it couldn't find her scent anymore.

With a shaky grin, she ran into the cave . . .

And fell.

Now she was wandering through a new maze. One of sounds. She heard the wingbeats of giant birds carrying thunderstorms in their feathers. Aasha thought of Zahril's lesson, when she had placed her hands over Aasha's eyes and told her to *listen*. Listen to the space between things, until she could hear steam pluming from a mug of tea. It had been the hardest lesson. Not because she couldn't learn to listen, but because she couldn't concentrate with Zahril's cold palms over her eyelids. They were so much softer than the rest of her.

Aasha pushed the thought from her mind.

She did what she remembered from Zahril's lessons. She closed her eyes to the riotous room before her. Sight would only trick her. Focusing on the sounds to guide her out. In front of her, rain fell sharply, sounding like pearls ripped loose from a sari and clattering loudly to the ground. *Not that way.* In the other direction was the *whumpf* of wings. A cold wind pushed her back, stinging her throat and making it hard to breathe. *Not that way.*

What did an exit sound like?

Aasha remembered Zahril forcing her to knock against a thousand gourds, to memorize the sound of crisp bread broken versus the sound of soaked bread ripped into pieces. *Don't roll your eyes at me, Aasha, this sound is the difference between life and death.*

The sound between life and death . . .

Silence.

She needed to follow the quiet.

She listened to another direction, trying to pinpoint her attention on one direction at a time. Then she heard it: *nothing*. But there was fullness to it, like walking down a completely empty street during a summer night where the air—so soaked through with damp—used you to bolster itself upright.

Without opening her eyes lest another sense betray her, Aasha followed the promise of quiet . . .

The other sounds faded.

Now when she opened her eyes, she was standing at the end of a gigantic feast table.

Aasha's stomach gave a desperate grumble. *Hungerrrr . . .*

She wished Zahril hadn't just left a cup of tea outside her door where anyone could have stepped on it. Then again, Zahril had told her that she never went to state banquets on a full stomach. It was the emptiness that heightened the senses. She told Aasha how some holy men and women would undergo rigorous fasting just to capture that euphoric transcendence that came from depriving the body. When one thing was denied, it felt and reached with all senses, frantic to keep itself alive.

The feast table groaned. Moths with wings of light darted overhead, transforming the ceiling into a glittering array of living stars. There was no one here. Not like the famous eaters that supposedly lived within Kubera's monstrous palace.

The food was tantalizing. But poisonous. Aasha could feel her star pushing against her skin, ready to burst free. For the first time during the examination, she exhaled. Relaxed. Nothing could kill her here. And yet . . . she looked around at the stone enclosure. The glittering ceiling. Even the wooden floor of interlocking stars that was polished to a shine as bright as a mirror.

Zahril was watching. Weighing.

If she chose wrong, she would know what Aasha was.

Aasha fought against touching her throat. She scanned the feast and its multiple dishes, all of which rested on rectangles of thinly hammered gold. Fat plums with rinds like dusk, shining with dew. Mounds of pearl-white rice, flecked with gold. Candied pistachios. Rose sweets wrapped in silver foil. Egg curries with translucent spheres of oil separating at the top. Aasha breathed in . . . she tasted without tasting. The trace of too much almond in the *palak paneer*. The rancid note that all that sugar in the carrot *halwa* could not hide. One by one, she touched the foods, careful to smell indirectly, lest she inhale poisonous fumes and be forced to fake a faint.

She circled the feast table until she realized . . .

All of it was poisonous.

The only thing that wasn't were the thin pieces of gold holding up the dishes of food. Even the plates and cutlery were dusted with finely milled apple seed. A poison that would leach into the skin.

She tore off a corner of gold. Ate it.

It tasted as she expected:

Like nothing at all.

And the moment she ate the piece of gold, the table cleaved in half. Beautiful dishes of food slid off and crashed onto the floor. A pair of stairs appeared. Aasha took them slowly. Only dimly did she realize what had happened. She had conquered sight, sound, taste, touch, and smell.

She had succeeded.

At the bottom of the stairwell, Zahril was waiting. Her arms folded. Aasha recognized the lines of worry that she'd never announce. The taut pull of her wide mouth. Even the extra flutter of her eyelashes, as if she had to look twice to acknowledge what she saw.

Aasha walked to her, and as she did, she felt as though she were holding her heart out. Zahril tensed. But she didn't move. She thought of Zahril's words to her when she told her that she sometimes wanted to kiss her. *It is fine to want things. It is far worse to need them. That is the risk of acting upon want.*

Going through that hell of an arena had only strengthened Aasha's resolve to look at things differently. And when she beheld Zahril's words through the lens of a victory, she saw another emotion unfold before her:

Fear.

The fear of loving and losing. The fear of letting a temptation become more than a luxury, but a lifeline. The fear of like ripening to love.

Aasha knew she was not in love. But she felt the stirrings of love's desire to live here, in her heart. As if it were a hand knocking on the door of her soul, waiting to be welcomed. She could love her. She *wanted* to. And not because Zahril had won her over with her kindness or her sweetness. But because she had awakened a fierce sense of belonging within herself. Because Zahril was a moon amongst stars, distant and inspiring. Enigmatic. Because she reminded Aasha of all the reasons why she had left the *vishakanya* harem, and all the reasons why she no longer cared to fit within Bharata's rules. Zahril belonged to herself. And Aasha carried a hope that one day they might belong to each other.

She kissed her.

It was not a first kiss for either of them. It was a kiss like a palimpsest, layered with near-invisible things. Aasha could taste Zahril's hesitancy laced with the mint-sweetness of her mouth. She could taste her wonder . . . and it was lightness upon her tongue, a sparkle on her teeth.

The kiss lasted two blinks. Maybe three.

When Aasha pulled away, she saw that some of the gold foil from the feast clung to Zahril's lower lip. The barest crescent of a smile curved Zahril's wide and lovely mouth. The smile wasn't a declaration. Or a promise.

But it was something.

And then she wrinkled her nose.

"Did you try rolling around in that rat dung before you went for the purple berries?"

Aasha nodded wearily.

Zahril sighed. "Let's get you a bath. You reek."

9

Aasha had been so worn out from the competition that she slept for a day and a half. Zahril brought her tea (Aasha poured it into a vase when she wasn't looking . . . Zahril had mistaken the salt for sugar). Aasha also caught her sitting stiffly at the foot of her bed, not sure whether this closeness was too strange. Or too soon. Once or twice as she dozed off, Aasha tried to tell her that this made her happy. But all she managed was a vague and unintelligible grumble.

When she woke up, Zahril stood on the opposite side of the room. Aasha's smile shrank. Had something happened when she slept? There was a sudden *cold* where there had been none . . .

"We must leave for Bharata immediately," said Zahril.

No greeting. No . . . nothing.

Aasha's cheeks burned.

"Are you all right?" she asked.

"I'm fine," she said. "There will be a formal hearing with the heads of state and the future monarchs where I will give my official recommendation. I am told there will be a feast to follow."

"And then what?" asked Aasha. "Will we come back here?"

Zahril hesitated. "You will need more training, of course. Whether they would prefer that is done here or at a tower of your own is not my decision."

"So it's my decision?"

"Perhaps."

Aasha sat up, pulling her blankets around her shoulders.

"Do you want me here?"

Zahril looked up at her then. "I don't want anything."

And with that, she left.

As the door closed, Aasha looked to where Zahril had been standing. Her heart fell. The painting of Bharata with the star balancing on a mountain's peak. Everywhere she looked, she was reminded that Zahril's heart had belonged to Sazma. Perhaps . . . perhaps it still did.

When the chariots came, Aasha sat at one side, ready to make room for Zahril.

The charioteer turned to her, brows tilted in confusion.

"Lady Aasha, you may take more room than that if you wish. The Spy Mistress always takes a private chariot."

"Oh," said Aasha, adjusting in embarrassment. "Does she travel to Bharata often?"

"I would not know, my lady," said the charioteer. He lifted a vial filled with pale liquid. "Even those of us who see her face quickly forget. It is part of the policy and part of our duty to Her Majesty, Queen Gauri."

Aasha sat quietly, her fingers twisting in the silk of her sari. What else had Zahril made other contestants for the position of Spy Mistress or Spy Master forget? Had she kissed them too, and then when she changed their mind, forced them to drink a draught that would cleanse them of the memory? Or worse . . . had she given it to herself? So that she wouldn't remember the press and part of Aasha's lips against her own. Maybe she was trying to rid herself of some guilt.

The days passed in a blur. The two chariots stopped and rested at alternating times, so that Zahril would reach Bharata faster. Aasha tried urging the charioteer to match them for speed, but he shook his head sorrowfully.

"I am under orders, my lady," he said.

Four days later, they reached Bharata. There was no grand welcoming for Aasha. But then again, no one was supposed to know when she left and when she returned. It was safer for Gauri and Vikram that way.

The moment she got out of the chariot, she made her apologies to the women of the harem who were insisting that she at least take a long, proper bath and change out of her travel clothes before she saw Gauri. Bharata moved in a flurry of activity. Servants carrying silver platters piled high with marigold garlands rushed in and out of the palace. The palace decorators shouted ridiculous orders for glass birds and sword flowers. Aasha frowned. She'd long since stopped questioning what Gauri and Vikram found delightful. It was their home, after all. Or at least, it would soon be their home.

The halls were empty. Not a single diplomat stood milling about, waiting for an audience with Gauri and Vikram. Aasha's heart raced.

The only way that the outer sanctum of Bharata would be empty was if *everyone* was inside . . .

Through the heavy wooden doors, she heard a steely voice. Two armed guards flanking the doorway moved to block her. Before, Aasha would have cowered, not knowing whether she was once more embarrassing Gauri or doing something inappropriate. This time, she fixed them both with a stern stare.

"You know who I am," she said. "Get out of my way."

And they did.

She pressed her ear to the door. She recognized Zahril's voice the way people recognize the hands of loved ones. From contours and texture and memory. In spite of her resolve to stay stoic and cold, Aasha felt her body give . . . and when she heard Zahril's words, the emotion gathering inside of her was a storm shaking itself loose from the sky.

"In conclusion, the Lady Aasha has my full and unwavering support as Spy Mistress. I accept that she will be my equal, and one day, my successor. I accept that her judgment lies equal to mine. And I dare any of you to refuse—"

A sound of dissent broke the sternness of Zahril's voice. Aasha couldn't catch the words, but she imagined she could feel Zahril's bristle of annoyance. She did not like being interrupted. And she certainly would not like the vague and flowery way that the courtier would present his dissent.

"If that is how you feel," said Zahril with terrifying calm. "Then I value your opinion as much as I value a dog's waste in the middle of the kitchen."

A roar of sound nearly made Aasha push back from the door. She heard outraged cries. Tutterings of displeasure. And through it, one deep, grumbling laugh. She grinned. *Vikram.* But the laugh was quickly cut off. Probably by a sharp glance from Gauri. Aasha could imagine them on the other side of the door. His face wry and tilting into a knowing grin. Her face calm and swooping into a smile that was unnervingly grim. A pang went through her heart. Though she didn't miss the culture of Bharata, she missed her friends.

"The Lady Aasha shows a remarkable empathy. Beyond just a calculating sense of knowing how to weigh and evaluate lethal situations with speed and grace, she has a way of reading people . . . of making them feel welcome. Of opening, even, the hardest of hearts. She could not be a brighter force if she carried a miniature sun in her arms. I will not hear less."

The hardest of hearts.

Aasha's smile could have lifted her heels off the ground.

She didn't stay to listen to more. She had heard enough, and it made her heart light.

With a curt nod to the guards, she went to the harem. Zahril had not seen her in days. She wanted to look as she felt—glowing.

"Vikram!" shrieked a voice.

Aasha jolted upright in the bath. She recognized the voice as Gauri's.

"You're not allowed in here!" hissed Gauri. "And could you please take off those silks? What does it mean that you almost convinced *me* you were a harem wife?"

"It means that my beauty is transcendent," said Vikram. "And why do I have to wait for you to see Aasha first? She's my friend too."

"Well I met her first."

"Oh, you can't be serious. I was *nice* to her first. You—"

"—is that a platter of *halwa?*"

"What? Where?"

The door to the bath chambers opened and slammed. Aasha turned to see Gauri barricading the door with a chair.

"I love you!" she called.

"I knew it was too good to be true," said Vikram, sounding distinctly betrayed. "That was cruel. Fine, I'm waiting out here."

"Good," said Gauri. "And please take off that dress."

"Absolutely not. You may like the sight of me in tight pants, but silk skirts just *breathe* with you. I think I'll go scandalize someone while I wait."

Gauri just shook her head and laughed, before turning to Aasha.

"I'm glad to see his confidence hasn't changed," said Aasha, laughing.

"I'm just glad to see you," said Gauri. She sat at the edge of the bath, appraising Aasha. "You look different."

"Better?"

"I don't think it's possible for you to look more beautiful," said Gauri.

"So worse?"

"Again. Impossible," said Gauri. "Just different. More . . . sure of yourself."

Aasha grinned. She did feel more sure of herself. All this time she had wanted to be human, but she had been wanting the wrong thing. What she had truly wanted was to be herself. To cherish her human curiosity, her *vishakanya* knowledge, and all the bits in between that she owed to no one. The way she saw the world. She had learned that in Zahril's tower. Or rather, unlearned her own fear.

"I suppose you're right," allowed Aasha.

But she would say no more about it.

When she had found a spare moment, she even tested herself. She stood in the middle of the courtyard, spinning wildly with her eyes closed until she tripped. She had expected and not expected it. Her heartbeat raced wildly; she stumbled. But even in her panic . . . even in her surprise . . . she did not lose control of herself. Because she knew herself.

"So," said Gauri. "Tell me everything. We weren't even surprised when Zahril announced that you were her choice."

Aasha smiled, but as she searched Gauri's face, she saw that her friend was not telling her the truth. Relief shone in her gaze. They may not have doubted that Aasha could do this, but it had been a victory for all of them.

"What is she like?" asked Gauri. "By tomorrow, everyone attending tonight's festivities, except you, of course, will have to take the potion that removes her face and voice from all of our memories."

Aasha raised her eyebrow. No wonder Zahril had not hidden her face from her the first time they met. She could have always taken it away in the end.

"What is she like?" asked Gauri. "What did you have to do?"

Gauri may have been renowned for her fierceness . . . but there was one weakness that always made her eyes round as a child's. Stories. Vikram had once lured her away from the training camp with the promise of a book of fairy tales that not a single advisor of Bharata had ever seen. She was furious when she found out it was a ruse, and less furious when she discovered that it was only so that Vikram could set up a surprise for her in the training arena.

Aasha let out a deep exhale. "Well . . ."

At the end of the story, Gauri might have looked like she was eight years old. Her legs were pulled to her chest, chin resting on her knees. A ridiculous grin spreading across her face.

"You're in love?" she nearly squeaked.

"Not *love*," said Aasha.

"I believe you were the one who first told me, 'I don't have to read desires to know what you're thinking' and I have news for you—"

"I like her," grumbled Aasha, as she toweled off her hair. And then more shyly: "You're not upset?"

Gauri just lifted an eyebrow. "What's there to be upset about?"

Aasha smiled. "Nothing. Nothing at all."

But then Gauri frowned. She drew her lip between her teeth, hesitating. "Does she . . . know?"

At this, Aasha turned.

"No."

They were silent. Gauri knew Zahril's story . . . how a *vishakanya* had stolen away Sazma.

"Are you going to tell her?" asked Gauri. "Now that you have the position, you should."

Now it was Aasha who hesitated.

"I couldn't at first because of the order . . . but now . . . now I wish I still had a reason."

"You're scared she'll hate you," said Gauri. "Scared she'll only be able to look at you and see the reason she lost Sazma?"

Aasha could only nod.

Gauri sighed. "It takes time for people to unlearn hate. I know that better than most." At this, she smiled, and Aasha knew that she was thinking of Vikram. "If she's not willing to give you a chance, then she's not worthy of your affection in the first place. Maybe she'll be angry. Maybe not. But everyone needs time."

Aasha sucked in a breath, hoping it might fortify her. The thing was, Zahril had had plenty of time. She'd been nursing this hate since the day Sazma had died a century ago. Maybe time couldn't erase all hate or soften any memory. Maybe sometimes time was fertile ground for certain hates, and in all that time, it had sprouted a tangle of thorns and knives so deep and sharp that Aasha would only cut herself if she tried to push past them.

10

Aasha had never seen Bharata so beautiful. Colored lights hung from trees. A tent of marigolds spiraled downwards from a translucent tent, bright as caught stars. Several bonfires threw ruby sparks into the air, and everyone—Ujijain citizen and Bharata native alike—linked arms and danced, their hands twirling in the air, heady nectar splashing onto the ground. Aasha felt her training settling into her skin. She had not eaten for the banquet, but had requested that food be brought in advance to her quarters. She watched Gauri and Vikram, listening to the crackle of the fire and kindling of dry wood. She smelled the air for anything out of the ordinary from the jasmine and amber oil that the wives and courtesans used to the sharp char of burnt fruit and rice that would be offered to the gods in honor of Gauri and Vikram.

A wide curving banquet table sat just outside the tent. Servants bustled back and forth, carrying great pitchers of fruit juice and mint water, and platters heaping with aromatic dishes. Aasha's stomach grumbled, but she did nothing.

At the end of the table, stiff and watchful as an owl, Zahril surveyed the crowd. Behind her stood a row of handsome statues painted in the likeness of heroes from the fairy tales. Someone had even sprayed them with water, so that their muscles looked like they were sheened in sweat.

Zahril had not adorned herself any differently for the occasion. Her hair was twisted away from her face, and she wore simple jewelry. A net of pearls and rubies at her throat. Dainty amethysts hanging from her ears.

And yet, for all of her practiced calm, Aasha felt her strain. She wanted to tell her that the future would be all right, that they could protect each other against all the world would dare to throw at them. After all, she had not imagined what strength she would find within herself. That the very act of trusting her own instinct above all would rescue her from her living nightmares. Her greatest fear had come and gone, and now all that was left was this . . . this fear to reach out and be reached for in return. It was the most delicious fear Aasha had ever known.

At that moment, Zahril turned to look at her. Aasha was impressed. She had trained for centuries not to make a single sound with her footfall. But Zahril could hear her through any chaos. Her eyes widened as she took in the brilliant red of Aasha's *salwar kameez*, the unadorned collar of garnets and pearls at her throat. Fashionable, and yet powerful as well. For it could hide her *vishakanya* star even when it was at full bloom.

Zahril took a deep breath. Her hesitance chastened Aasha.

Maybe all this time it hadn't been about her fear or rejection, but her worry . . .

They were standing in the same place—on the same *soil*—where Zahril had lost Sazma. Aasha sat down beside her, refusing the food and water offered. Together, they watched the festivities.

After awhile, Zahril said:

"I don't know how to be soft anymore. I used to know. I might hurt you, and scream instead of apologizing. I might run, and accuse you of abandoning. But . . ." and this time, she turned to look at Aasha. Really look at her. Aasha couldn't have felt more pinned by that mismatched jewel-toned gaze if they had caused manacles to wrap around her wrists. "I would give you all that I am. In time. If you let me. If you thought it . . . I . . . might be worth it."

Aasha didn't trust herself to speak for a whole minute.

It must have taken Zahril all five days just to speak that much. To *show* that much.

"I think thorns make a rose even more desirable."

Zahril stared at her. "On the one hand, I'm delighted. But we must do something about your sense of metaphors. I've heard courtiers so drunk they could barely remember their own names speak more compelling lines of poetry."

Aasha just laughed.

They sat in comfortable silence, each scanning the party.

"What kind of protocols have you ordered?" asked Aasha.

"The usual. Although the Ujijain Spy Master was insistent on his own methods for his half of the festivities, so I find myself on guard."

Aasha nodded. Though she felt guilty about it, she let her

vishakanya star rise onto her skin. Her stomach gave a squeeze of discomfort. It felt disrespectful to Sazma's memory, to summon the very power that had taken her life. Especially when she sat so close to Zahril that the bare skin of their arms occasionally pressed against one another.

The desires of the crowd were nothing out of the ordinary.

They wanted food. Drink. Each other.

But one thought reached Aasha, digging into her skin.

So close. Just her neck. So open.

A shudder ran through Aasha. She moved closer to Zahril, but the thought grew louder. A slight gust of air—the kind caused not from a wind, but by an arm moving swiftly—stirred the beads of her dress at the same time that she realized why the voice was so disconcerting:

It was coming from right behind them.

Zahril reacted only half a second after Aasha. She flattened herself against the table, just as Aasha reached out—poison brimming in her fingers—for the culprit. Her eyes fell on the lifelike statue. *Too* lifelike.

Someone had painted them. Enchanted them so that they could not move until the final moment. The gray man raised his stone sword. But Aasha could feel his pulse, and she knew that he was living.

"A knife!" shouted Zahril. "Here!"

But Aasha didn't take it.

After all, *she* was a weapon.

She closed her hand around the man's wrist just as his sword swung in a wide arc to her neck. It knocked her to the side, but it didn't go through. He slumped to the ground. Pushing herself up on her elbow, Aasha managed a shaky grin.

"Where's my thanks?" she asked hoarsely.

But Zahril was looking at her as if Aasha had taken the sword and plunged it through Zahril's belly. Aasha frowned. She pushed herself off the ground. Something glinted amidst the grass. Pearls. *Thousands* of little pearls. Her hand flew to her throat. But her collar of jewels did not meet her hand. Only *skin*.

And star.

Zahril looked as if she was a rendering of ice.

"I thought I'd met the worst kind of monster years ago," she said, her voice flat and affectless. "I was wrong."

In the days and weeks that followed, Zahril did not retract her appointment of Aasha.

Aasha was glad of this, for she had never seen Bharata and Ujijain plunged into more disarray. Now more than ever, Gauri and Vikram needed her nearby.

"Just until everything is settled," said Gauri wearily. "I am sorry."

"Don't be sorry," said Aasha. "I'm your friend. I am your friend before I am your subject, and so I will be here."

Besides, thought Aasha, *I have nowhere to go anyway.*

The treason of the Spy Master had sickened Gauri and Vikram. Aasha was called a heroine that day, celebrated throughout the two kingdoms.

No one but Zahril had seen the star.

And so her greatest secret was still . . . *hers.*

But though Aasha might have been victorious, the fledgling kingdom was mired with problems. Gauri and Vikram's victories were never without their losses, and yet no matter what kind of day they faced, Aasha always saw them walking hand in hand. Fingers laced. Eyes never straying from one another. As if they were the beginning and end of the universe, and everything else was just noise.

It cut Aasha.

Three cycles of the moon had passed without word from Zahril. Sometimes, while everyone was eating, Aasha would walk to the temple where the offering sat before the deities. Zahril always tasted the food of the monarchs before they did. But either her methods of enchantment meant that she never saw Aasha trying to talk to her, or she simply didn't care. Aasha didn't know what was worse.

The only benefit was that the courtiers of Bharata were on board with her appointment. Convinced even more by her multiple visits to the temple. *A pious Spy Mistress can only bring prosperity to the kingdom.*

"Aasha," said Gauri one evening. "The new Spy Master of Ujijain said that he is willing to take you on as an official assistant. You can stay here for the next year until you're ready to assume the new duties. But if you wanted to go somewhere else, I understand."

The meaning was clear.

She could return to Zahril.

Aasha shook her head. "I'm not wanted."

Gauri sighed. "Tomorrow is the final day. That's when both Spy Masters must submit an answer over who will mentor you."

Aasha said nothing. "Then I suppose I don't need to bother with packing."

After excusing herself, she spent the rest of the day in the royal kitchens. She no longer worried about the threat of her fingers. Her training with Zahril had made her so hyper-aware of her surroundings that nothing could frighten her anymore. At least not while she was awake. Aasha threw herself into the dishes . . . until her hair was streaked white with chickpea flour and her hands bore the battle wounds of many too-hot *rotis*. Aasha wanted to push herself to the point of exhaustion. She wanted a dreamless slumber, just *one* night where she wouldn't have to dream about Zahril beside her.

Zahril, who she would never hurt if she woke up from a nightmare, her body flooded with unwanted toxins.

Zahril, who could never quite get rid of the warmth in her garnet-black eye.

Night frayed the edges of the sky. Aasha pushed open the ivory door to her private villa, nestled amongst the fruit orchards of Bharata.

Zahril, she thought, *who*—

And then she stopped.

Because Zahril was standing right before her.

For several long moments, Aasha couldn't match the sight before her. There were the recognizable things in her room . . . the silk rug, and the pitcher of water that had somehow caught a mango blossom in its water. Those things made sense. But Zahril? Standing in her usual garb of cotton pants and a dark tunic? Aasha felt as if her sorrow had finally reached its breaking point and that her mind had hauled this illusion from the depths of her dreams.

"I understand why you did it," said Zahril.

Her voice was ice.

Aasha braced herself.

"That doesn't make it easier for me."

"I'm sorry," said Aasha.

"Sorry for what? Sorry that you followed orders that kept you and your monarch and the kingdom alive? Sorry that you . . . felt something?" Zahril laughed. But it was a hollow sound. "I taught you how to see and smell and touch and taste and listen."

Aasha nodded, unsure of where she was going with this.

"I taught you that the senses are more than what they seem. That they deceive. That they . . ." and at this, she hesitated. "They must sometimes be looked past. Or at least, seen through."

Aasha held her breath.

"You were willing to try," said Zahril.

Aasha stepped closer, convinced that this reality would shatter the moment she exhaled. But it didn't. She was close enough that she could see the sheen of light curving off Zahril's cheek. Close enough that she could study the crescent formed by her wide lips.

Zahril's eyes met hers. "I can too."

So simple.

Three words.

They were not the three words that Aasha so often dreamed Zahril would say. But it was like seeing with one's hands and listening with touch. It was a confusion of senses made glorious by their unexpectedness. It was . . . a way of understanding—and, perhaps, forgiveness—that was the only true magic Aasha had ever experienced. It filled her like a light.

She reached out, taking Zahril's hand, folding it between her own.

Sometimes words draw out conclusions.

Other times, one must infer through the senses. And that was what Aasha did now. She studied the sloping curve of Zahril's lips, not pressed tight with sadness . . . but determination. She listened to the sound of her breathing: tight and short. A thing of nervousness. She felt the velvet-skin of her palms pressing into her own, harder than she needed to, as if to say *I am here. I don't know how . . . but I am here.* She tasted the salt of her own mouth, as if it had filled to the teeth with unshed tears. She smelled the mint that Zahril must have chewed on her way here. And from all this, Aasha drew her conclusion. This was not an end, but a beginning.

Her answer was a wordless agreement . . .

A smile.

Given and . . . returned.

ROSE AND SWORD

PRESENT

Ten-year-old Hira would rather eat her own hand than listen to another minute of her sister's wedding preparations. First of all, there were too many people in the palace of Bharata-Ujijain. Which meant that she, along with her parents, the reigning raja and rani, had to stand for *hours* at the threshold of the palace entry and greet people that Hira had never heard of.

What she really wanted to do was sneak outside and go to her grandfather's study. He had kept so many stories there. Stories that not even her grandmother or parents had read. Sometimes there were little notes written in his hand. Hira liked to imagine that it was a secret conversation they were having together.

Hira's grandfather had been dead for years and she had never even met him. But she didn't feel so terrible about this because it was not as if Meghana had met him either. Not that Meghana cared.

In the past few months, Meghana barely thought of anything with all the bridal preparations swirling around her. She was too distracted. Nowadays, her sister was always leaning out of windows, sighing. She didn't want to play anymore. Not even when Hira pretended to be a *vanara* and wore a fake monkey tail and ran around the palace apartments shrieking about theft and blood deeds that must not go unpaid. Not even when Hira pretended to eat an apple (to which the cook had painstakingly applied gold flakes so that it looked like something out of her grandmother's stories) and turn ever so slowly into a great, big beast. One of the nursemaids had even made her a headpiece with bent pieces of iron from the blacksmith's quarters so that it looked like she had antlers! Meghana did not care.

And if her sister did not care, then neither did she. But sometimes . . . sometimes her heart ignored her wishes.

Last night, Meghana was directing her servants as to what they should pack in the chests that she would take to her new home. Hira felt her heartbeats snag together. Her sister was leaving. Just as their sister before them, Chandra, had left. It had not been so hard then. Chandra was sweet-natured and sang so beautifully that Hira imagined the stars leaned out of the night sky if only to hear her better. But Chandra had never played with Hira.

When Hira had seen her sister packing up those heavy, ornate bridal chests, she had only wanted to help. So she had collected her most precious toys: the fake apple with the burnished rind that turned little girls into little beasts, the glass bird with the bent wing that her grandmother said held a beautiful story, a bronze fox mask that turned one of them into the legendary Clever Fox Prince, and a jewel-bright silk cobra that the girls pretended would always know the difference between a truth and a lie. Hira had gathered them all together and then placed them into her sister's treasure chest.

When Meghana came into their rooms that night, Hira could hardly sit still. She wanted her sister to praise her. To be touched at the thoughtful gifts that Hira was parting with. Perhaps even for Meghana to invite her to come stay at the new palace . . .

But when Meghana had opened the chest and looked at Hira's gifts, she stood there. Her eyes widened, then turned glossy. And then, right as Hira stood up eagerly to point out all the different toys, her sister had kicked over the chest. It thudded painfully on the ground. The toys, once neatly wrapped in gauzy fabric, tumbled out. The apple scraped against the toy sword, the silk cobra unraveled, and the glass bird's bent wing caught against it. It was a silent riot until the glass bird shattered on the marble. Hira cried out. The candlelight stuck to the jagged edges. And even though Hira had not been injured, she felt inexplicably *cut.*

"What is *wrong with you?*" hissed Meghana. Her shoulders shook. "Why would I take *that* with me? Do you have any idea how . . . how . . ."

But Meghana couldn't even finish her thought. She sank into a chair, glowering.

"Get *out*, Hira! Just, just *go.*"

Hira hadn't waited another moment. Shame chased her shadow out of the room. She didn't even care that tiny splinters had somehow dug into her heel. She felt nothing at all until she finally stopped running.

That night, Hira slept in the blacksmith's study. Unfinished swords and blunted arrowheads lay all around her. Weapons dangled from the ceiling. The forge had long gone silent, and yet she could smell the echo of fire. For some reason, the smell of iron and fire and glass always comforted her. It was how her grandmother smelled. Like a strike of lightning.

Now, Hira swayed a little bit on the threshold. Her father reached out and caught her, frowning.

"Are you well, my child?"

Her mother took her face between her hands. Hira tried to avert her eyes, but her mother was too fast. Within seconds, she had sussed out her secrets in that eerie way of mothers.

"Why don't you take a break, hmm?" asked her mother. "Go give your Dadi-Ma some company. She might not miss these functions, but I am sure she must be lonely."

Hira tried not to bolt. She didn't have to be told twice to spend time with her grandmother instead of all these stuffy guests. Her father laughed, before sneaking her a candy with a conspiratorial wink. Her grandmother said that he was a lot like his father. Always managing to steal a handful of sweets when no one was looking and never getting scolded because his grin made you feel like you were in on the secret too.

"But come back before the feast!" shouted her mother. "Don't you want to say good-bye to your sister?"

"No!"

Hira shot a look over her shoulder. It was rather poisonous, and she might have gotten in trouble . . . but no one ran as fast as Hira.

She was out of the threshold, down the hall, and darting through the chambers within moments.

Her grandmother once said she got that from her grandfather.

"Running fast?" Hira had asked.

"No," she said, raising her eyebrow. "Mischief."

Hira knew that she was near her grandmother's quarters when she was finally out of earshot from the rest of the raucous wedding guests. Here, it was quiet. There was a small, burbling fountain in the strangest courtyard that Hira had ever seen. The hilts of swords glinted in a tangle of flowers. Meghana said that the old gardeners were still loyal to the memory of the former emperor and so they would add new swords. But Hira believed they truly grew out of the ground. That perhaps if she pulled one out ever so slowly, she would see silvery roots breaking off from the tip. Beneath wrought-iron arches fashioned into the shapes of birds with impossible wings and maidens dancing from spire to spire, *sweets* hung like impossible fruit.

It was Hira's favorite place in the world.

Hira paused to grab a tiny silver bowl of syrupy *gulab jamun* and was halfway across the courtyard when she doubled back and grabbed an extra bowl. Just in case. Cut-quartz lanterns swayed across the ceiling of her grandmother's chambers. She had lived here ever since she had ceded the throne to Hira's father when Meghana was just a baby. One day she announced that she had done all she could do, and that it was time to make room for the new generation.

Her father said that some courtiers had wanted the old queen to leave Bharata-Ujjijain and spend the rest of her days in religious exile. They said that she should be seeking penance in the great forests beyond. But the old queen had laughed off the notion.

"Penance?" she had famously declared. "After enduring the courtly politics of this kingdom for nearly a century, I am certain even the gods will agree that I have been through quite enough."

And that was that.

When Hira stepped over the threshold of her grandmother's living room, she heard a sharp gasp on the other side of the room.

"You're not supposed to be here," said her grandmother imperiously.

Hira's shoulders fell. First Meghana, and now not even Dadi-Ma didn't—

"Which makes me all the more delighted that you managed to sneak away," said her grandmother, winking. "Were you painfully bored?"

Hira nodded.

"Did you grab a sweet on your way inside?"

Hira nodded once more.

"Did you get one for me too?"

Hira grinned, and ran forward. She dropped off the bowl of sweets and then embraced her grandmother. Her grandmother held her tightly. One warm hand on Hira's shoulder blade and one cold hand against the back of her head.

"Let me see," said Hira, curling up beside her.

Her grandmother laughed and held out her hands.

Hira had never seen anyone else with hands like her grandmother. Her left hand was a warm brown the color of toasted spices. Her knuckles looked like the knobs of a tree, plump veins running across them like roots. But her right hand?

Her right hand was made of glass.

It was smooth and always cold to the touch. It made Hira think that while the rest of her grandmother was in one place, sometimes her hand belonged to another world altogether. Maybe in that world it was cold and there was a crust of frost on the ground. Maybe the other hand had just turned up its silver palm to catch one of the flakes before her grandmother had need of it in their kingdom.

But while it amused Hira, her grandmother's lips pressed into a line. It was the face she made whenever some memory caught her. And then, for the span of one blink, it was as if her grandmother were somewhere else entirely.

"Is something the matter?" asked Hira.

"Just a memory," she said with a faint smile. "The older you get, the more memories feel a bit like old battle scars. They will ache for no reason until you ease them away."

Hira frowned. "How do you do that?"

Her grandmother folded her strange hands in her lap.

"You relive them. You savor both the sorrowful and the sweet. You make peace with it, and as you do, you let it go, and it can have no power over you for a spell."

Hira glanced up at her grandmother. She was seated by the fire even though the afternoon sun blazed high in the sky. A silk shawl was pulled tight around her shoulders. Her hair was completely white, and thinned in some places so that Hira could see patches of her shiny, brown scalp. But no matter how old she seemed, her eyes were a lively and lustrous black.

"You will understand one day," said her grandmother. "Perhaps you will even think back on this day with some mixture of bitter and sweet. After all, your sister is leaving. I remember that day."

"You had a *sister*?" asked Hira, shocked.

Of all the things her grandmother had spoken of, her sister was not one of them. Hira tried to imagine her grandmother as a young girl . . . but she couldn't. She'd seen the portraits, of course.

Everyone had. Portraits of her grandparents, with her grandmother in her battle armor and her grandfather clutching a handful of scrolls. Where her grandmother's gaze was intense and grave, her grandfather always looked as if he was about to laugh.

"I *have* a sister," she corrected. "She is still alive. In fact, she looks like Meghana. Or perhaps Meghana looks like her. They are rather similar, you know. Beautiful and curious, with a touch of something rather mysterious about them. On her wedding day, I was miserable. Cried all night."

"What happened to her?"

"She married a king from a faraway land that we all must one day visit."

That sounded a little strange, but Hira thought better than to point that out. Sometimes her grandmother said strange things. Sometimes she could not even remember the story she was telling, and so Hira would have to tell her the story from the beginning just to find out what happened next.

"And you never saw her again?"

"I saw her. Once." Her grandmother rubbed absentmindedly at her glass hand. "And I will see her again. I will see many people again. Perhaps soon, I suspect."

"Can I come?" asked Hira.

Her grandmother snorted. "No."

"But why not? Mother and Father are busy, and Meghana . . . Meghana hates me. She doesn't want to see me ever again."

Her grandmother was silent. "Is that so?"

Hira nodded. And then, when faced with her grandmother's regal silence, she told her everything that had happened. Down to the broken glass story bird.

When she was finished, she waited for her grandmother to agree that Meghana had been cruel. But instead, her grandmother said:

"Have you ever considered that perhaps Meghana is scared?"

"*Scared?*" asked Hira, snorting. "Never."

The women of Bharata-Ujijain did not get *scared*. Besides, Meghana was—*used to be*, corrected Hira silently—daring. It was a well-known fact amongst the women of their family that they were immune to poison. No one was quite sure how. It was rumored that it had something to do with the small, blue star that each Bharata-Ujijain girl was born with. Her grandmother said that it was a gift from a friend who had long since left this world.

Meghana used to make a show of it by kissing serpents and laughing when they snapped at her.

Her sister was wild.

Invincible.

She would never be leveled by something as foolish as fear.

Her grandmother eased back against her cushions. She called for her water pipe, a nasty-smelling thing that Hira didn't quite care for because it turned people's teeth black.

"I rather like how it makes my teeth look like blunted fangs, don't you?" her grandmother had once said when they were little, baring her grin and snapping her teeth as if she were some forgotten monster. Then she would pretend to snap at them one by one because they were so delectable that she could not help but gobble them whole.

"I remember being very scared before my wedding," she said. "And it puts me in mind of another queen's wedding. She was very scared. Just like me. Just like, perhaps, Meghana. Though we all have different reasons for our fears."

There it was.

That faraway cast to her voice, as if it took all of her strength to pull it away from whatever memory she was living in. When her parents heard that cast, they would frown and call for the court physicians. But when Hira or Meghana heard it, it was a sign:

Dadi-Ma was about to tell a story.

"Why?" asked Hira, curling closer.

"Because the queen's bridegroom was about to die."

THE EXTRAVAGANCE
OF NORMAL

Gauri stared at her hands. One glass, one flesh.

Her hands were usually a cause for curiosity, but last night they had been the center of celebration. In preparation for tomorrow's wedding ceremony, Gauri had been sequestered in her apartments. Musicians and dancers had been brought in to entertain her and her female guests. And as the encroaching night pared the sun to a thin band of gold, an artist had been brought in to adorn her hands with henna. Well, at least one of them. No matter how hard the man tried, the paste refused to stick to the glass hand. It slipped off without drying. Her right hand would always be a cold and Otherworldly thing, not that Gauri minded.

Standing in the army training grounds, Gauri examined her left hand. The henna had darkened overnight to the color of charred wood. She brought it to her nose, inhaling that curious scent of spiced licorice. She traced the design delicately, as if she might disturb the intricate lattices and checkerboards, the maroon blossoms fashioned into the shapes of mango leaves and trellises of jasmine.

The artist had left something special in the design.

"Your future husband's name is concealed in the patterns," her friend Nalini had said with a sly grin. "He is a handsome one, my dear. I do hope he finds his name."

Gauri laughed. Among Bharata's wedding traditions was the test of the sharp-eyed groom. If the intended husband could not find his name hidden in the intricate pattern of his bride's henna, then he was not allowed to spend the night in her bed. Gauri suspected the tradition had been devised so that the groom would not be tempted to drink during the festivities and thus squander his chances.

"Reading is Vikram's favorite pastime," Gauri had said. "He'll probably find it instantly."

"I would not be so sure of that, my friend." Nalini leaned close and whispered: "Trust me, Gauri. When he sees you, he will forget all about reading. He might even forget the power of speech."

Gauri rolled her eyes. So many of Bharata's wedding traditions seemed foolish to her, although there was no harm in their fun. Besides, the test of the sharp-eyed bridegroom was far better than Ujijain's wedding traditions.

As Gauri was yet unwed, her unoccupied bed had become a matter of scrutiny. Many of their joint councils were curious. Just how, exactly, had she spent her time with the emperor of Ujijain while she had been away on her "mythical" adventure? To solve the problem, her council had suggested that different ladies-in-waiting would sleep alongside her, an Ujijain pre-wedding custom among royalty. Abiding another court's custom might have been fine had it not been for the fact that each wife of a courtier selected for that evening insisted on furthering her husband's agenda. The night before the henna ceremony, one woman could not help but talk in her sleep about the value of divesting treasury funds to a building project where her husband had played chief investor. She spoke . . . all night.

Maybe it was the sleeplessness that was affecting her so. In the past two days, something restless had grabbed hold of her between morning and night. There was a needle-sharp panic in her chest, something that she was not sure belonged to the anxiousness of a new bride or something . . . worse.

Ever since they had come back from Alaka and fought in the Tournament of Wishes, Gauri imagined that sometimes she could still *see* magic. A ripple in the air, like staring above the flames of a great fire and watching the sky warp from its heat. Or a rip, at times. A door where there should have been a wall. A glow in the trees that did not belong to the strange shine of creature eyes blinking open in the dark.

Perhaps it was exhaustion, she thought.

For the past three months, fatigue had sunk its teeth into every bone. Aasha and Nalini assured her that it would pass after the wedding, but judging by her planning experience, she doubted it. She was a girl pressed beneath glass. Even her dreams felt thin and transparent. She could keep nothing to herself, not even sleep. Every day, she and Vikram were placed under more scrutiny. Even in the moments where they could steal away from everyone else, the overwhelming emotion she felt was exhaustion. Not ecstasy.

Just last week, they had stolen a rare hour together. One precious sunlit afternoon where the music of the fountains and the birdsong from the menageries might have muffled out other sounds. Vikram had kissed his way down her jawline only to start snoring once his head dropped to her neck.

"In my defense, you are very warm and soft and inviting," he had said once Gauri had shaken him awake.

"You make me sound like a bed."

"If you were a bed, I would not wait a week to marry you."

She smiled at that. But even that smile set her nerves alight.

Would it always be like this? Would he always know what to say, and would she always know what to do? She had watched enough couples around her to know that there was a secret choreography to love. She was newly in love. Loving Vikram was startlingly easy.

It frightened her.

That afternoon, the rest of their hour together had not been unpleasant. He had tucked her against his chest, and even though she had loudly insisted that she was not tired, she had fallen asleep the second she closed her eyes. She could not remember when she had last slept so well.

Which was how she found herself here, running through the military drills on the eve of her wedding. She took a deep breath, closing her eyes as she felt around the grooves of her old practice sword. The tip was blunted. Rust striped the steel. It was the same sword that her father had caught her practicing with when she was a child. Back then, it had been so heavy that her fingers would cramp for hours and her whole body would feel bruised and tender after a day of practice. Eventually, the weight lessened. Her body adjusted. When she returned from Alaka with a glass hand, her body had adjusted again.

Gauri breathed deeply, slashing the sword out with her left hand.

When she breathed out, she forced out her fears . . . this weight upon her. These whispers that seemed to creep in from another world and fill her with a sense of *wrongness*. It was all just a weighted sword. Her body was merely untested. She would adjust. For the next hour, Gauri spun through the empty army barracks. There was no chance of someone coming inside because the entire militia was outside, participating in a pageantry of joined armies. This space belonged to her.

When she had finished running through her drills, she threw the sword across the arena. Sweat ran down her back. Her hair had unraveled from her braid and her lungs ached from breathing. But she smiled as she dragged her arm across her mouth. She was physically exhausted. Her limbs smarted, thighs burned. It was the kind of exhaustion that seemed to bring clarity to all her thoughts. Whereas the exhaustion she felt at the hands of the court made her thoughts resemble blown-out candle stubs.

Behind her, she heard the air part from the low whoosh of a blade.

Instinct took over. Adrenaline snapped through her veins, and Gauri felt all her senses buzzing. She stilled, gaze flying to the practice sword she had thrown just out of arm's reach. She could get to it in less than half a minute. But what if the intruder had an arrow? Without turning, Gauri cast about, looking for something, *anything* that could be turned into a makeshift weapon when she heard a low, familiar laugh.

Vikram.

He whistled, dragging a sword behind him. A dark blue silk *kurta* had been thrown over his night tunic and pants. He must have tumbled out of bed and come straight here.

Her heartbeats tripped and tangled at the sight of him.

"You smile when you see me, do you know that?" he asked, strolling toward her.

She had not noticed. She tried to pull back her grin, but a single smile from Vikram just tugged her lips into a wider crescent. He bent down to kiss her, but Gauri stepped out of the circle of his arms, looking about her.

"Someone could see us," she hissed.

"Who cares?"

"It is not proper."

He raised an eyebrow, gaze flicking from the practice sword, to the henna on her hands, and then to her face.

"That's different," said Gauri primly.

"It's the day before our wedding, my beastly princess. After that you will be my beastly wife, and then it doesn't matter who sees us."

"Beastly *wife*?"

"Beastly queen?" he asked, tilting her face up to meet his.

A vulpine grin lifted his lips. Up close, he looked as tired as she did. There were dark presses beneath his eyes. A wild shadow of stubble along his jaw. Usually, his eyes were bright. But today the light in his eyes had been thrown into shadow. Perhaps like her, he was just tired. Yet when he reached for her, she couldn't help but notice how hot his skin was to the touch. But then his fingers trailed up her spine, and her thoughts dissipated into the air.

She smiled. "Beastly queen is only a marginal improvement. I am wounded."

"Are you?" he asked. But the tease from his voice disappeared, replaced with something rougher. "Let me make amends."

His hands went around her waist, pulling her body to his. Gauri's eyes drifted shut. The sun had risen higher in the sky, warming her face. Her back had arched against his hands, and her whole body was ready to melt into a kiss . . .

. . . that was not happening.

She opened her eyes. Vikram watched her, his face dangerously close to hers. His eyes looked touched by fever.

"What are you doing?" she asked.

"Drawing out the inevitable."

"Yes, I can see that," she said. "May I ask why?"

"Because you are thoroughly spoiled. You expect to be kissed when you wish for a kiss, and you should be denied every now and then. Trust me. It will make them sweeter. Like a victory."

She frowned. "That can't be true."

"No?"

He kissed her.

And whatever she was about to say was snatched up by his lips. The touch of Vikram's lips filled Gauri with the same sensation it always did: a sort of drowsy hunger. He filled her with a want so dense she imagined she might sink her teeth into it. Gauri leaned into him, her fingers digging into his arms. Vikram answered by holding her so tightly that he nearly lifted her off the ground. And then, right when the kiss tilted on the edge of something dangerous . . . he pulled back and gathered his breaths.

"Was I correct?"

She said nothing. Which made him grin.

"Say it . . ."

"On my deathbed," she retorted, even as a smile tugged at her lips.

"Don't say that," said Vikram, his voice raw. "I don't ever want to imagine that."

Gauri didn't know what to say. What does one say to that? It was too immense. To return it would seem empty. To ignore it would be an insult. To thank him would be worse.

She loved him. This much she knew. What she did not know were the boundaries of what she felt. Was that good? Was that bad? What was she *doing*?

Again, that panic frosted any warmth the kiss brought. She couldn't see the end of this. Not that she wanted it to end, but love felt like wrestling the sky. It made her feel small and epic all at once, and it . . . confused her.

"It was just a jest," she said, embarrassed. She didn't look at him. Instead, she focused on something she considered wholly arbitrary. The sword hanging from his hip. "What's that for?"

"Ah," he said, a slight frown furrowing his brows. "Part of my joint-sovereign duties now include sword fighting. Our courtiers seem to think I will be cutting a path to my side of the throne every day."

"You might as well be," she said.

Plenty of people were eager to see the new sovereigns deposed. Even then, a thread of resentment wound through Gauri. She would have given anything to be at the barracks and training instead of—

"How was the library?" asked Vikram wistfully.

"My eyes were so assaulted by history texts that I did not recognize my reflection in the evening."

"Don't make me jealous," he said. Gauri bit back a wince. Here they were, complaining of the thing that the other would far prefer. "Ah well."

He tossed the sword, catching it in one hand and spinning it effortlessly. Gauri nearly pinched herself. In Alaka, he certainly had *not* been able to do that.

"What?" he asked. "Surprised I can lift a sword?"

"No."

Vaguely.

"You must have developed muscles from some activity," she reasoned. "Though I can't imagine which."

"A bit of running, a lot of reading. Holding up books is difficult. As is turning pages."

Gauri crossed her arms.

"To be fair, they were *very* heavy books," added Vikram.

Vikram glanced at her crossed arms, his gaze lingering on the henna designs winding up to her elbows. His grin dimmed, replaced with an inscrutable expression. Gauri would have crossed her arms tighter at this scrutiny, but that would not have helped. If anything, it would only have drawn attention to the designs. Vikram moved closer, tracing the cinnabar designs with a light finger.

"Tomorrow," he breathed.

She let out a shaky laugh. How did Vikram do it? Bits of wonder and awe always found their way to him as moths drawn to distant light.

"Tomorrow we are chained to each other's side," she said. "I do hope you like the tapestries on the throne room walls. We shall be staring at them until the day we die."

No sooner had she spoken did she realize she had said the entirely wrong thing.

He dropped his hand. "That's all that tomorrow means to you?"

A better person, a *kinder* person, would have spoken of the joining of souls and indescribable love. But she did not owe him such declarations. Everything she had done thus far showed that she loved him. She had spent her time with the Ujijain delegates, studied the history of his kingdom, ingratiated herself to his people. Those things were not demanded of her, but they were her love manifested. She wanted to love them as he did, not simply because it was diplomatically logical, but because she would vow to take into her heart what he did. Including, though it pained her, dull texts on city planning. Even if it did not light a spark in her heart, she would try. Just as, she thought—glancing at the sword on his hip and the new callouses along his fingers—he did.

"You know what I meant," she said, her shoulders caving.

"I'm not certain that I do," said Vikram, his voice a touch colder. "You seem to think that tomorrow is the start of an inevitable drudge toward death."

"I do not have time for this," said Gauri, picking up and sheathing her practice sword. "And neither do you."

"Wait. Time for *what*, exactly?"

"Time to pick apart words as you do. I *cannot*. I have been doing it for too long, from the council in the daytime to the strange women in my bed . . ."

His eyebrows shot up his forehead. "Can we revisit that last part?"

"One of your dreadful customs," she snapped. "To preserve my chastity."

"An alternative," said Vikram, pulling her back against his chest and speaking low into her ear, "is to be very obvious about possessing *no* such thing. Allow me to be of assistance."

"You're terrible."

"Terribly handsome."

"That too," she said, laughing.

He folded her against his chest, and Gauri breathed in the smell of him. These days, he no longer smelled only of parchment. He smelled of the cut grass in Bharata's palatial arenas, the sandalwood incense carried by Ujjiain's priests, and, as always, ink and parchment. For one stolen moment, the world no longer spun. Homesickness lifted off her heart. She hardly recognized her home with so many unfamiliar faces crowding the halls. Her home had to make room for so many more that her place within it had disappeared beneath the footfall of strangers. But here, in a universe bounded only by his arms, she found it once more.

She had only just begun to breathe easy when Vikram began to cough.

The cough dragged itself up through his body, rattling in his lungs. Gauri stiffened. Slowly, she pulled away, her hand traveling up his chest before stopping at his throat. His skin burned with fever. Gauri drew away her hand as if scalded.

"You're *sick*," she said.

"Only with longing," croaked Vikram.

He leaned forward, as if to kiss her. But then his legs crumpled. Gauri caught him around the shoulders.

"How long have you been hiding this?" she demanded.

Perhaps she should have been kinder, more worried. But Gauri only felt fury.

"Not long," he said. "I woke up feeling rather strange."

"*Strange?*" she nearly shouted.

Vikram frowned. "Where is your sense of nurturing? I thought you're supposed to become my wife tomorrow."

"And where is *your* sense of self-preservation?" she asked. "You shouldn't even be outdoors, let alone *out of bed*."

"I will"—he coughed—"get to bed with astounding speed if you join—"

He couldn't finish.

A film of sweat covered his skin. Vikram inhaled deeply, but it shuddered and broke apart in his throat. He hacked again, and then his head fell against her chest.

Gauri shifted him when she felt something wet against her hands.

She knew what was on her skin even before she saw the crimson shine of it:

Blood.

It was a warm shade of red. As red as the ruby that had won them entry into the Tournament of Wishes. As crimson as the roses that he had planted next to swords in a garden made just for her. As scarlet as his royal Ujijain robes when he had asked her to marry him.

Vikram's pulse leapt against her fingers . . . straining and furious, as if his blood could barely stand to move through his veins. His shadow wavered behind him. The shadow looked as though it were trying to pull itself from the seam of life tying it to Vikram. She knew. That was all it took. The realization pinned that moment beneath its weight, and time itself could not move forward.

All day Gauri had felt something . . . something that she recognized, but could not name. When she blinked, she saw a barren landscape running beneath her. She felt the flanks of a skeletal horse and the slow turn of its rictus grin as it dropped her onto the floor of a pale kingdom. She tasted the air of that land here and now, scalding her throat as her fingers tightened around Vikram. Only now could she name what she had sensed:

Death.

A single second stretched into infinity. Gauri knew this feeling. It was the infinity that belonged to those who sense the scope of their grief before it hits. The infinity of waiting for the strike that will come no matter what bargain is made, what tears are shed, what violence is wrought. This was what Gauri knew to be true of Death. It may take one life at a time, but that did not stop it from rendering skeletal the souls of the ones who had loved the departed.

"No, no, no," murmured Gauri.

She sank to her knees, folding Vikram to her. His sword clattered to the ground. Instinctively, she wanted to pick it up, slide it back into its sheath, to do anything of ritual that might transform this into something *normal*. She could see normal stretched out, extravagant as a horizon: an endless rotation of meetings, smiles stolen from outside the glances of courtiers and therefore all the sweeter, her spine against his chest and their limbs a labyrinth none could enter but they. Days that blended together, arguments that tilted to a fit of laughing, hands cobwebbing with the blue veins of a long life. No magic compared.

Gauri wanted to snatch back all she had said. Now, Vikram's words curled her mouth with bitterness.

That's all that tomorrow means to you?

If tomorrow still had his smile, then it meant all to her.

In her arms, Vikram was strangely light. Gauri gathered him tightly, as though to stop any more of him from escaping. Shock robbed her words.

But though she had lost her sense of time, her guards had not. Bharata-Ujijain officials flooded the courtyard.

She did not hear the sound of their trumpet sounding alarm. She barely felt the heavy shawl draped around her shoulders, the attendants' urgent hands forcing her to rise. All she felt was the sudden cold against her skin when Vikram was taken from her.

PRESENT

Hira frowned. "But I know this story! I thought you said this happened to you."

"It did."

"But I already know the ending. I don't want a story where I know the ending."

Besides, Hira could not imagine what this story had to do with Meghana and her wedding. Meghana had never even met her husband-to-be. Though that did not stop her from imagining that their souls had known each other from the moment they were forged.

Hira thought this sounded foolish.

"People can take a lot of roads to get to the same ending, and even with the same ending, sometimes it is quite a different story," said her grandmother.

"But everyone knows this story," said Hira, sighing. "Is this the one with the happy ending or the sad ending?"

Her grandmother did not smile this time. She did not look out the window wistfully the way she sometimes did. Instead, she reached for the strange necklace at her throat. It was fashioned like a snake. Sometimes Hira thought that it changed colors, switching its jewels from emeralds to rubies and sometimes sapphires, the way a person might select different silks from a wardrobe. But Meghana and her parents said that was just her imagination.

"It is the one with the true ending," said her grandmother.

THE BARGAIN FOR BREATH

Gauri crouched beside Vikram's bed.

Ever since the royal physician had visited Vikram, a steady parade of diplomats hesitated to knock at the door. But that did not stop them from lingering. And it certainly did not stop their words from traveling to Gauri where she sat hardly a foot away, leaning over Vikram. One courtier's wife wept loudly, declaring: *"Ah, so soon a widow! Her henna has not yet dried!"*

But Gauri was no widow. She was not even a wife.

Both kingdoms stirred restlessly.

Distantly, Gauri wondered whether the diplomats of Ujijain had already begun packing for their kingdom. Outside the chamber they spoke of broken treaties, and even foul play at the hands of a clever queen. After all, she was the last one who had seen him alive and well. And wasn't her glass hand rather cruel looking at times? Why did she not smile around the emperor the way he smiled around her? Perhaps her dark eyes had lured him. Perhaps not all of her had returned from that strange land they had visited. Perhaps, perhaps. All splinters of a tale twisting out of hand.

The physicians could not diagnose him.

Aasha declared that no poison had touched him.

Gauri smoothed the hair from his forehead, fussed with his sheets, rubbed his feet to bring warmth back to his skin instead of this burning fervor that had gripped it. She sat and loudly criticized his favorite books. She declared that she was utterly naked and entirely bored. She told him this was a game she did not wish to play.

But she recognized what she was doing. She had seen her enemies do the same. Polishing their armor, squinting at the sky, poring over plans that had already come to pass. Redundancies on the way to the inevitable.

Out of earshot, Gauri was called unseemly and theatrical.

She was never called grieving.

The physicians declared that their best hope was to wait and see. But Gauri did not miss the twist of their mouths. They pitied her. They thought he would die if not by tomorrow, then in a matter of days.

Scouts had brought back reports of a similar illness gathering souls outside of the city gates. One day, people coughed and fell asleep, burning with fever. They never woke.

Once the physicians had left, Gauri admitted no one but Aasha and Nalini. Nalini held her, wept the tears Gauri could not summon. More would come. By morning, Vikram's father would be here so that the ones Vikram had loved best would be there when . . .

No. Her mind could not bear the weight of those thoughts.

"I did this to him," she said.

Vikram had not moved in hours. His eyelids had ceased their twitching. The fever had lulled from a fire to a flicker, leaving his skin cold and wooden.

"Hush, don't say such things," said Nalini. "How could you have known?"

"But *I* sent him beyond the city walls. *I* told him that he should go on a procession, meet officials, shake *hands. I*—"

She broke off.

But Aasha stood still as a statue. She kept looking out the window, until Gauri finally snapped:

"Are you wondering why Death is taking so long to get here?"

Aasha fixed her with a calm stare. "That is not who I am waiting for."

But she would say nothing more than that.

O fficially, all wedding ceremonial preparations had been placed on hold in light of the emperor's illness. The palace officially said that everything would resume at the first flush of health. There was no mention of the physicians' dire gazes. Or the stillness of Vikram, the gradual cooling of his skin so that all that separated him from life and death were the stingy pulses of his heart.

The food was still prepared. The banners still painted. But the palace had started to make quiet shifts . . . marigolds to throw in a procession, sandalwood paste used only to prepare the dead, wood hewn for a funeral pyre. Whispers chased each other up and down the palace staircases, clambering up the walls until they threatened to spill over into the cities.

When night fell, Gauri heard the door open. Aasha stood there.

She walked forward and wordlessly placed a bite of food to Gauri's lips. Gauri opened her mouth mechanically.

How strange that only last night, she had not fed herself either.

Her attendants and friends had taken turns feeding her bites of creamy *rasmalai* and spicy *saag* because the henna for her wedding was still drying, and she was not allowed to touch anything lest she ruin the pattern.

"Why?" asked Gauri, finally. "How could he live through Alaka and all of its terrors only to . . . *here*. What did I do? Was I . . ."

She blinked. She thought of the warmth of his hand cupping her cheek. The way he steepled his fingers and pressed his brows flat when he thought. How he would pull her behind a pillar, covering her laugh with his lips until she did not want to think but only do this. Forever.

"What?" asked Aasha gently. Too gently.

"Was I too happy?"

And finally, Gauri wept.

She wept as Aasha rocked her back and forth. She wept as Vikram still did not move. And she only stopped weeping when Aasha whispered:

"There might be a way to save him."

Gauri stilled. She sniffed, dragging her arm across her face.

"What would you have me do? Plead my case to Death?"

Perhaps she was delirious. But when Gauri thought of Death, she remembered a man with cruel eyes and a sensuous mouth, a man who would not flinch from anyone's tears. Hers would make no difference.

"You know how the Otherworld likes its games," said Aasha.

"They think *this*—" said Gauri, flailing a hand at Vikram lying prone in his bed, "is a game?"

Aasha only shrugged. "Everything is a game when there is nothing to lose."

The offhanded way she spoke struck Gauri, but she knew that her friend meant no offense. Aasha was centuries older. She might look like a mortal, experience things like a mortal, but she was not of this world.

Hidden in her words was truth.

To an immortal being, Death was not even a fairy tale. It was a city they had no cause to visit. Death lent no urgency to their love affairs. It did not sweeten the taste of food with the fear that these might be the last flavors to sit upon one's tongue. It did not heighten colors with the dread that when they closed their eyes, this would be the last image to blaze through one's dreams.

"Do not leave his side," said Aasha. "When the *yamaduta* comes, follow him."

When she heard the name *yamaduta*, Gauri flinched. A *yamaduta* was a messenger of Death himself. Sometimes the messenger took the form of a dog with brindled fur and four eyes. Sometimes the messenger was a beautiful woman. For some, Death came in the shape of a loved one whose back was eternally turned. For some, Death came with blunted teeth and a baleful gaze. Gauri did not want Death to come at all.

"Make a bargain," said Aasha. "You have already seen the realm of Death, haven't you?"

Gauri nodded, sure of this even though the details of her visit had long ago softened into dreams.

"Then it cannot hide from you," said Aasha. "Strike a bargain. It has been done before, once."

Gauri knew the tale. It was the story of Savitri, a princess, and

Satyavan, her husband. Satyavan was fated to die a year and a day after their marriage. Because of Satyavan's piety, it was said that the Dharma Raja himself came to collect his soul. But Savitri refused to part with her husband. She followed him through the twisting lands of Naraka, extracting one boon after the next. Even though she had angered the Dharma Raja with her stubbornness, her devotion impressed him. At last, Savitri requested a boon with a catch: *Grant me a hundred sons by my husband.* And Death, perhaps exhausted from his ordeal with the clever princess or perhaps softened by her entreaties, had no choice but to let the soul of Satyavan return to the light.

"Maybe Vikram could outwit death," said Gauri miserably. "But I—"

"—*you* are an extremely ferocious individual," said Aasha. "I don't think Death would wish to converse with you at all."

Aasha's words dragged forth a light. And Gauri's soul strained toward the radiance of those words as if she were a plant newly freed of the ground's darkness.

No one would take her bridegroom from her.

Gauri's smile became a vicious slash.

Let them try.

"Bring me my best weapons," she said.

Gauri had laid many traps in her life. She had laid branches over trenches studded with iron spikes. Mimicked the birdcalls of spies to soothe her enemies' suspicions. Placed gaps in her speech that courtiers fell into, and spun their own words into chains.

But she had never laid a trap like this.

It would have to be enough, she thought. She settled down to wait.

By now, night had ripened to full dark. Time turned stingy. Seconds lasted for minutes. Minutes for hours. Hours refused to melt, holding their shape like frost on a winter morning. Sleep seduced Gauri's thoughts, but every time her chin dipped, the sharpened points of her jeweled choker jolted her from rest.

All through the evening, Vikram had not moved. Once or twice, Gauri had felt her gaze straying to him, but she willed herself not to look. Look at him, and the image would hold. She would be too scared to blink. Too scared that if she did, his soul would slip out from beneath him, and she would not catch it in time. But even lying there, Gauri could not ignore the taste of betrayal at the back of her throat. It seemed impossible to imagine that there was a world where she could not follow, a world that even now his soul leaned toward. As if that was where he belonged. And not by her side.

No sooner had that dark thought burst inside her did she feel it: The presence of Death.

Some might think death felt like a slowing down, the lull of closed eyes, the body settling in for sleep. But they were wrong. Death commanded urgency. Its presence squeezed life like a fruit. Her chest clenched. Her soul, frightened, curled in on itself and yet life sluiced out anyway. Life dribbled down the ridges of her anima. Life was a puddle of spilled ambrosia on the floor of a grand room, and in its reflection, every mundane action had been rendered golden by Death's secret alchemy.

Gauri gasped—

With one hand, she grabbed Death's messenger. She gagged a little, for when she looked down—dressed in Vikram's garments from the day—she saw a pearlescent arm sunk to the wrist in her own body. The arm snapped back, the hand empty and recoiling.

"What trickery is this?" demanded the *yamaduta*.

Gauri looked up. She stared. For this gleaning, the *yamaduta* had taken a cruel and beautiful form. In a way, she was humbled. Of course the one face that would lure Vikram to the afterlife was none other than her own.

Gauri stared at the creature that had stolen her face. It took a moment before she could remember that it was not human. She could stab it repeatedly with her weapons, but it could not die, for it was not alive. It was a command poured into the shape of that which would pull or punish the soul of that who it had come to retrieve.

"You . . . you are not the soul I am to take."

The messenger glanced around the room. But Vikram was nowhere to be found. Before night had fallen, Gauri had him removed from the room and placed him in her own chambers. But not before she had taken his clothes—an act that had scandalized her courtiers—pricked his thumb, and smeared her lips with his blood.

The messengers of Death are said not to look too closely, Aasha had warned. *It is said that they cannot bear to look into the face of a mortal lest they become too fascinated. They check only for the trace of someone's soul lingering in their blood and the scent of their mortal bodies.*

"You are correct," said Gauri.

She dragged her arm across her mouth, but the taste of Vikram's blood snuck onto her tongue anyway. His clothes were far too big on her, and the dangling sleeves and breadth in her shoulders made her feel like a child. Facing a being as old as time, she *was* a child.

"Reveal him to me. His soul has been summoned."

Gauri steeled herself. And then she looked into the creature's eyes. Her own eyes. Stern and dark and inherited from a father she had always known at a distance.

"You cannot have him."

"It is not up to you, oh Queen. You are not the first bride to be widowed before she is made a wife. You will not be the last."

"I said you *cannot* have his soul."

The messenger tilted her head to one side. A movement made all the more wrong on the creature for its borrowed features.

"How did you know?"

Now it was Gauri's turn to go still.

Know . . . *what?*

The *yamaduta* splayed her fingers like a king displaying a feast, and Gauri saw an image stretched out:

A Tapestry.

Some part of her knew it, but her immediate memory could not recall where. The Tapestry shifted and shimmered, recoiling from itself as if it were a living thing. And then the image sharpened, diving in unto itself and expanding upon a single thread. Gauri felt an answering tug in her heart. *Vikram.*

"The young emperor's life thread was split. The Dread Queen decided one path. Her Pale Consort decided another path. Their divergence created a gap. When two lives diverge, there is a small enough space through which I might slip through and grab his soul. But rules are rules, and I am bound to them just as anyone else. Because his life could not be decided by immortals, it allows for the meddling of one who is far more acquainted with death—"

"A mortal," breathed Gauri. She glanced into her own face. "A mortal can decide if Vikram's soul is taken?"

The false Gauri's hands fell at her side. The image vanished.

"In a way," it said.

It smiled. And in this, Gauri found the creature's flaw. Its smile was nothing like hers. It may have gotten nearly every detail of her face correct, but it had missed one thing. Her scar. Few knew the tale, and so most assumed that the scar was not a scar at all, but a dimple. A mark of beauty. Not a mark of a girl who had only found solace in sharp things. Gauri sensed the gap in the creature's words. She sensed the taunt of more knowledge, the slippery silence it left behind as if its cleverness had a residue. But for all its cleverness, it did not know her grin.

And so Gauri raised her chin and emptied her eyes of any guile. The barest touch of triumph crimped the edges of the creature's smile.

"The loop runs twofold," said the creature. *"You must steal your bride-groom's last breath from the final gate before Death. He is an aberration—"*

Gauri, now giddy with the chance that she might win him back, fought to keep a smile from her face. The creature would not want her life? Then it could have anything. Anything at all. She didn't care. Because the moment the messenger of Death started speaking, she had started *imagining*. She imagined like one starved of ideas, all of them tamped down so that she would not cause herself more grief. She could imagine Vikram leaning forward, elbows braced on his knees, all long limbs and sly grins and outrage at being called an "aberration." She could imagine *him*.

"—but take care, oh Queen."

Gauri's eyes snapped to the creature.

"I give you this single night to cross this land and go hence. But know now that the halls leading to the realm of Death are their own treachery." The creature paused. It grinned with all its teeth. Moonlight broke through the room, and its eyes glistened in the way of predators. *"You may find that you do not care to bring back your bridegroom's last breath after all. You can always turn around."*

PRESENT

Hira had hardly blinked the whole time her grandmother spoke.

"Why would the messenger of Death say such a thing?" she asked. "Why wouldn't the queen have wanted her bridegroom to return alive?"

Her grandmother did not look at Hira.

"Love changes," she said. "First bloom is not last breath. That is not a good thing, but a truth."

"So?"

"So, my little jewel, I pose the question to you. Imagine you had the most beautiful flower in all the world. Imagine that only you possessed such a wondrous thing. Now imagine that it has begun to wilt. Do you let it wilt? Do you let that stunning fragrance of freshness soften into rot? Do you let the petals fall one by one and know that you had loved it for as long as time gave you? Or do you drop it when the blooms are at their height into a preservation liquid? You may not be able to smell it anymore. But you can see the moment at which it is frozen, eternal. And perhaps, the longer that you cannot recall how it felt in your hand, how it made your very senses sing . . . perhaps in memory it becomes all the sweeter."

Hira thought about it, and found herself rather furious when she realized that she did not know. She huffed. "But what's the right answer?"

At this, her grandmother smiled.

"No such thing, my little love," she said. "The question is when you choose to let something go. And who can tell you the answer to that?"

"But what did the queen do?"

Her grandmother rubbed her glass hand. "She did what she thought was right."

THE FIRST GATE

The messenger of Death stomped onto the marble floor. The ground trembled. A neat circle dissolving into the stone as easily as sugar stirred into steaming tea. Logic told her that the entirety of the kingdom should have been thrown out of their beds by the force of the trembling. But the kingdom stayed silent, caught in the jaws of their dreaming.

The hole in the ground was nearly lightless.

And yet, Gauri caught the glimmer of details. A staircase. A tiny, muted glow at the very end of the steps. Even from where she stood, she could tell how the quality of the light would be thin and watered down. As if someone had skimmed moonlight off a pond, and not bothered with replenishing the light's luster for centuries. No stench of malice wafted from the ground. Not a whiff of decay could be detected, nor could she sense that hot iron perfume of old blood. But she did not sense any bliss either, for this was the space between the living and the dead.

To cross it took as long as an eon, and as short as a blink.

The land was as vast as an ocean, and as narrow as an alley.

The land had a name, but all who knew it promptly forgot.

"And where will you be?" asked Gauri.

The messenger of Death sat at the edge of the bed, its back unnaturally straight. But for Gauri, who had been a soldier for nearly as long as she had been a princess, the familiar posture needled her. The being looked around the room and then said:

"*Here. I shall sleep in your bed and run my hand across your clothes. I will pace the floors you have paced and touch my hand to the walls. I may go wherever Death may go, and Death is everywhere. Even now, Queen, I see his shadow on you. The gray that will touch your hair. The veins that will cobble your skin into a landscape. The ache that will slow your limbs. I see.*"

But if the *yamaduta* meant to frighten her, it had failed.

Gauri was not frightened of that kind of death.

What she was frightened of was something far quieter. It was the death of being forgotten to the one who loves you. The death of being left behind in a place that will forever hold more grief than glee. The death of laughter.

Gauri turned to the stairs, grabbed the railing, and started her descent.

Where was Vikram now, she wondered? Surely, if his soul had fled past hers and already begun its journey to the realm of Naraka, then something in her would have answered?

The steps forming the staircase were disturbingly uneven. Through the fabric of her slippers, Gauri felt slopes . . . ridges.

Things that might have once been a woman's sharp clavicle or a child's bicuspid now worn to the smoothness of a pearl.

Her eyes took an eternity to adjust. For here, darkness grew thickly when there was no one there to tend to it. At the bottom of the staircase, a long hall stretched forward. She looked behind her and saw an infinity of staircases, footsteps disappearing on the incline or descent. She realized then that she was not the first or the last mortal to visit this land. She was not the first to know grief so acutely that she would have fought Death. And for some reason, this offended her. It was arrogant, she knew, but then again perhaps all who had come here had felt the same fury at this realization. Every pain is its own world with its own language. None else could speak that unique dialect unless they had been born to it, or, as was more often the case, had borne it.

Around her, footfalls broke the silence, along with something else . . . the sound of something being *dragged*. Gauri had been sent only to recover Vikram's last breath.

What had the others been sent to gather?

The moment Gauri leapt down from the last step, hot breath ghosted against the back of her neck. She froze, one hand on a sword. It was the sword Vikram had practiced with when he fell down in the arena. Maybe it was no talisman, but anything else of his would have weighed her down with grief.

Something snorted behind her. A muzzle whuffed across her scalp, tugging at her hair.

"I know you," said a rasping voice. "I carried you on my back, inedible thing. You never said thank you."

Gauri turned and found herself staring face-to-face with a not-dead and not-alive white horse. Half of its body was in perfect health, its pearly white flanks shone, and muscles corded its body. But the other half? The other half was rotted and open, strips of flesh peeling off a giant rib cage, its garnet-dark heart beating at the shallow of its chest. Half of its face wore a permanent grin.

The sight of it summoned a memory that she had buried deep in her mind.

A not-dead and not-alive white horse racing across a barren landscape. A pale kingdom. A Tapestry on the wall that she could not bring herself to look at for too long.

"Thank you?" she said, uncertainly.

The horse tilted its head, examining her. It smacked its lips.

"You look unappetizing," it said. "You would taste dry as a sun-bleached bone. Where is your softness? Your whimsy? Bleh. Too salty. I feel thirsty just looking at you. I do not like it."

"Thank you," said Gauri, once more, this time with absolute certainty.

She took one step closer to the gate.

"This has been thoroughly alarming, and now I have to go," she said, turning on her heel and hoping the monstrous horse would not follow.

Men and women, children and beasts walked down the hall in either direction. Pale cave formations dangled from the ceiling. They glowed, but cast little light, and in the gloom they reminded Gauri of teeth. Perhaps this place was a monster's skeleton, hauled out, its body now a relic and a hall.

At first, Gauri thought that onyx pillars lined the walls. They were stately and black, flecked with bits of glittering stone. But then, she watched as a thin band of fire unraveled from its top. Light drib-bled slowly down the columns. Around her, everyone stopped. Their heads turned to the pillar closest to them.

"The sun is on its way," whispered one woman.

She was clutching something to her chest: a child's ragged doll.

"Where are you?" she called softly. "Where *are* you?"

Gauri looked once more to the pillars. She had been wrong. They were not onyx at all, but night poured into columns to create an hourglass of sorts.

When the pillar turned to gold, the sun would have risen.

And she would be out of time.

The sound of hooves clattered behind her. Again, that stench of decay. The horse had followed her.

"Where are you going? Can I come? Actually, I do not care for your answer. You move with urgency. How strange! What is urgency like?" asked the horse. "Does it feel like a fire? And if so, what kind of fire? A fire that flays the flesh? Cooks a person down to the mar-row? Or one of those ornamental fires that do not singe the flesh at all? I detest those. If it does not feed you, its purpose is hollow. What are you doing—"

Gauri looked at it sidelong. The horse's decayed side faced her and she did not like looking at its hollow eye socket.

"I have to get something," she bit out, hoping it would make the creature shut up.

The horse eyed her. Or maybe not. It was hard to tell when she could not see its eye.

"You are wearing bridal henna," it said. It huffed, and something red sprayed across its muzzle. A black tongue snaked out from its mouth and wiped it clean. "It smells too fresh. When was your wedding, inedible thing?"

Gauri grit her teeth. "It is tomorrow."

"Then what business have you in the space between life and death?"

She could sense, somehow, that the horse *knew* what she was doing. But why was it trying to force out the words? Was it taunting her?

But there was nothing for Gauri to hide. The truth was what it was.

"My bridegroom had a split thread," she said. "He already breathed his last. And his last breath is at the end of this hall. If I don't get it before morning, he will die."

"Everyone dies."

"It does not have to be so soon," she said.

The horse nodded once. And then, it *grabbed* her. Its blunted teeth closed around the fabric of her sleeve. Gauri tried to shrug out of her clothes. She would run naked down these halls if she had to, but the horse moved with inhuman speed, and moments later, she was on its back. She grabbed the pale wisps of its hair, holding on tightly as it ran through the hall.

"What are you *doing*?" she hollered.

The horse's head whipped to face hers. One hollow socket, one black eye. Its flesh pulled back at the lip in what Gauri imagined was a snarl, but turned out to be a smile:

"Helping!" it shouted.

The hall sped past. Light trickled down the onyx columns, swallowing the stars. Around her, the people moved like shades. The floor was littered with mementoes: scraps of paper with smudged names written in the edges, children's playthings, a woman's silk slipper, and even a *mangalsutra*. The necklace that a groom tied around his bride's neck. Her heart squeezed.

Unable to look any longer, Gauri shut her eyes.

And soon, the horse slowed to a stop.

Gauri slid off, quickly backing away and facing the horse so that it could not snatch her again.

"That was very difficult," huffed the horse. "I know you will taste bad, but I admit that I still wanted to break your skin. Just a quick sip, you see. Running makes me hungry. I much prefer just appearing behind someone when they least expect it."

It grinned.

Gauri stared at it. "Why are you helping me?"

The horse's withers rippled. Its ears swiveled and pointed at her.

"Because you need it."

"But why *you*?"

"Because," said the horse, and this time its voice reeked of something ancient, something that might have once been sinister but grew bored of malice and had landed at a strange medium. "I am trusted. Not everyone fights on behalf of those whose life thread is split. And perhaps you have more friends than you think."

Gauri's hand flew to her neck. It was a habit that she still could not shake, for it happened every time she thought of her sister, Maya. Once upon a time, her sister's necklace had dangled against her throat. A heavy sapphire pendant on a delicate string of seed pearls. But she had since stored it in her jewelry chest.

It did no good to wear a ghost around her neck.

The horse's words nudged at a memory that brought her solace.

In it, her sister told her a tale until the sun rose, and promised to see her again.

"Very well then," said Gauri uneasily. Trusted or no, that did not mean she had to face her back to the creature. "Where are we?"

"This is the first gate."

"How many gates are there before the threshold of the Kingdom of Death?"

"Two," said the horse. "The Gate of Names and the Gate of Grief."

Gauri had seen many gates in her life. And this did not resemble one. It looked like a grove gathered from scraps of children's nightmares. A sickly crescent moon hung in an unfinished sky, the ends of it unraveling into the solemn gloom that coated the entirety of this in-between place. Trees that looked more like twists of iron than any living thing grew in tight spirals. No fruit dangled from their branches. What swayed from their branches were voices. *Names.* Names repeated softly, deliriously, like a person who has lost all but this last cut of themselves.

The voices took all kinds of forms. The name *Chaya* transformed into a silver anklet when a young man reached for it. The name *Urvashi* dangled like a dried-out root. None reached for it.

People wandered through the grove. Plucking names and putting them back. Some looked stricken as they held the name to their ear. Others looked disgusted and turned around, leaving the Gate of Names instead of passing through it. Still more people wept when they held the name to their ear. But those who wept did not turn. Instead, they gathered the name to them, and walked into the grove and through the gate.

"Why names?" asked Gauri.

"Would you rather they have a Gate of Skin?" asked the horse.
Gauri recoiled. "No."

"Names are powerful things, my inedible bone!" said the horse.
"They are the gristle of destiny once fate has chewed a life down to
its death. Mmm, gristle. Names are sweet as blood spatter. Names
are cobbled-together hopes. Why else would someone name a wrinkled blanket of a newborn if not to impress some hope upon them
for what they might *be*? But, you see, my little bone girl, while a soul
can leave a name behind, a name cannot let go of a soul's hold. A
name can get enamored of a person. They're very sensitive." The
horse tilted its head in thought. "And also very tasteless. Pity. They
always seem so succulent in life. But that is why the discarded names
find their way to this place and affix themselves to this gate. Here,
they become a window of a kind. A way to view what might have
happened to the one who bore it."

In front of her, people twisted their way through the groves.
They held up the names as if they were inspecting fruit. Gauri
watched as one man flung a name down onto the dirt. Fury twisted
his features. Whatever he had seen in the name had made him aban-
don the soul who it had once belonged to. The man turned on his
heel. And then he walked out of the grove.

"What happens when someone holds a name?" asked Gauri.
"Does it show the future?"

"A little," said the horse. "It makes no pronouncements upon the
name-bearer's end. But it shows a direction that soul will encounter
should that name be allowed to ripen. It is up to the one who plucks
the name in this gate whether they believe it is a direction worth suf-
fering."

The horse turned its head, its unsettling gaze pinned to the man who had thrown the name onto the dirt and now stalked down the hall.

"You can always turn around and leave it behind."

No. She could not leave him behind. She would not. And yet that did not stop the shadows of her anxiety from falling across her thoughts.

Falling in love with Vikram was as easy and natural as drawing breath, but what about *staying* in love? What if ruling a country together changed them . . . what if the things that had once made them smile now made them scowl? And worse, how could she bear it if she saw that it was not time or circumstance that had made his heart falter, but *her*?

But she would have to. She would haul back his soul to the light even if she knew that she trailed her own devastation in its wake.

Gauri steeled herself. She needed a distraction, and so she turned to the horse:

"I never thought to ask if you have a name. Do you?"

The horse stamped its foot. "I am called Kamala."

". . . *lotus*?"

It tossed its mane. "A beautiful name for a beautiful *me*."

"Well—"

"And I chose my name myself," said the horse proudly. "Snatched it off a dead woman's tongue. Her blood tasted like apples. Tasty, tasty name. Tasty, tasty blood."

It smacked its lips.

"And your bridegroom?" asked the horse. "What is his name?"

"Vikram," said Gauri. She hated how her voice shook when she said it. She hadn't spoken it for a whole day and the echo of it sat thickly in her throat. "It means wise."

ROSHANI CHOKSHI

He used to tease her about it all the time. *Gauri, my very name encompasses all that I am. So trust me when I say that I should decide on this week's desserts. I'll be very judicious. I'll only help myself to a full serving of my own and then maybe half of yours too.* Her chest tightened.

"And yours, little bone?" asked the horse.

"My name means gold."

PRESENT

That's what your name means too, Dadi-Ma!" said Hira happily.

Her grandmother bowed her head in acknowledgement. "I know."

"And my name means diamond," said Hira, lifting her chin. "Which is a lot better than cloud."

Which was the meaning of Meghana's name.

Her grandmother laughed, and then cupped Hira's cheek. The cold crystal of her palm felt soothing in the day's heat. Hira leaned against it and breathed deeply.

"A precious name for my precious girl," said her grandmother.

"Is it bad that I like the horse? She makes me giggle."

"It is not bad," she reassured Hira, leaning close. "Even I like the horse."

SECOND BLUSH

It was not hard for Gauri to find Vikram's name in that grove of forget. It called to her. His name dangled playfully from its iron branch. First, it flashed silver, and then it transformed, turning pale, losing its sheen, before stretching into Vikram's favorite object in the world:

A scroll.

But there was no writing on the enchanted scroll. Gauri did not know whether to bring the name to her ears or hold it to her heart, but the moment she touched it, the paper shuddered. Words bled across the page. The words looked like no language that Gauri had ever seen. This was a calligraphy that did not belong in any earthly realm because it was destiny crimped into letters. The words shifted, living and supple as skin, and Gauri understood that *this* is what the horse had meant when it declared that the names did not show a destiny. It was like fate flexing a new muscle. A suggestion. A path.

A peek of what might happen should the bearer of the name return to the land of the living.

She did not read the words so much as she lived them.

They snuck into her mind, spreading across her vision:

Gauri and Vikram stood at opposite sides of their bedroom. Outside their window, the moon had waned to a sliver. Lamps burned low. The silk sheets had been pulled back in invitation, but neither of them made any move toward it. Vikram leaned against the wall. His truth-telling necklace, Biju, lay against his throat. A warning in yellow topaz. Gauri did not lean against anything. She stood with her arms crossed, still as a statue. The room was grand, but it was not so large that it should feel like a realm of its own. And yet, in that moment, it did.

"I spoke in jest," said Vikram carefully, as if he were speaking to an infant. "Perhaps you might have heard of this bizarre human development known as humor?"

"Don't talk to me like that."

"Like what?"

"Like I have clouds stuffed in my brain."

"See, I wouldn't mind that. Perhaps it would give you some damned levity."

Gauri's mouth flattened to a line. "Sovereigns are not known for their levity. They are known for their solemnity. For their respect to the art of ruling."

"Laughter and respect are not mutually exclusive."

"They are when it is said at my expense!" she shouted. "You humiliated me."

"You are overreacting!" said Vikram, taking one step forward.

Gauri took one step back. "You criticized my military strategy."

"On the contrary, my beastly wife, I praised it," said Vikram. In the past, the nickname had a touch of sweetness to it. But now, spoken in fury, the words seemed to have curdled in his mouth. He practically spat them out, and Gauri bit back a flinch. "I said that the only way that our militia could win a war any faster is if they kept your favorite dessert behind enemy lines."

"Everyone laughed."

"Because it was charming! We were speaking to our advisers, and it made you seem somewhat human for a change."

"I don't like that."

"You don't like anything."

Gauri dug her heels into the ground. "That isn't true."

"You don't like it when I laugh . . ."

"Again, not true."

"Very well, you don't like it when I make others laugh. You think it, what was it that you said last time? Ah, I recall now. It cheapens our social strata and undermines our rule."

She bit her lip. And then, very quietly, she said: "I like it when you make me laugh."

"But that isn't enough, is it?"

"I just don't see why you cannot keep your charm to matters outside of court."

"It's who I am," he said. "You have freed yourself of needing your people's love, but that does not mean you have to be so cold."

"It keeps me impartial."

"Just this morning, the gardeners told me that they had orders to move the Garden of Swords and Sweets into the courtyards of our residential quarters. Is that true?"

Gauri lifted her chin. "Yes."

"Are you ashamed of what I made for you?"

"No!" she said, her eyes widening. "Of course not!"

"Then why would you hide it from people?"

Gauri was silent for a few moments, and then she said: "Aasha."

"Aasha doesn't like it?"

"No, Aasha . . . Aasha has been reading people for me. Reading their desires. And spying too. No one wants to see me and think of a girl freshly in love. They want to see someone resilient, and it is too raw. They ask questions. Why the swords, why the sweets, and I do not owe anyone a piece of my heart."

"Is it truly that bad to reveal that you even have one?" shot back Vikram.

Gauri scowled and strode forward.

"Don't act as though you're somehow better than me," she said. "Have you forgotten that I'm a woman?"

"On the contrary, most nights that is a fact I usually savor."

She scowled.

"You can wear your heart on your sleeve and be called benevolent. You can sing and dance and be called artistic. But me? No. If I show emotion, I am called weak. If I do not keep myself at a distance from my own court, then they will think they have power over me. I have done this before, and I know how it is. Just because I hide some part of my heart doesn't mean that it means any less to me. I am not you."

"And I'm not you!" said Vikram. "I can't act as you do, and I refuse to. I do not imagine your burdens as anything light, but you're asking me to be someone I'm not."

"Fine! Be yourself! But that doesn't mean I have to like it."

Whatever playfulness lingered in his gaze vanished. "So what you are saying is that you do not like me. Is that right?"

He raised his eyes to Gauri. His gaze held a challenge.

Fight me. Fight with me. Tell me that isn't true.

But her eyes only hardened.

Vikram's jaw clenched. After awhile, he sighed. He walked toward her. At the same time, Gauri rocked forward on her heels, longing plain on her face. She wanted this to be forgotten. She wanted to not explain herself, and instead have it assumed that of course that was not what she meant. But instead of reaching for her, Vikram snatched a pillow from the bed.

"Since my presence is so offensive, I'll remove myself."

He left.

And she did not follow.

The scroll with Vikram's name seamed shut abruptly.

Gauri was left with the taste of that fight burning in her throat. It had not come to pass, and yet it was unquestionably real to her. This was a truth, and she was forced to look down its throat:

They would fight.

Then again, they had always fought. She wasn't entirely sure that they could help it. In the end, they always caught fire. When they collided—thoughts and dreams or lips and limbs—those sparks didn't just burn, but cast *light*. In the stateroom and surrounded by their courtiers, their fiery ideas burned down to the essence of each, combining along the way and gaining strength like some metallurgical alloy. And outside the stateroom . . . well. No inferno compared.

Yet, here was the underbelly of all that heat.

Here was the proof that they would not be invulnerable from their own flames.

And somehow . . . something marvelous reared up in the aftermath of her guilt.

Relief.

Even though their words were cruel. Even though the air crackled with unfinished fury. Even though she still felt the echoes of that anger . . . It had not stolen what lay beneath all of that, like some half-sunken jewel.

Love.

At least they fought. *At least* they faced each other with flames. *At least* they had not preferred the darkness of indifference.

And it was with this knowledge that Gauri reached for his name. The paper melded to her fingers, turning into a necklace that she then strung around her neck. The enchantment of his name burned cold against her throat, and she welcomed it. For a moment, it was as if his hands were at her shoulders, her back pulled against his chest. She tilted her head to one side, and felt the ghost of his stubble against her neck, his cheek pressed to hers.

The memory of a fight that had not come to pass still burned. She still fizzed with anger even as she walked out of that grove, and indignation chased her footsteps. But she welcomed this.

She welcomed not *knowing* what would happen next.

She welcomed this because what she knew was worth any unknown.

Gauri looked around her. The grove was still teeming with people. Some of them grabbed at the names, refusing to look at the contents, before sprinting down the line of trees and disappearing into what could only be the exit of the gate. Others hung the names back onto the branches, though a touch mournfully. But most people just stood there. Frozen. Holding the contents of a future that seemed a warped reflection of the present, and weighing its worth.

She did not wait to see what they would decide.

The horse, Kamala, had promised that it would find her no matter which side she chose.

Gauri started walking. She walked past the shade of strange branches, and past the names that called out to her, some of them sullenly and some of them longingly: *Manosh* and *Ilavati*, *Yasmin* and *Savitri*.

Eventually, the grove of names gave way to a barren expanse. There was no light, and yet it was not dark. Overhead, no constellations whispered of destiny. No clouds bore witness to the battle-grounds of her own heart. She left behind this gate with no ceremony and once more found herself staring at the edge of another hall.

At the entrance of the threshold, Gauri felt Vikram's name burning at her throat.

It was as if this act—of taking his name regardless of what she had seen and carrying it over this threshold—worked a magic of its own. In her mind's eye, a new scenario bloomed, one that had all the immediacy of just happening.

And in it, she saw the aftermath of their quarrel, and her heart broke.

The Garden of Swords and Sweets had been delicately uprooted and placed in a reclusive spiral far from the eyes of the courtiers. Vikram may not have verbally spoken to her in days, but the garden served as its own missive. Every day, fresh sweets dangled from the trees, painstakingly knitted in gossamer bags so as not to draw the attention of hungry insects or clever birds. A dagger with a jeweled hilt had "grown" near the foot of an acacia tree, and in a bramble of purple berries, Gauri found an arrow quiver ornamented in chased silver.

But he did not seek her out at night, even though the door to the bedroom was kept a demure width ajar. And he chose to take his meals alone. Even when they held court, he did not acknowledge her any more than he would a potted plant standing in his path. No longer did he furtively brush his thumb over her knuckles. He did not catch her eye and grin slyly until her thread of thought or conversation was entirely broken.

He was the picture of decorum and distance.

The very embodiment of what she had asked.

And Gauri hated it.

Every day she walked past the garden he had built her, and every day a new restlessness reared up to join the restlessness of the past. Vikram's message was clear:

Your move.

Very well, she thought.

Gauri planned in secret. This plan made her skin itch. She did not do things like this. She could barely bring herself to compliment her own reflection out loud, and yet she suspected that Vikram would not accept anything less than a raw piece of her heart.

Nearly a week of full silence between them had passed when she cornered him in the hall one evening. The moonlight danced through the cut stones of their residential quarters. He froze, looking this way and that before he realized it.

"Did . . . did you trap me?" he asked. He might be angry with her, but he couldn't quite hide that he was reluctantly impressed.

"Yes."

"Someone told me they had found an ancient scroll and strange light was pouring off the pages."

"Someone answers to the bribery of royalty," said Gauri, shrugging.

"Bribery?" repeated Vikram. "The oh-so-noble-my-own-shadow-refuses-to-fraternize-with-other-shadows queen resorted to cheap bribery?"

ROSHANI CHOKSHI

She nodded.

"On any other day, that might have been proof enough that you love me," said Vikram. But even as he joked, he sounded resigned. As if this was all he might truly expect from her.

Gauri took a deep breath. Her heart pounded. She felt rather ill, to be honest.

"I have better proof," she said in a small voice.

And then, not waiting for him to answer, Gauri turned on her heel and padded down the hall. She led him through a labyrinth of their rooms—past the columbarium and the messenger doves with their heads buried in their wings, past the receptacle that held the royal insignia and the sovereign jewels, and finally past the secret courtyard and her Garden of Swords and Sweets. Vikram kept a study there, a massive room cramped with books, where an artful architectural contrivance filled the room with light without allowing sunlight to spoil the pages.

Sometimes, it seemed to Gauri that Vikram's scrolls and books and treatises roosted. As if they were birds with heads tucked under their wings, nestled deep inside their alcoves and sleeping. She had told him this once, and he had laughed.

"I guess that's fitting," he had said. "Stories, knowledge . . . they set the mind alight."

That idea: levity brought on by the wings of a good book and a better story. That was what she had tried to show him.

When they entered the study, a flock of stories in mid-flight was there to greet him. Suspended from the arched ceilings by the finest gossamer thread were pieces of blank paper folded into extraordinary shapes. A winged lion, paper teeth cut to points. A peacock strutting across a bookcase, its tail fanned out and nearly sweeping the floor. A makara swimming across a ceiling newly painted with stars.

This was what he was to her.

To her, he was the tipping point of wonder to awe.

He made her see the world as pieces of unfinished magic, waiting to be transformed.

She knew she was . . . unyielding. She could not melt into humor the way he could. She didn't shout open declarations of love, but that did not mean that she did not feel.

Beside her, Vikram's eyes were wide. He walked beneath this sea of paper transformations, blank pages that looked like the beginning of a tale. The painted stars didn't shine, but Vikram regarded them as if they were real and somehow, the light changed. The force of his wonder was its own illumination.

"Vikram . . ." she started, the words knotting together.

He was standing at the far end of the room. If it had not been so silent, he might not have heard her. But he did, and he turned.

Last week, they had faced each other across a small room that felt as wide as a country. Today, they faced each other across a greater distance and yet they felt so tightly knit that the simple act of breathing in and out, of blinking slowly and regarding the other, of waiting, was like reaching out and drawing a line across the other's soul.

He smiled.

He crossed the study's distance in a matter of strides, and stood before her. Gone was his sly smile. There was something raw and unguarded in his eyes. And Gauri knew that if he looked closely, he would see that expression mirrored in her own. She tried to look elsewhere before he saw, but he caught her chin in his hand.

"I know you find these things hard to say," he said. "So at least allow me to see the truth of it in your eyes."

She relented. For long, horrible moments, Vikram's eyes held her in thrall.

They searched her thoroughly until it wasn't enough just to look at each other. Somehow, her hands went to the buttons of his silk jacket. Somehow, his fingers left her chin to travel down the bare slope of her neck, to the flimsy clasps of her nightsilk. Somehow, she pulled him or he pulled her, and now she was seated on top of the long, wooden table strewn with plans and papers.

"You never said sorry, you know," he murmured.

"And I never will," she retorted.

"Here's an idea. Perhaps you don't have to say it at all," he said against the hollow of her neck. "You could always show it instead."

"And why do I have to be the one doing all the apologizing? You have nothing to be sorry for?"

"I do," he said, toying with the ends of her hair.

"Then why don't you start."

Vikram's gaze flicked up to hers abruptly. There was no apology there. But something akin to . . . daring. Or hunger.

"That's only fair, my queen," he said. His voice seemed to borrow some of the darkness around them, and Gauri's heartbeat started to race, tangling together in anticipation. "I'll do my utmost to convey the very depths of my sorrow." He dropped his head to the slope where her neck met her shoulders and kissed her there. "Though I must warn you, it will be a long apology."

PRESENT

Hira tilted her head. "So they fought and then she made him a really pretty present?" She felt like she was missing something. "That's it?"

Her grandmother coughed abruptly. "Yes."

"They just . . . talked?"

That sounded very boring.

Her grandmother rubbed her temples. "May I finish the story?"

THE GATE OF GRIEF

It seemed fitting that at the threshold to the Gate of Grief, Gauri should weep.

The irony that what should slow her down was happiness instead of fear was not lost on her. Now, she feared her heart had become too heavy. If the first vision she had seen with Vikram's name had held bitterness with a core of sweet, this was sweetness with a bitter shadow. The name taunted her. The vision showed her not what she had to look forward to, bitterness and all, but how much she had to lose. Gauri saw her loss written out in a bitter calligraphy—all those paper marvels catching fire and crisping underfoot, the long dining hall where he might have laid down her down and covered her body with his, lips swallowing up laughter and false stars so drenched with human hope that they put forth their own light. *Love.* Love like secret choreography, a dance of limbs and laughter, a steady pattern made more beautiful by each passing day.

The name showed her what she could have, but only if she reached him in time.

Her fear grabbed her by the throat then.

Fear that she should not reach him in time, but be forced to return empty-handed to a world that would be ripped of all that might have been so sweet.

Her tears had not even begun to cool when the skeletal horse greeted her at the entrance. True to its promise, Kamala manifested the moment Gauri stepped over the boundary from one gate and through the hall that would connect her to the second.

"Ah, there it is," said the horse.

Gauri looked behind her, but saw nothing.

"What are you talking about?" she asked roughly, wiping at her face. "Let's go. We can't waste any more time, and I—"

"—yes yes yes, I know. You shall start dragging ghosts, but I would have a care," rasped the horse. "It is showing, you know."

Gauri rolled her eyes, and then pressed her fists against her face, as if she were terribly annoyed when what she was really doing was wiping away her tears.

"I thought you were sent to help me, and instead you're bothering me with this nonsense about invisible undergarments showing or what have you."

The horse tossed back its head and let out a sharp laugh.

"*Invisible undergarments?*" it repeated, delighted with itself. "Is that what humans call souls?"

"Souls?" asked Gauri. "Are you trying to tell me that my soul is showing?"

"But of course your soul is showing, my inedible bone!" said the horse. "It leans out! Can't you see it? Wilting and unbound! Did you see something that made your rib cage split with sorrow? Bad bad bad. That's how souls fall out, you know. And this is not a good place to start losing your soul."

The horse trotted forward. Its hollow hooves made a sound like dragging skulls on the stone floor.

"It is not always so bad to spend a moment just standing," said the horse. Its ears twitched. "I will not move until you do *not*. Ha! How clever I am."

Realizing that she would get nowhere with this bizarre creature, Gauri relented. She stood there. And as she did, she found that it was easier to breathe. She found that the vision of bliss did not expand painfully inside her chest, but instead felt like a hope held tight against one's skin. And though Gauri was almost certain that the horse was insane, the moment she merely stood there . . . and let her thoughts be gathered, she felt . . . better.

The horse stamped its foot. "I am rather disappointed."

"Why?" asked Gauri.

"There is nothing at all I want from you," it said, huffing. "I cannot have your blood on orders . . ."

Gauri wanted to ask *who* had ordered such a thing, but thought it best not to bait her own mortality.

". . . and I do not even wish to nibble a bit on your soul. It *smacks* of heroism. Bleh. Nasty residue. Full of pomp. Empty of originality. I detest it."

For the third time, Gauri found herself thanking the strange demon horse.

The hallway leading to the Gate of Grief might have looked just like the one that she had just left save for a disturbing difference. There were people in the walls.

Bodies tipped forward like the eaves of a building. Grieving faces and streaming hair and reaching hands formed a dome above those who wandered here. This place had wiped away the color of their skin, and left them the color of milk. But though they had no skin color to speak of, something grew across their features . . .

At first Gauri thought it was decay.

It unnerved her how beautiful decay could look. Ages ago, it had been her thankless task to join the scouts of Bharata after a war. They would walk through the battlefields days or sometimes weeks after a victor had been declared. Sometimes they were there to recover a soldier's armor, or retrieve coded messages left behind by a felled spy. On those trips, it was not uncommon to find a body in a state of unravelment. And though it disgusted her, she couldn't look away from the strange life that sprouted where another life had vanished. Fistfuls of mushrooms with satin caps. Mold with exquisite frills that were every shade of cream. Fungi like a nest of pearls.

The closer she looked at the faces above the hall, the more she saw that it was not decay at all.

But frost.

Gauri rose up on her tiptoes, straining. From a distance, the frost looked furred. If she had been in a fanciful mood, she might have imagined that these were beings in the middle of a transformation. Any moment now and great wings would shake loose from their shoulder blades and they would turn to swans.

That was not how death worked here.

Where the wall joined the floor, Gauri saw the final transformation of the faces. They were merely shapes of polished ice. All features smoothed away. A darker thought crossed Gauri's mind. Perhaps it was not frost that she was seeing, but the shape of forget spasming across the features of the long dead. This was their fate. If forgotten entirely, they would become no more than building blocks set to something greater than them.

The night pillars lined against the hall were less dark than they had been before. Now, golden daylight streamed down them in rivulets. In their new glow, Gauri was disturbed to see how much of the people's faces were see-through. Their skin was thinner here, and the light went through it as if it were a veil. She hesitated to look down at her own arms, scared to catch the glint of her own bone.

"Do you like happy things?" asked the horse, trotting at a fast clip.

"I'm no different from anyone else," said Gauri. "Of course I do."

The horse's ears swiveled. She could feel its withers rippling beneath her leg. Something like *pity* rolled off the creature.

"When you get to the gate, snatch your happiness by the teeth and do not let it go."

Strange, she thought. Then again, the horse never said anything of sense to her. Gauri looked around, bored. In the previous hall, Kamala moved as fast as the speed of thought. Now, however, she trotted at a fast clip but did not gallop. "Out of respect" it had said primly when Gauri asked why.

No one moved fast here.

There were less people marching toward the Gate of Grief than there were people wandering through the Gate of Names. But those who were here moved as if they walked through water. Every action exaggerated. Every expression twisted to extravagance. Gauri felt laid bare by their own rawness. And she hated it. *Close your heart and move forward*, she wanted to scold. But grief was a private world, and that was how it manifested here. She could yell and jump in front of a person. They would not notice.

"Why can I see them and they can't see me?"

"Family privileges," harrumphed Kamala.

Once more, Gauri just rolled her eyes. When Kamala said bizarre things, there was no use trying to decipher it.

"How much longer until we're there?" she asked.

"Oh, an eon and a blink!" laughed the horse.

She was trying her best not to let the thinning night pillars frighten her, but with every rivulet of gold dripping down the base, all she felt was that blissful memory pulling away from her. She wasn't even sure whether she was doing this right. Go past the two gates, and then what? Would Vikram's last breath be waiting for her? Would she recognize it? Would it be like a plume of smoke or . . . or *him* but pallid and rendered ghostly?

Ahead of her, someone screamed.

The sound of it made the hairs on the back of her neck rise. Kamala broke her trot for only a moment.

"Do not look too long," she said.

At what? Gauri wondered silently.

Ahead of her stood a giant construction of smoke. The smell of char stung her nose. The smoke swallowed up the frosted bodies once arching above them. This was the Gate of Grief. It was not wrought iron at all, but plumes of smoke that perhaps dreamed of being stone, for they looked hardy and cruel even as she could see straight through it to a land that was little more than scraps of shadow layered one upon the other.

"Steamed tears," said Kamala. "Very good building blocks. Nice tensile strength. But don't walk through it with your tongue out. Far too salty."

A gate of steamed tears?

Unlike the other gate, people walked in . . .

But not many walked out.

Save for one.

The owner of the scream.

Gauri was not the only one to see him. As one, every person turned and faced him. The man was older than Gauri, but not so old that his face bore any proof. His hair was disheveled. His robes marked him as a tradesman of some kind. Behind him walked a beautiful woman who was clearly dead. Wisps of smoke curled off her hair, teased by an invisible wind so that it looked as if she smoldered. Her skin was iridescent like a pearl's nacre. She held the man by the wrist, and tears coursed down her face. Her *mangalsutra*, that which marked her as a married woman, had broken in death and now dangled off her neck.

"Turn around," she pleaded. "Please, my love."

And in her voice, Gauri recognized the owner of the scream.

But not once did the man look at her.

"Why can everyone see him?" asked Gauri softly.

Kamala's ears flicked. "He is one who finds himself here quite . . . often. Every day he finds his way to the Underworld, and tries to bring his wife back to the land of the living."

There was a noticeable recoil from the people. They leaned out, giving the man and his wife a wide berth. Even Gauri found herself leaning to one side, eager for Kamala to get on with it and take her to the Gate of Grief.

Maybe it was cruel of her. Perhaps she should have been more impressed by the feat he'd accomplished. But in his face, it looked as if the price was far too steep. His own wife knew it.

"I can never stay past dawn and yet you drag me back," she wept.

Gauri wanted to shut her ears, but she couldn't, and she was forced to listen. The woman sounded desperate.

"Don't you love me?"

"You know I do," the man bit out gruffly, and still he marched forward, dragging his wife back toward the land of the living.

"Then why won't you turn around?" she asked, pleading. "Why won't you let me go?" Softer, this time, she said: "Only one of us can be a ghost."

He let out his breath. "I don't want to lose you."

"Am I lost simply because I am not by your side? Do you think if you drag me from hell that you have won?"

"Stop it," he said, trying to shake his hand loose from hers. But she did not let go.

"You do this every day," she said. "Every day when you wake up, you break yourself to bring me back. And even then, it is not a resurrection. It is a replacement."

"No, it's not," he said.

"Every night you will drag me up and every dawn I will have to leave."

"If I do this enough times, you won't have to go back."

She fell silent. The man's grief was a palpable thing, and Gauri bent over in her seat, feeling for all the world as if every wound she had ever suffered had opened up at once. She was not alone. Through her skin, she could feel Kamala's dark heart race. At either side of her, those who wandered through this limbo crumpled and sank to their knees.

The dead wife shrieked:

"You will always wake up alone. And one day, you will raise your hands to engrave your grief on your wrists and you will find that they are gnarled with age, and there is so little blood left in you that you might as well wait to join me," she said hoarsely. "And you will real-ize that time has tugged a blanket before your eyes. You will realize that you have squandered autumns and starved your eyes of stars. And you will hate me."

"I could never hate you," he said.

But he spoke the words dully, as one who had repeated some-thing so many times that its meaning had thinned.

"Turn," she said.

"Why?"

"Because you love me."

Gauri found herself sitting upright. She could not look away from this scene of grief played out before her. She wasn't even sure what she wanted in that moment, whether she would siphon off some secondhand victory if he did not turn.

But then, slowly, the man lifted his head. He turned slowly on his heel, his chest never once falling. As if all this time, he held in his breath. As if he were holding onto it just for her. Joy lit up his wife's face. When he turned to her, they beheld each other. Gauri felt like an intruder, but she could not look away from them.

The moment they turned to each other, Gauri saw them as they might have been once. For a blink of an eye, the woman had gone from eerie to earthen, her iridescent skin flooding with russet color. The wisps of smoke coalescing to black hair now silvered with age. Crease-lines, of joy, flared against the man's eyes. She held his face in her hands, crying as she smiled.

And then she disappeared.

The man stood there, his hands still raised in the air, molded to the shape of her. Desolation sucked the very air from the space around him. But he did not weep. Nor did he cross once more past the Gate of Grief. Slowly, he turned toward the land of the living. Slowly, he picked his way through the crowd, like one whose eyes are adjusting to the light. Slowly, he found the strength to leave her behind.

"You pity him," rasped the horse. And it said it with something like disgust.

They were nearly at the gate. Gauri would have jumped off and ran the rest of the way, but the floor had changed. Now, the reflection of the bodies overhead rippled across the liquid floor. Kamala may have been able to trot across its surface. But what if Gauri simply drowned? She forced down her impatience.

"So what if I pity him?"

"It is cruel to laugh at one's reflection."

Gauri felt struck. This was what her life had come to . . . being scolded by a being half-dead. It wasn't as though she was alone in pitying the man.

Everyone had recoiled. Part of her felt self-righteous. She would *never* be so beside herself with grief that she would waste her life dragging up the dead. Even the phantom of his own wife was exasperated.

But then again, wasn't that what she was doing? Fetching Vikram's last breath from hell's gates? If she lost him again . . . would she do *this*? Grate herself down to the marrow until she lost the very reason she had journeyed down to this bleak place?

"Grief is a land of its own, though here it squeezes itself into the shape of a gate," said Kamala. "Be careful what kind of citizen you make, little bone."

Kamala stopped trotting, and Gauri slid off its back. Vikram's name was warm against her throat. She wished she could wrap her whole body in that warmth.

"His last breath is in there," said the horse.

"And then what will happen?" asked Gauri. Her hand moved to the sword at her side. Would she have to fight for it? The way she had when they had fought in the Tournament of Wishes? She hoped she would have to fight for it. This place made her weak and useless.

"What will happen," said the horse cryptically.

"Will it show me the future?" she asked.

"Oh yes," said Kamala. "But this is no place for prophecy, it is a place for pain. And you will suffer the most for it."

Gauri turned. But the words *What do you mean?* died on her lips. The horse had disappeared. And with it, everyone else who had once stood around her. She had walked through the Gate of Grief without knowing, and inside she found a place that she did not expect. It was not bleak and stern like the Gate of Names. It was ... beautiful. Sharp.

Gauri was in a palace carved of white. Above her, the sky swelled with snow, its belly hanging low and trailing clouds as if daring the spires of this kingdom to pierce it. This was not a place she recognized in the land of Bharata-Ujijain. Yet it felt as familiar as home.

"Vikram?" she called.

A cloud snagged on a tower, and snow began to fall from the broken sky.

"Gauri?" he answered.

Something caught within her. She ran to the sound of him. Snow stuck to her skin and dusted her hair. Around her, enchantment fell away. Paper animals gathered themselves off the white walls and zoomed around her. She heard lyrics of ice that conjured twisted gardens encased in glass. Palaces of music unheard crumpling into fluted sighs of love. The air sounded as if it had been rummaged through, as if the fingers of some pale god had combed the atmosphere.

But the sound of love—the sound of Vikram's voice, the laughter straining at the seams of his words—was a found thing.

Like the way back home.

"Vikram?" she called again.

He did not answer, but the echo of his voice remained. Gauri ran past a set of open rooms before she found him. In each one, she glimpsed that which she might have had. In one, he tossed a child in the air. A boy with dark eyes like hers and a slow smile like his. In the next, they reclined against cushions. The light moved over them slowly and Gauri saw gray in their hair. In the room before she saw him, she glimpsed an unfamiliar elderly couple staring out a window. The kingdom they looked upon was vast, and the sunrise moved over it reverently, touching it with gentle light as if in awe that such a place existed. The couple held hands.

In the last room sat Vikram.

The bedroom looked much the same as their own with a single difference:

Gauri was already in it. She looked as old as Mother Dhina in this vision. Gray in her hair. Her veins raised. Her arms cradling an older Vikram on his deathbed. Age had wrought its ravage, but they were not so old that their own shadows should peel off them and wander elsewhere. Around the walls stood people with blurred faces. Family not yet made.

At the center of it all hovered a blue flame, wispy and quivering. His last breath. Here, for the taking.

Gauri stopped. For long moments, she could not bring herself to move. The grief of this place ripped through her. This was the truth. She would always lose him.

The only difference was the timing.

She walked closer, hearing herself speak. She sounded so old, and yet not old enough that she might follow him soon after. This was her grief: to be left behind.

"I told you not to go without me," she scolded.

"See, that was your mistake," teased Vikram, rasping. "You know I hate following orders. Even yours, my beastly queen."

His hand rose to her face and cupped her lined cheeks. With effort, he spoke:

"To possess even a single line in the legend of you is the greatest wish I could have made."

He did not speak again.

The image froze, hovering here, and therein lay her choice. As if through a filter of centuries, Gauri heard the messenger of Death's voice:

"You may find that you do not care to bring back your bridegroom's last breath after all. You can always turn around."

Such grief. Such bleakness as to lay waste to her soul. Past the image she saw so many empty days, more full of shadow than light. The drawn-out impatience of those who feel their life lingers on out of spite.

The messenger of Death had not doubted her ability to bring back Vikram. She had doubted her bravery. Who wanted that pain? There was pain regardless, but at least, if she walked away, she would never have to know the pain of loving someone so completely that the loss of him was an open wound upon her soul. She would never give herself entirely to that enthrallment, the seeds of which she already felt burrowing into her. She could love him more than she did now, and it might as well destroy her. But then she remembered his name at her throat, his hands in her hair, his shadow beside hers. Aasha had said that she would need to be brave to bring him back. But this was bravery new to Gauri. This was the bravery required to love the fleeting.

The bravery to hold loss in your heart and love anyway. The bravery to let go at the end.

And she knew, even as she reached for the flame of his last breath, that loving him would be the bravest thing she had ever done.

INHALE

The horse was not there when Gauri emerged from the wintry palace.

In truth, she had not truly expected to see it anyway, though she wished that she could have thanked it once more. Instead, the same staircase that she had descended now appeared before her. The image of what she had seen melted away, replaced with an infinite stretch of silvery brume. The mist coiled around her feet. An invitation. But Gauri grabbed hold of the staircase rail, and step by step, she pulled herself from hell.

When she emerged, she was standing once more inside the bedroom. The *yamaduta* sat in her bed, and looked up at Gauri with her face. It seemed as if all time and no time had passed. An eon and a blink, as the horse would say.

"*This is what I do not understand of mortals,*" said the messenger of Death. "*You suffer so greatly for a smile. Why?*"

In the room next to this one, she heard the rustle of sheets. A cough. And then, an irritated groan, like someone who had been shaken too soon from sleep. She knew those sounds. She smiled, even as her heart broke a little. She smiled, and the memory of the Gate of Grief receded to a faint kernel of knowing.

"I suppose it depends on who does the smiling."

TOMORROW

The night of their wedding was a night of discovery.

How long could a kiss last without the urgency of breathing? How long could a breath last without the urgency to kiss? It was a discovery of delicacy, like reaching for a bloom only to discover that it was a creature in camouflage with brilliant wings now catching the light as it danced out of reach.

Later, held tight in Vikram's arms, Gauri considered what she had said to him before she had descended to steal back his last breath. She had not told him yet, and she wasn't sure that she ever would. In the arena where she had practiced her swordplay, she had said:

"Tomorrow we are chained to each other's side. I do hope you like the Tapestries on the throne room walls. We shall be staring at them until the day we die."

She relayed this to him now, and he lay there silently.

"I remember," he said. "And I remember asking if that was all that tomorrow meant to you. Does it still?"

She curled a little closer to him and shook her head. What tomorrow meant . . . what *this* meant . . . was too immense to fit into words.

"This is an adventure, Gauri," Vikram whispered against her hair. "All of it."

"Even staring at the ugly wall Tapestry in our stateroom?"

He winced. "Unfortunately."

Gauri laughed. And though she was sure that there would be days when she could not, and perhaps even a stretch of years where she knew only the shadow, she took comfort in knowing that this laugh was just the first of many.

END

Their wedding was held with great pomp and ceremony," said Hira's grandmother. "Everyone who attended said they had never seen a more handsome bridegroom or a more beautiful bride. She even carried him over the threshold, which shocked a few people, but the pair of them thought it would be good to start shocking people early. Might make them more immune to the rest of the surprises they had in store for their kingdom."

Hira's heart ached, but she was not sure why.

It was a happy story, wasn't it? The bride who went to fetch her beloved and who returned victorious . . . but she still lost. In a way.

And for the first time since their fight, Hira's heart ached for her sister. Was it possible that she too felt lost? That maybe, when she had seen the toys Hira had left in her treasure chest, that she did not think of them as playthings but . . . reminders. Of something she was leaving behind.

"Did they live happily ever after?"

This question made her grandmother pause.

"They lived," she said carefully. "Mostly happily. Sometimes furiously. But always gratefully. It is, I think, the best way to spend existence."

Hira nodded, and hoped that she looked as wise as her grandmother sounded. *Spend existence.* What a strange phrase. It made her think that her own years were like currency. She had learned about currency and all of its strange magic when she had listened to her father's councilors. *This much armors our soldiers. This much paves the roads.* If *she* had currency, she would have spent it on something far more interesting: like *magic*. Sometimes her grandmother told stories like that. A place, called the Night Bazaar, whose currency dealt in years and memory.

"Does it still happen?" asked Hira.

"Does what still happen, my little jewel?"

Hira pulled her knees to her chest. This portion of her grandmother's window faced the royal grounds. And Hira saw a procession of chariots. Servants bustling through the growing crowd with trays of refreshment and sweet lime juice.

"Adventure," whispered Hira.

Her grandmother did not answer. Instead, she took off the necklace that she wore around her neck. The snake necklace that Hira swore turned different colors, though she seemed to be the only one who thought so. She clasped it around Hira's neck, and the weight of it felt like an oath.

"Did you know that when your grandfather wore this, it told the truth?"

"Really?" asked Hira.

"Oh yes," said her grandmother. "People lived in fear of him repeating anything they said. Honesty does not make for good politics. But it does make for loyal subjects. The snake had a name too. Biju."

"It doesn't tell the truth anymore?" asked Hira sadly.

"Well. It does not for me, at least," said her grandmother. "You might be different."

"How will I know if it's telling me a truth?"

"You'll feel it, my jewel. If you lie, it will tighten, ever so slightly. Like someone's hand squeezing yours. And if you tell the truth, it shall not move at all." Her grandmother kissed the top of her head. "Now go. You've spent too much time with me. Go talk to your sister. You won't have much more opportunity to do so."

Hira slid off the couch, her fingers tracing each individual scale of the necklace.

She couldn't wait to tell Meghana all about the story. Maybe they could test out the snake necklace before she left! Or maybe they could just sit beside each other. Hira was fine with that too.

She told her grandmother good-bye, and then raced out the door. As she did, she whispered to the snake:

"I will not live a life of adventure and magic."

Maybe it was just her imagination, but Hira could have sworn that she felt the barest *squeeze* right where the snake's tail looped over her collarbone. It felt like her grandmother's hand reaching down to guide her and say:

Oh, my love, you have no idea what magic awaits you.

EPILOGUE

It was right before dawn when she saw him.

Gauri had spent the day standing regally in the shadows, watching the ceremony for her grandchild's wedding. She loved weddings. She loved the dessert, and the laughter. She loved how the bride and groom snuck bewildered glances at each other. And she wished her family a life of joy. But after everyone had been embraced and alternately scolded or praised, she had retreated to her Garden of Swords and Sweets.

She could not lift a sword any longer.

Nor did she have any wish to do so.

It was enough to sit quietly on her stone bench and watch the sweets sway above her, and imagine a kingdom full of story birds. She did a lot of imagining these days. Which was why she almost dismissed the sight of him.

Vikram.

Sitting beside her on the bench.

He looked just as he had in his youth. Tall and lanky. Black curls falling over his forehead. His dark eyes touched with amber so that when the sunlight hit him and he smiled, it looked as though his eyes were made of topaz. Stunned, Gauri reached out to touch his face. Years had passed since she had touched him, and she had almost forgotten the hot silk of his skin. One touch and she remembered. She looked down at her own hand, this one flesh and not glass. It was unlined. Callouses gone. She was young once more.

She smiled, delighted to find herself in this dream.

Vikram clasped her hand to his face and grinned.

"I am almost too handsome to be real," he said. "It has clearly boggled your mind."

"You're not real," sighed Gauri. "I'm going to wake up and you'll leave again."

The smile vanished from his face.

"Not this time, my love."

"I'm tired," she said. "You've been gone a long time."

"I know," said Vikram guiltily. He ran his hand through his hair. "It wasn't like I had a choice. But I watched you . . . every day I slept beside you. Did you notice?"

She had, but she always thought it was a dream.

"I met your sister, by the way," he said. "She laughed at my jokes. I don't think her husband was particularly enthused, but he let me stay and wait for you. I refused to go without you."

Maya, thought Gauri. It had been even longer since she had thought of her sister's name. A door opened in her memory. Her sister both excited and resigned to see her again. Now she knew why.

"To a new life?" asked Gauri.

"On and on and on. Until we get tired of it and wish to leave."

"And you'll be there in the next life?"

"Always," he joked. "I'm very hard to get rid of. I'm like an infestation, really."

"Then you are my favorite pestilence."

"Music to my ears," he teased, and then helped her up.

She stood, and noticed herself left behind. It was not a bad feeling. It was like waking up and falling asleep all at once.

"Come on, my beastly queen," said Vikram, looping her arm through his. "Let's start a new adventure."

Read on for an extended excerpt

from Roshani Chokshi's next novel

The
Gilded
Wolves

Fléctere si néqueo súperos Acheronta movebo
If I cannot move heaven, I will raise hell.
—Virgil

O nce, there were four Houses of France.
Like all the other Houses within the Order of Babel, the French faction swore to protect and safeguard the location of their Babel Fragment, the source of all Forging power.

Forging was a power of creation rivaled only by the work of God.

But one House fell.

And the other House's line died without an heir.

Now all that is left is a secret.

PROLOGUE

The Matriarch of House Kore was running late for a dinner. In the normal course of things, she did not care for punctuality. Punctuality, with its unseemly whiff of eagerness, was for peasants. And she was neither a peasant nor eager to endure a meal with the mongrel heir of House Nyx.

"What is taking my carriage so long?" she yelled down the hall.

If she arrived too late, she would invite rumors. Which were a great deal more pesky and unseemly than punctuality.

She flicked at an invisible speck of dust on her new dress. Her silk gown had been designed by the couturiers of Raudnitz & Cie in the 1st arrondissement's Place Vendôme. Taffeta lilies bobbed in the blue silk stream of her hemline. Across the gown's low bustle and long tulle train, miniature fields of buttercups and ivy unfurled in the candlelight. The Forging work had been seamless. As well it should be given the steep price.

Her driver poked his head through the entryway. "Deepest apologies, Madame. We are very nearly ready."

The Matriarch flicked her wrist in dismissal. Her Babel Ring—a twist of dark thorns shot through with blue light—gleamed. The Ring had been welded to her index finger the day she became Matriarch of House Kore, successfully beating out other members of her family and inner-House scrambles for power. She knew her descendants and even members of her House were counting down the days until she died and passed on the Ring, but she wasn't ready yet. And until then, only she and the House Nyx patriarch would know the Ring's secrets.

When she touched the wallpaper, a symbol flashed briefly on the gilded patterns: a twist of thorns. She smiled. Like every Forged object in her home, the wallpaper had been House-marked.

She'd never forget the first time she'd left her House mark on an artifact. The Ring's power made her feel like a goddess cinched to human shape. Though that was not always the case. Yesterday, she'd stripped the mark of Kore off an object. She hadn't wanted to, but it was for last week's Order auction, and some traditions could not be denied . . .

Including dinners with the head of a House.

The Matriarch marched toward the open door and stood on the granite threshold. The cold night air caused the silken blooms on her dress to close their petals.

"Surely the horses are ready?" she called into the night.

Her driver did not answer. She pulled her shawl tighter, and took another step outside. She saw the carriage, the waiting horses . . . but no driver.

"Has *everyone* in my employ been struck by a plague of incompetence?" she muttered as she walked toward the horses.

Even her courier—who was merely to show up at the Order auction, donate an object and leave—had failed. To his lists of clear cut errands, he'd added: get fabulously drunk at L'Eden, that gaudy sinkhole of a hotel.

Closer to the carriage, she found her driver sprawled facedown in the gravel. The Matriarch stumbled backward. Around her, the sounds of the horses stamping their hooves cut off abruptly. Silence fell like a heavy blade through the air.

Who is there—she meant to say, but the words collapsed noiselessly.

She stepped back. Her heels made no sound on the gravel. She might have been underwater. She ran for the door, flinging it open. Chandelier light washed over her and for a moment, she thought she'd escaped. Her heel caught on her dress, tripping her. The ground did not rush up to meet her.

But a knife did.

She never saw the blade, only felt the consequence of it—a sharp pressure digging into her knuckles, the snap of finger bones unclasping, hot wetness sliding down her palm and wrist and staining her expensive bell-sleeves. Someone prying her Ring from her fingers. The Matriarch of House Kore did not have time to gasp.

Her eyes opened wide. In front of her, Forged moth-lights with emerald panes for wings glided across the ceiling. A handful of them roosted there, like dozing stars.

And then, from the corner of her vision, a heavy rod swung toward her head.

PART I

From the archival records of the Order of Babel

The Origins of Empire

Master Emanuele Orsatti, House Orcus of the

Order's Italy Faction 1878, reign of King Umberto I

T*he art of Forging is as old as civilization itself. According to our translations, ancient empires credited the source of their Forging power to a variety of mythical artifacts. India believed their source of power came from the Bowl of Brahma, a creation deity. Persians credited the mythical Cup of Jamshid. etcetera.*

Their beliefs—while vivid and imaginative—are wrong.

Forging comes from the presence of Babel fragments. Though none can ascertain the exact number of fragments in existence, it is the belief of this author that God saw fit to disperse at least five fragments following the destruction of the Tower of Babel (Genesis 11:4-9). Where these Babel Fragments scattered, civilizations sprouted: Egyptians and Africans near the Nile River, Hindus near the Indus River, Orientals from the Yellow River, Mesopotamians from the Tigris-Euphrates River, Mayans and Aztecs in

Mesoamerica, and the Incas in the Central Andes. Naturally, wherever a Babel fragment existed, the art of Forging flourished.

The West's first documentation of its Babel fragment was in the year 1112. Our ancestral brethren, the Knights Templar, brought back a Babel Fragment from the Holy Lands and laid it to rest in our soil. Since then, the art of Forging has achieved levels of unparalleled mastery throughout the continent. To those blessed with a Forging affinity, it is an inheritance of divinity, like any art. For just as we are made in His image, so too does the Forging artistry reflect the beauty of His creation. To Forge is not only to enhance a creation, but to reshape it.

It is the duty of the Order to safeguard this ability.

It is our task, sacred and ordained, to guard the location of the West's Babel Fragment.

To take such power from us would be, I daresay, the end of civilization.

•》 1 《•

SEVERIN

ONE WEEK EARLIER . . .

Séverin glanced at the clock: two minutes left.

Around him, the masked members of the Order of Babel whipped out white fans, murmuring to themselves as they eagerly awaited the final auction bidding.

Séverin tipped back his head. On the frescoed ceiling, dead gods fixed the crowd with flat stares. He fought not to look at the walls, but failed. The symbols of the remaining two Houses of the French faction hemmed him on all sides. Crescent moons for House Nyx. Thorns for House Kore.

The other two symbols had been carefully lifted out of the design.

"Ladies and gentlemen of the Order, our spring auction is at its close," announced the auctioneer. "Thank you for bearing witness to this extraordinary exchange. As you know, the objects of this evening's auction have been rescued from far flung locales like the deserts of North Africa and dazzling palaces of Indo-Chine. Once more, we give thanks and honor to the two Houses of France who agreed to host this spring's auction. House Nyx, we honor you. House Kore, we honor you."

Séverin raised his hands, but refused to clap. The long scar down his palm silvered beneath the chandelier light, a reminder of the inheritance he had been denied.

Séverin, last of the Montagnet-Alarie line and heir to House Vanth, whispered its name anyway.

House Vanth, I honor you.

Ten years ago, the Order had declared the line of House Vanth dead.

The Order had lied.

While the auctioneer launched into a long-winded speech about the hallowed and burdensome duties of the Order, Séverin touched his stolen mask. It was a tangle of metal thorns and roses gilded with frost, Forged so that the ice never melted and the roses never wilted. The mask belonged to the House Kore courier who, if Séverin's dosage had been correct, was currently drooling in a lavish suite at his hotel, L'Eden.

According to his intel, the object he had come here for would be on the auction block any moment now. He knew what would happen next. Light bidding would take place, but everyone knew House Nyx had fixed the round so that the object would go to them. But though House Nyx would win the artifact, it was going home with Séverin.

The corner of his lips tipped into a smile as he raised his fingers. At once, a glass from the champagne chandelier floating above him broke off and sailed into his hand. He lifted the flute to his lips, not sipping, but once more noting the ballroom's layout and exits just over the glass rim. Tiers of pearly macarons in the shape of a giant swan marked the East exit. There, the young heir of House Nyx, Hypnos, drained a champagne flute and motioned for another. Séverin had not spoken to Hypnos since they were children. As children, they had been something of playmates and rivals, both of them raised almost identically, both of them groomed to take their fathers' Rings.

But that was a lifetime ago.

Séverin forced his gaze from Hypnos and looked instead to the lapis-blue columns guarding the South exit. At the West, four Sphinx authorities stood motionless in their suits and crocodile masks.

Sphinx authorities were the reason no one could steal from the Order. The mask of a Sphinx could sniff out and follow any trace of an object that had been House-marked by a matriarch or patriarch's Ring.

But Séverin knew that all the artifacts came to the auction clean, and were only House-marked at the auction's conclusion when they were claimed. Which left a few precious moments between time of sale and time of claiming in which an object could be stolen. And no one, not even a Sphinx, would be able to trace where it had gone.

A vulnerable un-marked object was not, however, without its protections.

Séverin glanced at the North end, diagonally from him, where the holding room—the place where all un-marked objects awaited their new owners—lay. At the entrance crouched a gigantic quartz lion. Its crystalline tail whipped lazily against the marble floor.

A gong rang. Séverin looked up to the podium where a light-skinned man had stepped onto the stage.

"Our final object is one we are most delighted to showcase. Salvaged from the Summer Palace of China in 1860, this compass was Forged sometime during the Han Dynasty. Its abilities include navigating the stars and detecting lies from truth," said the auctioneer. "It measures twelve by twelve centimeters, and weighs 1.2 kilograms."

Above the auctioneer's head, a hologram of the compass shimmered. It looked like a rectangular piece of metal, with a spherical indentation at its center. Chinese characters crimped the metal on all sides.

The list of the compass's abilities was impressive, but it was not the compass that intrigued him. It was the treasure map hiding inside it. Out the corner of his eye, Séverin watched Hypnos clap his hands together eagerly.

"Bidding starts at 500,000 francs."

A man from the Italian faction raised his fan.

"500,000 to Monsieur Monserro. Do I see—"

Hypnos, of House Nyx, raised his hand.

"600,000," said the auctioneer. "600,000 going once, twice—"

The members began to talk amongst themselves. There was no point trying in a fixed round.

"Sold!" said the auctioneer with forced cheer. "To House Nyx for 600,000. Patriarch Hypnos, at the conclusion of the auction, please have your House courier and designated servant sent to the holding room for the customary eight-minute appraisal. The object will be waiting in the designated vessel where you may mark it with your Ring."

Séverin waited a moment before excusing himself. He walked briskly along the edges of the atrium until he made it to the quartz lion. Behind the lion stretched a darkened hall lined with marble pillars. The quartz lion's eyes slid indifferently to him and Séverin fought the urge to touch his stolen mask once more. Disguised as the House Kore courier, he was allowed to enter the holding room and touch a single object for exactly eight minutes. He hoped the stolen mask would be enough to get him past the lion, but if the lion asked to see his catalogue coin for verification—a Forged coin that held the location of every object in House Kore's possession—he'd be dead. He hadn't been able to find the dratted thing anywhere on the courier.

Séverin bowed before the quartz lion, then held still. The lion did nothing. Its unblinking gaze burned his face as moments ticked past. His breath started to feel sticky in his lungs. Part of him hated how much he wanted this artifact. He kept throwing his hopes into the dark and waiting for them to rot, but they persisted, sneaking back into his heart when he wasn't looking.

Séverin didn't look up from the floor until he heard it—the scrape of stones rearranging. He let out his breath in a rush. His temples pulsed as the door to the holding room appeared. Without the lion's permission, the door was Forged to remain unseen.

All along the walls of the holding room, marble statues of gods and creatures from myth leaned out of recessed niches. Séverin walked straight to a marble figure of the snarling, bull-headed minotaur. He'd planted one of his own L'Eden decorators to make sure the statue would be in this exact spot. Séverin raised his pocket knife to the statue's flared nostrils. Warm breath fogged the Forged blade. In one smooth line, Séverin dragged the blade's tip down the statue's face and body. The statue split open; the marble hissed and steamed as his Historian stumbled out of it and fell against him. Enrique gasped, shaking himself.

"You hid me in a *minotaur*? Why couldn't Tristan make a hiding dimension in a handsome Greek god?"

"His affinity is for liquid matter. Stone is difficult for him," said Séverin, pocketing the knife. "So it was either the minotaur or an Etruscan vase decorated with bull testicles."

Enrique shuddered. "Honestly. Who looks at a vase covered in bull testicles and says: *You. I must have you.*"

"The bored, the rich, and the enigmatic."

Enrique sighed. "All my life aspirations."

The two of them turned to the circle of treasure, many of them Forged ancient relics looted from temples and palaces. Statues and strands of jewels, measuring device and telescopes.

At the back of the room, an onyx bear representing House Nyx glowered at them, its jaws cracked wide. Beside it, an emerald eagle representing House Kore shook its wings. Other animals representing the other Order factions all around the world stood at attention, including a brown bear carved of fire opal for Russia; a wolf sculpted of beryl for Italy, even an obsidian eagle for the German Empire.

Enrique dug inside his costume of an Order servant and pulled out a rectangular piece of metal identical to the compass House Nyx won.

Séverin took the fake artifact.

"Still waiting on my thanks, you know," huffed Enrique. "It took me *ages* to research and assemble that."

"It would have taken less time if you didn't antagonize Zofia."

"It's inevitable. If I breathe, your engineer is prepared to launch warships."

"Then hold your breath."

"That should be easy enough," said Enrique, rolling his eyes. "I do it every time we acquire a new piece."

Séverin laughed. Acquiring was what he called his particular hobby. It sounded . . . aristocratic. Wholesome, even. He had the Order to thank for his acquisition habit. After denying his claim as heir of House Vanth, they'd blackballed him from every auction house so that he could not legally purchase Forged antiquities. If they hadn't done that, perhaps he wouldn't have gotten so curious about what objects they were keeping him from in the first place. Some of those objects were, as it turned out, his family's possessions. After the Montagnet-Alarie line was declared dead, all the possessions of House Vanth had been sold. In the months after Séverin turned sixteen and liquidated his legal trust, he had reclaimed each and every sold House Vanth possession. After that, he'd offered his acquisition services to international museums and colonial guilds, any organization that wished to take back what the Order had first stolen.

If the rumors about the compass were right, it might allow him to blackmail the Order, and then he could acquire the only thing he still wanted:

His House.

"You're doing it again," said Enrique.

"What?"

"That whole nefarious-whilst-looking-into-the-distance-thing. What are you hiding, Séverin?"

"Nothing."

"You and your secrets."

"Secrets are what keeps my hair lustrous," said Séverin, running his hand through his curls. "Shall we?"

Enrique nodded. "Room check."

He tossed a Forged sphere into the air where it hung, suspended. Light burst from the object, sliding down the walls and over the objects to scan them.

"No recording devices."

At Séverin's nod, they positioned themselves before the onyx bear of House Nyx. It stood on a raised dais, its jaws parted just enough so that the red velvet box holding the Chinese compass shone bright as an apple. The moment Séverin touched the box, he had less than eight minutes to return it. Or—his gaze went to the beast's shining teeth—the creature would take it forcefully.

He removed the red box. At the same time, Enrique drew out a pair of scales. First they weighed the box with the original compass, then marked the number before preparing to switch it with the decoy.

Enrique cursed. "Off by a hair. But it should work. The difference is hardly discernible by the scales."

Séverin's jaw clenched. It didn't matter if it was hardly discernible by the scales. It mattered if the difference was discernible to the onyx bear. But he'd come too far to back away now.

Séverin placed the box in the bear's mouth, pushing it in until his wrist disappeared. Onyx teeth scraped against his arm. The statue's throat was cool and dry, and entirely too still. His hand shook despite every effort to keep still.

"Are you breathing?" whispered Enrique. "I'm definitely not."

"Not helping," growled Séverin.

Now he was up to his elbow. The bear was rigid. It didn't even blink.

Why hadn't it accepted the box?

A creaking sound lit up the silence. Séverin jerked his hand back. Too late. The bear's teeth lengthened in a blink, forming narrow little bars. Enrique took one look at Séverin's trapped hand, turned paled and bit out a single word:

"Shit."

2

LAILA

Laila slipped into the hotel room of the House Kore courier.

Her dress, a discarded housekeeper uniform fished out of the dregs of storage, snagged on the doorframe. She grumbled, yanking it only for a seam to unravel.

"Perfect," she muttered.

She turned to face the room. Like all the L'Eden guest rooms, the courier's suite was lavishly appointed and designed. The only piece that looked out of place was the unconscious courier, lying facedown in a pool of his saliva. Laila frowned.

"They could've at least left you in your bed, poor thing," she said, toeing him so that he turned over onto his back.

For the next ten minutes, Laila redecorated. From the pockets of her housekeeper's dress, she threw women's earrings on the floor, draped torn stockings over lamp fixtures, mussed the bed and poured champagne over the sheets. When she was done, she knelt beside the courier.

"A parting gift," she said. "Or apology. However you see fit."

She took out her official cabaret calling card. Then she lifted the man's thumb and pressed it to the paper. It shimmered iridescent, words blooming to life. The Palais des Rêves' calling cards were Forged to recognize a patron's thumb print. Only the courier could read what it said, and only when he touched it. She slid the card into the breast pocket of his jacket, scanning the lettering before it melted into the cream paper:

Palais des Rêves
90 Boulevard de Clichy
Tell them L'Enigme sent you . . .

A party invitation sounded like a poor consolation prize for getting knocked unconscious, but this was different. The Palais des Rêves was Paris's most exclusive cabaret, and next week they were throwing a party in honor of the hundredth anniversary of the French Revolution. Invitations currently sold on the black market for the price of diamonds. But it wasn't just the cabarets that had people excited. In a few weeks' time, the city would host the 1889 Exposition Universelle, a gigantic world fair celebrating the colonial powers of Europe and the inventions that would pave the way for the new century. L'Eden Hotel was running at full capacity.

"I doubt you'll remember this, but do try and order the chocolate-covered strawberries at the Palais," she said to the courier. "They're utterly divine."

Laila checked the grandfather clock: half past eight. Séverin and Enrique weren't due back for at least an hour, but she couldn't stop checking the time. Hope flared painfully behind her ribs. She'd spent two years looking for a breakthrough in her search for the ancient book, and this treasure map could be the answer to every prayer. *They'll be fine*, she told herself. Acquisitions were hardly new to any of them. When Laila had first started working with Séverin, he was only trying to earn back his family's possessions. In return, he helped in her search for an ancient book. The book had no title she knew of . . . her only lead was that it belonged to the Order of Babel. Two years later, the team had moved from finding the sold possessions of House Vanth to acquiring for museums or colonial guilds that, while having outwardly allied with the Order, were like Séverin. Stealing back what had been stolen from them.

Going after a treasure map hidden inside a compass sounded rather tame in comparison to former trips. Laila still hadn't forgotten the time she ended up dangling over Nisyros Island's active volcano in pursuit of an ancient diadem. But this acquisition was different. If Enrique's research and Séverin's intelligence reports were correct, that one tiny compass could change the direction of their lives. Or, in Laila's case, let her keep this life.

Distracted, Laila smoothed her hands across her dress.

A mistake.

She should never touch anything when her thoughts were too frenzied. That single unguarded moment had allowed the dress's memories to knife into her thoughts: *chrysanthemum petals clinging to the wet hem, brocade stretched over the carriage footstool, hands folded in prayer, and then—*

Blood.

Blood everywhere, the carriage overturned, bone snapping through the fabric—

Laila gasped, but it was too late. The dress's memories caught her and held tight. Laila squeezed her eyes shut, pinching her skin as hard as she could. It made no difference. Nothing made the memories fade faster. But the sharp pain felt like a red flame in her thoughts, and her consciousness wrapped around that pain as if it would lead her out of the dark. When the memories faded, she opened her eyes. Laila pulled down her sleeve, her hands shaking from accidentally reading the dress.

For a moment, Laila stayed crouched on the floor, her arms around her knees. Séverin had called her ability "invaluable" before she told him *why* she could read the objects around her. After that, he was too startled, or perhaps too horrified, to say anything. Out of the whole group, only Séverin knew that her touch could draw out an object's secret history. Invaluable or not, this ability was not . . . normal.

She was not normal.

Laila gathered herself off the floor, her hands still shaking as she left the room.

In the servants' stairway, Laila shucked off the housekeeper uniform and changed into her worn kitchen uniform. The hotel's second kitchen was dedicated strictly to baking, and during the evening hours, it belonged to her. She wasn't due on the Palais des Rêves stage until next week, which left her with nothing but free time for her second job.

In the narrow hallway, L'Eden's waitstaff bustled past her. They carried chilled oysters on the half shell; quail eggs floating in bone marrow soup; and steaming *coq a vin* that left the hall smelling like Burgundy wine and buttery garlic. Without her trademark mask and headdress, not one of them recognized her as the cabaret star L'Enigme. Here, she was just another person, another worker.

Alone in the baking kitchens, Laila surveyed the marble kitchen counter strewn with culinary scales, paintbrushes, edible pearls in a glass dish and—as of this afternoon—a croquembouche tower nearly four feet high. She had been up at dawn baking choux pastry balls, filling them with sweetened cream, and making sure that each and every sphere was the perfect coin-gold of dawn before rolling them in caramel and stacking them into a pyramid. All that was left was the decoration.

L'Eden had already won all manner of accolades for its fine dining—Séverin would accept nothing less—but it was the desserts that lit up the guests' dreams. Laila's desserts, though absent of Forging, were like edible magic. Her cakes took the shape of ballerinas with outstretched arms—their hair spun sugar and edible gold, their skin pale as cream and strewn with sweet pearl dust.

Guests called her creations "divine." When she stepped into the kitchen, that was exactly how she felt. Like a deity surveying the scraps of a universe not yet made. She breathed easier in the kitchen. Sugar and flour and salt had no memory. Here, her touch was just that. A touch. A distance closed, an action brought to an end.

An hour later, she was putting the finishing touches on a cake when the door slammed open. Laila sighed, but she didn't look up. She knew who it was.

Six months after Laila had started working for Séverin, she and Enrique had been playing cards in the star-gazing room when

Séverin walked in carrying a dirty, underfed Polish girl with eyes bluer than a candle's heart. Séverin set her down on the couch, introduced her as his Engineer, and that was that. Only later did Laila discover more about her. Arrested for arson and expelled from University, Zofia possessed a rare Forging affinity for all metals and a sharp mind for numbers.

When she first came to L'Eden, Zofia spoke only to Séverin and ran—or rather, sprinted—in the opposite direction when anyone else approached her. Laila noticed, however, that when she brought desserts for meetings, Zofia only ate the pale sugar cookies, leaving all the colorfully decorated desserts untouched. So, the next day, Laila left a plate of them outside her door. She did that for three weeks before she got busy one day in the kitchens and forgot. When she opened the door to air the room, she found Zofia holding out an empty plate and staring at her expectantly. That had been a year ago.

Now, without saying a word, Zofia grabbed a clean mixing bowl, filled it with water and guzzled it on the spot. Zofia dragged her arm across her mouth. Then she reached for a bowl of icing. Laila smacked her hand, lightly, with a rolling pin. Zofia glowered, then dipped an ink-stained finger into the icing anyway. A moment later, she began absentmindedly stacking the measuring cups according to size. Laila waited patiently. With Zofia, conversations were not initiated so much as caught at random and followed through until the other girl grew bored.

"I set some fires in the House Kore courier's room."

Laila dropped the paintbrush. "*What?* You were supposed to wake him up without being in the room!"

"I did? I set them off when I stepped outside. They're tiny."

When met with Laila's wide-eyed stare, Zofia abruptly changed the subject. Though, to her, it probably did not seem abrupt at all. "I don't like crocodile musculature. Séverin wants a decoy of those Sphinx masks—"

"Can we go back to the fire—"

"—the mask won't meld to human facial expressions. I need to make it work. Oh, I also need a new drawing board."

"What happened to the last one?"

Zofia inspected the icing bowl and shrugged.

". . . you broke it," said Laila.

"My elbow fell into it."

Laila shook her head, and threw her a clean rag. Zofia stared at it, befuddled.

"Why do I need a rag?"

"Because there's gunpowder on your face."

"And . . ."

". . . and that is mildly alarming, my dear. Clean up."

Zofia dragged the rag down her face. The ends of the cloth caught on her strange necklace, which looked strung together with knife points.

"When will they be back?" asked Zofia.

Laila felt a sharp pang.

"Enrique and Séverin should be here by nine."

"I need to grab my letters."

Laila frowned. "This late? It's already dark out, Zofia."

Zofia touched her necklace. "I know."

Zofia tossed her the rag. Laila caught it and threw it in the sink. When she turned around, Zofia had grabbed the spoon for the icing.

"I need that!"

Zofia stuck the spoon in her mouth.

"Zofia!"

The Engineer grinned. Then she swung open the door and ran off, the spoon still sticking out of her mouth.

Once she finished the dessert, Laila cleaned up and left the kitchen. She was not the official pastry chef, nor did she wish to be, and half the allure of this hobby job was that it was only for pleasure. If she did not wish to make something, she didn't.

The farther she walked down the main serving hall, the more the sounds of L'Eden came alive—laughter ribboning between the glassy murmur of the amber chandeliers and champagne flutes, the hum of Forged moths and their stained-glass wings as they shed colored light in their flight. Laila stopped in front of the Mercury Cabinet, the hotel's messaging service. Small metal boxes marked with the names of the Hotel staff sat inside. Laila opened it with her staff key, not expecting to find anything for her when her fingers brushed against something that felt like cold silk. It was a single, black petal pinned to a one-word note:

Invidia.

Even without the flower, Laila would have recognized that cramped and slanted handwriting anywhere: Tristan. She had to force herself not to smile. After all, she was still mad at him.

But that would not stop her from accepting a present.

Especially one that he had Forged.

Forged. It was a word that sat strangely on her tongue when she'd first arrived in Paris. The empires and kingdoms of the West called Tristan and Zofia's abilities 'Forging,' but the artistry had other names in other languages. In India, they called it *'chhota saans,'* the small breath, for while only gods breathed life into creation; this art was a small sip of such power. Yet, no matter its name, the rules guiding the affinity were the same.

There were two kinds of Forging affinities: mind and matter. Someone with a matter affinity could influence one of three material states: liquids, solids or gasses. Both Tristan and Zofia had matter affinities, but whereas Zofia's Forging affinity was for solid matter—mostly metals and crystals—Tristan had an affinity for liquid matter. Specifically, the liquid present in plants.

All Forging was bound by three conditions: the strength of the artisan's will, the clarity of the artistic goal, and the boundaries of their chosen mediums' natural and elemental properties. Which meant that someone with a Forging affinity for solid matter with a specificity in stone would go nowhere without understanding the attendant chemical formulas and properties of the stone they wished to manipulate.

The affinity manifested in a child no later than thirteen years of age. If the child wished to hone the affinity, he or she could study for years Most Forging artisans studied for years at renowned institutions or held lengthy apprenticeships. Zofia and Tristan, however, had followed neither of those paths. Zofia, because she had been kicked out of school before she had the chance. And Tristan because, well, Tristan had no need of it. His landscape artistry looked like the fever dream of a nature spirit. It was unsettling and beautiful, and Paris couldn't get enough of him. At the age of sixteen, the waiting list for a commission stretched into the hundreds.

Laila often wondered why Tristan stayed at L'Eden. Perhaps it was loyalty to Séverin. Or because L'Eden allowed Tristan to keep his bizarre arachnid displays. But when Laila stepped into the gardens, she *felt* the reason. The perfume of the flowers thick in her lungs. The garden turning jagged and wild in the falling dark. And she understood. Tristan's other clients had so many rules, like House Kore, which had commissioned extravagant topiaries for its upcoming celebration. L'Eden was different. Tristan loved Séverin like a brother, but he stayed here because only in L'Eden could he lift marvels from his mind, free of any demands.

Once she stepped into the gardens of L'Eden, she was inside Tristan's imagination. The gardens were no paradise, but a labyrinth of sins. Seven, to be exact.

The first garden was Lust, or *Luxuria* as it was known in Latin. Here, red flowers spilled from the hollow mouths of statues. Life-sized shrub sculptures of damned lovers like Paolo and Francesca clung to each other only to be yanked apart by the vines rippling invisibly beneath the grass. In one corner, Cleopatra coughed up garnet amaryllis and pink-frilled anemone. In another, Helen of Troy whispered zinnia and poppies. Laila moved quickly through the labyrinth. Past Gluttony, or *Gula*, where a sky of glossy blooms that smelled of ambrosia closed tight the moment one reached for them. Then Greed, or *Avaritia*, where each plant and stem and leaf appeared encased in gold veneer. Next came Sloth, or *Acedia*, with its slow-moving shrubs; Wrath, or *Ira*, with its fiery florals; then Pride, or *Superbia*, with its gargantuan, moving topiaries of green stags with flowering antlers and regal lions with manes of jasmine, until finally she was in Envy. *Invidia*. Here, a suffusion of greenery. The very shade of sin.

Laila stopped before the Tezcat Door propped up near the entrance. To anyone who didn't know its secrets, the Tezcat looked like an ordinary mirror, albeit with a lovely frame that resembled gilded ivy leaves. Tezcat Doors were impossible to distinguish from ordinary mirrors without, according to Zofia, a complicated test involving fire and phosphorous. Luckily, she didn't have to go through that. To get to the other side, she simply unlocked it by pinching the fourth gilded ivy leaf on the left side of the frame. A hidden doorknob. Her reflection rippled as the silver of the Tezcat Door's mirror thinned to transparency.

Inside was Tristan's workplace. Laila breathed in the scent of earth and roots. All along the walls were small terrariums, landscapes squeezed into miniature form and frozen. Tristan made them almost obsessively. When she asked him once, he told her that it was because he wished the world were easier. Small enough and manageable enough to fit in the hollow of one's palm.

"Laila!"

Tristan walked toward her with a wide smile on his round face, dirt smudged on his clothes and—she breathed a sigh of relief—no sign of his gigantic pet spider.

But she did not return his smile. Instead, she lifted an eyebrow. Tristan wiped his hands down his smock.

"Oh . . . you're still mad?" he asked.

"Yes."

"Would giving you a present make you less mad?"

Laila lifted her chin. "Depends on the present. But first, say it."

Tristan shifted on his feet. "I am sorry."

"For?"

". . . for putting Goliath on your dressing table."

"Where does Goliath belong? And for that matter, where do *all* your pet insects and whatnot belong?"

Tristan looked wide eyed. ". . . not in your room?"

"Close enough."

He turned to the work table beside him where a large, frosted glass terrarium took up half the space. He lifted the cover, revealing a single, deep purple rose. The petals looked like snippets of nighttime. She traced their velvet edges softly. They were almost exactly the same shade of Séverin's eyes. The thought made her draw back her hand, as if stung.

"Voila! Behold your present, Forged with a little bit of silk taken from one of your costumes—"

When he caught her frantic gaze, he added:

"—One of the ones you were going to throw away, promise!"

Laila relaxed a bit.

"So . . . am I forgiven?"

He already knew he was. But she still decided to draw out the moment a little longer than necessary. She tapped her foot, biding her time.

Then: "*Fine.*"

Tristan let out a *whoop* of happiness, and Laila couldn't help but smile. Tristan could get away with anything with those wide, gray eyes.

"Oh! I came up with a new device. I wanted to show Séverin. Where is he?"

When he caught sight of her face, Tristan's grin fell.

"They're not back yet?"

"*Yet,*" emphasized Laila. "Don't worry. These things take time. Why don't you come inside? I'll make you something to eat."

Tristan shook his head. "Maybe later. I have to check on Goliath. I don't think he's feeling well."

Laila did not ask how Tristan would know the emotional states of a tarantula. Instead, she took her Forged rose and headed back inside the Hotel. As she walked, unease shaded her thoughts. At the top of the stairs, the grandfather clock struck the tenth hour. Laila felt the lost hour like an ache in her bones. They should have been back by now.

Something was wrong.

3

ENRIQUE

Enrique scowled as he held apart the bear's jaws. "Remember when you said 'this will be fun'?"

"Can this wait?" Séverin grunted through clenched teeth.

"I suppose."

Enrique's tone was light, but every part of his body felt leaden. The onyx bear held Séverin's wrist between its teeth. Every passing second, it bore down harder. Blood began to run down his arm. Soon, the pressure of the creature's jaws wouldn't just trap his wrist.

It would snap it in half.

At least the emerald House Kore eagle hadn't got involved. That particular stone creature could detect "suspicious" activity and come to life even when its own object was not in question. Enrique nearly muttered a prayer of thanks until he heard a soft caw. Air gusted over his face from the unmistakable flap of wings.

Well then.

"Was that the eagle?" winced Séverin.

He couldn't twist his body to turn.

"No, not at all," said Enrique.

In front of him, the eagle tilted its head to one side. Enrique pulled more strongly on Séverin's trapped wrist. Séverin groaned.

"Forget it," he wheezed. "I'm stuck. We need to put it to sleep."

Enrique agreed, but the only question was how. Because Forged creatures were too dangerous to go unchecked most artisans would have added a last-minute security measure, a failsafe known as 'slumber mode.' But even if he found it, it might be further encrypted. Worse, if he let go of the jaws, they'd only crush Séverin's wrist faster. And if they didn't get out by the eight-minute limit, the Forged creatures would be the last of their worries.

Séverin grunted:

"By all means, take your time. I love a good slow, painful death."

Enrique let go. Steadying himself, he circled the onyx bear, ignoring the ever-closer jumping of the obsidian eagle. He ran his hands along the bear's body, the black haunches and shaggy feet. Nothing.

"*Enrique,*" breathed Séverin.

Séverin fell to his knees. Rivulets of blood streamed, dripping down the creature's jaws. Enrique swore under his breath. He closed his eyes. Sight wouldn't help him here. With so little light in the room, he would have to feel for any words. He trailed his fingers across the bear's haunches and belly until he caught something near its ankles. They were chipped away depressions in the stone; evenly spaced and close together as if it were a line of writing. The letters and words came to life beneath his touch.

Fiduciam in domum

"Trust in the House," translated Enrique. He whispered it again, running scenarios through his head. "I . . . I have an idea."

"Do enlighten me," managed Séverin.

The bear lifted one of its heavy, jet paws, casting a shadow over Séverin's face.

"You have to . . . to trust it!" cried Enrique. "Don't fight it! Push your wrist farther!"

Séverin didn't hesitate. He stood up, and pushed. But his hand remained stuck. Séverin growled. He threw himself against the creature. His shoulder popped wetly. Every second felt like a blade pressed tight against Enrique's skin. Just then, the eagle took off in the air. It circled the room, then swooped, talons out. Enrique ducked just as the jewel claws grazed his neck. He wouldn't be so lucky the next time. Once more, claws rasped at his neck. The eagle's talons tugged him upwards, his heels lifted off the ground. Enrique shut his eyes tight.

"Just mind the hair—" he started.

Abruptly, he dropped to the ground. He opened his eyes a crack. A bare ceiling met his gaze. Behind him, he heard the shuffling of talons on a podium. He raised himself up on his elbows.

The eagle had gone statue still.

Séverin heaved and rose to a stand. He clutched his wrist. Then, yanking his arm, he swung it forward. Enrique grimaced at the wet *snick* of joints popping back into place. Séverin wiped the blood on his pants and yanked out the Forged compass from the mouth of the still onyx bear. He slid it into his jacket, and smoothed back his hair.

"Well," he said, finally. "At least it wasn't like Nisyros Island."

"Are you *serious?*" demanded Enrique. He limped after his friend to the door. "It'll be 'like dreaming' you said. As 'easy as sleep!'"

"Nightmares are part of the spectrum of sleep."

"Is that a joke?" demanded Enrique. "You do realize your hand is mangled."

"I am aware."

"You almost got eaten by a bear."

"Not a real one."

"The dismemberment would've been real enough."

Séverin only grinned.

"See you in a bit," he said, and slipped out of the door.

Enrique lingered to give Séverin a head start.

In the dark, he felt the presence of the Order's treasure like the eyes of the dead. Hate shivered through him. He couldn't bring himself to look at the looming, "salvaged" piles. He might help Séverin steal, but the greatest thief of all was the Order of Babel, for they stole more than just objects . . . they stole histories, swallowed cultures whole, smuggled evidence of illustrious antiquity onto large ships and spirited them into indifferent lands.

"Indifferent lands," mused Enrique. "That's a good line for later."

He could use it in the next article he submitted to the Spanish newspaper dedicated to Filipino nationalism and reform from 300 years of Spanish rule. This room, thought Enrique, was where the fight for reform . . . not in political arenas or the thresholds of churches, but surrounded by the objects of history. As a historian, maybe he could fight against injustice too. So far he didn't have the connections that made anyone think his thoughts were worth listening to. This acquisition could change that.

But first he had to finish the job.

Enrique counted down the thirty seconds. Then, he straightened the borrowed servant's outfit, adjusted his mask, and stepped into the darkened hall. Between the gaps of the marble pillars, he could just make out the flutter of fans stabbing into the air.

Right on time for his meeting, the Vietnamese diplomat Vũ Văn Đinh rounded the corner. A falsified letter poked out of his sleeve. Though he had hated doing it, Tristan was exceptionally good at faking people's handwriting. The diplomat's mistress was no exception.

Just last week, Enrique and the diplomat had shared a drink at L'Eden. While the diplomat was distracted, Laila had fished out the mistress's letter from Đinh's jacket and Tristan had copied her penmanship to orchestrate this very meeting.

Enrique eyed Đinh's clothes. Like so many diplomats from colonized countries, he had outwardly allied with the Order. Once, there had been versions of the Order all over the world, each dedicated to their country's source of Forging power—although not all of them called the artistry Forging and not all of them credited its power to the Babel Fragments. Not anymore. Now, their treasures had been taken to different lands; their artistry changed; and their ancient guilds given two choices: ally or die.

Enrique straightened his false suit, and bowed. "May I assist you with anything, Sir?"

He extended his hand. Fresh panic reared inside him. Surely Đinh would look. Surely he would *know* that it was him. The very tips of his fingers brushed Đinh's sleeves.

"Indeed you may not," said Đinh coldly, drawing away his arm.

Not once did he look him in the eye.

"Very well, sir."

He bowed. With Đinh still waiting on a meeting that would never take place, Enrique walked to the back of the ballroom. He dragged his fingers down his face and neck. A slight prickling sensation rolled down his face, neck and arms, and a thin film of color floated above his skin and clothes, swirling to match the appearance and apparel of ambassador Vũ Văn Đinh.

Provided no one looked too closely, he now looked identical to the ambassador.

The powder on his fingertips, made from the pale crystals of Japan's Kishu region, was Mirror Powder. The substance itself had been banned and confiscated and so the Order had not bothered to ward their meetings against it. They hadn't counted on Séverin being friendly with the officer of customs and immigrations.

"Ambassador Đinh," said a servant, bowing.

In true diplomat fashion, Enrique did not acknowledge the man. He moved quickly through the crowd. The Mirror Powder would only hold for a minute longer.

Enrique jogged down the main staircase. At the base was a Tezcat Door that seemed to date back to a time when the Fallen House had not yet been ousted from the French faction of the Order of Babel, for its borders held the symbols of the original four Houses of France. A crescent moon for House Nyx. Thorns for House Kore. A snake biting its own tail for House Vanth. A six-pointed star for the Fallen House. Of them, only Nyx and Kore still existed. Vanth's bloodline had legally been declared dead. And the Fallen House had . . . fallen. It was said that its leaders found the West's Babel Fragment and tried to use it to rebuild the Biblical Tower of Babel, thinking it might give them more than just a sliver of God's power . . . but the actual power of God. Had they suc-ceeded in removing the West's Babel Fragment, they might have destroyed the known civilization. Séverin thought it was a rubbish rumor and believed the Order had destroyed the Fallen House as a power grab. But Enrique wasn't so sure. Of the four Houses, the Fallen House was said to be the most advanced. Even the Tezcat doors Forged by the Fallen House did more than just camouflage an entrance. Rumor went that they were capable of bridging actual distances. Like a portal. For years, the Order had tried to discover what had become of the Fallen House's Ring and massive treasure, but none had been able to find it.

Today, thought Enrique, that might change.

Through the Tezcat, Enrique could see glittering corridors, a handsomely dressed crowd and the glint of far off chandeliers. It always unnerved him that though he could see the people on the other side, all they would see was a slim, polished mirror. He felt strangely like a god in exile, filled with a kind of hollow omni-science. As much as he could see the world, it would not see him.

Enrique stepped through the Tezcat and emerged in one of the opulent halls of the Palais Garnier, the most famous opera house in all of Europe.

One man looked up, stunned. He stared at the mirror, then Enrique, before scrutinizing his champagne flute.

Around Enrique, the crowd milled about obliviously. They had no idea about the Forged ballroom the Order kept secret. Then again, everything about the Order was kept secret. Even their invi-tations only opened at the drop of an approved guest's blood. Any-one else who accidentally received one would see nothing but blank paper. To the public, the Order of Babel was nothing more than

France's research arm tasked with historical preservation. The public knew nothing of the auctions, the coffers full of treasures that stretched for kilometers deep beneath the ground. Half the public didn't even believe the Babel Fragment was a physical thing, but rather a dressed-up Biblical metaphor.

With the glamour of the Mirror Powder gone, Enrique was left in his servant costume. He strode through the crowd, tugging his lapel as he walked. The servant costume shifted, the threads unraveling and embroidering simultaneously until he was dressed in a fashionable evening jacket. He flicked his watch, and the slim band of Forged leather burst into a silk top hat that he promptly spun onto his head.

Just before he stepped outside, he blew a kiss to the Verit stone bust of Clio, the muse of history from Greek mythology. Verit stone was more expensive than a kilo of diamonds. Only palaces or banks could afford to build thresholds of Verit, which always revealed the presence of weapons or hidden objects.

Outside, Paris was a touch humid for April. Night had sweated off its stars, and across the street, a black hansom glinted dully. Enrique got inside, and Séverin flashed him a wry grin.

The second Séverin rapped his knuckles against the hansom's ceiling, the horses lurched into the night. Reaching into his coat pocket, Séverin pulled out his ever-present tin of cloves. Enrique wrinkled his nose. On its own, the clove smell was pleasant. A bit woodsy and spicy. But over the past two years that he'd been working for Séverin, cloves had stopped being a scent and become more of a signal. It was the fragrance of Séverin's decision making, and it could be delightful or dangerous. Or both.

"Voila," said Séverin, handing him the compass.

Enrique ran his fingers over the cold metal, gently tracing the divots in the silver. Ancient Chinese compasses did not look like Western ones. They were more like magnetized bowls, with a depression in the center where a spoon-shaped dial would have spun back and forth. A thrill of wonder zipped through his veins. It was thousands of years old and here he was, *holding* it—

"No need to seduce the thing," cut in Séverin.

"I'm appreciating it."

"You're fondling it."

Enrique rolled his eyes. "It's an authentic piece of history and should be savored."

"You might at least buy it dinner first," said Séverin, before pointing at the metal edges. "So? Is it like what we thought it'd be?"

Enrique weighed the half of the compass in his hand, studying the contours. As he felt the ridges, he noticed a slight deformation in the metal. He tapped on the surface and then looked up.

"It's hollow," he said, breathless.

He didn't know why he even felt surprised. He knew the compass would be hollow, and yet the possibilities of the map reared up fast and sharp and dazzling in his head. Enrique didn't know what, specifically, the map led to . . . only that it was rare enough to send the Order of Babel into a furtive clamoring. His bet, though, was that it was a map to the lost treasures of the Fallen House.

"Break it," said Séverin.

"*What?*" Enrique clutched the object to his chest. "The compass is a thousands of years old! There's another way to prize it, *gently*, apart—"

Séverin made a grab. Enrique tried to snatch it away, but he wasn't as fast. In one swift motion, Séverin grabbed both sides of the compass. Enrique heard it before he saw it. A brief, merciless—

Snap.

Something dropped from the compass, thudding on the hansom's floor. Séverin got to it first, and the minute he held it up to the light, Enrique felt as if a cold hand had pushed down on his lungs and squeezed the breath out of him. The object hidden within the compass looked like a map. All that was left was one question:

Where did it lead?

· » 4 « ·

ZOFIA

Zofia liked Paris best in the evening.

During the day, Paris was too much. It was all noise and smell, crammed with stained streets and threaded with hectic crowds. Dusk tamed the city. Made it manageable.

As she walked back to L'Eden, Zofia clutched her sister's newest letter tight to her chest. Hela would find Paris beautiful. She would like the linden trees of Rue Bonaparte. There were fourteen of them. She would find the horse chestnuts comely. There were nine. She would not like the smells. There were too many to count.

Right now, Paris did not seem beautiful. Horse shat marred the cobbled roads. People urinated on the street lanterns. And yet, there was something about the city that spoke vibrantly of life. Nothing felt still. Even the stone gargoyles leaned off the edges of buildings like they were on the verge of flight. And nothing looked lonely. Terraces had the company of wicker-chairs, and bright purple bougainvillea hugged stone walls. Not even the Seine River, which cut through Paris like a trail of ink, looked abandoned. By day, boats zipped across it. By night, lamplight danced upon the surface.

Zofia peeked at Hela's newest letter, sneaking lines beneath every shining lantern. She read one sentence, then found that she could not stop. Every word brought back the sound of Hela's voice.

Zosia, please tell me you are going to the Exposition Universelle! If you do not, I will know. Trust me, dear sister, the laboratory can spare you for a day. Learn something outside the classroom for once. Besides, I heard that the Exposition will have a cursed diamond, and princes from exotic lands! Perhaps you might bring one home, then I will not have to play governess to our stingy stryk. How he can be father's brother is a mystery for only God to ponder. Please go. You are sending back so much money lately that I worry you are not keeping enough for yourself. Are you hale and happy? Write to me soon, little light.

Hela was half-wrong. Zofia was not in school. But she was learning plenty outside of a classroom. In the past year and a half, she had learned how to invent things the École des Beaux Arts never imagined for her. She had learned how to open a savings account, which might—assuming the map Séverin acquired was all they'd hoped it to be—soon hold money to support Hela through medical school when she finally enrolled. But the worst lesson was learning how to lie to her sister. The first time she had lied in a letter, she'd thrown up. Guilt left her sobbing for hours until Laila had found and comforted her. She didn't know how Laila knew what bothered her. She just did. And Zofia, who never quite grasped how to find her way through a conversation, simply felt grateful that someone could do the work for her.

Zofia was still thinking about Hela when the marble entrance of École des Beaux-Arts manifested before her. Zofia staggered back, nearly dropping the letters.

The marble entrance did not move.

It was a testament to the quality of Forging taught in École des Beaux-Arts. Not only was the entrance Forged to appear before any matriculated students two blocks from the school, but it was also an exquisite example of solid matter and mind affinity working in tandem. A feat only those trained at the École could perform.

Once, Zofia would have trained with them too.

"You don't want me," she said softly.

Tears stung her eyes. When she blinked, she saw the path to her expulsion. One year into schooling, her classmates had changed. Once, her skill awed them. Now it offended them. Then the rumors started. No one seemed to care at first that she was Jewish. But that changed. Rumors sprang up that Jews could steal anything.

Even someone else's Forging affinity.

She should have been more careful, but that was the problem with happiness. It blinds.

For a while, Zofia was happy. And then, one afternoon, the other students' whispers got the better of her. That day, she broke down in the laboratory. There were too many sounds. Too much laughing. Too much brightness escaping through the curtain. She'd forgotten her parents' lesson to count backwards until she found that kernel of calm. Whispers grew from that episode. *Crazy Jew.* A month later, ten students locked themselves in the lab with her. Again came the sounds, smells, laughing. The other students didn't grab her. They knew just the barest touch—like a feather trailed on bare skin—hurt her more. Calm slipped out of reach no matter how many times she counted backwards; or begged to be let go; or asked what she had done wrong.

In the end, it was such a small movement.

Someone kicked her to the ground. Another person's elbow clashed into a vial on a table, which splattered into a puddle, which pooled out and touched the tips of her outstretched fingers. She had been holding a piece of flint in her hand when fury flickered in her mind. *Fire.* That little thought—that snippet of will, just as the professors had taught her—traveled from her fingertips to the puddle, igniting the broken vial until it bloomed into a towering inferno.

Seven students were injured in the explosion.

For her crime, she was arrested on grounds of arson and insanity, and taken to prison. She would have died there if not for Séverin. Séverin found her, freed her, and did the unthinkable:

He gave her a job. A way to earn back what she'd lost. A way out.

Zofia rubbed her finger across the oath tattoo on her right knuckle. Oath tattoos were signs of contractual promises between equals, ink-Forged so that when one sought to break the terms of an agreement, nightmares would plague that person until the agreement was dissolved. Most employer-employee relationships used a different, cruder binding where the parties involved were not equally weighed. That Séverin had used this . . . a sign of equals . . . was something she would never forget.

Zofia turned on her heel and left Rue Bonaparte behind. Perhaps the marble entrance could not recognize when a student had been expelled, for it did not move, but stayed in its place until she disappeared around a corner.

In L'Eden, Zofia made her way to the star-gazing room. Séverin had called for a meeting once he and Enrique got back from their latest acquisition, which she knew was just a fancy word for "theft."

Zofia never took the grand lobby's main staircase. She didn't want to see all the fancy people dressed up and laughing and dancing. It was too noisy. Instead, she took the servants' entryway, which was how she ran into Séverin. He grinned despite appearing thoroughly disheveled. Zofia noticed how tenderly he held his wrist.

"You're covered in blood."

Séverin glanced down at his clothes. "Surprisingly, it hasn't escaped my attention."

"Are you dying?"

"Incrementally. But no more than usual or expected."

Zofia frowned.

"I'm well enough. Don't worry."

She reached for the door handle. "I'm glad you're not dead."

"Thank you, Zofia," said Séverin with a small smile. "I will join you momentarily. There's something I'd like to show everyone through a Mnemo bug."

On Séverin's shoulder, a Forged silver beetle scuttled under his lapel. Mnemo bugs recorded images and sound, allowing projections like holograms should the wearer choose. Which meant that she had to be prepared for an unexpected burst of light. Séverin knew she didn't like those. They jolted her thoughts. Nodding, Zofia left him in the hall, and walked into the room.

The star-gazing room calmed Zofia. It was wide and spacious, with a glass-domed vault that let in the starlight. All along the walls were orreries and telescopes, cabinets full of polished crystal and shelves lined with fading books and manuscripts. In the middle of the room was the low coffee table that bore the scuff marks and dents of a hundred schemes that came to life on its wooden surface. A semicircle of chairs surrounded it. Zofia made her way to her seat. It was a tall metal stool with a ragged pillow case. Zofia didn't like things touching her back. In a green velvet chaise across from her sprawled Laila, who absentmindedly traced the rim of her teacup with one finger. In a plushy armchair crowded with pillows sat Enrique, who was balancing a large book on his lap and reading intently. Of the two chairs left, one was Tristan's—which was less of a chair and more of a cushion because he didn't like heights—and one was Séverin's, whose black cherry armchair Zofia had custom-Forged so that an unfamiliar touch caused it to sprout blades.

Tristan barged into the room, his hands outstretched.

"Look! I thought Goliath was dying, but he's fine. He just molted!"

Enrique screamed. Laila scuttled backwards on her chaise. Zofia leaned forward, inspecting the enormous tarantula in Tristan's hands. Mathematicians didn't frighten her, and spiders—and bees—were just that. A spider's web was composed of numerous radii, a logarithmic spiral, and the light-diffusing properties of their webs and silk was fascinating.

"Tristan!" scolded Laila. "What did I just tell you about spiders?"

Tristan puffed out his chest. "You said not to bring him into your room. This is not your room."

Faced with Laila's glare, he shrank a bit.

"Please can he stay for the meeting? Goliath is different. He's special."

Enrique pulled his knees up to his chest and shuddered. "What is so special about *that*?"

"Well," said Zofia, "as part of the infraorder of Mygalomorphae, the fangs of a tarantula point *down* whereas the spiders you're thinking of have fangs which point and join in a pincer-like arrangement. That's rather special."

Enrique gagged.

Tristan beamed at her. "You remembered."

Zofia did not find this particularly noteworthy. She remembered most things people told her, and besides, Tristan had listened just as attentively when she explained the arithmetic spiral properties of a spider web.

Enrique made a *shoo* motion with his hands. "Please take it away, Tristan. I beg you."

"Aren't you happy for Goliath? He's been sick for days."

"Can we be happy for Goliath from behind a sheet of glass and a net and a fence? Maybe a ring of fire for good measure?"

Tristan made a face at Laila. Zofia knew that pattern: widened eyes, pressed down brows, dimpled chin and the barest quiver of his bottom lip. A pattern of supplication by way of rendering oneself infantile. Ridiculous, yet effective. Zofia approved. Across from her, Laila clapped her hands over her eyes.

"Not falling for it," said Laila sternly. "Go look like a kicked puppy elsewhere. Goliath can't stay here during a meeting. That's final."

Tristan huffed. "*Fine.*" Then he murmured to Goliath. "I'll make you a cricket cake, dear friend. Don't fret."

Once Tristan had left, Enrique turned to Zofia:

"I rather sympathized with Arachne after her duel with Minerva, but I detest her descendants."

Zofia went still. People and conversation were already a cipher without throwing in all the extra words. Enrique was especially confusing. Elegance illuminated every word the Historian spoke. And she could never tell when he was angry. His mouth was always bent in a half-smile, regardless of his mood. If she answered now, she'd only sound foolish. Instead, Zofia said nothing but pulled out a matchbox from her pocket and turned it over in her hands. Out the corner of her eye, she saw Enrique roll his eyes and turn back to his book. She knew what he thought of her. She had overheard him once. *She's a snob.* He could think what he liked.

Minutes ticked by. Laila handed out tea and desserts, making sure Zofia received exactly three sugar cookies, all pale and perfectly round. Calm washed through her. She settled back in her chair, glancing around the room. Eventually, Tristan returned and dramatically plopped onto his cushion.

"In case you're wondering, Goliath is deeply offended and he says—"

But they would never know the tarantula's specific grievances because at that moment a beam of light shot up through the coffee table. The room went dark. Then, slowly, an image of a piece of metal appeared. When she looked up, Séverin was standing behind Tristan. She hadn't heard him enter.

Tristan followed her gaze and nearly jumped when he saw Séverin. "Must you creep on us like that? I didn't even hear you come into the room!"

"Appearing as if out of nowhere and cloaked in shadows is part of my aesthetic," said Séverin, dangling a Forged muffling bell.

Enrique laughed. Laila didn't. Her gaze was fixed on his bloodied arm. Zofia knew he was alive and well enough, so she turned her attention to the object. It was a square piece of metal, with curling symbols at the four corners. A large circle had been inscribed upon the middle. Within the circle were small rows of stacked lines shaped like squares:

"That's what we planned for weeks to acquire?" asked Tristan. "What is it? A game? I thought we were after a treasure map hidden in a compass?"

"So did I," sighed Enrique.

"My bet was that it was a map to the Fallen House's lost stash," said Tristan.

"My bet was on an ancient book the Order lost years ago," said Laila, looking terribly disappointed. "Zofia? What'd you think it'd be?"

"Not that," she answered, pointing at the diagram.

"Looks like all of us were wrong," said Tristan. "So much for blackmailing the Order."

"At least because all of us were wrong none of us have to play test subjects to whatever strange poison Tristan makes next," pointed out Laila.

"Touché!" said Enrique, raising a glass.

"I resent that," said Tristan.

"Don't call it a loss yet," said Séverin, resolute. "This diagram could still be useful. There has to be a reason why the Patriarch of House Nyx wanted it. Just like there has to be a reason why all of our intel was on high-alert with this transaction. Enrique. Care to enlighten us on what this diagram is? Or are you too preoccupied with praying for my immortal soul?"

Enrique scowled and closed the book on his lap. Zofia glanced at the spine. He was holding the Bible.

"I've given up on your soul," said Enrique. He cleared his throat and pointed at the hologram. "What you see before you might look like a board game, but it's actually an example of Chinese cleromancy. Cleromancy is a type of divination that produces random numbers that are then interpreted as the will of God or some other supernatural force. What you see in this silver diagram are the 64 hexagrams found in the I Ching. I Ching is an ancient Chinese divination text that loosely translates to 'Book of Changes.' These hexagrams—" he pointed at the small squares composed of six stacked lines in an eight by eight arrangement "—correspond to certain cryptic words, like 'force' or 'diminishing.' Supposedly, these arrangements translate fate."

"What about the spiral things on the edge?" asked Tristan.

The four symbols bore no resemblance to the Chinese characters or sharp lines forming the hexagrams.

"That . . . That I'm not entirely sure," admitted Enrique. "It doesn't match anything recognizable from Chinese augury. Perhaps it's an added on signature from whoever possessed the compass after it had been made? Either way, it doesn't seem like a map to anything. Which, honestly, is disappointing, but that doesn't mean it won't fetch a good price on the market."

Laila drew herself up on her elbows, tilting her head to the side a little more. "Unless it's a map in disguise."

"Why not?" mused Séverin. "Any ideas?"

Zofia counted the lines. Then she counted them again. A pattern nudged against her thoughts.

"This is nothing we haven't seen before," said Séverin cheerfully. "Remember that underwater Isis temple?"

"Distinctly," said Enrique. "You said there wouldn't be any sharks."

"There weren't."

"Just mechanical leviathans with dorsal fins," said Enrique. "Forgive me."

"Apology accepted," said Séverin, inclining his head. "Now. When it came to that code, we had to rethink the direction. We had to question our assumption. What if what we're looking at is not just a map, but a hint to what it might lead to?"

Tristan frowned. "A bunch of divination lines do not a treasure make, dear brother."

"Lines," said Zofia distractedly. She tugged at her necklace. "Are they lines?"

"*That*," said Séverin, pointing at her. "Is exactly the type of reasoning I'm talking about. Question the very assumptions. Good thinking."

"What if you shine it under a different light?" mused Tristan.

"Or do those symbols at the four corners correspond to something that's a hint?" asked Enrique.

Zofia kept quiet, but it was as if the pattern had peeled off the metal square. She squinted at it.

"Numbers," she said suddenly. "If you change the lines to numbers . . . it becomes something else. We did a similar procedure last year with the coded Greek alphabet riddle. I remember because that was when Séverin took us on that expedition to Nisyros Island."

All five of them collectively shuddered.

Tristan drew his knees to his chest. "I hate volcanoes."

Zofia sat up, excited.

"Each of those hexagrams is made up only of broken and unbroken lines. If you make every unbroken line a 'zero,' and every broken line a 'one,' then it's a pattern of zeroes and ones. It looks like some kind of binary calculus."

"But that doesn't tell us anything about the treasure," said Tristan.

"The ancients *were* obsessed with numbers," said Enrique thoughtfully. "It's clear in their art. Which makes me wonder what else might be here. Maybe it's not a strange calculus after all."

Enrique tilted his head. "Unless . . ."

He pointed at the symbols tucked into the four corners.

"Séverin, can you alter the image and break off the four corners?"

Séverin manipulated the Mnemo hologram so that the four corners broke off. Then, as if the image were real, he shrank the I Ching diagram, enlarged the four corners and placed them beside one another.

"*There*," said Enrique. "I see it now. Séverin, place them in a block and rearrange the order? Turn the first symbol sideways, attach it to symbol two, symbol three should hang down, and the fourth symbol goes on the left."

Séverin did as asked, and when he stepped back, a new symbol took shape:

"The Eye of Horus," breathed Enrique.

Tristan leaned out of his chair while Laila, suddenly alert, rose up off her elbow. Envy flashed through Zofia.

"How . . ." she said, under her breath. "How did you see that?"

"The same way you saw numbers in lines," said Enrique smugly. "You're impressed. Admit it."

Zofia crossed her arms. "No."

"I dazzle you with my intelligence. You're secretly infatuated with me."

Zofia turned to Laila. "Make him stop."

Enrique bowed, and gestured back to the image. "The Eye of Horus is also known as a *wadjet*. It's an ancient Egyptian symbol of royal power and protection. Over time, most Horus Eyes have been lost to history—"

"No," said Séverin. "Not lost. *Destroyed*. During Napoleon's 1798 campaign to Egypt, the Order sent a delegation tasked specifically to finding and confiscating all Horus Eyes. House Kore sent half its members, which is why they have the largest supply of Egyptian Forged treasures in Europe. If there's any Forged Horus Eyes left from that campaign, it's with them."

"But why was it destroyed?" asked Laila.

"That's a secret between the government and the Order," said Séverin. "All official documentation I've ever found suggested the Horus Eyes could reveal something. My guess is that certain Forged Horus Eyes showed all the slumber mode locations on Napoleon's artillery. If everyone knew how to make his weapons useless, where would he be?"

"What's the other theory?" asked Laila.

"Napoleon thought all the Horus Eyes were looking at him funny and so he had them destroyed."

Enrique laughed.

"But then why have a Horus Eye on an I Ching diagram?" pressed Zofia. "If it's a calculus of zeroes and ones, what would it even see?"

Enrique went still. "*See.*" His eyes widened. "Zero and one . . . and *seeing*. Zofia. You're a genius."

She raised her shoulder. "I know."

Enrique reached for the Bible he'd left on the coffee table, and started flipping through the pages.

"I was reading this earlier for a translation I'm working on, but Zofia's mathematical connection is perfect," he said. He stopped flipping. "Ah. Here we are. *Genesis 11:4-9*, also known as the Tower of Babel passage. We all know it. It's an etiological tale not just meant to explain why people speak different languages, but also to explain the presence of Forging in our world. The basic story is that people tried to build a tower to heaven, God didn't want that, so He made new languages, and the confusion of tongues prevented the building's completion. But He didn't just strike down the building." he said, before reading aloud: "*. . . and they ceased building the city. Therefore its name is called Babel, because there the Lord confused the language of all the earth, but the Lord delighted in his creation's ingenuity and deposited upon the land the bricks of the tower. Each brick bore his touch, and thus left an impression of the power of God to create something from nothing.*"

Something from nothing.

She'd heard that phrase before . . .

"*Ex nihilo,*" said Séverin, smiling widely. "Latin, for 'out of nothing.' What's the mathematical representation of nothing?"

"Zero," said Zofia.

"Thus, the movement of zero to one is the power of God, because out of nothing, *something* is created. The Babel fragments are considered slivers of God's powers. They bring things to life, excluding, of course, the power to bring back the dead and create *actual* life," said Enrique.

Across from her, Zofia noticed that Laila's smile fell.

Enrique leaned out of his chair, his eyes uncannily bright.

"If *that's* what the diagram is really about, then what does that mean about the Horus Eye?"

Laila let out a long breath.

"You said looking through the Horus Eye revealed something . . . whatever it could see had to be dangerous enough that the instrument couldn't be kept in existence. What would be dangerous enough to threaten an entire empire? Something that has to do with the power of God?"

Séverin sank into a chair. Zofia felt a numb buzzing at the edge of her thoughts. She felt as if she'd leaned over a vast precipice. As if the next words would change her life.

"In other words," said Séverin slowly. "You think this might be telling us that looking through a Horus Eye reveals a Babel fragment."

•»5«•

SÉVERIN

Séverin stared at the luminous dark of the Eye of Horus. In that second, the air smelled metallic. Like a prelude to a thunderstorm. He could almost see it. Gray rippling the sky as if it were hectic with fever. Fanged teeth of light flashing in the clouds—a taunt to snap. He couldn't stop what would come next.

And he didn't want to.

When he first heard about the compass, he imagined it would lead them to the lost treasure of the Fallen House, the only cache of treasure that the Order longed to grab hold of and would do anything to possess. But this . . . this was like reaching for a match only to find a torch. The Order had covered up their hunt for Horus Eyes, and now he knew why. If someone found the West's Fragment, they could disrupt all Forging not just in France, but Europe, for without a Fragment to power the art of Forging, civilizations died. And while the Order might know the Horus Eyes' secret, the rest of the world didn't. Including many colonial guilds that had been forced into hiding by the Order. Guilds with knowledge of the Babel Fragments' inner workings that rivaled the Order's. Séverin could only imagine what they'd do to get their hands on this information, and what the Order would do to keep it out.

"We're not . . ." Enrique trailed off, unable to finish his sentence. "Right?"

"You can't be serious," said Laila. She was pinching the tips of her fingers repeatedly, a nervous habit of hers. If she could help it, she never touched an object when she was distracted. "This could *kill* us."

Séverin didn't meet Laila's gaze, but he could feel her dark eyes pinning him. He looked only to Tristan, his brother in everything but blood. In the dark, he seemed younger than his sixteen years. Memory bit into Séverin. The two of them crouched behind a rosebush, thorns ripping at the soft skin of their necks, their hands clutching one another's while the father they called Wrath screamed their names. Séverin opened and closed his hand. A long, silver scar ran down his right palm and caught the light. Tristan had a matching one.

"Are you?" asked Tristan softly. "Serious?"

All this time, they'd been after an artifact that would be a bargaining chip to the Order. An artifact that would force the Order to restore his lost inheritance. Instead, he had information that was either a dream or a death sentence . . . depending on how he played this game. Séverin reached for his tin of cloves.

"I don't know enough to be serious. But I'd like to know enough to have options."

Tristan swore under his breath. The others looked shocked, even Zofia blankly stared into her lap.

"This information is dangerous," said Tristan. "We'd be better off if you just threw the compass at House Nyx's door."

"Dangerous, yes, but the most rewarding things are," reasoned Séverin. "I'm not saying that we approach the Order tomorrow and tell them we've got hold of one of their secrets. I have no intention to rush anything."

Enrique snorted. "Slow and painful death is far better than getting it over with quickly, sure."

Séverin rose to his feet. For a decision like this, he didn't want to be eye-level. He wanted them to look up. They did.

"Think about what this could mean for us. It could bring us everything we wanted."

Enrique dragged his palm down his face. "You know how moths look at a fire and think '*oooh! shiny!*' and then die in a burst of flames and regret?"

"Vaguely."

"Right. Just checking to be sure."

"What about Hypnos?" asked Laila.

"What about him?"

"You don't think he'll notice what went missing? He has quite the reputation for . . . zealousness when it comes to his possessions. And what if he *knows* what the compass really contained?"

"I doubt it," said Séverin.

"You don't think he could figure it out?" asked Laila.

"He can't. He doesn't have you." When Laila's eyes widened he caught himself and gestured to the whole group: "*All* of you."

"Awww . . ." said Enrique. "What a sweet sentiment. I shall take it to my grave. Literally."

"Besides, Zofia and Enrique made a perfect fake artifact. There's no way that Hypnos can trace it back to us."

Enrique sighed. "God, I'm brilliant."

Zofia crossed her arms. "I am too."

"Of course you are," soothed Laila. "You're both brilliant."

"Yes, but I'm *more*—" huffed Enrique.

Séverin cut them off with two sharp claps. With each clap he felt the cold iron of the oath rings hitting his palms. One for Zofia. One for Enrique. Laila insisted she worked *with* rather than *for* him, and there was no need for Tristan since no iron band compared to their bond.

"Now that we have the piece, let's examine it thoroughly. We make no plans beyond that. We don't make any speculation about what we might do. We don't do *anything* until it's clear what we're working with. Understood?"

The four of them nodded. Just like that, the meeting was concluded. They rose slowly. Enrique was the first to head to the door.

He paused in front of Séverin. "Just remember . . ."

And then Enrique hooked his thumbs together and made a strange waving motion with his hands.

"You're a bird?"

"A *moth*!" said Enrique. "A moth approaching a flame!"

"That's a very alarming moth."

"It's a metaphor."

"It's an alarming metaphor too."

Enrique rolled his eyes. Behind him, Zofia smuggled more cookies on her plate.

"How are the Sphinx masks coming along?"

"Why?" she asked, eyes narrowed.

"Might need them sooner than later."

"Mmf."

Zofia shoved the rest of a cookie into her mouth as she left.

Even before he turned back to the room, Séverin knew who was approaching next. Laila. Everything in the room always rushed to her: every beam of light, every last pair of eyes, every atom of air. Maybe that's why he sometimes couldn't breathe when he saw her. Though the room was nearly dark, whatever light clung to its corners now raced to illuminate her. Usually, Laila had a habit of being almost relentlessly radiant. She hated seeing someone hold an empty plate and always thought everyone was hungry. She knew everyone's secrets even without having to read their objects. At the Palais des Rêves, she turned that radiance into an allure that earned her the name, L'Enigme. *The Mystery.* But this evening, she spared him no smile. Her dark eyes looked like chips of stone.

Uh oh.

"No tea and sympathy for me?" he asked. He lifted his hand. "I am wounded you know."

"How thoughtful of you to delay the hour of your death so that I might witness it firsthand," she said coldly. But the longer she looked at his wrist, the more her shoulders softened. "You could've been hurt."

"It's the price one pays for chasing wants," he said lightly. "The problem is I have too many of them."

Laila shook her head. "You only want one thing."

"Is that so? Enlighten me."

He meant it teasingly. But Laila's posture changed almost immediately. More languid, somehow.

"Very well," she said.

Laila moved closer. She slid her hand down the front of his jacket.

"I will tell you what you want."

Séverin held still. This close, he could count her eyelashes, the starlight gilding her cheek. Her skin was so warm he could feel it through the linen of his shirt. What game was she playing? Her fingers slipped into the inner breast pocket of his jacket. She pulled out his silver tin, popped the latch and withdrew a clove. Eyes still locked on his, she dragged her thumb across his lower lip. He didn't remember parting his lips. But he must have because a moment later, a sharp clove hit his tongue. Laila drew back. Cold rushed in to fill the space. All in all, it took no more than a few seconds. The whole time her composure had stayed the same. Detached and sensual, like the consummate performer she was. He could see her staging an identical routine at the Palais des Rêves—reaching into a patron's jacket for his cigarette case, placing it on the man's lips and lighting it before she took it for herself.

"*That's* what you want," she said darkly. "You want an excuse to go hunting. But you have mistaken the predator for prey."

With that, her skirts swirled around her heels as she left. Séverin bit down on the clove and watched her leave. He waited a moment before turning back to Tristan.

He knew what argument they would have. He had prepared for it, and yet, it still wrenched something from him to see the shine in Tristan's eyes. In that moment, Séverin felt far older than his eighteen years.

"Just tell me," he said wearily.

"I wish that this was enough for you."

ROSHANI CHOKSHI

Séverin closed his eyes. It wasn't about *enough*. Tristan would never understand. He had never felt the pulse of an entirely different future only to see it ripped from his grasp and smothered in front of him. He didn't understand that sometimes the only way to take down what had destroyed you was to disguise yourself as part of it.

"It's not about enough," said Séverin. "It's about balancing the scales. Fairness."

Tristan didn't look at him. "When you came of age, you promised that you would protect us."

Séverin hadn't forgotten. The day he said that was the day he realized that some memories have a taste. That day, his mouth was full of blood, and so his promise would always taste like salt and iron.

"Let's say this whole venture doesn't kill us. What if you get what you want? If you get back your House you'll be a patriarch . . ." His voice pitched higher. "What if you become like—"

"Don't."

He hadn't meant for his voice to sound so cold, but it did, and Tristan flinched.

"I will *never* be like our fathers."

Tristan and Séverin had seven fathers. An assembly line of foster fathers and guardians, all of whom had been fringe members of the Order of Babel. All of whom had made Séverin who he was, for better or worse.

"Being part of the Order won't make me one of them," said Séverin, his voice icy. "I don't want to be their equals. I don't want them to look us in the eye. I want them to look away, to blink harshly, like they've stared at the sun itself. I don't want them standing across from us. I want them kneeling."

Tristan nodded tersely.

"I protect you," said Séverin softly. "Remember that promise? I said I'd protect you. I said I'd make us a paradise of our own."

"L'Eden," said Tristan miserably.

Séverin had named his hotel not just for the Garden of Paradise, but for the promise that had been struck long ago when the two of them were nothing but wary eyes and skinned knees, while the houses and fathers and lessons moved about them as relentless as seasons.

"I protect you," said Séverin again, this time quieter. "Always."

Finally, Tristan's shoulders fell. He leaned against Séverin, the top of his blonde head tickling the inside of Séverin's nose until he sneezed.

"Fine," grumbled Tristan.

Séverin tried to think of something else to say. Something that would take Tristan's mind off of what the five of them were planning to do next.

"I hear Goliath molted?"

"Don't pretend like you care about Goliath. I know you tried to set a cat on him last month."

"To be fair, Goliath is the stuff of nightmares."

Tristan didn't laugh.

Over the next week and a half, Laila spied on the Order members who frequented the Palais des Rêves, looking out for any signs of unrest or rumors of theft following the auction. But all was quiet. Even the notorious Sphinx guards who could follow the trail of any House-marked artifact had not been glimpsed outside the city residences of House Kore and House Nyx.

Séverin was sitting in his office when his butler came in with the mail.

"For you," said his butler, a concerned furrow on his forehead.

Séverin glanced at the envelope. An elaborate letter H was emblazoned on the front.

Hypnos.

He dismissed the man, and then stared down at the envelope. Bits of brown flecked the front, like dried blood. Séverin touched the seal. Instantly, something sharp stabbed into the pad of his finger, a Forged thorn concealed in the melted wax. He hissed, drawing back his hand, but a drop of blood hit the paper. It sank into the envelope, and the elaborate letter H shivered, unraveling before his eyes until it opened into a short missive.

I know you stole from me.

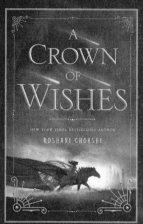